3 4
HAR

D1220470

1-15

THE GOLD AND THE GLORY

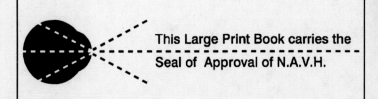

This Large Print Book carries the
Seal of Approval of N.A.V.H.

A MARTHA PEMBERTON WESTERN,
BOOK 1

THE GOLD AND THE GLORY

CHET CUNNINGHAM

WHEELER PUBLISHING
A part of Gale, Cengage Learning

GALE
CENGAGE Learning®

Detroit • New York • San Francisco • New Haven, Conn • Waterville, Maine • London

GALE
CENGAGE Learning®

LIBRARY OF CONGRESS CATALOGING-IN-PUBLICATION DATA

Cunningham, Chet.
   The gold and the glory : a Martha Pemberton western. Book one / by
Chet Cunningham. — Large print ed.
      p. cm. — (Wheeler Publishing large print western)
   ISBN-13: 978-1-4104-4552-0 (softcover)
   ISBN-10: 1-4104-4552-6 (softcover)
   1. Large type books. I. Title.
PS3553.U468G65 2012
813'.54—dc23   2011043948

Published in 2012 by arrangement with Chet Cunningham.

Printed in the United States of America
   1 2 3 4 5   16 15 14 13 12
FD026

THE GOLD AND THE GLORY

PROLOGUE

CHAPTER ONE

San Francisco, June 1872.

"Now I wouldn't come right out and say that the girl is *wild,* if you know what I mean, but Martha is certainly close to it," Mrs. Ruth Warner said, a flat, stale smile decorating her matronly face. "I don't spread stories, but from what I hear that girl gives her poor mother pure and total anguish. The last time I was at the Pemberton house Martha came home from the library, leastwise that's where she *said* she had been. Oh, she was all fuss and feathers, and just high and mighty and touch-me-not, her face all flushed and bright and those black eyes dancing. Somehow it didn't fit with a girl who was supposed to have been reading all afternoon."

The occasion was the gathering of the San Francisco Tuesday Literary Society, and Amy Schenck had just finished giving her report on a group of short stories by some new writer called Mark Twain. The consensus was that he did seem interesting in a common sort of way, but that he had no style, no flow of words, and that he would never do anything really important in the field of literature.

Amy had lost the spotlight and she waited for a small break in the conversation, then plunged in. "Well, I heard that Martha kissed that Anderson boy right out in public. It just isn't right for a girl of her good family and all to go around kissing. We all know what that leads to." Amy ducked her head and put one hand over her face to hide what she hoped was just a hint of a blush. There were several murmurs of agreement around the circle from the occupants of the thickly upholstered chairs.

"Poor Abigail," said Mrs. Wendell Horn, frowning down her aquiline nose and over the top of her glasses. "I know she must be simply crushed. Now a real scandal a family can live down, grow above, but this constant *threat* of something happening — well, poor Abigail must be miserable. Having a daughter like Martha is a terrible strain."

"She told me she didn't feel well enough to come to our meeting today," Ruth Warner dropped in casually. It made her the center of attention, which she wanted. "Wild. I really dislike to use the word about the daughter of one of the oldest and very best members of the Literary Society, but we must face facts. It wasn't two months ago she was caught in her father's study with the door closed and she was with one of her cousins. Willy Henderson, and you all know what a young hellion he is. They say her skirts were rumpled and her blouse was askew." Mrs. Warner shook her head. "I just suppose the girl is wild. There is some strange, unsettled streak in her that nobody thought was there. She's bound to come to no good, you mark my words. And it grieves me to see poor Abigail suffer so because of her."

The seven women set their mouths and frowned almost in unison. Only Rebecca Kent-James had a questioning look.

"She's always seemed the perfect little lady to me — Martha, I mean. She's such a pretty girl, with that beautiful long dark hair and flashing black eyes. Isn't her hair a wonderful shade?"

Mrs. Warner sniffed. "Rebecca, dear. You haven't been here long enough to really *know* the child, I'm afraid. The good Lord knows we're all trying our best to help turn this wilderness into some kind of a civilized country. But that Martha Pemberton isn't doing her duty. Oh, yes, the girl was promised once, and to a boy from a very good family. But six months later she said it was all a mistake. She said she didn't think he was serious. She said she *wasn't ready* to marry!"

"Disgusting."

"Scandalous!"

"I never realized it went that far."

"The little hussy!"

Mrs. Warner smiled grimly at the round of support. "Well, all I can say is that Abigail must be extremely careful with that young lady, or I shudder to think what might happen to her. I've heard Martha goes walking down around the docks."

"Isn't her father's business firm down there?" Mrs. Kent-Jones asked. "I thought she was the daughter of Harold L. Pemberton, the man who owns the Pacific Steamship and Trading Company." She looked around at the frozen faces. It was high time somebody tried to stand up for the girl. "Well, isn't that right?" Mrs. Kent-Jones asked.

"Yes, dear," Mrs. Warner said with a quick little eyes-closed nod showing that Mrs. Kent-Jones was forgiven for mentioning it. "But it still isn't the place for a nice young girl of good breeding to walk around alone!"

There was a murmur of agreement.

"Oh, yes, and I've seen her with my own eyes," Mrs. Warner continued. "There was that trunk to pick up from Hawaii, and I wanted to make sure it was not damaged, so naturally I had to go down to the dock myself, to help oversee the drivers. It is simply impossible to get good help these days. Anyway, Martha Pemberton was walking past as big as life and wearing some old clothes that I'll wager her mother had thrown out long ago. I hardly recognized her. Hussy, a brazen hussy for sure. I don't know why else she would be down there. No, I'm not ready to label anyone, but the girl does make you wonder, doesn't she? What does she do down at the docks, anyway?"

Amy Schenck passed the platter of small cakes and followed around with her silver coffee service. She spoke as she moved, giving her a commanding conversation weapon.

"Now, I try to be as up to date as I can. I'm all for this Susan Anthony woman back east and her woman's suffrage and all that, so you see I don't hold with doing things one way just because I've done them that way for twenty years. But there is a limit. After all, this is the year eighteen hundred and seventy-two, and all sorts of wonderful things are happening. But when it comes to a young girl's reputation, a mother simply can't be too careful. If that Miss Pemberton were my child, I'd lock her in her room for a few days until she minded me." Amy looked at the raised eyebrows around the room.

"Well, I sure would! It's better to use the rod a little more than to spoil the child — especially a girl. Just remember, one wild night, or even one wild *hour*, and a young girl can be ruined for life. You all know that: damaged goods. Do I have to remind you about Josephine Brannon?"

The name brought an immediate hush to the room. No one wanted to talk about Jo Brannon and the disgrace she had brought thundering down on her family just two years previously.

Mrs. Warner cleared her throat. She never used that tactic unless she had to, but she was president of the society and it was her duty to keep the members on the subject of literature. This was going too far afield. "Now, Amy, I don't think we need to bring that up. Some of our finest young men were involved . . ." She broke off, looked quickly at Mrs. Horn, then glanced away. Helen's eyes were downcast, her fingers twisting the napkin on her lap.

Mrs. Warner hurried on. "So, now, perhaps we should continue discussing the true-to-life qualities of this Mark Twain's writing. What a strange name that is."

"Names don't really count, you know," Louise Smith said, speaking for the first time. She was a large woman with a small round face, narrow-set dark eyes, and a voice that was strident to the point of discomfort. But she was wife of the district judge and one of the best money raisers for charity in all of San Francisco.

The Literary Society members usually listened closely when she spoke. Mrs. Smith smiled faintly as the rest of the heads turned toward her. When she was satisfied she had every eye, she spoke rapidly.

"My husband says many people change their names these days. It isn't difficult. It can be done legally, but most men just drop a name they don't want and use a new one. Usually they're trying to cover up something in their past."

Mrs. Warner coughed, her stare turning cold. "There seems to be no reason to bring up the subject, Louise. You know we have a rule about maligning members of this society."

"Ruth Warner, you had your turn, now

it's mine. I only mention the facts." Her tone was sharp, and she stared directly at Mrs. Warner for any argument. She received none, so glanced around at the rest of the women, who all watched her expectantly. She went on.

"The facts are that Martha Pemberton may be an adopted daughter. She is certainly not the natural child of the couple who claim her."

Gasps exploded around the room as the seven women showed various degrees of surprise. Then heads began to nod and pairs of women whispered together.

"It was all done fifteen years ago, very quietly. Some young girl came to town and claimed the Pemberton girl was hers. She went to the police and had documents that seemed to indicate a real question existed as who Martha's true mother was. The police took it to the district attorney who consulted with my husband. So there was a closed hearing.

"The woman was little more than a girl herself, a dark-haired sloe-eyed one who was so dark everyone knew she was a gypsy, and she spoke only Spanish. She was slender with a provocative figure and a walk that made men turn and stare at her. My husband said she came into court dressed only

16

in a thin blouse he could almost see through and a short flouncing skirt that showed all the way over her knees. He said he guessed she wore nothing under her outer garments.

"But she had a document, a piece of paper signed by a priest in San Diego that listed the girl as the mother and one Harold L. Pemberton as the father of a baby girl. The date was listed and it was only a week from Martha's birthday.

"That was where it became more interesting. It turned out that Harold Pemberton had made several business trips to San Diego on his ships, including two around the time the baby would have been conceived. He also moved to San Diego shortly after that and stayed there for over a year setting up his operations there. During that time, Martha was born. The little girl was two months old when the Pembertons moved back here."

"All this came out in the closed hearing, of course. Hal Pemberton swore on the Bible that Martha was his natural child and that he had never known or seen this dark-eyed beauty before. Abigail was in the chambers the whole time. She sat dry-eyed and stoic, and she too swore that Martha was the child she saw pulled squalling from her womb.

"That settled it. Hal Pemberton told my husband he would pay the girl's passage back to San Diego, or to Seattle or even Denver, but he asked that the girl be restrained by the court from ever contacting him again about this matter.

"It ended that way, with Hal giving the woman a thousand dollars and rushing her out of town on his next boat to San Diego."

Ruth Warner felt her anger building with her frown. She walked to the big bay window and looked down across the scattering of mansions spaced toward the blue sweep of San Francisco Bay. When she turned she had control of her voice.

"Louise, dear, the story doesn't prove a thing. Both the Pembertons swore the child was their natural issue."

Mrs. Smith nodded. "Yes, Ruth, that's correct. But remember the line from William Shakespeare: 'Methinks the lady doth protest too much.' Why was Hal Pemberton protesting so? Why did he have a formal hearing? Many rich men are pestered by this sort of female strumpet with a squalling brat in tow demanding money, support, a settlement. He could have shipped her to one of those South Sea islands his ships go to all the time. But Hal wanted it all settled legal and proper and hushed up."

18

"But, Louise, to say the child may not be Abigail's . . ."

Louise Smith straightened her back and stared hard at the other woman. "Look at the three children. Randy Pemberton is the eldest, must be about twenty now and he's a blond and more fair than his mother. The youngest is Penny, so white-haired she looks like she hasn't a spot of color on her. Abigail is a Norwegian blonde, and Hal has a touch of German blond in his hair. So where did all of that jet black hair come from on Martha Pemberton's pretty head?"

The women gasped in unison, staring at Louise. She had done it again. She always had some choice bit of information to share with them. Of course nobody ever breathed a syllable of it outside the room. This one was a bombshell. The very idea that Martha Pemberton could be half gypsy and illegitimate at that. *A bastard!* No wonder Martha was half wild.

Ruth Warner rapped her small gavel on the pounding board that came with it and cleared her throat. "Ladies, this has simply gone far enough. Not a word of this is to leave this room, is that clearly understood?"

Every head in the room nodded agreement.

"All right, then, let's get back to our

19

author of the week, that strange one, Mark Twain."

Four miles from the scene of the regular meeting of the Literary Society, the object of the ladies' concern dismissed her carriage with an admonition to the driver that she would be ready for him to pick her up promptly at five o'clock in front of the San Francisco public library. She walked up the steps and into the building, going straight to the ladies' convenience room. There she took an old shawl from her large purse, threw it around her shoulders, then unpinned her hat, letting it flop around her face so it would be hard for anyone to recognize her. She smiled at herself in the wavy mirror and went back to the main section of the library and on out to the street by the side door. Her step quickened as she walked toward the waterfront.

She wanted to giggle. A proper young lady did not walk alone near the docks. But she knew this area, had played here since she had been a child. Didn't her daddy own half the ships in the harbor? No one would dare harm her. She was as safe as if she were in her own drawing room up on the hill. She paused at Front Street, then plunged across just behind a team of six towing a big wagon filled with freight from one of the ships at the embarcadero. The wagon was one of her father's. She smiled softly to herself, walked another block and came toward the *Star of the Sea.* The ship, a huge three-master, was riding high in the water. Martha knew most of the crew was on shore leave. She walked up the short gangway and stepped onto the polished deck. The ship seemed deserted. Martha turned to the left, went into a dank little hall — what did they call it? — a companionway, and near the front of the ship, she knocked on a door. There was no response. She knocked again.

Someone coughed behind her. Martha spun around, one hand half-way to her mouth, then she saw who the man was: Allen Cornelius, the first mate. He was second in command of the ship.

"I fear the captain isn't here, Miss," he said, his voice rich and deep. She had never heard him speak before. She had seen him on other occasions when she visited the captain. For a moment she was frightened. Captain Swartout was not here to protect her, defend her. He was old enough to be her father. She pushed the fear from her mind. Martha had seen this young man several times before. He wasn't much over twenty-five, she guessed, and nearly six feet tall with blond hair and wide shoulders heavily muscled and a trim, hard-looking body.

"Oh, well. I see," she said weakly. "He was teaching me how to play Mah-Jongg, that funny Chinese game with the little tiles. Do you play?"

"No, Miss, I'm afraid not."

"Maybe I could teach you," she said, then blushed and hurried on. "I mean some time when the captain is here, of course."

"Of course." His smile was insulting. She noticed how he had examined her closely, his eyes probing through the bulk of her shawl to look at her figure. It was shameful, but she didn't move. She should be leaving, yet she stayed, watching him. Quite unexpectedly, she found him fascinating.

"Could I offer you some tea?" he said quickly. "I'm afraid I became used to it in China when we were ported there for repairs for two months. I could brew some for you quickly."

"Oh, no, I couldn't. Not without the captain . . ."

"He won't be back today, or tonight, I'll wager, if I'm any judge of an amorous look in his eye," Allen laughed. "I'm sorry, I didn't mean to offend you, but you must know the captain is quite a ladies' man."

"And what about you, Mr. Cornelius?"

He chuckled, and she liked the sound. "You are something, aren't you? I've heard that you always speak your mind — and that's not exactly fashionable for women these days, is it? Well, no, I'm not known as a ladies' man, although I have a strong appreciation for a beautiful woman, even though I can't say hello to her. That was my position with you up today, but now that you're here, and the captain isn't, and the Mah-Jongg board is locked up in his cabin, why don't you honor me by sipping a small cup of the tea I bought myself in Hong Kong not six months ago?"

"At least you are gallant, Mr. Cornelius. And bold. Do you know who I am?"

"Oh, yes, Miss Pemberton, I most certainly do. That's why you are doubly safe with me. One word from you and my career with the company could be shattered . . ."

"Or greatly enhanced?"

"Such an idea . . ."

She was the one who laughed now. "Mr. Cornelius, I would like very much to have tea with you. On the deck, I suppose?"

"Ah, well, no. All of my things for making tea . . ."

"Are in your cabin. I expected they were, Mr. Cornelius." She shook her head, making her long black hair sway. A smile crept onto her face as she watched him from steady eyes. "Mr. Cornelius, I would be pleased to accept your kind offer of a cup of tea — in your cabin." She felt very worldly and very wicked.

He was pleased. "Good, Miss Pemberton. I am honored. Right this way. Do you prefer the lighter green tea, or something in a black with more body and bite?"

"I really don't know, Mr. Cornelius."

So they had tea.

In the next few weeks they met often, sometimes in the library, sometimes in a carriage. Once they had a picnic lunch in the big park by the bay. As she learned more about this handsome first mate, she realized he was strong-willed, had a streak of sternness, and that he faintly disapproved of her because she was a Pemberton.

Once she asked him why he didn't come courting formally, so she could meet him in her parlor. He laughed, kissed her roughly and then turned angry. "Because your father would have me thrown out of the house. He would also have me chucked off my ship and I'd never find another job at sea again except as an ordinary seaman. No, my sweet. I enjoy my position too much to jeopardize it that way."

Then, quite suddenly, his ship was getting ready to sail. The *Star of the Sea* was newly outfitted, her canvas repaired and her seams tightly calked. She would take a load of goods for trade in the South Pacific.

They met that afternoon in the far corner of the library reading room, then went out separately after she put on her disguise. He held her arm as they walked across the street, then down two blocks and up a side street where Martha had never been before. He turned her into a doorway. In back of the outside door rose a flight of steps. There, in the privacy of the closed area, he bent and kissed her on the lips. Martha felt her curiosity rising. She responded to his kiss and touched his cheek. He broke away and caught her arm, piloting her up the steps.

"A friend of yours lives up here?" she asked.

"Oh, yes, a very good friend." His smile was quick, a strange catch in his voice.

Down a short hall he used a key and opened a door. Inside she saw it was simply a one-room lodging with a big bed, a washstand and pitcher of water and a small closet.

"Land O' Goshen!" she breathed, when she heard him closing the door and locking it.

He came to her and held her from the back, his arms tight around her waist. "I told you I had a surprise for you — remember?"

She nodded, unable to do more. The room seemed unbearably hot after the coolness of the spring day outside.

"It's a surprise I hope you'll always remember, and if not exactly treasure, appreciate."

"No!" she flung the word at him, now knowing what he intended. How had she been so blind, so trusting, so naive?

"Yes, my sweet love. Yes. Your time of teasing is over. My sweet, you have led me on once too often. Today you find out where playing around with a man's affections leads. The next time you'll know if you want to stay in the game or not."

"That's not fair! It's horrid! I'll scream!"

"I rather hoped you would. The whole building is empty. We're near an alley where no one ever goes. It would spice up the affair a little if you did scream and cry and wail and promise me anything but your lovely body."

"I'll tell father. He'll throw you in prison. You know he can do it. You'll never work again."

"Think, Martha. We've been discreet. You

can't even prove that I know you. No one can testify that we have met anywhere, or that we've ever been together. I might have seen you once or twice on the ship when you came to see the captain. It would be an empty and easily disproven charge. You'd lose, and you'd look ridiculous, and be ruined for life. No, you'll say nothing to your parents. Screaming a little is all you have left. Why don't you scream, Marty."

"Don't call me Marty! If you want me to scream, I won't." Her black eyes snapped at him. "And I won't give you the satisfaction of raping me. I'll . . . I'll . . . help you. I'll undress myself . . ." Then the tears came, silent tears. He picked her up like a lost child and lay her on the bed. At first she gasped, realizing where she was, but the sobs won out and she cried softly. As she wept he took off his coat, tie and shirt. The sight of his undershirt was shocking to her, so she shut her eyes. When his hands first touched her, Martha pulled back.

He bent and kissed her lips and she groaned, not in passion, but in surprise and protest. He began to talk softly, telling her how long he had waited for this day. How he had watched her each time she had come on board to play Mah-Jongg with the captain. How he had planned to be there when

27

he knew the captain was gone.

"So, you see, I trapped you from the very start. But you're so beautiful, so remarkably beautiful, I could do nothing else. I'm the hunter and you're the fox. There was no way you could escape. But we have plenty of time — all afternoon. I won't rush you."

She sat up at once and threw off her coat. She ripped at the delicate buttons on her blouse until it was half open, then her fingers wouldn't work any more. He kissed her soft lips, and this time she couldn't pull away. But tears came again, quietly and with less force. His lips held hers for a long time before she leaned away.

"Allen, for so long I've dreamed of doing this with a man I truly love. How can you shatter my dreams this way?"

"Because you do love me. This will prove it. You wouldn't have come up the steps if you didn't know what was going to happen. Now, no matter who else has you, you will always love me the most, because I was the first. And one day when I return with a ship of my own, I'll capture you, and with or without your father's blessing, I'll sail away with you."

"That's romantic."

"This is a romantic time." He kissed her again, his tongue fighting to enter her mouth. His fingers continued to work on her buttons, and when they were all open, Martha caught his hands. "No, Allen."

"Yes, little Marty. Yes, Martha. Marty with the bright black eyes, the beautiful face and narrow waist with two luscious, tempting breasts just crying out to be petted. Yes, Martha." His hand touched her wrapper over one breast and she yelped.

"Oh, no, Allen!"

His kiss quieted her. She wondered why she wasn't screaming at him, fighting him, kicking, hitting him. Why did she let him do this? Kissing was bad enough, but the rest! His hand rubbed her breast and she hated it. But somehow it didn't seem so bad after a few moments. How could she ever undo the damage she had done by tearing at her blouse? For a moment she was afraid she had aroused him so much he wouldn't stop. She had heard how even the most gentle of men could become savage beasts. She should never have come up here. What had she been thinking about?

His lips against hers made the terror of it all die in her breast. Why did she feel this way? Suddenly it was so strange, a kind of soft warmness she had never known before. What did it mean? She sighed and looked up at him.

"Allen, you did plan this . . . this part of it too?"

"To love you? Of course not. How can a person plan to fall in love, or not to fall in love? Now be quiet. Don't try to think so much. Just let that wonderful warm feeling sweep over you, let it carry you along, feel how grand it is."

How did he know how she felt? How did he know that she was already brimming with a glowing warmth that was unusual but delightful? She felt his hands on her wrapper, rubbing gently. Then one hand slid under her corset and she gasped. When his hand touched her bare breast, Martha knew she was going to swoon. There was nothing she could do now to stop it. She lost her balance and fell backward, her eyes fluttering closed. She knew it was the worst thing she could do, to be lying down on the bed, but she couldn't help herself, and she couldn't stop him now. Not even if she wanted to. Did she want him to stop? It was so new, so exciting, so delightful!

She felt strange, warm and moist, as if her body were perspiring, but it wasn't. Martha knew her heart was beating wildly, and her breath came hard and fast. Her breasts burned, flaming at his touch, and now she moaned in pleasure. She had never felt anything so delicious in her life. She didn't ever want him to stop touching her that way.

Martha didn't remember all of it later, but her corset came off, and her skirt and hose, until they were both lying on the bed naked. She wouldn't look at his body. He talked to her softly, gently, telling her what to do, showing her, and she did it, like some schoolgirl. But he was so persuasive, and it all felt so strangely, wonderfully marvelous! He parted her legs and there were a few moments of sharp pain, then she groaned again in delirium, in rapture, in absolute glory!

Above her she heard his long panting gasps before he collapsed heavily against her, crushing her into the mattress. For a moment panic stormed through her, but she relaxed and fought it back and lay there in a dreamy, softly-white-and-gold world that she hoped would never go away.

Later he roused and came from her, sat on the edge of the bed, then dressed silently. She lay there, not knowing what to say, not knowing if she should pretend to be sleeping. Should she cover herself? Should she talk to him? Could she look at him? Was one supposed to talk afterwards, or simply let that beautiful feeling surge through one's body as long as it would? He dressed slowly,

31

watching her, smiling. Then he touched her arm.

"Are you all right?"

"Yes, really."

"Was it pleasing to you?"

She didn't know what to say. Should she tell him how beautiful it was, how rapture and ecstasy had joined in her very soul? Or should she scream and scold him?

"Some women don't enjoy making love at first. I certainly enjoyed it. Did you?"

She nodded.

His face broke into a smile and she realized he had been near to frowning as he spoke. He relaxed.

"Well, then, why don't you get dressed, and we shall go out for one of the finest meals San Francisco can offer!"

"You mean it?"

"Of course. If you'll go with me."

"Oh, yes! I'll go."

She began dressing and with a start realized she was not the least bit embarrassed. She was absolutely naked, sitting on a bed beside a man she hardly knew, and she wasn't the least bit upset by it. She glanced down at her breasts. They looked just as they had before, but he had said they were beautiful, he had touched them and even kissed them tenderly. How marvelous it had all been!

Martha dressed quickly, letting him help her with the corset hooks, then she washed her face in the bowl and combed out her hair. She left the old shawl in the room and pinned back the hat. She was proud to be seen with Allen Cornelius now.

The irony of it struck her at once. Less than an hour ago she had hidden her face when she was with Allen. Now she wondered why.

It was the most memorable dinner of her life. Many times she had been to famous and expensive restaurants in San Francisco, but this night had been the absolute best. They sat close together in a small eatery with a candle on the table and the lamps low. She couldn't remember the name of the place or what they had eaten, but it was beautiful.

When Martha burst in the front door of her father's big house on Nob Hill after eight that evening, she was radiant. She glowed and felt like a queen. Her mother and father were both out, and the maid said she had dinner ready. Martha pushed it aside and hurried to her room. She fell on the big feather bed and luxuriated in wave after wave of total joy that flooded over her. She had made love with the most wonderful man on earth, and she would marry him. She was sure he would ask her the next day. There would be no formal courting as such, only a brief period before her marriage. Then she would have a house of her very own.

Martha rolled on her back and saw him naked again, felt him touching her, caressing her, making love. So wonderful. It would be like that for always and always.

A vague sense of uneasiness crept into her joy. She fought it down, but it was still there. Then the word came out and she sat up, stunned.

Babies.

She hadn't even considered . . . she hadn't even thought about . . . Martha covered her face with her hands and wanted to cry. What had the girls said about babies? Oh, they had talked about it several times, but none of them knew many facts. At first they thought it might take five times to make a girl pregnant. Then they heard about a girl who got in trouble by "doing it" just once. Maybe once was enough! She knew so little about such matters. It simply wasn't discussed at home or at school, or by "polite" society. "After you're married you'll learn about all that," her mother had told Martha darkly one day when she was fourteen and her periods had just begun. Her mother turned furiously red at Martha's questions about pregnancy and stormed out of the room.

There was no one else Martha could ask who knew.

Pregnant!

Tomorrow she would go to the library and do some research. She knew one librarian who would help her. She would find out about those things. There must be books about it. Why wouldn't there be books about it?

She tried to recapture her happy mood, but it had vanished. Oh, yes, she could remember it in detail, every moment now. The joy of reliving her love-making would never fade, but the sense of wonder she had known just a few minutes ago was gone. Would it ever come back?

Martha sighed. Tomorrow she would go see him on the ship, or get a message to Allen. Allen. What a wonderful name! He was so tall and strong, and he had told her he was twenty-five. Mature. Yes, and he must have some money. They would be married right away. They really must, after what had happened this afternoon. She shuddered in fear, but couldn't stop a slow moan escaping her lips. As soon as the date was set for sure they could make love again. But not until then. She promised herself that making love was for married people, *only* for married people.

No, she couldn't be pregnant. It just wasn't fair, so it wouldn't happen to her. But what if it did? No. After all, she was a Pemberton, so it couldn't happen. Tomorrow she would send word to the ship to have Allen come calling. She would introduce him to her mother and tell her they met by chance on the ship and that she wanted him to come courting. It would all be arranged and formally correct, and Allen could court her as long as the ship was in port. Then they would announce their engagement.

Martha didn't care what her father might say.

She set her chin. She would tell him she was almost eighteen and she was a grown woman and would make her own decisions. She would tell him after she arranged it with her mother. But not a word about what happened in that bedroom this afternoon! Not even the hint of a thought about that.

"Pregnant!" She said the word out loud and shivered.

The next day, when she tried to send word to Allen, the messenger came back. The *Star of the Sea* had sailed that morning with the

36

tide. She was outbound for China, and not expected back for almost nine months.

Martha heard the news silently on the front porch where she had waited for Allen to come. She thanked the messenger and went straight to her room. First she locked the door, then threw herself on the bed and exploded with tears. He had taken advantage of her, made love to her, maybe ruined her for life, and then cast her aside like a worn-out shoe! He had deserted her. As first mate, he would know the exact time and date of the ship's sailing. So he knew yesterday. He knew all along. He knew before!

All the time he was pretending to love her, he knew.

All the time he was touching her, undressing her, he knew.

All the time he was pressing deep inside her, he knew.

She beat at the pillows with her fists. Her feet pounded the mattress and covers.

He had deceived her. He had mistreated her, abandoned her with no more than a casual glance. And he was gone now for six to nine months. Martha gasped at the time — the same as for a full grown human baby to be born.

She cried again, huge tears rolling down

her cheeks, staining her satin pillow cover.

She would go to her father at once, have Allen pulled off the ship and brought back here to stand charges. Or she could hire some men to kidnap him, torture him and slowly kill him.

No. She wanted that pleasure for herself. She would find him and shoot him with one of those little guns her father kept in his desk upstairs. Yes, that was it, she would kill him herself — only he wouldn't be back for nine months! Just thinking about the nine month span sent her into another seizure of violent crying. Her mother knocked on the door, pleading to come in. Martha paid no attention to her.

At last the tears stopped and her anger and hatred solidified into a rough form of action. If she ever saw Allen Cornelius again, she would kill him. There were many, many ways — gun, knife, even poison. Yes, she would do it.

She opened the door to her mother, undressed and went to bed, explaining she had the worst kind of pains in her back and head. Over her protests, her mother called the family doctor.

Martha stayed in bed for a week. No pleading by her father, her mother or the doctor did any good. She told them she was ill and might never recover. She ran a slight fever, looked terrible, but refused all mirrors. When the door closed each time and she was alone, she cried.

Time and again she probed her flat little white belly with her fingers. Was it true? Was there life growing inside of her? She could think of nothing else. Had her greatest moment of rapture turned into such a horrendous, mind-jolting catastrophe?

Facts. What she needed were facts! All her life she had prided herself on her ability to look at a problem and figure out the conditions. Then she solved it. Now she would do the same. She rang for the maid and ordered her to heat water for a bath. By noon Martha was at the San Francisco public library on Market Street.

Mrs. Gruber, the assistant librarian, was most kind. She was a mother of two, a widow, and said she thought any young girl about to be married deserved to know all the facts about themselves and their bodies and reproduction. She found three books for Martha from the restricted section and put her in a small private room where she could read them alone.

Two hours later, Martha closed the last book, waited for her high color to recede, then stood. She had learned everything she wanted to know about herself and her body. They even had drawings of men's and women's organs! She blushed again, just thinking about them. But they had been factual. If her next menstrual period arrived on time, she could be sure she was not pregnant. She had a little over four days to wait. Then she would know for sure. Then her life would continue, or she would be in for some drastic changes. The girls had been wrong. Doing it just once was plenty! She took the books back to the counter, turned them so the man behind her couldn't see the titles, and hurried out before Mrs. Gruber got back. At least now she knew. Why hadn't anyone ever told her?

In her room at home, Martha refused to see anyone. She sat and read, and wrote one long furious letter after another to Allen, only to burn up each one in turn. She would wait until the four days were over. Then she would know.

What if she were with child? She should make some plans now. She felt a new sense of being grown-up as she considered the problem. She would face it head-on. She would not tell her mother, but would go directly to her father in his office. She had done that in the past with minor troubles. He had always treated her like an adult with a real situation to deal with. Now she would simply tell him she was with child and that she wanted to go away somewhere, maybe to San Diego for a year. He would give her money, and she would go. It would be quite simple . . . *if* she were pregnant. With that planned, she settled down to wait out the three more days of torture.

Thursday morning came and she found a small red stain on her nightgown. It was blood. Martha wept silently for joy.

That weekend she received suitors. She had never been so radiant, so beautiful. Her mother marveled at the change in her, and smiled at the way she led on the three young suitors without ever committing herself to any one of them. Abigail often had differences with this headstrong daughter. She was so much like her father that it made Abigail wince. But Martha was a good girl, strong and bright. She would make some man a fine wife, even if she would be a handful for a few years. Now, Mrs. Pemberton was bound and determined to find her daughter a fine catch of a husband before something untoward happened. Goodness sakes, it certainly could these days with women prancing around showing off their ankles. It was disgusting. She shook her head and watched Martha trying to teach some young swain with two left feet to do the waltz. It was wasted effort. They swirled behind the drapes for a moment and Mrs. Pemberton leaned forward, but the pair came out at once, Martha with a little teasing grin on her face.

Jamison Horn walked away from the Pemberton mansion late that Saturday afternoon cursing silently to himself and kicking at stones in the street. He had been completely put down, put off and treated like a little boy who was bad so he didn't get any candy. It made him furious.

He stared at the other two hopefuls with him, Andrew Luston and Matthew Schenck. They all had one purpose and all had failed miserably at it — courting Martha Pemberton.

Jamison was a stoutly built young man of twenty-one, with a full head of flaming red hair, wide-set eyes and a broad face often given to song and laughter. Right now he wasn't doing either.

"I don't know about you two, but I'm getting damn tired of playing games with that little lady." He sent a long hateful look back at the mansion. "Why, she's nothing but a first-class flirt. She's all promises and teasings and then when it comes right down to a decision on something . . . nothing."

Andy Luston, almost twenty-three and the oldest of the trio, grinned at such inexperience. "A flirt, you say? Aye, that she is. Flirting is bargaining, man. Ever think of it that way? And she sure does have the goods to bargain for." He sighed, rubbing one gray leather glove across his chin. "But what a handful she's going to be for the man who finally wins her. But not soon. No, our Miss Pemberton is having too much fun right now to think of getting wed."

"Then why does she let us come courting?" Jamison asked.

"The sport of it. Men hunt, gamble, drink, wench around. A young girl likes excitement, too, and what better game than to have three men trying to wed and bed her?"

"It's all a game with her?" Jamison asked.

"That's what she told me by the curtain," Luston said. He stood half a head taller than the others, and thin as a ponderosa pine tree. His nose was too long, and bent interestingly to one side as a result of a tavern brawl. He grinned at the other two. "That's when I kissed her, when we swirled the curtain around us."

"You did *not* kiss her!" Matt Schenck howled. He turned and faced Luston. "You take that back!"

Andy Luston laughed. "Schenck, you're acting like a grammar school ninny. Are you fighting for the honor of your lady fair? Grow up, kid. That 'lady' is twice the tiger any of us is, or ever will be. She could chew us up and spit us out for breakfast. *Of course* I didn't kiss her. If I had, I wouldn't be bragging about it, I'd be sneaking back for a hundred more and then finding out just what that sleek little body of hers looks like without all those damn clothes on." He shook his head. "Don't worry about Miss Martha Pemberton. Even without her money, she could take care of herself nicely, and I'm sure she'll marry extremely well. Since none of us fit into that money category, forget her."

"Forget her?" Schenck yelped.

"Good idea, Schenck. That little female is going to cause more than one man to go through pure hell, and it won't be the man's fault." He stopped near his buggy and waggled his gloved finger at the pair. "This is my last night wasted on that doorstep, I can tell you that. I thought I had a chance a month ago. Now I know I don't. I could really use some of that Pemberton money. But it's hopeless. I saw that tonight. She's changed, become tougher, more sure of herself somehow. And I'm not about to hang around and entertain the young beauty."

"But . . . but she's got to marry *some-body*," Jamison said.

"Probably, but not one of us. Not one of the three here standing will ever touch one of her saucy, bouncing breasts. She has her eye set on much bigger quarry, even if she doesn't know it yet."

Matt Schenck took one step backward, then looked at the Pemberton mansion before he turned to Luston. "You talk as crazy and as fast as she does. She's just a kid — a silly little girl. She's only eighteen!"

Andy laughed and slapped Schenck on the back. "Sure, Schenck, sure — a mere child. You stay right there in the traces, old man, and keep on entertaining her. I didn't mean to run both of you off. What in hell would she have to do all Saturday and Sunday afternoons?" He paused and lit a black cigar. "Eighteen? Schenck, I've had whores younger than she is, damn good women they were, too. Now, that Martha is all girl, I guarantee it. She just needs to be aroused. After that first time, look out! I don't care how old her mother says she is. Her body says she's plenty old enough. That tiny waist and those beautiful legs . . . oh, Lord, get me away from here before I waste another three months." He stepped into his one-horse chaise and unwound the reins.

"You men go to it, but neither of you will win. She's fair game, damn fair. *Adios*." He snapped the reins, and the rig wheeled down the street.

CHAPTER TWO

Allen Cornelius got back to his ship extremely late that evening. He saw an old friend after dropping Martha at her father's house, and there was no way he could avoid a round of drinks. That first round soon developed into several rounds, and by the time Allen weaved carefully on board the *Star of The Sea,* he wasn't sure of what was happening.

Two hours later he was awakened by the ship's apprentice, Josh, who said Captain Swartout demanded to see Mr. Cornelius at once.

"The captain? He's out whoring," Allen said.

"He was, sir. He's been rousted out, too. Special orders, I hear, of the company. We're to sail with the morning tide."

Allen pulled on his boots and jacket and tried to rub the sleep from his eyes. Sail with the morning tide? They were out of their minds! No, the ship's stores were all on board. He'd supervised the completion of that the previous morning. And the cargo for trading had been secured for a week. Still, there were a hundred chores to be done.

"Roll out the crew, Josh. Do it any way you can!" He ran for the captain's cabin.

After that he had no time even to think. There were dozens of jobs to be finished. It was his job to make sure they were done before the ship left the embarcadero. First the fresh water tanks had to be topped off and a special cask put in each of the officers' cabins. Then there were the stores to double check against theft. He checked the lashing-down of the cargo, and moved to verify each and every manifest.

The watches were posted, and he slumped at the rail, trying to figure out what to do next. The eastern sky began to glow with that dull gray of first dawn. There would be enough breeze with the high tide in an hour to lift them out of the bay. Then he would strike a course for the Hawaiian Islands and they would be off.

It was always a treat for Allen to push off on a new voyage, the thrill of adventure, of challenging the sea, of working with physical skill, strength and knowledge against the mighty, unrelenting and unforgiving might of the oceans. It would be great to be at sea again.

It wasn't until the aft lines were cast off and they edged away from the dock under partial sail that he thought of the afternoon before, and the soft luxury of Martha Pemberton's sweet young body. Just thinking about her made his blood race.

"Oh, God, no!" He said the words out loud, and two seamen looked at him startled, then glanced aloft.

"No, lads. No, it's all fine here. Steady as she goes." It was Martha he was thinking of. She had said last night she wanted him to come calling today. She'd sent word for him to come at a certain hour so her father wouldn't be there but her mother would. "Oh, no!" he said softly to himself. She would be furious. She would think he had known all the time he was sailing, as a first mate should, that he had purposefully waited until the last night to seduce her, then abandon her. There wasn't even the possibility of sending word to her now.

He cursed silently to himself as he paced the small deck. Why did the fates treat him this way? The girl was a gem, a jewel. He knew she would be a handful as a wife, but he was fully determined to win her hand.

But now . . . what a damnable time to be sailing. She would think he had made love to her and run away, not waiting for her reaction — just loving and leaving.

Allen swore at the crewmen who had not turned the capstan exactly right. He raged at them, then left for his quarters. The captain would take the craft out of the harbor, that was his way. Allen could storm at himself below decks for half an hour.

Furious, outraged — she would feel he had purposely cast her aside. She would never speak to him again! No. He must find a way to contact her. But how? Tell the captain he had to get off a letter? Impossible. There was no way to get a message to her until they reached Hawaii. There he could leave a letter at the Pacific Steamship and Trading Company office, hoping it would be returned to San Francisco by the next Pemberton ship heading home. He could hope, but the mail across the Pacific was notoriously bad. It was at best a slim hope. Still he dug into his kit and took out a writing pad and quill pen and began to write. He preferred the quill to the modern steel tips. Twice he tore up a page. Three times he started again, and at last he decided it was as good as he could make it. He told her exactly what had happened, explained that he was sick about it, that he wouldn't have let it come about for the world, but that now there was simply nothing he could do about it. He would return at the soonest possible moment.

Allen prayed fervently that he would be back soon, and that the months would fly by like a week for his love and she would be waiting for him with open, loving arms when he docked again.

Then he would make his peace with her, and together they would launch a campaign to woo her mother, then her father, and in that way they would win the right to marry. It wasn't as if he were some ordinary seaman right off the docks. He was one of the Boston Corneliuses, well known in shipping circles. He would write and have his letters of credit sent to a San Francisco bank. He must have well over a hundred thousand dollars on deposit by now.

Allen thought how he had come here. It had been on a special letter from his uncle addressed personally to Harold L. Pemberton himself, president and founder of the Pacific Steamship Lines. The two men had met and had some business dealings. The letter only said that young Cornelius had been in a "disagreement in management policy" and for the good of the Boston firm and the young man's future, it was requested that Allen be given employment in some secondary management level with the Pacific Steamship and Trading Company. There had been more to it than what the letter said, and Pemberton knew it, but he didn't press the issue.

For Allen, the problem had been his cousin. He had been totally surprised that afternoon at his uncle's Boston home. Most of the family had gathered for a birthday party for an aging aunt. Melinda caught his arm and said she needed him to reach a book for her from high on a library shelf. It was after dinner, and everyone was scattered throughout the big house. She went into the library with him and abruptly locked the door, then smiled and walked up to him and kissed him on the lips.

"Did that surprise you, Cousin Allen? I've loved you for just years. Didn't you know that?"

She was seventeen, fully developed, with large breasts, but she was simply not a pretty girl. She smiled at him and put her arms around him, pushing her breasts against his chest.

"Do you like that, Allen? Does that feel good?"

"Yes, of course, but if anyone should . . ."

"Scaredy cat. I locked the door, and nobody ever uses the other one." She pulled him over next to the door where she leaned against it, then kissed him again, standing on tiptoe. She grinned, feeling the hardness at his groin where she pushed against him. "You do like that. I can tell you like it."

"Melinda, now stop that."

She stuck her tongue out at him, leaned back and caught his hand. She pulled it up and placed it over her breast. Her smile was teasing. "If you're not afraid, cousin love."

"Look, it isn't that. I work for your father, and if he even knew we were alone in here with the door locked . . ."

She moved his hand inside the loose neckline of her blouse and under the top of her corset directly on her bare breast.

"Oh, Melinda, don't do that."

"I want to, darling Allen. I want you to touch me, feel me." She smiled. "Darling Allen, haven't you ever touched a girl before? I've been touched. Don't worry, you won't break me."

His hands began to move. He couldn't stop. Allen knew the risks, but the soft, pink girl-flesh was so willing, it swayed him. He fondled her breasts.

"Since you're playing with me, darling . . ." She put her hands down to his waist and began opening the buttons on his trousers.

"Hey!"

"You are afraid."

"Just of your father."

She laughed, opened her shirt front and pushed one breast out of the wrapping. "Kiss it, darling. Kiss it and make me feel good!"

Allen could only remember one woman who had been so blatant, so sex-hungry as this one, and she had been on the docks at Boston. He and two seamen had bought her for the day, and she had worn all three of them into limp lumps.

Melinda had just popped her other breast out of her dress and was pulling at his trousers fly, when the private, always locked door into the library from the other side opened and Archibald Cornelius strode into the room. He stopped in mute surprise when he saw his daughter undraped.

Allen left for San Francisco the following day.

Now, on the gently swaying ship, Allen tried to shake off the memory. Outside, the gathering light outlined the hills of San Francisco. He could almost see the big Pemberton house on the hill. Soon he would be back there, campaigning for the

54

hand of the woman he loved.

But now there was work to be done. He had to snap out of his chagrin, his depression, and get his work done. When he came back to port, he would attack his new problem.

Quickly he got on deck.

"Ben, you shirker, up the ratlines, help out on the main. Can't you see they're short-handed topside?" His bellow brought a man out of the jumble of lines around the forward mast and scurrying up the lines.

That night in his cabin before he checked the watch, Allen reaffirmed his resolve to challenge the powers and plot a course to win Martha's hand. He had been two years at Harvard. He could navigate a tall ship across the Pacific with only a glass, a compass and his wits. He had spent a year in the bookkeeping side of the business in Boston and knew many details about shipping, prices, profits, net, gross, and partial loads as well as contracts. Besides, the lady in question had found him attentive and attractive. He had a good family background and a sizeable fortune in the bank. And he had made love to her. That was the strongest argument in his behalf — but he couldn't use it.

He admitted to himself that he had seduced Martha. He had set out to trap her, planned it carefully from the very first day he met her when he knew the captain would be out. His usual attention to small matters, like courtesy and thoughtfulness, had won the day and the bed. His blood heated again as he thought of her, stripped of her clothes. Delicious. Absolutely delicious. He had never known a woman with her honesty, her openness, her lack of embarrassment, and with such a built-in fire. Her heat of passion singed him again now as he remembered it.

Never had he possessed a woman with so much enthusiasm in making love, and she was just learning. No limp rag, his Martha! For a moment he thought she had been more interested in being seduced than he was in doing it. Not that she had flaunted herself at him the way Melinda had. No indeed. She was controlled, and so confident that it made him smile, remembering.

In that respect she was much like her brother, whom Allen had seen only twice. He was blond, aloof, in school at the University in San Francisco. He kept above the common riff-raff like first mates, and only talked with ships' captains. Randy Pemberton was twenty years old, and Allen knew that some day he might be working for him.

He thought back to Boston. It might be

just as well he was gone from there. Everything here was so new and growing, so open, so ready for development. The land was virgin, the towns small, the population so scant it was almost a wilderness. Maybe he should thank his cousin Melinda for her help after all. He smiled thinking about Melinda. She would make out all right, if she didn't get pregnant first. She was no raving beauty, but she had more suitors than any other girl her age. She also had more money, and would inherit millions. That night, after her father had surprised them in the library, she had wept and run to her room. She locked the door and soon sneaked out her window. When Allen arrived home in minor disgrace, he had found Melinda lying naked in his bed. She was very good at getting in and out of first-floor windows. Melinda stayed most of the night and proved to Allen that she was not just a tease. He grinned, remembering how good she was at making love.

Allen looked back at the stack of books he had brought for the trip, but pushed it aside. Perhaps this was the time to leave the sea and go into the shore side of the Pacific Steamship firm. He had been there for two years now, and this would make almost two and a half at sea. He would need another three or four before he could get in line for a ship of his own. On land he could surely progress faster in the company.

Although here he had authority. It was his job to run the ship, to make port and take care of all unloading, and loading of cargo. The captain handled the bargaining, haggling and the making of payments. Sometimes Allen thought the captain wasn't as sharp as he should be, but his trips always made a profit for the company, with a share for the captain.

Captain Swartout was a good Mah-Jongg player and could drink half the crew under any table. In foreign ports he could always find a girl who wanted a free ship ride. He usually got one at the first port of call, used her for a month or two and deposited her at the last port before sailing for Hawaii. It was strictly against Pacific Steamship and Trading Company rules, but who would turn in his own captain? Allen had almost asked the captain if he could bring a girl on board during the last trip. She was a tiny Japanese girl of whom he was very fond, but his better judgement won out and he left her on the island. At least Captain Swartout never beat his girls, and they always left the ship richer and wiser than when they had boarded.

■ ■ ■ ■

Three months later, Allen came on deck
early one morning to check the watch just
before dawn. They were only a few days out
of Hong Kong. Allen made his usual rounds,
talking briefly with two men on watch,
discussing the weather, girls, what the
sailors would do on their first shore leave.
He rounded a stack of cotton bales and realized his mistake. He had cut around them
sharply to save time, and almost lost his life.

The marlinespike smashed down toward
his head, and only his quick lunge to one
side saved him. The heavy iron spike glanced
off his shoulder, numbing his left arm. He
flailed out and caught the assailant who was
still moving forward. Allen used the man's
own momentum and smashed him against
a bulkhead, where his skull cracked open
like a walnut under a heavy hammer.

A shot blasted forward.

Allen dropped to the deck and squirmed
behind the baled cotton. The clouds had
covered the half moon. He could see little.
His right hand moved to the holster and
pulled the .44 he always carried in these
waters. He had the new type, with cartridges. A man eased along the far rail, a

pistol in one hand, a short saber in the other. The man's cat eyes picked out Allen near the cotton, and he fired. The heavy ball missed. Allen returned the fire and saw his bullet spin the man around. Allen jumped up and rushed to where he leaned against the rail. But the man came to life, whirled with the saber and slashed Allen's left arm, which still hung limp at his side.

The saber rose again and Allen realized he had come in too close, that the sailor had a one-shot pistol and had to rely on his short-range weapon. Allen fired again, the big .44 slug catching the mutineer in the chest, splattering two ribs as it bored into his heart and slammed him backwards four feet where he crumpled to the deck, blood gushing onto the wood as the man died.

A dozen seamen poured out of their quarters, several with hurricane lamps. They searched the deck and found one more dead man, a seaman on watch who evidently had refused to join the mutiny. Captain Swartout stumbled out of his cabin and took charge. He called out the entire crew, found two men missing and organized a search. One was spotted aloft. He refused to come down. A second man had hidden in a sail locker where he had unloaded his pistol and tried to hide it. He had been an unwilling participant. He said that if he didn't help, he would have been shot at once.

Dawn had eased on them as they searched. Now they watched the man aloft as the light strengthened. The captain ordered the man hiding in the locker to go topside and bring down the fourth mutineer. He stared at the captain for thirty seconds, then nodded. He knew it was his only chance for survival.

In the rigging, the two men faced each other and talked for a moment, then the fight began. Each man had a six-inch knife and his wits. The battle moved higher and higher in the rigging until both stood on the top spar. Knives bit into flesh. Both men knew they faced hanging if they crawled down the ratlines. Possession of a pistol was in itself a hanging offense on board a Pacific Steamship ship. Drops of blood spattered on the deck. All hands watched the fight aloft.

The battle raged back and forward along the spar, then on down ratlines to the lower spar and back up again. For each man it was a life-and-death struggle. Soon both bled from minor wounds, but nothing fatal had landed.

Then the man who left the deck to roust out the mutineer lunged forward, holding on by one hand, kicked at the other man, missed and swung past him. The knife drove in firm and deep into the attacker's chest. He screamed, clung to the line for a moment, then his foot slipped and he fell, careened off a line as the boat rolled over in a huge swell, his body splashed into the sea a dozen feet from the rail.

One seaman ran to the stern, and watched the spot as the ship sailed past.

"No sign of him, sir," the seaman reported. Allen nodded.

They looked aloft again. The man there had shrugged out of his shirt and sweater, throwing them aside. He bent and kicked off his boots, then looked at the water. He stood 130 feet off the water. No one said a word. The mutineer judged the distance, waited for the roll of the ship to swing the mast out over the sea. Then he dove. But luck turned on him. An unusual cross-swell righted the ship just before he left the spar. The big square-rigger swung sharply the opposite way, and a moment later the men on deck scurried out of the way.

The mutineer's dive carried him clear of the lines, and as he came down they saw him furiously trying to alter his direction, to clear the ship. But he couldn't. His arms, then his head hit the main deck four feet from the rail, shattering his arms, smashing his head open. His torso buckled, snapping his spine in a dozen places. Leg bones broke audibly as his whole body smashed into the unyielding wood, then toppled forward slightly. Half the bones in his body had been broken or crushed.

A half-hour later the body had been dumped overboard without benefit of burial services. Three other bodies were likewise committed to the deep with only a few words, and Allen returned to his quarters to make out a report. He was shaken. It was the first violence he had seen at sea, certainly the first attempted mutiny. He still couldn't raise his arm. Josh, the apprentice working to be a ship's officer, had bandaged his arm and smeared it with some kind of poultice. The slash near his shoulder wasn't deep but painful, and the bash on the shoulder was the disabling part. The intent of the mutineers was obvious. Close to port, they had tried to seize the ship, kill the five officers and dump them into the sea, allow any who did not want to join the mutiny to debark at a nearby uninhabited island, then sail the ship into Hong Kong and sell the trading goods. If they were smart enough, they might have kept the ship, re-rigged her, changed the name and registry and have gone into the trading business on their own with the profits on the sale of goods.

Only they had failed. And they had died.

Now there was little chance for time to drag. Allen had to get the craft ready for the first port of call. From that point on he would be working sixteen hours a day. But always he found time to write in his journal, which he would give to Martha when the ship returned. He hoped the journal would help vindicate him from the villainous role he had been forced into, which had been totally out of his power to prevent.

He worked hard, drove the crew and saved a day here, another day there, and hoped he could make up a week or more by the time they were ready to leave for the long trip home. He saw the women at dockside, but didn't take shore leave. One day the captain grew tired of his girl and gave her to Allen. She came to his cabin and undressed slowly, seductively, but Allen could not bring himself to make love to her. After Martha, this girl seemed plain, ugly, flat-chested and uninspiring. He put her back ashore.

When the final cargo was stowed and clearances made, he didn't even double check the stewards on the new supplies of food. He was too anxious to be off and headed for home.

Allen could only wonder what had taken place during the nearly seven months it would be since he had seen the lovely Martha Pemberton. He longed for that first sighting of San Francisco.

CHAPTER THREE

The South Pacific, 1872.

Captain Peter Dyke walked the rolling deck of the steamship *Pacific Gem,* a dark frown distorting the open, usually smiling face. The captain was still angry with himself because of a snip of a girl who had ridiculed him in front of his employer, and the memory even now rankled him.

Peter Dyke stood over six foot three. His head was topped by a crop of red hair and a full red beard completed the frame of his square-cut, handsome face. Now he shook his head in disgust. If she had been one of his hands, he would have applied the lash to her bare back himself!

The thought of the girl naked to the waist played on his mind as he paced, and he tried to imagine how she would look. He cursed the wide Pacific Ocean. He had been too long at sea. Still the vision of the black-eyed wench clung in his mind as his seaman's legs compensated for the roll of the steel-hulled ship, and his seaman's mind noted the direction of the wind and the fact that the waves were smaller now than they had been half an hour before. The mild blow was wearing itself out.

He was still two days out of Rapango, and once there he would be working around the clock, to be sure the loading and unloading all went well. He couldn't trust his first mate farther than he could throw a hatch cover, and his purser would be tied up, trying to keep the paperwork straight.

Captain Dyke watched the waves break over the bow of the two-hundred-foot-long *Pacific Gem.* She was a good ship, one of the first of her kind in the South Pacific, and sailing out of San Francisco.

She carried a forty-five-foot beam, and her holds dropped down thirty feet from the deck. He was justly proud of her, and that he had been named her first captain. He had worked his way up through the line on other ships and he knew the South Pacific like the inside of his cabin. Now he had command of the big ship, the biggest and best in the whole ocean in 1872.

In fact, the big ship had changed the name of the firm from Pemberton Sailing Company to Pacific Steamship and Trading

Company. It was a timely change. Within twenty years all the ships would be steel-hulled and steam driven.

Again his thoughts went back to the long black hair and darting eyes, the sensuous young body and swaying breasts of the girl back in San Francisco. There had been many other women in ports, even some in home port when he met the girl, but the only one he remembered now was Martha. She had struck such a response in him that he had been unable to speak when he first saw her. She brushed past him, laughing at his sudden affectation, and he only saw her from a distance after that. She dazzled him. Soft skin the color of new ivory, glorious billowing midnight black hair that fell around her soft bare shoulders, and breasts so surging and straining against her tight white dress that he longed to set them free.

Captain Dyke shook his head, clearing it of the wild thoughts he had, the fantasies, and walked with a rolling gait to the bridge and checked the compass. They were on course and not quite two days out of Rapango.

They would lay in the deep water lagoon for over a week, taking on cargo. Rapango had no dock, so everything would be ferried out in the two small work boats now lashed to the deck. It would be slow, back-breaking work, even with the new winches and loading booms, but it would still take more than seven days to load.

As he stood on the bridge, Captain Peter Dyke found himself thinking more and more in terms of how long it would be before he sailed into San Francisco, how long before he could see the woman he now knew he must have, one way or the other.

She was bewitching, young, with the very devil shining out of those black eyes. She would be one who needed taming on a wedding night. His brows jolted upward as he stared at the oncoming seas. Never before had he thought of marriage, but now he knew that marriage was the only way he would ever have her. Martha Pemberton, the daughter of his employer, who was the owner of the Pacific Steamship and Trading Company, would not be an easy mark.

She was fair game for a chase, and in the final moments after the capture she would be like other women he had taken — but the chase would be more than enough diversion.

Now his mind was made up. When the *Pacific Gem* touched in San Francisco, he would go at once to Mr. Pemberton and ask permission to court his daughter. She would marry someone — why not a captain? Why not keep the marriage and the money that went with it inside the business structure of Pacific Steamship?

He left the bridge and paced the outer decks again, thinking about the girl. She was spirited, perhaps with a touch of wilderness, but he knew how to break a bucking horse — it wouldn't be much harder handling this woman.

He was no mean catch himself. He knew of at least a dozen young ladies who would be eager for him to ask permission to court. Two of them had been more than willing to go to bed with him as an incentive.

He paced again. The girl's round, sweet face haunted him. Why did he suddenly want only her? It had been a year ago that he saw her last, at the owner's house. He had teased her, and she had flirted shamelessly. She must have changed a lot in that year. He was anxious to see her.

But first, work, and Rapango. The tiny island held a warm spot in his heart. He wasn't king of Rapango, but almost. The speck of land in the Pacific lay to the east of Papeete, on the very fringes of the French protectorate. Officials weren't sure if Rapango was in their sphere or not, and that was partly how Captain Dyke had made his deal. It had been five years ago, when he was still running his own small trading ship between the islands. He and his mate were in Papeete waiting for a cargo to transship and had stopped at a small cafe-tavern. They had been watching three native girls bare to the waist dancing the Tahitian hula, and Frenchy, Dyke's only crewman, was disgusted.

"They call them tiny sluts dancers?" Frenchy exploded. "I've seen a better figure on a palm tree."

Peter Dyke blinked slightly red eyes watching the three brown forms. "Damn, is this why we busted our asses for three days, to get back here?"

Frenchy had changed his mind. "Well, now, Cap'n, you take that middle one. She's not 'alf bloody bad."

Peter Dyke drained the whiskey bottle and banged it on the table. He stood, grabbed the Frenchman's shirt collar and pulled him around the table.

"Come on, you dumb sailor. We'll go for a walk and find ourselves some young stuff."

The captain started to push Frenchy ahead, but stopped when he heard a small noise behind him. He turned toward the entrance to the cafe and his mouth gaped open as he stared at a white woman. She

71

had just stepped inside when he saw her, a quick flash of pink and white, dotted by the lightest blue eyes he had ever seen. The long pink dress brushed the floor, pinching in tightly at her waist. It hid almost nothing. At first he couldn't see her face behind the frilly parasol. Then she turned toward him. Her face was small, round, very French, with features a little sharp, but dominated by liquid blue eyes. The neckline of the expensive dress plunged delightfully low, exposing on each side a generous mound of pink flesh, with the rest discreetly hidden by a froth of lace.

He stared openly at her, knowing he had not seen anyone so pretty in a year. There was only one Frenchwoman on the island so young and beautiful — Petite Cousteau, daughter of the governor of all Tahiti.

She did not come into the cafe, but stood surveying the dozen men inside. When her eyes found him, she stopped looking and motioned to him. He walked slowly toward her, drinking in all the delights he knew were just under the dress.

"Captain Dyke?" she asked. He nodded. "I wish to charter your vessel for a week's trip. Is it available?"

"Yes?" he said, his eyes never leaving her breasts.

"Come at 8:30 tonight to the west entrance of the governor's house to sign the contract."

"Yes, ma'am."

She watched him, and her eyes danced, then she spoke so low no one else could hear. "I'll have a surprise for you," she said, and turned and went out the door.

That evening at precisely 8:30, Captain Peter Dyke knocked at the west door of the mansion, and was ushered in by a native girl in a blue uniform. Although the governor's house was the biggest and best in all Tahiti, the hallway he entered was simple, stark. A short way along the passage, the servant girl knocked on a door, then hurried away.

The panel opened a crack, then the same voice he heard that afternoon asked him to come in.

As he pushed open the door, a flood of delicious scents poured over him, but he forgot them at once as he saw the luxury of the room. The color scheme was soft pink, with feathers and huge ostrich plumes on the wall. The rug was so thick that he stumbled. The large bed, with a canopy and four decorated posts, stood to one side. A long couch piled with pillows took up one side of the room.

The girl stood beside the bed. His eyes widened, and Captain Dyke sucked in his breath when he looked at her. She wore a simple Chinese robe of fine silk, woven so loosely it was transparent. It showed every detail of her stunning body: small feet, trim legs rising in perfect contours to small thighs, and a bush of brown hair protecting her crotch. Above, a tiny waist, a flat stomach and the quick outthrust of small, finely-sculptured breasts.

"I'm glad you came, Peter Dyke," she said, sitting on the bed.

"About the ship — she's the *Paradise* . . ."

She laughed. "Peter, I don't want your smelly old boat. I thought surely you understood that." As she said it, she pushed the thin robe off her shoulders and patted the bed, then lay back. Captain Peter Dyke walked to the bed and looked down at her.

Back on the shifting deck of the *Pacific Gem,* Captain Dyke quit his exercise walk and returned to his cabin. He would never forget that French girl. It had been like a disease with her: she demanded to be loved twice a day. He stayed for a week, and refused to leave. At last the governor granted him exclusive trading rights on the island of Rapango, and gave him a hundred gold pieces.

An inspection party was due from Paris, and the governor wanted Captain Dyke out of his daughter's bedroom well before the inspectors arrived.

So he and Frenchy sailed for Rapango. He knew the island well, a sheltered cove, but with no dock. Plenty of copra for sale, and very little tribal government. He could take over the island, and live like a king if he wished. There would always be enough to eat, enough copra to sell, and an unending supply of willing fifteen-year-old virgins.

The real force on the island of Rapango was Tapo, the old priest, who communicated with dozens of gods and laid down the laws and taboos. No white men lived on Rapango. It measured only five miles wide and fifteen miles long — just a speck of green in the broad Pacific Ocean.

Old Tapo had been a sailor in his youth for two years, and had learned to speak French and some English. The last time Captain Dyke had visited the island of Rapango was on his own small trader looking for cargo.

Tapo had sat in his palm hut watching for sign. He was well past his fiftieth rainy season, and his hair was as white as the top of a crashing wave. But Tapo had much soul, much *po,* and was the sacred priest for the whole tribe on Rapango, or the Island of a Thousand Breadfruit, as his people had called the land for over twenty generations. He had trained from childhood to be a priest, but now he said he felt he had learned nothing, that he knew less about the gods than the breadfruit trees or the golden fishes that swam in the lagoon.

"Captain Dyke, for the past twenty-four high tides I find bad sign and ill omens. They all show the gods from the mighty Oran to the gods of the surf and rocks and wind, hold my people in disfavor. Two nights ago, Robolo, a lesser god of the trees and plants, came to me in a dream, and spoke from the side of his mouth, showing great unhappiness."

"Evil and sickness tread upon the Island of a Thousand Breadfruit, old friend Tapo, the great god told me. He said the young men no longer cut the ripe wood for huts, the roots go uneaten because no one digs them. Fruit falls wasting from the trees, and I see young girls lie with their brothers and lift their *ti* skirts willingly."

Captain Dyke pulled at the whiskey bottle and shook his head at Tapo. "You can't fight the gods, Tapo."

"Now I know, but what was I to do, Captain? I rose from my pandanus mat and walked the beach for hours, pondering what the dream meant. Surely it is true, or Robolo would not say it. But why did he tell me at that time?"

Tapo sighed, remembering. "I went to the waves and found more sign, which rushed toward me on the foaming waters in the moonlight. They all warned of danger. I picked up a rare and beautiful Glory of the Sea cone shell and my hand shook. It is the most powerful omen our people know. It is so rare, that in fifty rainy seasons I had never seen one before. Thilu, the great goddess of the sea, lives in the rare shell, and only for unusual and terrible events does she ever permit her shell to wash ashore as a sign."

He went on to tell the captain that he had crept to his grass hut trembling. His fear was stronger when he dreamed again that night that he saw the great white shark, his top fin splitting the waters in the lagoon. The *mano* came closer to shore and watched Tapo. *Mano* was spokesman of many gods, and Tapo knew him well.

"Why did you permit the men and women of your island to ignore the old gods, Tapo? You have forgotten Kilu, and your temple has no stone for this great god. He is most angry. He has waited many rainy seasons

77

for your signs of obedience. He has now lost patience, and has told me to warn you of his wrath."

Before Tapo could question him, the *mano* turned and swam out to sea, past the reef and out of sight, which in itself was another great and bad omen.

Tapo woke and sat on his mat the rest of the dark hours. He was sure *mano* had brought a great warning, but from which god? From the goddess of the sea or of the wind? From the god of fire or Robolo — or was it from the mighty Oran, the god of the sun and fertility? Kilu? Who was this ancient god, Kilu? In another day Tapo could have asked the old men in the village, but now he was the most ancient. He would have to discover Kilu for himself.

For ten days and ten nights, Tapo lay in the temple on the hard stone, refusing to eat and drinking only enough water to keep alive. At the end of the fast he came to his own hut and collapsed. The old women of the tribe nursed him back to health with herbs and roots and tea made from the *tium* leaf. When he could walk again, Tapo went to the cliff calling to King Matono for permission to speak. The king asked him to walk up the sacred stairs.

"Oh Great King, the smaller gods are

angry," Tapo said after he had recounted the many signs and omens he had found. "In my cleansing at the temple many gods came to me and warned me that we have much evil. They told me what we must do to prevent a powerful misfortune, and they told me who the god Kilu is."

The king listened with growing uneasiness. Never had Tapo been so fearful, so anxious, and never had he brought such terrible news.

"Oh Mighty Matono, we have forgotten the great god Kilu, he whom our fathers and our fathers' fathers worshipped as the most powerful and feared of all our gods."

King Matono thought of the old gods, but could not remember the name of Kilu.

"The great god of the burning rocks!" Tapo wailed. "He who sent whole rivers of fire against our people, a hundred rainy seasons ago."

"But Kilu is dead," said the king. "Our fathers watched him die from the place of tears. He has not talked to us or sent his burning rocks toward us for three generations."

"Still he lives, and is angry. He waits for us to become evil, so he may destroy us. Kilu is a vengeful god."

"Is there any way we can appease Kilu?"

the king asked.

Tapo turned so his side was toward the king, a great show of respect, and bowed his head to the mat. "Only one way, great king. We must find the most beautiful maiden in our village upon whom no canoe has ever sailed, who sings like a bird in the hush of dawn, and whose beauty makes every man in the village yearn to lift her *ti* skirt and steal away into the bushes with her. On the thirteenth high tide from today, we must present her to Kilu, offering her from the place of tears, casting her into the very jaws of the mighty Kilu!"

"No!" King Matono roared. "During three generations we have not offered maidens as human sacrifices. The killing has stopped. I will not let it begin again. Let Kilu strike me dead this instant if he is so powerful and I am wrong!" Matono glared at the walls of his palace and turned, shaking his fist toward the mountain where Kilu lived. But his life was spared.

Tapo fell on his face and crawled from the presence of the king. Outside he hurried down the hill on old legs that trembled so he could hardly keep from falling. He crept into his hut near the temple and fell on his mat.

The king would not permit the sacrifice.

How else could they appease the angry god? Could the whole tribe stop doing what angered the fire god? But what was that? Tapo sat with legs crossed, arms folded, thinking of every aspect of village life.

It could not be the temple itself. It had been placed four generations ago in the best place to worship all the gods. It was directly in line with the mouth of the lagoon so the first rays of the morning sun slanted across its roof before any of the other huts in the village was touched. It was open to the sea on two sides so Thilu could float in and out on the moist sea air and refresh herself. It was close to a stand of fine coconut palms and breadfruit trees. The six corner posts of the temple were carefully consecrated according to ancient custom. Each hole was blessed with fish from the sea, breadfruit and coconuts and specially treated pieces of tree bark. The posts were set only when the sun shone directly into the bottom of the hole. It had taken three months to consecrate the temple. Now Tapo suddenly was worried. Had they made some mistake back there for which his people must suffer now?

He beat his head against the soft sand until he became dizzy. When his mind cleared, Tapo went into the village and studied his people to find the cause of the disaster.

Much later Tapo looked up at Captain Dyke who sat beside him in the warm, dry sand.

"Old friend Tapo. It is well known that the gods think in strange and mysterious ways. They even argue and fight among themselves. But what they all agree upon is that we must get all the cargo on board the *Pacific Gem* quickly. The god of the wind is often angry this time of the year, and we must be out of the lagoon within five days."

Tapo smiled. "Sometimes, Captain Dyke, you twist my words and make the gods smile on your own pleasures. But it will be done. My people need the cloth and iron tools you bring, and you need the copra and fruits."

He made a strange series of lines in the sand, all interlocking. When he looked up, his smile was gone, and Captain Dyke felt a quivering of fear brush past him.

"Captain, for now we are friends, but some time soon I fear that all may change. In the end the gods will have their way, and neither you nor I will have our way."

Even now as he sat on his bunk in the large captain's cabin on board the *Pacific Gem*, Peter Dyke shivered as he remembered that last talk with Tapo. He wondered if the old native did have some ability to see into the future.

Captain Dyke didn't worry about it for long. He would be back at Rapango soon to take on more cargo before sailing for home. In a month or a little more he should be in San Francisco, looking into Martha Pemberton's black eyes, watching her sleek young body and trying to win her hand in marriage.

■ ■ ■ ■

Book One

■ ■ ■ ■

CHAPTER FOUR:
A LEARNING TIME

Martha Pemberton laughed gaily and dodged behind an ornate, overstuffed chair in the big parlor of the Pemberton mansion. The Oriental rug had been rolled back from one end of the beautifully furnished room and she had been trying to teach three Saturday afternoon suitors how to waltz. She jumped nimbly one way, then the other, and skipped around the chair as the young man pursuing her stumbled and fell over his own feet. Martha stopped and covered her mouth with one hand as she giggled.

"Matthew, you just look so silly when you fall down that way. How am I ever going to teach you to dance the waltz?"

He got to his knees, her ridicule running off him so quickly he never even recognized it. Matt Schenck only grinned, stood and held out his hands in the proper position to touch a lady when doing the waltz. Martha shook her head.

"No, Matthew. I'm sorry, but your turn is over. Now, let's see if Andy has remembered anything about the waltz . . ."

Andy jumped to his feet and walked quickly toward her. He bowed low. "May I have the honor of this waltz, Miss Martha?"

She beamed. "Now, that is just perfect, Andy. You are a good student." Her smile turned to an impish frown. "But can you count all the way up to three?" She tittered and stepped into his arms, his right hand gently touching her pinched-in waist, his left holding her hand stiffly in front of them.

Andy began to sweat. He'd danced with her twice before this way, and each time he wanted to pull her tightly against his aching body and kiss her soft red lips. But he had resisted. Right now she smelled so sweet he thought he was in a rose garden.

Andy went into the waltz steps slowly, then gained confidence as he remembered and whirled her around the bare section of the parlor floor.

"My, my, Andy. You must have been practicing," Martha said, her voice amused, a little high, trying to let him know that she wasn't very impressed, that she didn't care a fig for him.

Andy whirled her once more and they were in the big front hall and shielded from the other two suitors. Quickly he pulled her slender form against him, his mouth pressing hungrily against her lips. The kiss was quick, not perfectly on target, but it still caused Andy to moan deep in his throat.

Martha was so surprised that she couldn't speak for a second. Then she exploded in fury. Her fingernails raked down Andy's cheek, gouging out enough skin to draw blood. She slapped his face as hard as she could, and jumped back.

"Andy Luston . . . you . . . you *beast!* How dare you? You get out of this house at once, and I never want to see you again. Never, do you hear me? You are not welcome here *ever* again. Do you hear me? You are not welcome here ever again!"

Andy had shrunk back, surprised at her sudden outburst, startled that she reacted so violently. He touched his cheek and felt the blood. Quickly he ran to the parlor, picked up his hat and gloves, and with one anguished glance backward, hurried for the front door.

Martha took several deep breaths as she stood in the hallway before she went back into the parlor. Matt Schenck and Bradley Cooper sat on the sofa staring in open-mouthed surprise. Matt jumped up first.

"Martha, are you all right?"

She flipped one hand at him. "Well, of course. I can handle the likes of that Andy Luston any day." She took another breath and turned toward Bradley Cooper.

"Now, Mr. Cooper, I believe it's your turn to dance. I know it is just silly, silly, silly, not to have music to dance to, but we count, do you know, Mr. Cooper? And it all works out just dandy. Come on now, Mr. Cooper. I'm sure you won't be as ungentlemanly as that Andy Luston."

The man stood, started to put his feet in the wrong place, and then corrected himself. He walked up, bowed, asked if he could have the dance, and held out his arms. She moved into them, letting his right hand slip a little way around her waist before they moved away to her chanted cadence: "One, two, three. *One,* two, three. *One,* two, three."

"My, yes, Mr. Cooper, you are doing just fine! Now, once down the hall and back." They twirled into the hall and to the far end. There Martha stopped dancing and leaned against the surprised young man, pushing her big breasts hard against his chest. She smiled, reached up and kissed him. Martha held the kiss deliciously long, and purred as she felt warmth surge all through her body. It was such a wonderful feeling that she didn't know how to describe it. At last she pulled free, patted him on the shoulder, and put his hand back loosely on her hip as they waltzed back into the parlor.

"Not a word about that kiss," she whispered in Cooper's ear. He grinned and nodded. Back in the parlor she whirled out of Cooper's grasp and sat on the couch. She patted the places beside her and motioned for the two swains to sit down. They did, obediently, Cooper still with a satisfied smirk on his handsome face.

"Now we shall talk about cultural matters, like the opera or the symphony. There is always literature, as well." She looked at both of them, but saw only blank stares. Martha giggled. "I really don't know much about any of those things, either. Why don't we talk about Susan B. Anthony instead? Three years ago, in 1869, she began her drive for equality for women. She says women are more than the property of their husbands, that we should be totally equal under the law, able to vote and to hold office."

Matt shook his head. "Golly, Miss Martha, you surely don't believe wild ravings like that, do you?"

She glared at him. "Of course I do, Matthew Schenck. Miss Anthony is my idol — my heroine. I believe everything she says.

Now, if you don't mind, I've developed a pounding headache, and I must lie down for a rest. Would you be so kind?"

They both stood, kissed her offered hand and retreated out the front door, glad to get away with no more than a gentle rebuke. Bradley Cooper decided not to tell Matt that he had kissed the queen bee herself, and hadn't even got stung. He must really be the favored one of her many suitors — at least right now.

Martha ran to her room and dropped on her big feather bed. She could still feel Cooper's lips against hers, but all the time she had pretended they were Allen's lips, and that Allen was holding her. She wished desperately that it had been Allen kissing her, that she had been holding him so tightly that her breasts ached.

Martha moaned just thinking about him, remembering the delicious way it had been when they lay closely together, when his hands caressed her body and undressed her, and then how he had loved her with such tenderness and awe.

Oh! She hated that man!

She hated Allen Cornelius for seducing her and then running away with the morning tide so he never even knew if he had made her pregnant or not. Because he had left her alone to wait and wonder and worry and then at last be relieved that she wasn't with child and that no one knew of their tryst. So she was available, eligible, and not quite yet an old maid. She was still "unspoiled" and not "damaged merchandise" or "ruined" in the eyes of polite society.

Again she tried to recapture the marvelous feeling of Allen's hands touching her bare breasts, but the powerful surge of emotion wouldn't come back. Instead tears arrived, rolled down her cheeks, and she cried silently into her pillow.

She really loved Allen Cornelius. Wouldn't he ever come back? Nine months was an eternity. How could he make love to her so sincerely and then run away? Men! She hated all men.

But she loved Allen. She simply had to wait for him. These silly suitors who came courting were like pathetic puppies clamoring for attention. They disgusted her.

When Allen came back she would arrange for him to come courting, and the very next week they would go to her father and Allen would ask for her hand, and her father would agree. It would be a marvelous wedding, the grandest that San Francisco had ever seen. It would last three days like the Spanish weddings, with feasts and games and at last the ceremony. They would be deliriously happy, and have five fine children, three girls and two boys, and they all would dance and sing and the boys would become famous doctors and the girls would marry well and provide her with fifteen grandchildren . . .

Oh, how she hated that Allen Cornelius! If she ever saw him again she would scratch out his eyes. The bounder. The cad. The opportunist. He knew he was going away the very next morning, and he picked that day to seduce her. She hated the man . . . but she loved him more. How could that possibly be?

She sat up and rubbed her eyes dry, then selected a shawl, threw it around her shoulders and found her mother in the sewing room.

"I'm going for a ride down by the bay, Mother. I want to look out over the water. It should be beautiful today." She held up her hand when her mother started to give her the usual warning about being careful. "Yes, I know, Mother. I'll be most careful. Jacob is driving, so I'll be in responsible hands. I want to sit and look out at the water for a while. I'll be home well before dark."

As she rode in the surrey, Martha tried to

understand her own mood. She had never felt this way before — a yearning, a longing for the man she loved. She felt sad, worried that he might never come home, and that he really had known the ship was leaving with the early tide. She had built up the notion that he must have been as surprised about it as she had been, and had had no time to get a message to her. But what if it hadn't been like that? What if he had known all along?

No, she wouldn't accept that idea. Not today. Today she was going to remember, to walk past the room where he had taken her, go down the same streets, look out at the bay and try to see his ship, to dream, to remember exactly what he looked like and how delicious had been their love in that little room.

She left Jacob at Front Street and told him to vanish into a tavern or somewhere and to be sure to pick her up at that same spot in exactly two hours. He nodded, used to her sudden flights and her solitary walks. His purse was fatter because of it. She always gave him a dollar gold piece for his silence.

Martha walked. Her route was the same one she had taken from time to time with Allen, away from the ships, into the retail area, past the warehouses, then curving back toward the bay.

She paused as she went by the door of the rooming house where they had spent those glorious two hours. Would it ever be the same? Would it ever happen again? What about the thrill, the surging, powerful, ecstatic floodtide of feeling?

She sighed and wandered back toward the docks. A big three-master had tied up since she had been by earlier, but it wasn't the *Star of the Sea,* Allen's ship. She sat on a piling, wrapped her gold and black skirt carefully around her, and stared out across the bay. Somewhere to the west, far, far out there across the sea, was Allen.

She thought again about that last evening with Allen and lost all track of time. When she heard a seagull cry as it swept closely past her, she shook her head and came back to the present. The sun was fast sliding into the sea. How had it become so late so quickly? It would be dark soon. She jumped down from the piling and looked around. She was late meeting her driver, Jacob. He would be cross, her mother would be upset . . .

She hurried.

Martha started along the docks. The dusk had settled so quickly. She could save two blocks if she went straight along the wharf for a block, then cut up toward town. The warehouses loomed huge on the side of the street beyond. There was nothing to fear. She and Allen had walked this way many times, even later at night. As she moved down the dock toward the shadows, the dusk closed in more on the port town.

She almost turned back, then shook her head, found a short stick and struck out quickly for the other end of the street, where the first of the brightness of the gas lights glowed.

Martha was halfway along the dark block bordering the wharf when she sensed someone behind her. A man jumped to the dock on the bay side, and laughed. He was less than fifteen feet behind her.

Martha ran. She turned to look at the man, but he was not chasing her. When she looked ahead again she only had time to see a large man with a peg leg before she stumbled into him. One of his huge hands covered her mouth, the other slid around her waist, lifted her off her feet as though she were a rag doll and carried her over the planks to a platform near the water, then swung along a board walkway back the way they had come. Soon he dropped to the still wet sand where the tide had receded from under the dock. She could see little, but here the pilings were dry. She knew at high tide they would be well underwater.

Twice she tried to scream. Nothing came out past the tightly clasped hand over her mouth. She kicked at him, but hit nothing but a piling. He gave her a hard swat on her behind. She went limp. The man carrying her didn't mind. He simply flopped her over his shoulder and continued his walk.

With her head hanging down his back, Martha screamed, then found herself quickly muzzled again by the foul-smelling hand.

A hundred yards later they entered a crossing section of big wooden pilings, turned inland between more wooden poles, and at last came to dry land under another pier or a building, she couldn't tell which. It had been built into a crude shelter, with the front thrown together from old packing crates, flotsam lumber and chunks of boards. Behind the makeshift wall was a large room about twenty feet square with two lamps burning, and a dozen men lounging around on blankets and old mattresses spread on the dirt floor.

Her captor carried Martha to the end of the cave-like room, where a blanket divided off a smaller area, and pushed inside. There was a real bed, a chair and an old dresser.

"Scream all you want now, sweetheart," the man said. "Nobody ever gonna hear you from down here."

He dumped her on the bed with sagging springs. She sat up and stared at the man, half curious, fully in a rage, and determined to scream despite what he said. She did, four times, but was sure he was right. Overhead the foot-thick timbers of the dock let no sound penetrate. She stared at her kidnapper. He was over six feet, with one leg gone just below the knee where his wooden peg leg was fitted. He wore dirty work clothes and a scraggly beard that looked as if it had been trimmed haphazardly with scissors. One cheek showed an oozing red and yellow sore. His eyes were dark and he wore a seaman's cap over his head. One eye socket seemed empty, with the eyelid sagging into the vacant area. The man's hands were twice as big as hers, huge bear paws she knew could knock her halfway across the room with one swipe.

Martha stopped screaming, but the man only stared at her. He hadn't hurt her so far. Maybe he only wanted to watch her, talk with her. Perhaps if she could get him to talk, she could reason with him and make him see what a dangerous situation it could be for him. Martha shivered as he stared at her from his one eye.

"Poor little bitty is cold, I'll wager," he said.

She tried to ignore him. "The police will kill you when they find you down here," she said. No, that was wrong — not at all the thing to say.

He laughed, a roaring humorless laugh. "Police will never know. They don't even know we're here. Even if they did, we got lookouts. We be gone to hell and back by the time they come here."

Now keep it civil, she thought. Be dignified, be a lady. She watched him. "How long have you lived down here?"

"I been here three years. One winter we even had a stove. Smoked some, but it were warm."

His eye watched her breasts. Each movement she made he followed, staring at her.

"Money. I have a lot of money. If you let me go I'll get as much as I can for you. Then you can live on top, rent a hotel room somewhere."

"Ain't about to let you go, sweetheart. Not after we went to all that trouble to snatch you. Ain't about to. Four of 'em who helped got time coming with you."

She shivered again. What did he mean,

four of them? A figure, a big amount of money, more than he had ever heard of. "I can give you ten thousand dollars if you'll let me go right now."

The big man laughed and scratched his crotch. Martha looked away quickly, too embarrassed for any rational thought.

"Ten thousand dollars, huh? Yep, you just might do that, sweetheart, but then again, you might not. I got you here, right now, just waiting. What the hell I do with money? Just spend it or lose it." He rumbled a low laugh. "But now a pretty little bit like you got gonna be sure to give a man a tarnation of a wild time between his legs. Now there's a memory that's gonna last me one hell of a long time."

Martha shivered, sure now of what he wanted. She tried not to listen. He wouldn't do that. He simply wouldn't. He was frightening her. But as she watched him, saw the desire in his black eye, noticed the way his big hands moved, she was convinced he was going to rape her. Force her to submit. The other time there had been tenderness and understanding and at the end, love. But now . . . here. She shuddered. She would fight him, fight with every muscle. The thought of his diseased face, his wooden stump of a leg, and that one missing eye, combined with the stench of his clothes and the filthy way he lived made her nauseous. But she had to be strong and firm. She had to stand up to him.

"Look, I know what you want, and it's impossible. My father is a very rich man. He will pay you enough so you can buy your own brothel. Then you can have a different woman every night. If that's what your interest is, I can guarantee that you will have all the girls you want."

He shook his head.

"I told you, my father is a very rich businessman. He can make you wealthy. You can trade one girl now for a hundred later."

The big man glared at her, slid out of a sweater, then pulled off a filthy shirt he must have been wearing for a month. He still had on dirty, greasy long underwear.

"Look, I don't know if the name will mean anything to you, but my father is Harold Pemberton, he owns the Pacific Steamship and Trading Company."

For a moment the huge man stared at her, his bearded face hiding his reaction, then his eyes glazed, his nostrils flared and his mouth opened, emitting a roar of anger.

"Admiral Pemberton's kid? That lousy sonofabitch?" He leaped at her, grabbed her and pushed her down on the bed, then fell on top of her. It took him only a moment to pull away her shawl, then to rip off her shirtwaist, buttons popping, tearing off one sleeve. He ripped away her chemise and threw it to the floor, panting and staring down at her bare breasts.

"Gutless Pemberton's got a daughter this old, and so well built, huh? Well, he's gonna get damaged goods in return, that's for damn sure!"

The furious man continued stripping off her clothes until Martha lay huddled naked on the dirty blanket.

"Now, high and mighty Pemberton, try to tell me what to do now! Tell me there's no way to save my leg. Tell me I've got to let the doc cut it off. Tell me I've got to be a peg-leg the rest of my life, forever banned from earning my living as a sailor!"

His face around his beard was livid with anger. She had never seen eyes with such hatred in them. His mouth showed ragged black stumps of teeth and his breath came out foul. She turned her face away.

He grabbed her chin and pulled her head back.

"Look at me, Pemberton! Look at me while I take you. And then tell your father it's all his fault. It's all his goddamned fault for doing me like he did!"

She saw him pull open his clothes, then he pushed her higher on the bed and before she knew what he was doing, he had tied one of her hands to the bed. She pounded him with her fist but he hardly noticed it. He caught her other hand and tied it to the other side of the bed. She couldn't even kick him.

Martha began to cry. Tears spilled out of her eyes, and down her cheeks.

The man laughed at her. "Won't do no good 'tall, little Pemberton witch. Tell your daddy. I want him to know how you fought and suffered, and you tell him it's all 'cause of me."

Then his hands moved over her body. She was surprised how gently he began, how softly he caressed her breasts. He pried her legs apart and spread them wide and before she could even yell out in protest he had plunged into her and she screamed at the sudden tearing pain. For a moment she fought to maintain consciousness. She fought against the panic, the raw pain and the fury that gripped her. He was raping her!

She caught the words and held them, held them to maintain her sanity and her consciousness. She would fight him any way she could. But how?

His body and his rough clothes churned against her. She wanted to scream again, but she knew now that she shouldn't. It would be over quickly, then he would send her home to let her father know of his revenge against the Pemberton family. Or would he let her go so quickly? Would he hold her there a month, six months? He could. No one knew where she was. Jacob would be out of his mind, and out of a job as well, by now.

It took the big man several minutes to gain his satisfaction and her breasts and legs were rubbed raw from his filthy stiff clothing. But at last he grunted and sighed, and fell on top of her in a kind of total exhaustion. Her mind was working, trying to figure a way out. This would be a good time to attack him. But how? Her hands were still tied, and there were a dozen or more others just outside, waiting, watching, leering, perhaps hoping that they might be next. She pushed that idea from her mind. It was simply too terrible to consider.

Martha tried to concentrate on more pleasant thoughts, but her mind went back to his forcing himself on her. To her surprise, her overriding emotion had been anger and fury with thoughts of revenge. She had not been as terrified as she had often thought she might be in such a situation. Grimly she made her plans. She would wait, get untied, then escape. There must be a knife, a club, some weapon, and she would get away tonight, late, when they were all in a drunken stupor or sleeping. She would, she must! Before she could stop them, silent tears rolled down her cheeks.

Twice more that night he dropped on her and took what he demanded. Her wrists were still tied to the bed. She pleaded with him to let her go, to untie her, but he wouldn't. She kept all her other emotions tightly locked inside of herself. Sometimes she felt as if it all were happening to someone else. That she could lie there, yet be away from her body, and watch and wonder, and not feel a thing.

After the third time, when he rolled off the bed and sat on the floor panting, she spoke.

"Please untie me. I have to attend to a call of nature."

"No."

"You want me to soil your bed?"

He sighed, stood and untied her hands from the bedstead. She rubbed them, hoping the circulation would come back. She had no idea what time of night it was.

"Where?" she asked.

He pointed under the bed where a white porcelain chamber pot sat. She hadn't seen it before. Martha took it to the far side of the hovel-like room, turned her back to him and relieved herself. As soon as she stood, he growled for her to get back on the bed.

"Please don't tie me up again. I can't stand it. I can't go to sleep that way."

He watched her for a minute, shrugged. "You ain't going anywhere, and you ain't gonna need to worry about sleeping anyway. My little friend Joe wants to have a chance with you. You be nice to Joe, or I'll break your arm." He called the man's name softly, but no one came. Martha sat on the edge of the bed waiting. On her trip to the far corner she had seen a weapon, a two-foot-long piece of wood about two inches square. If only she could get it.

"Joe musta gone to sleep. You sit right there, bitch, and wait for us. You move, I'll whack your backside. I'll be back in a jiffy." He went to the blanket partition and looked out, looked back inside at her. He buttoned up his pants, then pushed through the blanket door.

Martha leaped off the bed, ran silently to the corner and found the stick, then ran back near the slit in the blanket where the peg leg man had vanished. She held the stick back over her shoulder, hoping to hit him somewhere vital, on his head, maybe. She closed her eyes. She couldn't stand to think about it. She'd never harmed a human being in her life. But he had just raped her three times. He deserved anything she could do to him. She heard voices, then a laugh that didn't sound quite right. A moment later she heard someone moving toward her. Martha guessed the big man would come in first, so she held the club higher over her shoulder, waiting.

The curtain parted. A small man came through, looked at her and laughed. He was barely four feet tall, but she could tell in a glance that he was in his thirties and dim-witted. Behind him came the peg-leg. He looked toward the bed as she swung the club. It whooshed over Joe's head and before the tall man could throw up his hands, the club slammed into his throat.

She had swung it with all her might, and the blow crushed his windpipe. He tried to scream, but only a hoarse croak came out, and he staggered toward the bed and fell, his hands at his throat. His terrified eyes turned toward her in the faint light. She knew he couldn't hurt her any more.

She looked at the second man, alert,

wondering if she would have time to hit him too.

Joe stood watching her, staring at her breasts. His hands were at his sides, a silly grin on his face.

"Girl?" he said.

He was a child, dim-witted. She wouldn't need the club. She reached for his hand and led him to the bed.

"Sit down, Joe, and let's talk. Yes, I'm a girl, Joe. These are my breasts." She looked around for her clothes, found her skirt and pulled it on. She talked quietly to the slow-witted man. When she put on her chemise, he looked sad.

"Joe, you and I have to go out and get some food. You understand? So I have to put my clothes on. When we come back, I'll undress for you again. Do you understand?" He nodded. She put on what was left of her shirtwaist. It didn't cover her. She looked at the clothing in a heap on the floor and found a man's shirt that wasn't too filthy. She slipped into it and buttoned it, then put on her shoes.

The peg-leg man lay near the blanket door. He had crawled toward them, making gestures with his hands. His breathing came like a croupy child's, a rasping of each breath as he struggled to pull enough oxygen through his shattered tubes to satisfy his lungs. She walked around him and took Joe's hand.

"Now, Joe, we must be very quiet so we don't wake up any of the others. They must be sleeping. Now, you lead me out the quickest way, and we'll buy some food."

He nodded and they pushed the blanket aside and walked through the room. More than twenty men lay sleeping on the floor, on dirty blankets, some on old mattresses. They stepped over several, but once Joe's foot came down on a hand. The man groaned in pain and rolled over, an empty wine bottle rolling from his hand.

Another dozen feet and they would make it.

"Hey, hey there!" a voice said behind them.

She whirled, her heart trying to pound through her ribs, but she saw no one. Evidently someone had been talking in his sleep. They walked on, passed through the last blanket door and were in the dank darkness below the docks.

Joe led her through ankle-deep water along the pier, then to one side where he climbed up a half-rotted ladder that led to the top of the wharf. Martha followed him, not sure where she was even when they stepped on the hard planks of the dock. He walked ahead now and soon she saw a warehouse, then a street, but she couldn't read the sign.

They walked farther, but now even the gas lights had been turned out and it was solid blackness. Joe turned to her.

"Food?"

"Yes, Joe. Take me to a food store."

He nodded, caught her hand and led her along another street, down a block, then up two more streets. They came to a storefront with pictures of food in the window. It was a wholesale grocery store.

She had a vague idea where she was now. If only she could find a policeman. She told Joe to sit on the step and wait for her, telling him she had to get some money. He nodded, trusting her completely.

Martha walked in the general direction of her father's offices. She knew that two or three men worked there all night. If only she could find the right street.

She had gone half a dozen blocks, sure that Joe would not try to follow her. A carriage clattered by a block up and she ran toward it but the rig vanished in the darkness before she got there. She stopped, then realized she was just across the street from the main office of the Pacific Steamship and

Trading Company. She ran to it, tears streaming down her cheeks.

Desperately she looked for the sign that said "Night Bell." When she found it at the far side of the door, she pulled the chain a dozen times.

She was still yanking it when an angry man opened the door.

"What in hell is going on here? What . . ." He paused.

"Oh, please, sir. Please help me. I'm Martha Pemberton, and somebody kidnapped me. Please let me come inside where I'll be safe!"

Five minutes later, messengers were sent rushing to the police and to the Pemberton household. Word of the missing girl had been kept quiet, but the police had been notified.

An hour later Martha soaked in a tub of hot water at home, letting all the fear, the terror and the anger wash out of her. Dr. Paulson, the family physician, had hovered over her for fifteen minutes, asking questions, examining her. She hadn't told anyone she had been raped, but the doctor must have known after his examination. Or would he? She didn't know if it would leave any kind of a mark or sign.

Martha had cried all the way home in her father's arms. It was a delayed emotional reaction, and the relief of knowing that now she was truly free of that ghastly man.

The doctor had a talk with Mr. Pemberton, then left. Her father went into Martha's room, sent her mother into the hall and spoke frankly with her. Martha snuggled down in her bed and listened.

"Martha, did any of those men rape you?"

"Yes, Father, one of them. A big man with a peg leg. He said that years ago you ordered his leg cut off after an accident at sea."

Harold Pemberton frowned, trying to remember such an incident, but he could not. "If I did that, it was to save the man's life. Now tell me exactly where you were, where this underground rat's nest is located."

She told him as well as she could, pinpointing the piling she sat on, then the way she walked. He nodded, said he knew the spot, and told her to go to sleep and try to forget the whole thing. He left her room with a quick and purposeful step.

An hour later ten men from the San Francisco police department swept into the hiding place and routed the men sleeping there. Mr. Harold Pemberton went along as a guide to direct police and identify the men. In the scuffle that resulted four men who tried to escape were shot, including one identified as Stewart Sheffield, a former sailor with one wooden leg and a crushed windpipe. In the police report no mention was made that Pemberton had a pistol or that he stormed into the second room alone and that he indicated Sheffield had tried to escape. Sheffield had been shot twice in the heart.

The other men were charged with drunkenness and vagrancy and the next morning were put in a wagon and driven outside town and left there.

CHAPTER FIVE

Martha pushed away the breakfast tray and sighed. It had been a week now since her kidnapping, and her mother still wanted her to stay in bed and recuperate. Heavens, her mother should know she wasn't hurt, at least not physically. Martha threw back the sheet and got out of bed. She dressed quickly in a light blue frilly print gown and tied a sheer white scarf around her neck and went downstairs. It was a beautiful day, and she wasn't going to be penned up in her room all the time.

Her father stared at her as she went down the stairs. She could see that he was ready to go to his office.

"Could I talk with you for a moment, Father?"

"Yes, of course."

When they both were seated and the door closed, she looked straight at his eyes. "Father, I would guess you are wondering if

I am with child after the incident last week. I can assure you that I am not pregnant. My menstrual flow started two days after that incident, so I can't possibly be with child. It is simply physically impossible. I hope that relieves your mind, Father."

"Yes, yes, it does — greatly."

He was embarrassed to be talking about such delicate matters with his daughter. But she had to go on.

"Does Mother know about everything that happened?"

"Yes, she insisted knowing if you were violated."

"Then I'll tell her that I'm not pregnant. It should be good news for her, too."

Harold Pemberton seemed to relax, as if a chore had been taken from him. He smiled. "Martha, I'm glad you're not going to be further involved because of that terrible night. Now I hope we can get things back to normal around this house. If you will tell your mother, I would appreciate it." He smiled, bent and kissed her cheek, then strode out of the house to his carriage, which waited at the front door.

Martha watched him get in, noticed that Jacob was not driving, and remembered that he had been discharged the night of her capture. She was sad about that. It had been her fault, not Jacob's. She would try to find him and give him a sizeable gift.

Her mother walked into the front hall. "For goodness' sake, child, what are you doing out of bed?"

"Mother, I am not a child, and I am not sick. I'd like to talk with you for a moment." She led the way into her mother's sewing room. The curtains there were new again, some more of her mother's handiwork, made of some filmy white material that let the sun stream into the room. They both sat and Martha looked at her mother seriously.

"In case you have been worried, Mother, I am not pregnant."

Her mother gasped.

"I am not going to have a child, so there is no reason to pamper me any more. As I understand it, almost no one knows about the incident, except that I was missing for a few hours, and I'm sure the gossips in town will not be able to make much out of that."

"Well . . . I mean . . ." Mrs. Pemberton paused, flustered. Then tears formed in her eyes. "Oh, darling, I was just so worried that . . ."

"Worried that I'd been ruined, that I was damaged goods?"

Her mother nodded, biting her lip. "I was so frightened."

"Well, you don't need to be any more, and I think I should go on seeing my suitors just as usual."

Her mother didn't respond.

"Mother, surely you don't think that just because I was raped I *am* ruined, do you? Mother, he didn't damage me!"

Mrs. Pemberton looked up. "How can you be sure?"

"Mother, two days afterwards my monthly flow began. It has just ended. There is no possible way that I could now be pregnant. You should understand that!"

"Thank God! Now that we are sure, I am satisfied." She left her chair and kissed her daughter's cheek and hugged her. "I'm so grateful." She sat down again. "Now it is time for us to launch you into a social season with the express purpose of finding an appropriate husband. I want no protest or complaint from you. This has been a very close call. If word of this got out you would be simply ruined here in town, you know that. You'd have to go to Los Angeles or San Diego, and even there your prospects would be bleak. Believe me, Martha. I know the people in this town."

"Yes, Mother," Martha sighed. She had expected this, but not so suddenly. She dreaded it. She had thought it through carefully and decided this would be her mother's answer. With the danger past, there would be a concentrated effort to marry her off before anything else happened. Martha was resigned to it. There was simply no way she could tell her mother she wanted to marry a junior officer on one of her father's ships who was now in Hong Kong. Not the slimmest chance.

"Now, tomorrow we will have the dressmaker here, and the next day let's have that hairdresser in who has all of those styles, French switches and little wigs that blend in so well with your hair. Saturday night we will start with the first party. After that it is going to be a twice a week until something happens."

"Yes, Mother."

"Now, I want you to be sure to stay out of the sun so your skin will be a lovely creamy white. When you go outside, wear a bonnet to protect your face, and be sure to have long sleeves on and wear high-necked dresses all the time." She paused. "You do see what I'm trying to do for you, don't you, Martha? I want you to have a fine marriage to an intelligent and, if possible, wealthy young man, who can give you everything in life you deserve."

"Yes, Mama."

The first party was that following Saturday night. It was a champagne gala with hors d'oeuvres and a six-piece orchestra to play Strauss waltzes. Martha was radiant, smiling and laughing, surrounded by six of the most eligible bachelors in town that her mother could find. She insisted on asking Andrew Luston, over Martha's protests. But during his first dance with Martha she leaned in and whispered that he was forgiven and that he could come courting. Later that night she found a screened spot in the garden and kissed Andy, then insisted that they go back inside.

Martha danced every dance, and was momentarily interested in a tall Spanish-looking man whom she found out was the son of a Spanish don who had once ruled half of California. His name was Don Obisbo and he was visiting from San Diego. He showed her how they could dance a Spanish step to the Strauss music and she laughed, delighted.

"Do you come to San Francisco often?" she asked.

He smiled, amused by her coquettishness. "Not often. I live in Mexico City now, where my father's businesses are situated."

Martha smiled politely and crossed him off her list. She knew that in a month or so her mother would demand that she pick out the most likely suitor and indicate to him that he might ask for her hand. She would have to have some idea of which man would be the least objectionable.

Martha begged off the next dance with Matthew Schenck. They sat near the windows of the large parlor and watched the couples dancing. Her mother had invited twelve older couples and six bachelors. There were no unattached women or young girls, which made an interesting evening for Martha.

She had to admit that every person her mother had invited to the affair had come. That was proof enough of her mother's social standing. But Martha didn't care at all what other people thought. She'd rather marry a man she loved. She tried to follow the logic behind the two statements, but found none, and decided that love is never logical. Allen Cornelius — now that made sense. She wondered where he was.

"Are you rested enough now to continue the dance?" Matt asked. She nodded, hoping she could pretend that Matt was really Allen and they were gliding around the room as gracefully as a pair of young swans.

It was well after one in the morning when the musicians stopped playing and the guests finally went home. Martha sat with her shoes off and her feet up on a chair.

Her mother came to her and smiled. "Well, dear, did any of them look like possibilities?"

Martha shook her head. "No, Mother. The Spanish gentleman was interesting, but he lives in Mexico City. Anyway, I think he's married."

"Well, just wait until next week, dear." She urged Martha to go to bed so she would be fresh for the tea the next afternoon. "There will be about twenty ladies here, Martha, and some of the very finest families in town will be included. I want to impress them with you so they'll send their sons to the next party I have planned, a grand ball in the biggest hotel ballroom I can find. It won't be for two weeks yet, but I want hundreds of people there. I told your father about it, and he didn't even say he thought it was too much money to spend. For a man of some wealth, your father sometimes can be very close with his money."

"Yes, Mama."

She went to bed dreaming of Allen Cornelius, wondering what he was doing at that exact instant, wondering where he was, and the question of questions: had he really known his ship was leaving the next morning after they had made love?

The next day was the tea, then invitations to other affairs, and within a week Martha felt as if she were on a social treadmill that would never stop. Everyone in town with an eligible daughter or a promising son seemed to be holding an event or a party. At least Martha didn't have time to get bored, or time to worry about Allen.

There was a tennis party, a circus outing, a sail on the bay, one huge picnic, a day in the country with horse races, a pair of dances and a party at the boating club.

By the time her own ball arrived at the Dorchester House, with its grand ballroom over two hundred feet long, Martha was at the point of collapse. She spent all day in bed before the grand affair, getting up at six for a final coiffure and gown fitting. The gown was emerald green, swept to the floor and made of fine silk and lace, dangerously low cut in front, showing some cleavage, with puffs on the sleeves, and pinched in tightly at the waist. The corset she wore with it nearly killed her, but she planned on not fainting from the lack of breath by sitting out every other dance.

When she arrived at the ball in the best carriage, Martha felt ready for anything. She walked up the steps and to the ballroom on her father's arm, and felt a thrill when the captain at the door tapped his cane on the marble floor and in the silence which followed announced her name:

"The guest of honor, Miss Martha Pemberton!"

Her mother had told her that they had invited over three hundred people, including every eligible bachelor from every family with any social standing. There would be dozens of unattached young men and women at the affair, and Martha was looking forward to it.

A hush touched the crowd as she walked down the marble stairs into the grand ballroom. At once the orchestra struck up for the first number. There were thirty musicians in the group, and it was the very finest orchestra on the Pacific coast.

The whirl began. Matthew Schenck claimed the first dance and they were off. The food and wine and special champagne flowed, and as the evening began she was afraid it was going to be much like the others. Only this time there were many more people.

An hour into the evening, and after Martha had taken two glasses of champagne, a tall, sunburned man stepped in front of her and asked for the next dance. She had not noticed him before. As she remained seated, her father moved in, smiling.

"Yes, yes. I was hoping you might come, Captain Dyke. May I present my daughter, Martha Pemberton. This is Peter Dyke, the captain of our *Pacific Gem,* the largest and finest iron-hulled vessel afloat in all of the Pacific Ocean!"

She put out her hand.

Captain Dyke smiled and kissed her hand.

"Thank you, sir, for introducing me. I had the impression the young lady might not want to dance with me. Perhaps she remembers my teasing her the last time I saw her, about a year ago. It's good to see you again, sir."

"Fine, fine, Dyke. I hope you have a good time."

Captain Dyke nodded, held out his arms to Martha, and waltzed away with her. So she had met the captain before. When? At one of those small parties her mother used to give at the house, probably. Captains were always coming. She didn't remember this one. He wore a stiff white collar, with a folded silk neckcloth and a severe black suit that fit him perfectly. She guessed he had had it hand-tailored in Hong Kong. For a moment the word brought back thoughts of Allen. She pushed them aside, and instead smiled up at Captain Dyke. He was older than she, probably twenty-eight, she guessed — maybe thirty.

"So we have met before, Captain Dyke?" she asked.

"Yes, about a year ago. It was at your home. A small dinner party. You pleaded a sudden, convenient headache, as I remember. I was disappointed."

"A year ago, I was only a child."

"But I remembered you on every watch on the long trip to Rapango and back."

"You are an excellent dancer, Captain."

"And so are you, Miss Pemberton."

"Thank you, sir."

"I'm going to marry you, Martha Pemberton."

She darted a glance at him. His face was serious, attractive, and so suntanned he looked almost foreign. His red hair stood out like a beacon, but she couldn't laugh at his words.

"You haven't even approached my father yet."

"Of course not. That's what will take the time, the courting, the visits, the dinners. Then I'll ask the old boy."

"You're confident, that's obvious. But what about all of the competition, the suitors with both money and family?" She frowned, suddenly wondering. "How on earth did you ever get an invitation? You're not on any of my mother's lists, I'm sure."

Peter Dyke laughed and spun her around twice, then walked her off the floor to a small alcove where he stood her against the wall.

"Invitation? I didn't have one. I just attached myself to a small group coming through the door and waltzed right in, as you might say. Your father likes me."

"You're much too old for me."

"Now, Kate! Did you ever read the *Taming of the Shrew?*"

"Yes, by Mr. Shakespeare . . . you mean I'm a shrew?"

"Now, I didn't say that. But you will take some training." He laughed and watched her. "But what a great time I will have as I do the training. I'll love every minute of it."

"You are impossible."

"The very words Kate used herself." He took her hand and they waltzed back onto the floor, circled the big room, and as the music stopped, walked back to the soft couch she had claimed as her own for the evening, and in front of which a line of hopefuls stood, waiting for a dance.

"Thank you very much for the waltz, Kate, and I will be back soon. As for now, I must to Padua."

Martha laughed in spite of herself as he left with a little flourish of an imaginary hat and cape. His body seemed firm enough, but his senses were rattling around in his head.

As she danced with four other young men who had lined up for a turn, she kept thinking about what Peter Dyke had said: "I'm going to marry you." Just like that, not "I want," not "I wish," not "Maybe," but a flat statement. Martha smiled, wondering who she was waltzing with now. She really didn't care. Captain Dyke would at least make his campaign for a wedding ring an interesting one.

Just after midnight, Martha was dancing with some inept man she remembered only as Harry, who had unpleasant breath, when at the far end of the floor someone cut in. Captain Peter Dyke replaced the man smoothly and Martha found it curious that without missing a step she was dancing with a new partner.

"That's not good form in San Francisco, Mr. Dyke."

"In Papeete it's done all the time. I paid him to stand in line for me, to dance with you, just so I could cut in."

"That's underhanded and sneaky, and it

just isn't done here. I think you should stop dancing right now and leave."

"But you're smiling."

Martha giggled. "You, Captain Dyke, are devious and unprincipled. That's the kind of trick *I* would have thought of. And it worked."

"It always does." He swung her wide into an alcove and behind a screen. For just a few moments they were alone. He bent and carefully kissed her soft lips.

Martha knew she should be outraged, knew she should at least slap him. Instead, when his lips left hers, she smiled up at him.

"That was very nice. You've kissed lots of girls, haven't you?"

"A few."

"How old are you?"

"Twenty-eight."

"That's not so old."

"We'll remind your father about that when the time comes." He swept her away and back into the whirl of the dance floor. They stopped at the champagne table and he was in the middle of telling her about the island of Rapango when an unhappy young man tracked them down.

"Miss Pemberton, it's my dance," he said. "You didn't come back to your couch."

"Oh, dear, I'm terribly sorry." She handed

her half-filled champagne glass to Peter. "Would you hold this for me, Captain? Finish it yourself, if you like."

He took the glass. "For now, Kate, for now," he said. She glared at him as she danced away in the other man's arms.

Peter Dyke watched her go, a glint in his eye that he couldn't quite explain. Something about the girl fascinated him. Those full breasts peeking daringly from the top of her gown, the tilt of her head when she was annoyed or angry, her smile, so perfect, yet touched with devilment, and her long black hair so like the native girls on Rapango. He would marry the girl in a minute if he could, but it wasn't to be done that way. He must surely suffer through a month or more of parties and outings, and regular courting as well. But his mind was made up. Come high seas, cross winds or rip tides, he would wed and bed the wench.

Martha watched Peter standing with both glasses. Served him right. The "Kate" remark had caught her completely unprepared, and she hadn't thought of a thing to throw back at him. At least he had her attention, which was what he was trying to get. He was a clever one, and old enough to know exactly what he was doing. No stumble-footed eighteen-year-old he. No eager, clumsy, tongue-tied bumpkin seeking his first real kiss. In many ways he reminded her of Allen — except for the flaming red hair. Peter Dyke would stand out in any crowd, by his red head alone.

Interested. Yes, she was interested in the captain, and wondering what he might do next to keep her attention.

Twice more that night he danced with her — the only man in the room who waltzed with her more than once. He swept her away one time when she waited for her partner to go to the punch bowl for her. She told Peter how naughty he was, but giggled when they kept at the far end of the big floor, avoiding an anxious search. Another time he cut in on an unsuspecting man and told him there was a messenger at the door to see him about something urgent. There was no urgent message, but while the flustered swain left to find out, Peter danced away with Martha.

The ball lasted until two in the morning, and Captain Peter Dyke was still there when Martha went up the marble steps on her father's arm, heading for the big house on the hill.

He watched her go and waved. She smiled and waved back, and Martha realized for the first time that she had thought of Allen only once all evening. It had been a wonderful party.

During the next three weeks, Captain Peter Dyke showed up at every party, dance, or ball where Martha was the hostess or guest. She had no idea how he managed it, but at the end of the third week, he had convinced her that if she did have to choose a husband, he would be the one. Then her mother came down with the ultimatum.

"Martha, you've seen every eligible young man in our city. Your father and I both believe that it is time that you pick out one and get married."

No amount of pleading would change her mother's mind. Martha realized her mother was terrified about another accident that would ruin her daughter. Martha had run out of excuses and run out of time.

"Which of the suitors do you like best, Martha? Which has the best chance at your hand?" her mother asked.

"Right now? You want me to blurt out a name on a minute's notice, and then I'll have to live with that for the rest of my life. How can you do this to me?"

"Martha, if it were up to me, I'd simply select the best husband for you and make you marry him. At least this way you have your choice."

Martha remained silent.

"Who is the lucky man to be, Martha? This is the time."

Martha sighed, thinking about Allen. Should she tell her mother about Allen, and plead to wait for him? Or would that only make matters worse? Could she pick out one of the suitors, and when Allen came back, find out for sure if Allen loved her and then quietly get a divorce? It was being done more often now. Then she'd be free to marry Allen. Divorce was a serious step, but if others could do it, why couldn't she? That decided, she turned back to her mother.

"The only one I could possibly marry is Captain Peter Dyke."

Her mother jumped back in surprise. "But he doesn't even have a family here. He's a sailor. He works for your father."

"Then he'll always have a good job, won't he, Mother?"

So it was decided. The following Sunday, Captain Peter Dyke came to the house for a family dinner, and after the meal he and Mr. Pemberton vanished into the den, where cigars were lit and the talk began. Captain Peter Dyke asked for Martha's hand, and her father gave it. They soon came out with the good news and a date for the wedding was set; one month from that day, on a Sunday afternoon in early August. Certain business arrangements were made as well. The *Pacific Gem* would make one more journey under a new captain, then return home to be refitted, and the captain's quarters expanded, doubled in size and another room added. It was to be furnished luxuriously and would set sail right after the ceremony to the South Seas, on a combined business trip and honeymoon.

Then the parents left the room, allowing the couple to be alone for a few minutes.

"I told you I would marry you when we had that very first dance — remember?"

"Yes, you did say that."

Dyke chuckled. "And now you have resigned yourself to a fate worse than death — marriage to me."

She looked up and sighed. "No, Peter Dyke, it's not that at all."

"But you're unhappy. You don't look like an excited, thrilled bride-to-be in love."

"What if I love someone else . . . ?"

"There's always someone else. Someone from our dreams." He moved closer to her. "I could grab you and say, kiss me, Kate. Will I have to do that?"

She moved toward him, put her arms around his neck and found his mouth with hers. It came as a sudden tingling shock when his tongue brushed her lips. He had pulled her tightly against his chest, and she thought he would crush her. For just a moment her eyes closed, and she dreamed it was Allen in her arms. Then she saw Peter's red hair, the start of red whiskers on his cheek, and she tried to relax. For better, for worse, her fate was sealed. She would be a sea captain's wife, and he would be on the ocean two-thirds of the time, and probably each time he left she would be pregnant. She edged away gently.

"I think we had better save any more than that for the wedding night."

"Now, that's more like my Kate."

"I am *not* your Kate. I am *not* some character from one of Mr. Shakespeare's plays. I am me. I am Martha. Please don't ever call me Kate. If you don't think Martha is enough, then you still have time to withdraw your offer."

"I'll withdraw nothing." He pulled her back roughly and kissed her soundly, his hand cupping a breast this time. She could not get away from him, and in a moment she gave up struggling. When he let go she was furious, but she didn't let him see it. This would be a short marriage. That she could almost guarantee.

CHAPTER SIX

Preparations moved along for the wedding. It was to be the largest event San Francisco had ever seen, a two-day affair with feasting and dancing and parties, climaxed by the wedding on Sunday afternoon. Martha was lost in the flurry. But she found time to whisper a secret regret to Allen, wherever he might be.

Two weeks before the wedding day, Martha was told she had to christen a ship the Pembertons were launching that afternoon. She tried to beg off but there was no way around it.

Now she sat on a high stand over the water and looked at the boat. She was not an iron-hulled ship at all, rather, an ugly wooden vessel that would be used in the coastal trade. An iron plate had been fastened to the bow where she would be christened. Then she would slide into the harbor backwards.

Martha watched the sky and the seagulls, then the bay itself, and wondered where Allen was. She didn't listen to the speeches, not even to her father's. Then someone was touching her shoulder. It was time to do the bottle-swinging. As she came out of her daydream, the first thing she saw was the light brown face of an extremely handsome man. He touched her shoulder again.

"Time come to do it, Miss," he said with a strange accent, a curious lilt to his pleasant, low voice.

She blinked, smiled, and stood where he indicated. He handed her a bottle of champagne that had a stout string tied to it in case she dropped it.

Somebody else spoke, then everyone looked at her. The brown man nodded at her. "Just say: "I christen thee *Empire Builder.*"

She said the words.

"Now swing bottle hard, hit iron plate. Swing with gusto!"

She did as he said, and the bottle smashed, splashing her and the ship and the man beside her with the bubbling wetness. A cheer went up from the shipbuilders and those seated in chairs at the edge of the ways. The ship shuddered, then far below, men with huge hammers knocked out braking blocks and the hundred and fifty foot long craft began to slide away from her. It picked up speed, then hit the water stern first, and a moment later it floated in the bay, right side up and high in the water. A crew at once began hoisting sails as the *Empire Builder* moved off.

"That's all there is to it?" asked Martha.

The brown man beside her nodded. "Yes, Miss. That's all."

"Oh, I'm sorry. I'm Martha Pemberton."

"Yes, Miss. I know. I'm Johnnie Laveau. I help around the yards."

"You're from some foreign land?"

"Yes, Miss. Jamaica."

"Oh! Then you're one of my father's favorite people. I remember he said he found you on one of his ships and brought you to shore. Aren't you the manager of the shipyard now?"

"Yes, Miss. But sometimes I think I'd rather be back at sea. The clean salt air. The sound of the wind in the rigging, and the alive feeling it gives you when you're running in front of a thirty-knot gale."

She watched him as he spoke, and saw that he was living every moment of it again. He was a man who truly loved the sea, and probably couldn't wait to get back on it.

"But the work here is so much more

important, and you must earn much high wages here."

"Oh, yes, Miss Pemberton. That is true."

"But you'd rather be back at sea."

"Oh, yes, *mon,* oh yes!"

"Then . . . why?"

"Mr. Pemberton, he good man. But he say he wants *mon* to do one thing here, *mon* had better do that thing." He put his hand over his face, embarrassed. "Forgetting, Miss, that you know big boss, Mr. Pemberton, too."

Martha was laughing. She felt more alive, more excited about just living, than she had for a week. "Johnnie, would you have time to take me on a guided tour of the shipyard? You could show me how you build the ships and what materials you use, just everything about it."

"I surely don't know, *mon.* I ask Big Boss, you ask Big Boss. He say go, I go."

She watched his face, so smooth, such a delicious light shade of brown, wide dark eyes so much like her own, and a smile that lit up the whole platform.

"You wait right here, Johnnie Laveau, I'll ask Father. I may never have another chance to tour a shipyard. Now you stay put."

She worked her way across the platform

until she caught her father's eye. He waited for her.

Johnnie could see the two talking. He had known about the beautiful daughter for some time, and he also knew he was an outsider, a Jamaican, so a lower order somewhere. What he was most sure of was that he was not one of the eligible bachelors invited to any of the parties or fancy balls. But he had admired the girl from afar. Now he was deliciously close to her beauty. White girls were not his favorites, but this one was different. Sleek, trim body with surging breasts that caught a man's eye even before he looked at her face. Her beauty was perfect; not a mark, not a mole, nothing to mar her exquisite pink-scrubbed face. Wide-set eyes, a snub of a nose and sweet lips half of San Francisco clamored to kiss. He saw her father motion to him, and he was moving quickly around and past the guests and workmen who had already begun to take down the platform so a new ship could be started.

Johnnie listened to the instructions of his employer, then grinned and stepped back.

"Yes, sir, Mista Pemberton. Safe as a little babe in her mother's arms. Yes, sir. I know my head, he's on da block. I mistake anywhere make and it's a whooshing drop of the blade right through my neck bone."

Martha frowned slightly at the strange language, then brightened when her father patted her hand.

"Now, Johnnie is your guide. You do what he tells you, and you be home with the carriage in not more than two hours. Johnnie will drive you right to the front door."

"Oh, Father, don't be such an old fuss-budget. I'll be fine. And Johnnie will take good care of me." She touched his shoulder. "Lay on, MacDuff!"

He turned, surprised. "You have read *Hamlet*. An interesting play, isn't it?"

"Yes, interesting," she said, wonder in her voice. There was a lot more to Johnnie Laveau than his strange English and his seamanship.

The tour was interesting to Martha, but it was over sooner than she wanted it to be. An hour before she was due, she was back at the Pemberton mansion, where Johnnie saw her to the front door, bowed, said he was delighted to be her guide, and left.

Martha watched him walk away, straight and tall, with no backward glance. She wondered if she would ever see that fascinating man again.

Martha fingered the parting gift he had given her. It looked like a finely braided necklace of some strange material with a small leather pouch on the bottom. Johnnie told her to wear it around her neck for the next two weeks. To please him she had slipped it on, but she had not thought of wearing it longer. She took it off now and studied it carefully. If she didn't know better, she would think the braid was made of human hair. But that was highly unlikely. She took it up to her room, dropped it in a small drawer, and promptly forgot about it.

Captain Peter Dyke took dinner with the Pembertons each evening the week before the wedding. It gave them some time to get to know each other. What usually began in strained silence warmed into an over-jolly affair as each tried to outdo the other in good fellowship. Often it withered down into a contest of tall tales about life at sea, between Captain Dyke and Mr. Pemberton.

But after dessert, Martha and Peter were herded into the library and the door discreetly shut, all but an inch. There was no couch in the library, and Mrs. Pemberton felt fairly sure that nothing untoward or premature could happen there.

Martha was nervous the first evening as the door closed and Peter came over and put his arms around her.

"I've been waiting all evening to do this,"

he said. Then he kissed her, and Martha tried hard not to pull away. He held her close and kissed her a second time, and then it was better, she felt something, a slight faraway stirring, a remembrance, and she knew it would be all right, at least for a while. She returned his kiss and felt his hand moving toward her breast. She pushed away and shook her head. "Not yet, Mr. Dyke. You have no shipping rights over those waters for a week yet."

He gave in gracefully, and they sat down in matching chairs near the cold fireplace and talked. "There's so much about you I don't know," he said. "You read a lot, but do you like dogs? Can you ride? What about swimming, diving? How many children do you want? Where will we live?"

They talked for two hours, then he kissed her again and said he was due back at his ship to handle an inspection on some new work. It was moving along well, and they would be ready to sail on Sunday.

After six days of dinner and talk with Peter Dyke, Martha realized she had made a lucky choice. He could be a rough and tumble seaman, and she was sure he had patronized brothels from Seattle to Hong Kong, but he also had an inquiring mind and a searing ambition to succeed in his chosen profession.

Once she asked him if that was why he was marrying her — to help him in his career.

He had shaken his head. "I wish it were. That would make it simpler. I'd have no hard nights walking the decks, wondering where you were, how you were feeling. I wouldn't have to worry about how to treat my father-in-law who is also my boss." He held her hand. "You have no idea how many sleepless nights you caused me on my last trip. And when I did get to sleep, I dreamed of nothing but you."

"Peter Dyke, how can you say that? With all of those half-naked native girls running around on Rapango, you wouldn't even be *thinking* of me!"

His kiss came hot on her lips and his hand found her breast, and almost before she knew it her whole body was on fire. She gasped and pushed him away gently, not wanting to.

"Peter, not yet. Just two more days. Is that such a long time to wait?"

He drew her close and kissed her cheek, then stood to go. "It's a damned long time, and you feel it as much as I do."

The wedding was the biggest California had

ever seen. Two days before it began, people flocked into town and stayed at hotels as the guests of the Pembertons. Parties and receptions and then a huge gala ball the night before the ceremony left everyone bleary-eyed the next morning. The wedding itself was in the biggest church in town and Martha went through the motions in a dazed condition. The night before she had cried for hours, dreaming that Allen would rush in at the last moment and stop the ceremony. He didn't. She said the right words and felt Peter's lips hard on hers as the ceremony ended and the music from the pump organ swelled as they walked up the aisle and out of the church.

The after-wedding dinner was held in some hotel. She couldn't remember which one. Her father became a little drunk. Two fistfights broke out, and in the middle of it all, Peter Dyke swept Martha into his arms and carried her out to the buggy. A half hour later they were on board the *Pacific Gem.* Their luggage had been put on before. She sat on the bed in the captain's cabin and stared in surprise at how small and cramped it was. And this was after it had been expanded!

She heard a sound and rushed to the small round window. As she looked out she saw that they were moving. The dock and the warehouse slid away from her. She was alone with a man who was practically a stranger to her, and now they were moving out to sea. What on earth should she do now?

For a few minutes she lay on the bed and cried. Why hadn't she told her mother the whole thing? She would have understood. But Martha couldn't at the time, and she knew she could not, even now. She had married falsely, to satisfy her family, to cover up any social problems. She was a fraud.

The lock on the door jangled as a key opened it. She brushed the tears away and sat up, putting on a smile for her husband. It would be Peter. He had said that no one else but he would ever be coming through that door. It had a double lock so it could be locked or opened from either side.

He burst through the door grinning, his face indicating his pleasure at being back at sea. "We're underway," he said. "The first mate will guide us out of port and to sea. This is the start of our honeymoon to the South Pacific. Sometimes I wish we could just stay there on Rapango, stay there and never come home."

She watched him. He would be a good husband, and she would be a good and faithful wife.

"Come out on deck. We can watch San Francisco fade into the dusk to the east and on the west we'll see the golden sun sink into the waves. Your first sunset on shipboard should be an exciting event."

He led her up a steel stairway the men called "ladders" and to the "bridge" where the first mate was giving orders and calling to the men far below in the engine room. They stood in the soft breeze and watched San Francisco fading away. For a long time she could see Nob Hill, where her home — her former home — sat. Then it, too, was gone, swallowed in the mists and the coming dusk.

She shivered, and he put his arm around her. "Just a few more minutes to sundown. I think you'll enjoy it."

The horizon fractured into a dozen different strata of clouds and as the sun sank it exploded each ridge and line into a different shade of pink, orange, red, violet, and then deep purple, before it faded to black. When the last tint of color drained from the clouds, the couple went back into the captain's quarters and he gave her the grand tour. There was a big sitting room more than twelve feet square, a bedroom about the same size, and a small galley where they could make light snacks, coffee and tea.

"This is the most elaborate captain's quarters of any ship I've ever seen on the high seas," said Peter.

He led her to an easy chair, and returned quickly with a bottle of chilled champagne. "It's been soaking in the ocean since last night, so it should be pleasantly chilled." He popped the cork, lost some of the sparkling liquid and then poured them each a stemware glass full. Before she could drink, he held up his glass in a toast.

"To this marriage. May it be happy, fruitful, and may it last as long as the sun rises over the sea."

She lifted her glass, sipped, and then drank the champagne, which always tickled her nose. She watched him as they both drained their drinks, then put down the glasses. He lifted her from the chair and kissed her nose, then her eyes. His arms went around her, and he touched her lips with his. The kiss seemed to grow hotter by the second. Peter picked her up and carried her toward the tiny bedroom.

"No more champagne, darling. I don't want to be tipsy. I want to remember every second of this night clearly."

They sat on the edge of the bed and she took his hand and placed it over her breast.

Then she reached up and kissed him.

They explored cautiously, slowly, undressing each other in natural stages. Much later they made love gently in a tender union that was so moving Martha cried in joy. Their second love-making was more passionate, with a mounting urgency that soon consumed them both, left them panting and totally spent.

Toward morning, Martha woke and found Peter's big hand still covering her breast. She smiled and kissed his cheek, but he slept on. Martha felt a soft glow spreading through her whole being. She was happy. Now she was sure that the decision to marry Captain Dyke had been right. They would be immensely happy together, work out any problems calmly like adults, and she would bear three fine children. They would build a mansion of their own on Nob Hill and have a dozen grandchildren running all over it.

For the briefest second Allen Cornelius tried to intrude, but she shut him out. It was all over with Allen. He had missed his chance. He could have refused to sail. He could have dived overboard into the bay and come to her. There were a hundred ways he could have seen her before he sailed, if he had been strong enough.

"Peter." She said his name again. He

moaned in his sleep, his hand caressing her breast. She kissed his lips, then kissed his chest and felt him stir. Her hands worked lower and a moment later he was awake and reaching for her.

"My God, woman. Are you trying to wear me out the first night?"

She kissed him again, then lay on top of him, and he groaned in delight.

The fourth day they did not make love. She sat by the porthole looking out at the sea, trying to see a flying fish take off from the top of a swell as its fright overwhelmed its caution and it shot out of the wave and soared away from danger on its finny wings for twenty, even thirty yards, before it dove back into the sea. She had seen two the first day, but none since.

Martha moved to the big chair and began reading her book, but put it down. Charles Dickens held no charm for her today. Four days married, and not a bruise yet. She wondered if he would hit her. Yes, he just might. They had argued already — a bit of a fight. She couldn't remember what it had been about. Then suddenly she did, and in spite of herself she blushed. He was a strong man, she'd give him that. And she had no thoughts of trying to dominate him.

But what about after the voyage? What then? Would she settle down in some little house, already big with child, and wait for the blessed event? Life with Peter Dyke would not be easy, she knew that. She realized now that he must have been a womanizer, to have gained such specialized knowledge. Some of the things he said and some of the things he told her to do with him . . . she had been so shocked at first that she simply could not speak. He was a drinker, and she guessed a brawler. She had to face the fact that he was a sailor, with all of the accompanying vices. Now that some of the love-blindness was wearing off, Martha realized that this would not be a marriage made in heaven, that there would be rough spots, but she was strong enough to glide over them. There would be little chance that marriage and a family would change Peter Dyke's habits, which had built up over a dozen years.

She tried Dickens again, read a chapter, then walked up to the forward deck, where she had permission to wander without a guide. She loved the wind in her face. They had been at sea now for almost five days. She wondered how she would like it after a month.

Peter had shown her their course on the

charts. They had turned almost due south once they left San Francisco, would miss the Hawaiian Islands by 800 miles and were heading straight for Tahiti in the South Pacific 3,660 miles away. She shivered. That was more water than she had ever thought existed. Why was there so much water, anyway? It wasn't any good. You couldn't even drink it. It simply took up space, and there must be land underneath it.

For the next two weeks she read her books, stitched on some sewing her mother had packed in her bags, and made love to her husband. Gradually he introduced her to new elements in their lovemaking, delights she would never have thought of, sensations that left her breathless but curiously pleased. Now she snuggled down in the feather bed and watched her husband strip off his clothes. What a hard, muscular body he had! So suntanned that he could pass for a native except for his mop of red hair. In the tropics, he told her, he wore only cut-off pants. He slid out of his trousers and she looked away automatically, then glanced back, fascinated by her man as she always was.

He knelt and kissed her breast, holding it in his hand, then he opened his mouth and chewed gently.

"Oh, darling, careful, that makes me want to dissolve when you do that. I might even faint."

He chuckled and rolled over her. "You'll do a lot more than faint today before I'm through."

It was the forty-fifth day when they arrived just outside the harbor of Rapango. A solitary canoe put out from the shore and rowed toward the big ship. Martha saw that it had poles in the water with a float on them. An outrigger, Peter called it. Sitting in the front of the canoe was a white-haired man who looked very old. A young man wearing nothing but cut-off pants rowed the canoe.

The old man climbed up a rope ladder which had been let down over the side. She was amazed how easily he went up the swaying ladder. She had tried it once, on board the ship, and found it almost impossible.

The old man went through a doorway below and she didn't see him again until he left the boat. Martha used Peter's new binocular field glasses and watched the old man get into the canoe. He looked frail. She turned the glasses to the canoe. She looked through the glasses to the shore and saw natives there watching the boat, others

153

working with knives, some getting ready to fish. She couldn't see plainly, but Martha was certain that the women wore nothing above their waists.

A few minutes later Peter came into the cabin looking thoughtful. "That was old Tapo, did you see him? He's the priest and the medicine man. He tells me there has been a small pirate boat around with ten white men who spoke English. They killed one man in his tribe and carried off three young women. Tapo's six temple guards with their spears could not even defend themselves against the pistols the pirates carried. Tapo said he thought the sailing ship had set a course back to Tahiti."

"When can I go ashore?" Martha asked, her eyes glittering.

Peter laughed. "Not until we're safely anchored inside the lagoon, at least. We've got a lot of work to do making room for the cargo, and getting the tools and cloth and other material ready to go ashore. After we're all set here, I'll get someone to take you ashore for a day."

She jumped up and kissed him. "I'm so anxious to get on land again, and to see how the natives live."

"It's different there. It's a primitive society. They don't have houses like we know, they don't have beds or chairs or even windows. Don't expect roasts and knives and forks and bone china dishes. They even worship a dozen gods they say live in rocks, and trees, even in the wind."

"Really? That *is* exciting! I want to learn as much as I can about them, how they live, what they believe."

Peter nodded. "Tomorrow. Maybe tomorrow, after we get the unloading underway. It's a slow process, since there's no dock here. We have to do it all with the whale boats. We send in trading goods and supplies, and the boat brings back a load of copra."

"I'd like to go just as soon as I can."

"Martha, I really don't think you're going to like Rapango very much. Now, when we get to Tahiti, I'll introduce you to the governor of the island. It's much more civilized there. Here it's different. If you can do without good food and drink, and a soft life, the rest of it isn't so bad. The people work only as much as they must to live, and that's about it. I have an awful time getting them to produce enough copra to make it worthwhile to stop here every six months." He waved. "I've got to get down to the holds and be sure everything is set. Then we have to wait for the very top of high tide so we can scrape across the reef out there and get into the lagoon."

The next day the unloading started and Martha went ashore. Billy, one of the cooks, was her guide. He was a thin youth of fifteen, and was on his third trip with Captain Dyke. He found Mirani, a girl about Martha's age. She was a head shorter than Martha, with long black hair to her waist. She wore a loose-fitting kind of shirtwaist, only it had no sleeves, and ended three inches from her waist. The neck was open and three buttons held it together down the front.

"Bonjour," Mirani said.

Martha nodded and smiled. The cook jabbered at her for a few moments in French, then took their hands and put them together.

"Friends," he said in English, then said the same word in French. Mirani said the word, trying hard to pronounce it correctly. The young cook said a few more things to Mirani, then turned to Martha.

"Her name is Mirani, and she says she will be pleased to show you about the village, so you can see how her people live. She will meet you whenever you come to shore and see that you are well cared for and taken back to the ship at night. Mirani is one of the few girls on Rapango who has been to Papeete and gone to the mission school there. That is where she learned to speak French. She can also read and write French, which is more than I can do."

He spoke again to Mirani, then to Martha. "Mirani says you are to think of her as your sister, and to ask any questions you wish. She is proud to be your guide."

"Tell her I am most pleased and I appreciate her giving me so much of her time and attention."

He translated for the dark-skinned girl. She smiled and laughed easily, then caught Martha's hand, and they walked along the sandy beach.

It was a day of wonders for Martha. From the soft white sand they went into the trees. Many were coconut palms with the big fruit hanging overhead. The island was in the tropics, and every conceivable kind of tree, fern, grass and plant that had ever been brought there flourished.

Mirani walked through the open place below the coconut palms, in what Martha realized was a kind of street, to one of the grass huts. Like the rest of them, this one had been built of native materials. Inside, the floor was made of woven reeds and tough dry leaves from some of the trees.

The huts had no doors. The windows were only holes in the walls, and there was no way to have fire inside the huts. Mirani showed Martha where the beds were, and to her amazement they were only woven mats, made of some softer material than the floor mats.

The tour continued. Outside, Martha saw a fire ring, where rocks had been arranged in a small circle and an iron grate placed over it as a place to cook. Some of the huts had no such cooking fire area.

Children ran everywhere. Martha lost count of them. None of them wore clothes, their young brown bodies busy at games of tag and hide-and-seek, but the most popular game was eating. It seemed that they ate whenever they were hungry, with no set time for meals.

When the boys reached a certain age, about twelve, Martha estimated, they began to wear a loincloth. A few had cut-off trousers. But the girls were older before they put on any clothing. Then they wore thin skirts of *ti* leaves, but they remained bare-breasted. Only the grown women wore the small white blouses such as Mirani had.

Martha saw many things she wished she could ask questions about. She tried by signs, but they couldn't communicate very well. When the sun neared the peak of its morning climb, Mirani took Martha into the edge of the jungle, where they broke off a hand of ripe bananas from a tree and ran with them to the lagoon. They found a spot to lie down on the fresh green grass and ate the bananas, then stared at the sky.

Mirani jumped up and ran to the water, made splashing sounds, and came back, trying to convince Martha they should go swimming. Martha knew she could not. She still wore her high necked shirtwaist, a chemise and wrapper and a skirt with three petticoats that swept the ground. Her shoes were sturdy, laced up and ankle high. Mirani quickly stepped out of her *ti* skirt, unbuttoned her blouse and dropped it on the grass. She ran and dove into the lagoon, swimming twenty yards out, then stroking back.

She knelt beside Martha, a frown on her face, questions in her eyes.

"But I have no bathing clothes," Martha said. "I can't swim without them. What if someone should come?"

Mirani pointed to both of them again and shook Martha's clothes and indicated she should take them off and put them on the ground. Martha couldn't. At last she removed her ankle-high shoes and then her hose and lifted her skirts up over her ankles and waded in the warm water. Oh, it would feel good to jump in and swim the way they had when she was a child in San Francisco Bay. But she certainly would not swim without the proper bathing clothes.

Martha watched Mirani splashing around in the water and when the woman walked out and back toward Martha, it seemed perfectly natural that she should be naked. For her it was acceptable and right — but it would not be for Martha.

Mirani wiped the water off her slender brown body with her hand, then put on her clothes. They continued walking around the lagoon. Soon they came to a little cove where a dozen boys and girls were swimming. They were from five to thirteen years old, and all were naked.

Martha would need a lot of time to get used to that sort of thing. It just didn't seem right. Martha scolded herself. She was in a different culture from the one she had known. These people were doing what they had done for hundreds of years. She must learn to accept that.

During the next four days, as the small boats worked back and forth between the *Pacific Gem* and shore, unloading trade goods and bringing back copra, Martha stayed on shore with Mirani. She was trying to absorb as much of the culture of these people as she could. She talked with old Tapo, who was the only one in the village of over two hundred who could speak English. Gradually she and Mirani each learned a few words of the other's language, and on the fourth day Martha brought a bathing suit with her, a long full body suit that covered her completely, and she and Mirani swam. Mirani was like a frisky sea otter in the lagoon, and Martha enjoyed the warm, clear water and was fascinated by the color-ful fish and the many kinds of shellfish and plants on the bottom.

When Martha realized there were only two more days before the ship sailed, she asked Peter if she might spend the last night on shore with Mirani. Peter, busy at his office desk on the *Pacific Gem,* agreed, and she took a few of her clothes in a suitcase and left on the small boat. It would be the first time she had been away from her husband overnight since they were married.

That day, Mirani and Martha took a long walk along the shore and saw the endless rows of coconut palms that a Dutchman had planted many years before. Now the trees were bearing and the men and older women worked a few hours daily harvesting the ripe nuts and turning them into copra.

"Why don't you work more, so you can buy lumber and windows and build real houses?" Martha asked, through some words and signs.

They came around a bend in the trail and Martha gasped in surprise. It was a house with window frames, a hinged door, a chimney and once-painted boards, but it was falling to pieces.

Mirani took Martha inside and showed that the tropical climate had rotted the wood five years after the house was built — right through the paint. In another year it would all fall down except the chimney, and the jungle would claim it. Mirani got the idea across that different places need different types of houses. Their open-air grass huts served them nicely, and all the materials needed to build them were there in the jungle, free for the gathering.

That night Mirani, Martha and most of the crewmen from the *Pacific Gem* were invited to the village to a farewell feast. Tapo presided as a hundred-and-fifty-pound pig was given its final hour of roasting over a long spit.

After the feast there was singing and the old traditional dances were performed as well as the vigorous Tahitian hula. Martha covered her face in embarrassment as the girls danced bare-breasted, wearing only their *ti* skirts. Then, when no one else seemed to mind, she watched in open amazement. The girls moved in the Tahitian hula in a way that the human body simply could not. It seemed impossible to shake the hips so fast with the upper body remaining perfectly still. No one could dance that way, but she had seen it. Passing around the circle of men and older women were bottles of some kind of native drink fermented from coconut milk and berry juices. The more the bottles passed the more the men and women alike began to call for a "changing dance." When the shouting for the changing dance became too loud, Tapo rose and spoke sharply in the native tongue, and the talk stopped at once.

Martha asked Mirani what it was all about, but the dark girl only smiled and said that perhaps some day Martha would find out. After the feast, Martha went to Mirani's hut, a larger one that sat apart from the others. Tapo had told her that Mirani's mother had been a much-loved queen of Rapango. She had died many years ago, and king Matono had ruled since then.

Martha watched the stars, saw the last of the small fires in the village burn out and all activity cease. She wanted to remember this night for ever and ever. At last she lay down on her reed mat and went to sleep. Tomorrow she would be up early and out to the *Pacific Gem* so they could sail promptly with the noon-time high tide.

A mile away, on a hill overlooking the lagoon, a white man built a small fire that could be seen seaward. He let the fire burn for a minute, then put it out. He built the fire again and let it burn for a minute, again dousing it. Three times the minute-long fire burned. Two miles at sea, in the shadows of the South Pacific darkness, a two-masted sloop rode easily in the swells. A lookout high on the mast grinned as he climbed down and told the captain the good word. The big steamship was still anchored in the lagoon.

CHAPTER SEVEN

Captain Peter Dyke sat in his cabin checking the label on a bottle of wine when he heard a shrill cry.

"Boarders! Boarders! We're under attack!" Before he could say another word, the lookout in the bridge fell as a rifle bullet slammed through his chest, pounding him back against the bulkhead. He died as he slid slowly to the deck.

Dyke grabbed his two revolvers, the latest type six-gun he could buy in San Francisco, and rushed on deck. His first shot brought down a man going up a ladder to the bridge. His second round toppled a man over the side.

Captain Dyke crouched by a steel ladder watching his ship. He was sure the cry had sent crewmen tumbling from their bunks in the forward quarters, but would there be enough of them? Tapo had said there had been ten men in the pirate sloop which had left a week earlier. It must have come back and waited until the ship was loaded before attacking. None of Dyke's men had guns, and only a few owned knives. It would be a one-sided fight.

He saw movement near a hatch cover and stared intently at the shadow. His man or theirs? Then he saw a naked torso and a rifle. Dyke held the six-gun in both hands and aimed deliberately at the center of the shadow. He fired, then shot again and saw the man roll into the moonlight and lie still. As soon as the gun went off the second time, Peter dove for a new position behind a huge air vent.

He searched below him, then looked above. Two of his men charged out from the forward companionway. One was cut down by four bullets, all fired from close range. The other man dove to the deck and grappled with one of the pirates.

Peter moved to get closer to the enemy. He didn't know where the gunmen were. A searing missile slammed into his shoulder as he left his protection, spinning him to the deck. Peter lost one of his guns but held on to the other as he shook his head, rolled to his knees and felt a terrible pain in his left shoulder. Captain Dyke picked up the six-gun, found he could still use his hand

and arm, and ran quietly to the bulkhead he had picked out as his shield. Now someone was behind him. He slid between the wall and a protecting funnel, then looked behind. Movement. He watched it until it came again. Peter Dyke brought up both six-guns and fired at the spot with each weapon. There was a scream of anger, then silence.

Peter left his haven and worked his way toward the stern. It was up to him to drive off the attackers. He had put four down, but that probably left six. He vaulted a low railing and crept along the deck that led toward the number one hold. His shoulder throbbed with a staggering pain. He couldn't let down now. To give up was to die. He pressed near the edge of the deck and looked over at hold number one. A body moved from the hatch cover toward a ladder just beyond. The moonlight glinted off a gun in the man's hand. Peter shot twice, then dropped to the hard deck and rolled, forgetting his wound. Agony ground through him. For a moment he couldn't see as he came close to fainting. Peter wasn't sure if he could stand.

Carefully he struggled up to his knees. The six-guns were like fifty-pound weights in each hand. He could feel blood gushing down his arm now, under his shirt, all the way into his pants.

He saw a man edging around a bulkhead in front of him. There was no chance the pirate would not spot him. Peter slowly lifted his right hand with the six-gun and pulled the trigger. His aim was wide, the lead slamming into the bulkhead and off into the night.

Peter Dyke heard a vicious chuckle, saw a leering face and then a bright orange flame in front of him, and felt something knock the gun from his hand. His wrist billowed with fire.

Captain Dyke fell on his back and tried to roll over, but his shoulder exploded with pain and stopped him. The whole scene began to shift and change. Sometimes he could see nothing. Then it was as bright as if he saw him only half the time in the flickering of a campfire.

Peter's hand wouldn't lift the weapon. His left arm failed to function at all. The face came again, now only a dozen feet away from him, laughing, snarling, the mouth making sounds, but Peter could hear none of them. The leering face steadied, and Peter saw the man lift his weapon again. The orange-bright flame leaped from the gun, the bullet pinning his right shoulder to the deck, breaking the joint, dropping Peter into the deepest blackness he had ever known.

A toe jolted his side until his eyes opened. The laugh came from farther away, but the toe was still there. The orange flame blossomed once more, and a .44 caliber bullet sped toward Captain Peter Dyke, boring a hole in the soft underside of his chin, continued into the cavity beyond and plunged through the roof of his mouth where it dug a wide swath among the thousands of vital nerve endings in his brain.

Suddenly everything was cold. Peter Dyke felt a hand grasping at him, squeezing his heart. White-hot heat raced into his brain, then billowing sound shook him, which in turn was overshadowed by such brilliant lights that he knew his eyes would be burned out. Then his eyes were embers and his last breath sucked into greedy lungs before the scalding blood cascaded down over his mind and he lived no more.

The gunman shot Peter Dyke four more times. The bullets shook his body as they plunged into the lifeless hulk accompanied only by the trapped air in his lungs escaping in a final wheezing death rattle.

For a moment the *Pacific Gem* was quiet. Then a man groaned.

Marcel Navarre's green eyes swept the

moonlit expanse of the big ship. Never had he hoped to capture a prize so easily. This man was surely the captain. Who else would be permitted two guns on a ship at sea? With the captain gone, the others would be sheep.

"The battle is over. Your captain is dead. You are ordered to lay down your weapons and assemble on deck by the first hold at once!" Navarre's voice boomed into the void.

Only silence answered him. A knife sped through the air and struck the bulkhead beside him. He spun and snapped a shot at a white blur of the man who had thrown it. The lucky shot hit the man in the back and he went down.

"Enough of the killing. Come out and you'll live to fight and love another day. You don't owe your lives to this scow!"

"I'm coming out. Don't shoot!"

"Me, too. Hold your fire."

Navarre smiled. "All right, lads, let them come, but keep them under your guns all the time."

Five minutes later it was over. Eleven men had been rounded up and forced to lie down on the hatch cover. None was armed.

Navarre counted his men. Four were dead. Three of the enemy crew were awaiting burial, including the captain. He hefted the two revolvers he had taken from the captain. They were balanced beautifully. Both had six-inch barrels. They were excellent weapons. He would save them.

Navarre left two of his men to guard the captives and took the rest of his crew on a tour. They found lamps and prowled around. It was an immense vessel. The captain's cabin fascinated Navarre. When he found the women's clothing he scowled, because they had discovered no woman on board. Then he thought that she might have stayed on the island. If she were there it would not be hard to find her. He would enjoy bedding a white woman again. It had been too long.

When the touring party came to the engine room, they held their lamps up in surprise. The huge steam engine had been sabotaged. The long side-lever arm had been disconnected from its regular position. Neither Navarre nor any of his men knew anything about steam engines, and he suspected it would take an expert repair crew to fix the engine so the ship could be put back into action. Just as he headed for the deck, he heard a shot and cries from above. When they stormed up to the top deck, they were too late.

One of his guards was dead, the other disarmed, and the eleven captives were all gone. They had slithered down ropes into Navarre's sloop, and even as he watched, the sailing craft slipped away in a light breeze, making for the mouth of the lagoon. Every man fired at the retreating sailboat but they could not stop her.

Marcel Navarre watched the sails vanish into the night and swore. Now *they* were stranded! This big hulk of iron wouldn't move with her engine disabled. She had no sails, and none of his men could operate her anyway. He left one man on guard and told the rest to sleep wherever they could. Navarre retreated to the captain's cabin and lit two coal oil lamps, still amazed at the luxury of the place. That was when he decided for sure that the captain's wife must have been on the trip with him. He prowled the rooms looking for hidden money or jewelry. Navarre did not worry about being stranded for long on Rapango. He could rig a small boat if he had to, and get back to Papeete that way. Right now he was more concerned with ways he could repair the *Pacific Gem* and sail her to a friendly port far from Tahiti, where he could sell both ship and cargo.

He ripped a small desk apart looking for

secret compartments, found nothing of value, and dropped onto the big bed. He was surprised at the featherbed's softness.

Navarre let his one hundred eighty pounds sink into the feathers, and tried to relax. He wore a full beard, which was now tinged with streaks of gray. His hair was black and his eyes were green. Navarre was forty years old and had been making his living by his wits ever since he jumped a French ship in Hong Kong, fifteen years ago. He hated losing the sloop, but the trade of vessels should work out ultimately. He had to concentrate on getting that engine back into operating condition.

Navarre relaxed in the big bed, wondering what the captain's wife looked like and how well she would perform in bed. He went to sleep with a smile on his face.

Early the next morning, the four remaining men in his crew threw the dead overboard, after stripping all valuables and clothing from them. Next, they would go ashore, establish their authority and find the white woman. Navarre decided he might as well live on board the ship until the galley's supply of food ran out or they got the engine repaired.

Shortly after dawn, Navarre and his four

men rowed from the *Pacific Gem* toward shore. All were armed. They saw a group of six native men waiting for them. Each man had a spear. When Navarre was sure they were spears, he ordered one of his men to fire into the group with a rifle. One native went down, mortally wounded, and everyone else on the beach vanished into the trees. At the sand, Navarre placed his men around him with their guns drawn.

One solitary figure came toward them. It was the old priest who could speak French, and whom Navarre had talked to before.

"Tapo," Navarre called out in French, "come closer and talk. If you do what we ask of you, no more of your people will be harmed."

"*Awee! Awee!* Why do you return to plague us?" Tapo asked. "We have no gold, no money — nothing to steal."

"Quiet, old man. We have come looking for the white woman, the captain's wife. We must talk to her about her husband."

Tapo watched the man, remembering how he had killed the palace guards, and stolen three young women for his boat. Tapo did not believe this Frenchman. There had been gunfire on board the big ship last night. Everyone in the village had heard it. Now, when these men rowed from the ship this morning, it must mean the friendly crew was either dead or had run away. Tapo wondered which. It was reported that the small sloop was nowhere to be seen on this side of the island.

"Is Captain Dyke sick?" Tapo asked.

"Oh, yeah, he's sick. Very sick. That's why we must talk with his wife. Bring her to us and we will go back to the ship and leave you here in peace."

"I know of no white woman," Tapo said.

Navarre fired a pistol round into the sand beside the old native's foot. Tapo did not flinch.

"Tell us true, old man. Where is she? We will pull your fingers off one by one until you tell us."

Tapo shook his head. "You will not harm me, for if you do, you lose all talk with my people. No other here can speak French, so you would have to use signs and motions. No, you will not harm me, and I say I know not where the white woman is. Everyday she came to shore, and then returned to the ship at night. Did she not last night?"

"We didn't find her."

"Perhaps she knew you were attacking and fled in your ship. The small sloop is gone. Perhaps she is on it."

"Impossible. The *Pacific Gem's* crew escaped and stole our sloop when we were below decks. No woman was with them." Navarre wished he had another native there. He would start cutting off fingers until the priest told him where the white woman was. But the old man was right. He couldn't permit the priest to be harmed. He needed Tapo.

"We'll search the village, Tapo. When we find the white woman, we'll kill everyone in the hut where she's hiding."

"She is not here," Tapo said, but this time his voice did not carry as much conviction.

Navarre studied the slim old native, wondering what he was thinking. He was lying, that was for sure. The woman had to be close by. She wasn't on the big ship, and she hadn't gone away in the sloop. He began speaking in English now, shouting toward the village. He had found out the captain's name on the *Gem,* so he used it.

"Mrs. Dyke, we know you're in the village. The captain wants to speak with you. He's wounded and he's calling for you. Come so we can take you to him."

There was no response. Navarre led the entourage off the sand and up to the first huts. The pirate shouted his message. Now for the first time the natives began to appear around the huts and the edges of the trees. He told them in French what he had said in English, and it seemed that some of them understood.

After he called out his message for the third time in English, he saw movement in the trees and a white woman stepped out. She was dressed as he would expect, in clothes from chin to toe, but her waist did pinch in alluringly, and she was young. She might not be too bad.

As she came toward him he saw she was dark-haired with a strikingly beautiful face, and the swell of her breasts under the shirtwaist delighted him.

"Mrs. Dyke?" he asked.

She looked up, nodded and kept walking toward him.

"Mrs. Dyke, your husband's been wounded and would like very much to see you," he said in English.

She stopped two yards from him and stared up into his face, defiance gleaming from her eyes, her chin lifted a little too high.

"Sir, why should I believe you? You are a pirate and a murderer. You killed two natives on this island, stole three young women, and this morning we saw your men throw several bodies into the lagoon. Why should I not assume one of them was my husband?"

"Because I said so, Mrs. Dyke. Because there is honor even among men like me who have to scratch out a living the best way we can. Now, you will come?"

She looked around the village, then stared at Tapo. The priest shook his head, as his advice. She stared at the ground for a moment, then walked forward.

"If my husband is not on your boat, if he is indeed dead as I have assumed, I will kill you. I promise you that!"

Navarre wanted to laugh. This small, slight beauty was threatening him with death. It was a joke. He remained serious.

"Madam, if your husband were dead, why would I risk showing myself to come here on an errand of mercy? Why wouldn't I simply sail the *Pacific Gem* away as a prize? Come now, let's hurry and get to your husband."

Navarre's men were leering at the woman. There was nothing the pirate captain could do to prevent it. She ignored them, kept her chin up and walked ahead of them to the longboat, which had been used only the day before to transfer cargo. Martha sat in the bow and held on as the men launched the boat. All five of the pirates got into the craft and the men rowed toward the big ship.

She stared forward, not wanting to talk or even to look at the men. They were all ragged, dirty, unkempt, the dress of the Pacific.

Mirani had urged her to remain hidden. She indicated that the bad man had stolen girls and killed temple guards. He was bad, very bad. But the wifely urgings had been too strong. If Peter had been only wounded in the fighting they had heard last night, then it was her duty to go to him and comfort him. It could be as Navarre said. Mirani had told her what the pirate had said to Tapo in French, so she had stepped forward. She did not want harm to come to Mirani or her people.

Martha was the first to climb the rope ladder as the boat scraped against the iron hull of the *Gem.* It was hard work for her, but she made it, and ran at once to the captain's cabin, before any of the others got on board. She closed the door and locked it. When she looked around she saw the rooms had been ransacked, probably in a search for money and valuables. Peter was not there, as she had guessed he would not be. She had been tricked. Martha sagged onto the bed and let the tears come. What was she to do now? She was a captive, at the very least.

Someone pounded on the heavy door.

"Mrs. Dyke, your husband isn't in there. He's down on the aft deck over on the port side, resting on a mattress. He asked that we not move him."

She listened through the door. It would take the men hours to batter it down. But again her instincts told her that she had to go to Peter. If there was even the smallest chance that Navarre was telling the truth, she must go and find out.

"How badly is he wounded?"

"In the shoulder and in the thigh. Painful, but not fatal. The pain was why he wouldn't let us move him. It is intense."

"What color is my husband's hair?"

"His hair? The battle was at night. How could I see his hair? This morning it was still dark. Oh, let's see. Yes, now, I do remember, his hair is red, flaming red hair."

Slowly she reached for the bolt. She slid the heavy iron bar back and slipped the lock. Martha pulled the door open slowly.

"Take me to my husband," she said.

When the door was fully open, Navarre lunged into the room, caught her by one arm and swung her around so she fell back on the bed. At once the shirtless man dropped on top of her, his hands catching her flailing fists and pinning them deep into the featherbed.

"So young and sassy, and so full of action," Navarre said, his face only an inch from hers. "This is going to be one damn fine romp! Five times I should guess before I wear out and pass you on to my second." He leaned back and watched her chest heaving up and down from her struggles. The top three buttons had torn free from her shirtwaist and he could see the soft white flesh below her neck.

"It's been so long since I've had a white woman, I almost forgot how sweet and clean they smell." He pushed his face between her breasts. When he rose he looked at the door.

"Rogers, you bastard, close the damn door and wait your turn!"

Martha was crying again. Huge tears rolled down her cheeks. She sobbed and knew it made her breasts heave and shake, but she couldn't help it. He kept her hands pinned down. Only his lips violated her, kissing at the tears, forcing down hard over her mouth, making her short of breath. She felt his arousal as he pressed against her. How could she escape? She knew there could be no way. Even if she could get to the rail and jump, his men would swim after her and bring her back. She tried to stop crying. Between sobs she managed to ask a

181

question.

"Peter Dyke is dead?"

"Aye, pretty one. Shot full of holes and fed to the sharks. So don't you worry your pretty little head about him."

"Liar!"

"Aye."

"Cheat, pirate, killer, *monster!*"

"Aye, when I see them, and I can spot a pretty woman every time."

She let his words slide off her, not paying attention. She tried to think. A dozen plans charged through her mind. She could fight him all the way, because she was sure he intended to rape her. She could submit and pretend to go along with it, hoping to find a weapon — but no handy two-by-two board was in sight. She could bargain her favors for half the value of the ship and cargo. She might try to deceive him, cooperate, promise to be his woman and only his, then slip into the water and swim the two hundred yards to shore at night. She was still making plans when he let go of her arms and sat up, his legs straddling her waist.

"So what is it to be, pretty one? Will you fight me, or do you want to have some fun too?"

"I'll kill you!" Her words crashed out without any conscious thought.

He was not impressed. "Aye, I'm counting on you trying. But the doing is a bit harder. So, right now, this minute, wench, is it to be my tearing off your fine clothes, or will you just relax?"

She had seen the elongated bulge in his trousers now just below his broad belt. As he talked she clenched her fist and suddenly swung it with all her strength at the target. Surprise helped, and he had not yet started to turn before her fist slammed into his enlarged penis.

Navarre roared in pain, his hand slapping her cheek hard as he fell forward, his chest smashed into her face, driving her head into the goose feathers, almost suffocating her.

The rules of the game were set.

He grabbed her hair and rolled over, pulling her on top of him, pinning her waist with his legs. He caught her shirtwaist in back and ripped it sideways with both his big hands, tearing buttons and seams as it came apart down her back and chest, the cloth dangling in shreds from her arms. He pulled her chemise apart, then the wrapper she wore around her breasts, and a moment later they swung undraped and free. Her hands had been pounding at his shoulders and head, but he grabbed them now and pushed her away from him, watching her breasts.

He rolled her over into the bed and sat on her hips, then before she could react, he dropped his head and chewed on each breast. Her hands got free and beat on his shoulders, but they were like iron. He caught her hands and held them again. He was the strongest man she had ever seen. Helpless, she turned her head to one side and let the tears come again.

Now he straightened, ripped her skirt and petticoats from her waist and threw one of his massive legs across her stomach, pinning her to the bed. He jerked the last of her clothing off and threw it on the floor. He didn't bother with her shoes or hose. She was still helpless under his heavy leg. Martha's tears continued and he laughed at them.

"Don't think crying will stop me, my pretty. I like it when a witch like you cries. Gives me more of a challenge, more of a go."

He unbuckled the four-inch-wide leather belt around his waist and kicked out of his pants. She turned her eyes away before his trousers came down. She heard his boots hit the deck, but she kept her eyes away from him.

"Look at me, bitch," he commanded. "Afraid you'll like what you see?"

She stared defiantly at his face, with a scar on his cheek extending out of his short black beard. His piercing green eyes held her, challenged her.

"Look at the rest of me, woman."

She had forgotten her tears. This was a tougher fight. His upper body was heavily muscled, shoulders wide, thick arms with biceps that bulged. His chest rose full and massive, tapering quickly to a smaller waist than she had imagined. Then she looked away.

"So you can't look at my staff of life. Look, damnit!" She had turned on her side, facing away from him. But now she looked over her shoulder at his crotch, then down his well formed and rugged, muscular legs. She had seen a naked man before.

"Am I good enough for a fancy lady like you?"

"You're a contemptible violator."

"And you like it. You like what you see. Admit it."

"A killer and a rapist and a pirate. You should hang."

"You'll really like it before I'm through. You'll be begging for it."

She tried to hit him again, but he caught

her fist, brushed her onto her back and lay on top of her with all his weight. She thought she would be crushed.

Furiously she tried to block it all out. She tried to think of something else. She would not react to his manhood, his rugged maleness. She simply would not. She would not let her body betray her. She would think about all the wonderful times she had had growing up, swimming in the big bay, going for boat rides, she was better at games than her brother — of course, he was younger than she was. She would not feel his hands on her, never!

She remembered one picnic in the sun, back before she had to worry about keeping her skin soft and white, when they had played games all day. She fought down the urge to open her eyes to discover exactly what he was doing, to watch his tongue caressing her nipple. Martha won. Her eyes remained tightly closed.

Allen! She wondered where Allen was now. She knew he had no idea his ship was sailing that morning, and that he had important duties to perform, that was why he couldn't get a message . . . no, no, keep your hand away . . . oh, God!

It was a long time later that she lay there and waited for him. She lifted her parted knees and watched him, almost ready to ask him to enter her and to bring her own desire to a conclusion. She had never felt such a range of emotions in the span of an hour. From the jolting realization that this man had killed her husband, to fury, then murderous anger and determination not to yield to him, to make him force her every step of the way.

And now, such a burning, demanding desire! Such a wanton need for him inside her. She held out her arms to him. "Oh, please, now, please. I need you." Navarre moved his hands away from her and bent over her to finish what he had begun. He had a knowing, satisfied smile on his face as he thrust forward.

Later she wasn't sure how many times they had clung together in the delicious spasms of pure ecstasy. Four, perhaps five times. He had sent to the galley for food and wine, and as they ate she remembered clearly what she had to do. Her strategy was still the same. She would stay with him for a while, then escape and plot ways to kill him and recapture the ship for her father. She knew that the others had escaped in the sloop. It was only a three-day sail to Papeete, Mirani had told her. So in six days the French could come back with many guns and perhaps a warship and regain control of the *Pacific Gem,* then hang the pirates.

Should she stay on board for the week or more before the French could get there, or should she escape? She sipped the wine and knew she would swim away at her first chance. Tonight, if possible. In the darkness they wouldn't be able to find her in the water. But first she had to get away from Navarre and his men. She must find a way.

"Will the ship stay here long?"

He looked up from a plateful of salt pork. "Stay here? Hell, we can't move. The crewmen wrecked the damn engine before they surrendered. We're dead in the water."

"But won't the crewmen get to Papeete?"

"In that sloop? Be a miracle if they make it to Tahiti. She was leaking bad, that's why we turned back here. The old tub was in bad shape."

"Oh. Well, then, you'll fix the engine and then set sail?"

"With you in my bed, right? I'll try." He watched her. He wasn't sure of her, but she had responded well to his first treatment. He would have her watched closely.

CHAPTER EIGHT

Marcel Navarre dressed slowly, enjoying the woman watching his every move. He fastened his wide leather belt, pulled on his boots and pushed both six-guns in the band.

"Woman, you stay right there. I've got to go in and have a talk with the king who rules this God-forgotten island. Since we'll be here a while, we might as well have an understanding with the old boy."

He walked to the door and looked at her lying still naked on the bed.

"Don't do anything stupid. This might work for both of us. I've taken off the lock on the inside of the door, and put a heavy bolt on the outside. You can't get out of the cabin, so don't try. And tonight, you and I will have another long, long party on that featherbed of yours."

Martha watched him as he went through the door, heard the bolt slide into place, and knew this might be the right time to try her escape, with Navarre and most of his men gone.

She searched her mind for some idea, some trick to use on her guard. Slowly she began to dress, a pair of long bloomers, a cool skirt, a wrapper, the new chemise from her dresser and a loose-fitting blouse on the outside of her skirt. She put on her hose and buttoned up the shoes he had taken off her some time during the morning. Martha decided it was only a little after midday. That would give her plenty of time.

Now she searched the cabin for some kind of weapon. The guns were gone: both of Peter's big six-guns and the small Derringer he had hidden in the desk. Even the desk was demolished. On the floor she found what might work. It had come from one of Peter's shore leaves, perhaps in India. It was an ivory letter opener with a six-inch blade-type shaft, not really sharp, but with a good enough point and a solid carved ivory handle. The weapon was heavy enough to cause massive damage. Quickly she opened the fasteners of her blouse and took it off and the chemise and the wrapper she used to hold her breasts firmly in place.

Next she went to the door and began thumping on it. She hit it with the leg from the desk and after five minutes attracted someone's attention. A rough voice shouted through the door.

"Yeah?"

"Hello?"

"I said, Yeah. What 'n hell you want?"

"I've got a problem."

"Sure you have, locked in."

"No, that's not it. I'm going to live with Marcel. He's a fine man. That's not my problem."

"What is?"

"The chamber pot. It's embarrassing, but it's almost full and just smells so bad. I mean, I can hardly stand it. Could you empty it for me?"

"I don't empty no slop jars."

"I would be ever so grateful. I need to sleep and I just can't. The smell is just so . . . look, I know he told you not to open the door for any reason, but I'll set the chamber pot over by the wall, and I'll stay on the bed. You can see me, and I won't be any danger to you. Wouldn't that be all right?"

Evidently he thought about it a while.

"Hell, might be all right. Just how much of you am I gonna see?"

"Sir! I'm a married woman!"

"Ma'am, you were. Now you're a widow."

"Oh, yes, well, even so . . ."

"You show me yourself and I'll empty the damn thing."

"My . . . my breasts?"

"Yeah, that's right."

"And you wouldn't touch me? I am . . . I mean we just . . ."

"Christ, no, I won't touch you. Just let me look at them bare and hanging out."

"Well, I don't know."

"Look, don't matter to me. You want to smell that slop all day, you go right ahead."

She waited. He spoke next.

"Look, lady. Nobody else is on board so you can't talk anybody else into getting the thing. You show 'em to me or smell it."

"Well . . . all right. But you stay right by the door. Wait, now, I'm moving the chamber pot over there." She carried it to a spot near the door. There wasn't much in it but that would have to do.

"You ready yet?"

"No, I have to undress. Wait a minute." She took the blouse and laid it on the bed, hiding the letter opener under the clothing so she could grab it quickly. Martha looked down at her bare breasts and sighed. At this point escape was the most important thing, not false modesty.

"All right, I'm ready. But only for a quick look."

"Yeah, yeah." The bolt slammed open and she saw the door swing inward. The man was not as large as she had imagined. He had a full black beard and she could smell his body odor from across the room. He glanced down at the white chamber pot, then looked at her. The man stepped into the cabin, his eyes riveted on her breasts.

"My God! Look at you!" He took a step toward her.

She didn't want to scare him off, but he had to get close enough so she could use the ivory letter opener.

"My God!" He began rubbing his crotch.

"You said . . ." She let it trail off.

"Beautiful, I ain't never seen none that big before."

"You said you'd only . . ."

He didn't hear her. The man took another step toward her.

"Hey, you been with the captain all morning, how about a quick one with me? I ain't had no white gal for two years."

"Well, really! I only agreed to let you look . . ."

"Come on, the cap'n'll never know. How could he know? I ain't gonna tell him." He walked closer, his hand rubbing a lump in his pants. "How about it, sweetie, just one little time? What's it gonna hurt? I need it."

She let him move forward, her hand edging under the blouse and grabbing the ivory handle. Another two steps.

"Well, maybe I could let you touch me, feel me."

"Hey, now, that's a good girl."

She sat up taller, thrusting her breasts out more, forcing his hands to lift to them, which exposed more of his belly to her attack.

His hand curled around one breast and Martha shivered.

"Hey, puss, I won't hurt you. It don't hurt a bit. Hell, after this morning . . . His left hand cupped her other breast and she shivered again. He put his head back and laughed, his eyes closed in rapture.

At that moment she pulled out the letter opener, holding it like a saber with the blunt handle end in her palm and lunged forward, jamming the opener into his chest just under his rib cage and slightly upward. She continued to push with the palm of her hand until the blade stopped and he staggered backwards, collapsing on the floor, agony tinged with surprise on his face as he screamed.

For one dreadful moment she watched him. He grabbed the handle and started to pull, then realized that would make the injury worse, make it bleed more. He slumped on his back on the floor, his hands pounding the carpet in frustration.

Quickly she put on her blouse, forgetting the chemise and wrapper, and stepped around the man, heading for the door.

"Don't . . . go!"

She stared down at him. "Why not? You killed my husband, shot him down, not giving him a chance. At least you have a chance." She went out the door and to the side of the big ship. The rope ladder was over the side closest to shore, so she couldn't get to the water that way. She looked out from the port side at the far shore. It was about a quarter of a mile to the edge of the lagoon, well away from the village, and hidden from the village by the ship. She would go there.

The rail was twenty feet from the water, and she had never dived that far before. Then she saw a rope on the deck, and tied it to the railing and let it dangle over the side. The line came within three feet of the water. Martha sat down on the deck and took off her shoes, knowing she would never make it to shore wearing them. She shrugged and slid out of her skirt as well. Now she only had on her bloomers and blouse. It would have to do. Gradually she let herself over the side, holding onto the rope, and edged down the iron hull of the ship. She "walked" down, leaning far back, holding the rope tightly, which helped take some of the pressure off her hands. She let down slowly, not wanting to fall. When she was within five feet of the water, her hands gave up and she dropped into the sea.

Martha came up from the blue-green water of the lagoon, took two big breaths and swam away from the ship toward the tall coconut palm on the far shore. She had swum much farther than this in San Francisco Bay, but here it was different.

At once she realized she had a problem with her blouse. It tangled with her arms, seemed to scoop up and hold the water. Without it, swimming would be much easier. She kept trying. Then she knew that by wearing the blouse she might not make it to the far shore. Martha floated on her back and unbuttoned the blouse, then swam out of it. For a moment she thought of Mirani swimming bare-breasted, and that reassured her. At once she felt a new freedom, and her swimming was now easier. The bloomers had pasted themselves against her legs and didn't seem to cause any problems.

She swam with a steady crawl stroke for a hundred yards, turned on her back and rested. Again she swam and rested, floating longer the second time. As she rested after her third hundred-yard swim, she saw that she was within thirty or forty yards of the shore. The spot was well to one side of the village, in the opposite direction from the coconut plantings. She had never walked this way with Mirani. Martha swam to the shore and came out of the water as naturally as if she were fully clad in her bathing dress. She moved across the sand quickly and into the jungle growth. Plants and small animals that would have frightened her a week before seemed harmless now. She found a banana tree and picked off two ripe fruits and ate them. As she sat on the grass she realized that she was practically naked. The thin cotton bloomers were not yet dry and clung tightly to her legs.

She could think of only one solution to her plight: Mirani. But how could she contact the woman? For a moment Martha felt a rush of anger, hurt and despair, but she pushed the tears back and wiped her eyes. She had to know what was happening in the village. How? Could she work up to it cautiously?

For a moment the idea of a city girl sneaking up on these natives in their own jungle was funny. She laughed, then frowned.

There must be some way. She would move along as close as she could and wait for someone to walk by. That was better — if she could find some kind of trail. Martha moved along the edge of the jungle near the beach, never getting too far from the white sand. She had gone a quarter of a mile when she heard voices ahead. She hid behind a tree and waited. Who could it be?

When Navarre found she had escaped and wounded her guard, he would be furious. She had to be ready to hide on the island for a long time. She would not stay in the village because that would put the villagers in danger of Navarre's wrath.

She began moving forward again. There were people out there, and she had to find one whom she could make understand that she needed Mirani.

Marcel Navarre took his three best men with him as he went into the village just after noon. He felt sexually satiated. What a woman! Once he got her excited he couldn't get her stopped. And she was safe in the locked cabin. He decided he would keep her for himself. No sense in sharing a jewel like her with the others. Let them get native girls. They didn't care very much anyway. That decision made, he checked both of his six-guns and stood up in the boat to see what was happening on shore. The natives were moving about as usual. Lazy bastards. Worked an hour or two a day when they felt like it. No wonder so many of the older ones were fat as pigs. If he had control of this damn island for a few years, he'd make some changes.

The thought sparked an idea. Why didn't he take over Rapango? It was on the fuzzy fringe of the French protectorate area. Not even the French were sure they had authority here. He could move in, tell the king to obey orders or he'd lose his head, and then put the natives to work. He would turn out a fortune in copra in just a few years. The big ship? Hell, he could say it had broken down and he had salvaged it. The crew had deserted or died. He'd bring in an expert and get the steam engine running again, and he could use it to move his own copra to market.

He'd change the ship's name. He'd have somebody get to work on that, first thing tomorrow. Change the name everywhere it showed — in the log, everywhere. Hell, he'd made up enough "old" logs before. He could show he'd been skipper of this ship for three years, with trips all over the Pacific. Home port could be Seattle. Damn, why not? First came the king.

Navarre had no idea who the king was or what kind of guard force he might have. Each of Navarre's men carried two pistols in belts and a rifle. It was more firepower than these natives had ever dreamed of. He'd convince the king to go along with his ideas. Then it would be easy sailing with old Tapo, who would control the people. The priest was right, though. He did need him around as an interpreter, especially with the king.

Tapo met Navarre's boat at the shore. This time there was no group of men with spears. Tapo sat in the warm sand, holding a shell in each hand. Navarre stared down at him.

"Old man, get on your feet. We're going to talk to the king, and we need you to help us."

Tapo shook his head slowly. "The king does not talk to foreigners. He has no interest in you or your boat or your problems. He wishes only that the big iron ship be removed from his lagoon as soon as possible, so it will not spoil the water and kill the fish."

Navarre signaled two of his men, who picked up the priest and carried him between them on the way to a small hill to the north of the village where Tapo had once indicated that the king lived.

"This is bad, this is very bad," Tapo said.

"Shut up, old man, and do what we say. Will you walk now?"

Tapo nodded. It would be a bad omen if he were carried to the king's palace. Indeed he must walk, and precede these men. But first he had to warn them.

"Navarre, there are certain customs. No one dares to touch the king. No one may have his head higher than the king's. No one may move toward the king. If the king signals for us to leave, we must go quickly and silently."

"How many guards does he have around the palace?"

Tapo ignored the question. "When we go to the throne room, we must all sit with our sides to the king, to show proper respect."

Navarre nodded, letting the priest think he would do as he suggested. Actually he had no intention of following any of the suggestions. He'd give the king a chance to play the game, but if he didn't . . .

The men moved up a trail through dense growth toward a cliff. At the base of it, Tapo called out in a loud voice in his native tongue, asking permission to approach the king for an audience. The request was granted.

They went up a trail cut in the small cliff to a plateau. In the center, under soaring palms, stood a building made of bamboo and coconut logs, and topped with a roof of palm fronds. An open space had been left below the floor and between the top of the walls and the ceiling so air could pass freely through and around the room. The windows were simply openings.

"The house of the mighty Matono, our king," Tapo said in French. "He does not speak your tongue, so I offer myself as interpreter for you."

The steps of the king's house were heavy and elaborate, the swinging doors fastened with hinges made of tough shark hide. Inside the first room, pandanus mats covered the floor. The king sat in the second room on a small cushion, his eyes closed.

King Matono was a compactly built man with light brown skin and black hair worn long, tied in back with a piece of sennit. His brow was high, and when he looked up, his eyes showed dark brown. He did not smile.

"Ask him how many natives are on the island," Navarre said.

Tapo sat down and turned, indicating the others should sit. They did, on Navarre's order, but only Tapo sat with his side toward the king to show respect. Tapo began talking rapidly to the king, telling him how the strangers had killed two of his guards, how the men threatened the people and were pirates.

"Just ask the question," Navarre snarled.

Tapo did, then answered. "Twenty times the number of the king's fingers," Tapo said.

"How many warriors does the king have?"

The priest relayed the answer. "We have no warriors, only four temple guards you saw before."

"Is Matono a good king?" asked Navarre.

The old priest smiled. "Yes, he is just and fair. He is strict in enforcing the tabus. We hope his new wife will bear him many sons."

"Tell Matono that he is no longer king. That I, Marcel Navarre, now own this island. It is my kingdom, and I rule by the whip and the gun. If he would stay alive, he must leave this place and return to the village."

Tapo shook his head, tears springing to his old eyes. "I cannot say those words! I cannot repeat such terrible statements."

"Say them or die on the spot, Tapo." Captain Navarre drew and cocked his six-gun and aimed it at the priest.

Tapo began, choked up, and stopped. He was telling the king that this pirate and killer demanded to be king, and that the great

Matono was in terrible danger.

King Matono scowled and looked at Navarre for the first time. He rose and stood spraddle-legged, his hands shaking with anger. Matono bellowed a string of words Navarre could not understand. Then he sprang for a small table, grabbed a ceremonial sword and lunged toward Navarre.

The pirate shot the king six times, the heavy .44 caliber bullets stopping his charge, then pounding him backwards. He was dead as he slid to the pandanus mat.

Tapo leaped to his side. *"Auwe! Auwe! Auwe!"* The old priest picked up his king's head and cradled it in his lap. He knew the king was dead, and that life on Rapango would never be the same. He cried, tears dripping onto the royal chest. One of Navarre's men pulled Tapo away from the body and forced him to stand in front of Navarre.

"You must kill me next," he told the pirate. "For I did not defend my king, so I am automatically a dead man."

Navarre shook his head. "Not so, old man. You've got to stay alive to help your people. Without you here to caution me, I might kill half your people just for sport. Your duty is to protect your people, not to think of yourself." Navarre let that penetrate the native's skull. Then he went on.

"Now, your next job is to get rid of the body. I may want to come to live here. Get the body out of here and dispose of it. After that, you must double the production of copra daily. I don't care how you do it, but tell the people there must be twice as much as before."

Tapo's heart cried as he went to the village and brought back four young men to carry the body of King Matono to the burial place, the valley of heartache. There he was laid to rest with the traditional honors due a king. Only when Tapo returned to his village and sat in front of his modest hut did he truly understand what the new orders from Navarre meant. *Twice the copra!* He meant to work the villagers like slaves, taking everything, giving nothing in return. Captain Navarre was indeed an evil man, but how could the natives fight against the fire sticks?

On the way back to the ship, Navarre told his three seamen to go into the village and pick out three girls to take back to the ship. Having the girls on board ship would save time and satisfy the lust of the sailors at the same time. When not otherwise occupied they could cook and clean and wash the men's clothes. Navarre hurried the men, anxious to get back to the ship to see how

Martha was getting along, and to get the name off the ship's side. He hoped during the next lesson he gave Martha that she would learn faster. What a find he had made, what a truly magnificent woman he had claimed as a prize of battle.

As Martha moved stealthily along the shore of the lagoon, she became aware that the voices she heard were coming from the water side. The closer she went to the sounds, the slower she moved, not wanting to be seen or to give away her presence in any way.

At last she parted some heavy reeds at the very edge of the water and looked through. Children! It was the place where she and Mirani had seen the children swimming before. And as before, they were all naked, splashing, swimming, playing tag, diving for shells. Some of the larger girls had breasts that were swelling, and some of the boys were already well developed. Her problem was, how could she get the attention of one of the girls without alerting all of them?

Again, she was distinctly aware that she was bare-breasted. She would be embarrassed if any of the boys saw her, or if any adults were close by.

She was also concerned that as few of the

villagers as possible should know that she was on the island. She made up her mind how she might contact one of the girls, went back into the jungle and worked closer to the village on the other side of the swimming lagoon, then moved back towards the water until she found the trail the children used to get to the swimming place. She stood behind a tree and waited. Two nude boys came past, laughing and talking. Martha stared at them curiously, then turned away in embarrassment. She let them go by.

Soon three small naked girls came by. Martha guessed they were about six, too young to understand. She waited for a half-hour more and saw a young girl with budding breasts walking along the trail. When the girl was fifteen feet away, Martha stepped into the trail. The girl gasped, then smiled in greeting. Martha had seen her in the village, and now used the one word in the native language she remembered, meaning "friend." She reached for the girl's hand and led her into the jungle.

It took Martha half an hour to make the girl understand that she should bring Mirani to her. Martha tried to tell the girl that no one else must know, that she was hiding from the bad man, Navarre. The word brought a look of fear to the girl. Martha went over it again: *"Mirani, Mirani."* At last they both smiled and the girl ran down the trail. Martha now had hope that she would see Mirani's friendly face before the sun went down.

Martha faded back into the jungle again, to a place where she could see the trail but not be seen, and waited. She was totally alone, almost naked, and she had no idea how she could survive once Navarre came hunting her with his revolvers and rifles. She was certain that he would come. He had enjoyed her body too much to let her escape. She only prayed that Mirani would get there first.

Less than half an hour later, Mirani came running along the trail with the young girl. Martha called softly and Mirani turned into the jungle and found her. The woman spoke rapidly to the younger girl for a few moments, and she darted away.

Martha put her arms around Mirani and hugged her, then told her with sign language all that had happened on the ship and how she escaped.

As they worked at communicating, Mirani gave Martha one of the short white blouses that the older women wore. It was tight across the shoulders and breasts, but it made Martha feel more dressed. Mirani also gave her a *ti* leaf skirt, showing her how to slip it on and fasten it with a piece of sennit. It covered her bloomers, which were almost dry by now.

Mirani took her hand and led Martha through the jungle. Soon Martha was lost and couldn't even tell where the ocean was. After walking steadily for an hour they came to a small hill in what Martha decided must be the center of the island. She heard the ringing of a machete as they approached and held back, but Mirani smiled and urged her forward.

The growth on the small hill was less dense, and as they came toward a stand of coconut trees, Martha saw the beginnings of a shelter being made. It was a simple peaked affair, about six feet tall in the center and built so it would blend in with the rest of the foliage.

Hard at work was a young man she had seen in the village. When he saw them, he put down his long knife and ran to meet them. Mirani said something to him, and he smiled and bowed. She explained by sign language that this was Tero, her intended husband. Soon they would have their own hut and be married. At one side Mirani showed Martha a treasure more valuable than gold, her suitcase which she had taken

209

to shore the day before and left in Mirani's hut.

Martha opened it to see what she had brought. Two dresses, two skirts, a blouse, three pairs of bloomers, and a blessed pair of shoes! Her feet had been suffering on the long barefoot walk. She hugged Mirani again. Mirani told her that she would be safe there, at least for a few days. She and Tero had to get back to the village before they were missed in the search she knew Navarre would start. At the side of the shelter was a reed basket filled with several kinds of fruit and a portion of poi, the cooked taro root that was a native food staple. The two natives told Martha that one of them would be back as soon as possible, and a moment later they were gone.

Martha was hungry. She tried to eat the poi, found it strangely tasteless, but ate as much of it as she could, then ate a banana and two other strange-looking but delicious fruits.

She wanted to cry, but she knew that once she started she might not be able to stop. She understood enough about the jungle not to be terrified of it, even at night. There were no vicious animals here, and she had shelter. She had no fire because she knew that would be a beacon to any searchers.

Martha sat on the sleeping mat Tero had left. Suddenly she wanted to change into real clothes. She took off the white blouse and *ti* skirt and hung them on a branch, then put on a clean pair of bloomers, a long skirt and a blouse. At least now she felt more civilized.

Tears pressed against her eyelids again but she forced them away. She was alive, she was free, and she had two good friends. Mirani and Tero would help her, she knew that. There was nothing to worry about. The sloop would get to Papeete and the French would come back and capture the pirates. So in a week at the most she would be safely back on board the *Pacific Gem,* and it would sail on to Tahiti and the next stop on their trading journey. These terrible days would become only a distantly remembered nightmare. One day at a time, she just had to make it through twenty-four hours before she worried about the next day.

Until the French came, she could manage it.

She lay down on the mat, and before she knew it she fell asleep.

When she awoke it was dark. For a few seconds she did not remember where she was. When she did, she sat upright on the mat and looked around inside the shelter.

211

She heard the many night sounds of the jungle, some closer now — birds, small lizards and rodents, big frogs and insects, each chanting its individual notes to add to the chorus.

Tomorrow Mirani and Tero would be back. They would have good news, she was sure. Mirani said Tero would come and help her complete her small camp. She was sure they would be there. Martha only hoped that the three persons who knew she had made it safely to shore were not harmed by Navarre and his murderous crew. All she could do now was pray for their safety.

Martha lay on her back watching the darkness. She listened to the now familiar buzzes, chirps and other night sounds. Tomorrow she would ask Mirani exactly what made each sound, then she would not in the least be afraid. How could you be afraid of the chirping of a cricket after you saw a cricket?

Slowly, emotional fatigue crept up on her again. She had never felt so drained, mentally and physically. The swim alone would have been enough to put her down. This had been the most exhausting and the most terrible day of her whole life. She couldn't even think back over it. That very morning she had awakened in Mirani's hut, happy, ready for an interesting morning ashore before getting ready to sail. Then Mirani had explained to her about the shots during the night. When Navarre came she had fled with Mirani. *Navarre*. She shuddered. The man was so evil, he did not deserve to live. She remembered her threat to kill him, her promise to kill him if Peter were dead. She had always tried to keep her promises.

Martha closed her eyes. The blackness was no more dark than it had been with her eyes open. The clouds hid the moon, which meant it would be raining soon. She hoped that the hut would keep out the rain.

CHAPTER NINE

Sometime during the night a brief rain squall blew over the island, drenching everything with the daily watering. Martha woke suddenly when a drop of water splashed on her face. She rolled over and looked at the blackness, realizing that the quick shelter Tero had thrown up was keeping her dry. Only a few drops came through. She sat on her suitcase. Most of the night sounds had quieted. She waited out the quick rain, and when it stopped she lay back on the mat, still surprised at how warm the rain was in the tropics. Rain in San Francisco meant a chill wind, a lowered temperature and often a case of the sniffles. Martha closed her eyes and went to sleep quickly.

The sun slanting through the open door of her shelter finally awoke her. When she looked outside she saw Tero and Mirani there already at work. They had doubled the thickness of the palm frond thatch on her hut without her hearing, and now cleaned a small area where Tero worked on a bench and a small table for her.

Martha ran to Mirani and hugged her.

"Thank Tero for me for putting up such a fine little house and so quickly," she bubbled before she realized that Mirani couldn't understand most of her words. The two women sat down on the grass and began exchanging words. "Friend, me, you, go, come." Finally they each understood what the word "search" was in the other's language.

Mirani nodded when asked if Navarre had searched. She indicated he had been furious, had screamed, raved. Said the white woman must be found and surrender, or the daily quota of copra would be doubled again.

They talked of other things then, and soon Mirani indicated that she must go back to the village, because Navarre was watching her. Tero could stay most of the day and not be missed. She said Tero would help her find fruit trees and show her how to use roots and berries for food. Mirani left a large cooked fish and said it would spoil after overnight, so she should eat it that day. They embraced again, then Mirani left.

Tero motioned to her and they searched

for a good spring. He found one nearby, pure fresh water bubbling up from the ground. Tero showed her how to clean it out and dig a small hole which would soon fill up and clean itself and collect water, so that she would have a continuing supply. Then they found mango and papaya trees with ripe fruit and carried some back to the hut. There were two banana trees with ripe fruit at the edge of the clearing. Tero also gathered a dozen ripe coconuts, and showed her with his machete how to cut them open for the meat and how to save the sweet milk by punching the eyes.

Martha talked to Tero continuously, well aware that he couldn't understand what she was saying, but feeling lonely for someone to talk to.

"How in the world am I ever going to get away from here, Tero? What if the sloop really *was* leaking? What if the crewmen from the *Pacific Gem* are lost, the boat sunk, the men drowned? What will happen to me, stranded way out here?"

All day Tero showed Martha how to live in the wilderness. He gave her a knife with a six-inch blade, and made a small sheath from pliable palm fronds for her, with a belt to hang it on. She was amazed at how easily he did these remarkable things. When she thanked him, he grinned in delight. Before the first day was over she had learned more phrases in the native dialect, including "thank you, please, and excuse me."

When Tero indicated he must go, she said "thank you" in his language, then reached up and kissed his cheek. He smiled, acted embarrassed, ran lightly into the jungle and was gone.

Martha took out the knife and tried to whittle on a stick the way she had seen Tero do. He had carved small figures so easily. But Martha gave up, and cut open a mango instead, eating it slowly and deliberately. Tero had left her a tin cup, and she filled it with fresh cool water and placed a clean leaf over the top. As she sipped the water, she wondered now if she would ever see San Francisco again. It seemed such a long time since she had slept in a real bed. But it had been less than two days.

Either Tero or Mirani came to her daily, and they talked and learned more of each other's words. A week passed, but there was no furious search by the armed pirates. Martha held on, knowing the French would come soon. But the next time Mirani came, Martha asked her if the French had arrived, and Mirani had to tell her there had been no word at all from Papeete. They both knew that if the French did not respond at once, it could be several weeks or even months before they got around to it.

In the village Navarre had been making changes. He and the pirate crew had moved to shore, taking all of the stores and provisions from the *Gem* with them. They had given up repairing the steam engine, knowing that even if they got it ready to run, none of them knew how to operate the big ship. So instead they concentrated on forcing the natives to produce more copra.

Mirani said the work crews of all able-bodied men and women were marched out every day to work in the coconut harvest. The men went up the trees and cut down the ripe nuts and the women cut them open so the meat could dry in the sun. They worked four hours every day, which was an unheard-of work load for anyone on the island.

After the second week, Martha gave up trying to keep her cotton and linen dresses clean. She wore the *ti* leaf skirt more and more. It was actually much more practical, never needed washing, and when it wore out she would throw it away and have Tero make her a new one.

She took a daily bath in the small stream a hundred yards below, where she had scooped out a spot she could sit in. It reminded her of her bathtub back home.

Gradually she began to explore around her area. She was adept at finding good things to eat, and Tero helped her build a small fire pit and brought up armloads of dry wood which would burn with almost no smoke. They worked out a system by which she would start her cooking fire just at dusk, and by the time the meat or fish was cooked, the little smoke there was would dissipate in the darkness and leave no tell-tale trail for any searcher to follow the next morning.

Mirani said that Navarre was losing interest in his search for Martha. He had explored nearby areas with his three men as guards, and with native guides, but had found nothing. At last he took three native girls into the king's palace and settled down to working on increased copra production. He had thought about sailing one of the work boats to Papeete to find out if the *Gem's* crew had made it to the islands. But he put it off. It would mean he might find out he was hunted for piracy, and he would have no good defense. After another month or so, he would go.

Every day Martha learned more about primitive living. Each time Tero and Mirani came to her hut, they taught her something else about the jungle, about the birds and the small animals, and how to take care of herself. Tero taught her how to throw her knife. She practiced by the hour until she could stick it in a palm tree close to where she was aiming. He fashioned a bow for her, strung it with sennit and made some arrows. For a full week she practiced with it until she could put an arrow precisely where she wished, from fifty to seventy-five feet. She realized Tero was teaching her how to defend herself, how to wound or even kill the pirates, if they finally did find her hut.

She had discarded the bloomers that she had worn at first under the *ti* skirt, and often when she was alone, she left off the small white blouse Mirani had given her. It seemed so natural to slip around the jungle bare to the waist and clad only in the *ti* leaf skirt. Gradually her feet hardened until she was more comfortable without shoes. When Mirani or Tero came she wore the blouse, but she was not embarrassed if they arrived while she was bare-breasted. She would simply go into the hut and put on the blouse. How much she was thinking like a native! Her skin had tanned beautifully, and now she was a light brown all over her body. With her dark hair and *ti* leaf skirt, she could almost pass as a native.

In the sixth week she grew restless. Mirani said the pirates seldom went to the big ship any more. The two work boats were beached on the sand, and the pirates had discovered the native fermented drink called *tacora*, made from coconut milk and the juices of several native berries and fruits. Often, three of the pirates were drunk at one time.

Martha decided she wanted to go out to the ship. Mirani said it would be too dangerous. Martha shook her head.

"I want you to go with me, and Tero, too. I want to see if I can find any of my combs and other personal things. The pirates will never know that we've been there." At last she convinced Mirani that it would be safe. They met Tero at the children's lagoon the following day just at dusk. Tero reported two of the pirates were in a drunken stupor and the captain and first mate were in the palace drinking.

Both Mirani and Martha took off their white blouses before they stepped into the water and began swimming for the ship. They swam quietly, and when they came to the ship, went around it to the village side where they hoped the rope ladder would still be dangling down to the water line. It was. They climbed the ladder quickly, and once on board, Martha led them to the

221

captain's cabin.

It looked much the same as it had the day she had left. She even found a bloodstain on the carpet.

She wished for a torch so she could see better. Instead she worked her way around the room by touch, examining her dresser. With a small cry she let them know she had found something, her set of combs and brushes which she held to her chest in delight. She even discovered a small hand mirror and some of her inexpensive jewelry. She prowled the room for more than an hour, but found nothing else she wanted. The clothing was there, but she had no use for it. Maybe someday, when she left the island, she would claim it.

They went to the galley and found several knives. She took three of them, selecting ones which she could throw well. She found a small compass, which she took, as well as some thin rope. She put all her treasures in a pillowcase. In the galley she found two cans of beans and two of canned peaches, which she added to her loot.

Then she was ready to go. Tero had found a large cork float which he tied to the pillowcase of goods and lowered it over the side on a rope to the water. Mirani and Martha hurried down the rope ladder and untied the rope so Tero could put it back where it had been. No one would realize they had been on board.

When the rope was safely put away, Tero dove from the rail, cleaving the water with only a whisper, and surfaced near them. He pushed the float on the swim back to the children's lagoon.

Martha told them she wanted to go into the village.

Mirani shook her head. "Pirates catch you," she said.

Martha laughed. "They won't even know I'm there."

They walked cautiously, with Tero ahead. He reported that the captain and his mate were still in the palace, and the other two pirates were in a drunken stupor. In the village, Martha slipped up to the open window of the hut which one of the pirates had taken over. He was bearded and blond, she could see in the bright moonlight. She saw a bottle of *tacora* still in his hand and a native girl sleeping beside him. For several seconds Martha stared at the pistol lying near the man's hand. It would be simple to slip in and take it. But she knew the villagers would be whipped if the gun were missed. She didn't want to cause them any more trouble.

Outside the village she talked to Mirani about escaping to Papeete. One of the work boats could be rigged with a sail, and with the compass she had they could sail to the nearby French islands. They discussed the problems. Getting a boat out of the lagoon would be the hardest part. It would have to be done at night, when Navarre was sleeping. But the biggest drawback was that none of the native men knew how to sail a boat. Only old Tapo knew how to steer and sail, and there would be no time to teach anyone else.

Martha frowned, holding back the tears. "Soon the French will arrive," she said. "Then everything will be fine."

Mirani took Martha halfway back to her hut, then Martha insisted that she knew the rest of the route home and they parted. As she walked alone through the dark jungle, Martha realized she had "gone native," that she could move about in the jungle as well and as quietly as most of the natives on the island. Now there was no reason why her hideout had to be so far from the village. She would build a new hut, a lean-to closer to the village, so it would not be such a long walk. She was determined that it was time for her to begin her campaign of harassment against the pirates. Mirani had told her that the man she had stabbed with the letter opener had died. Martha felt no remorse.

The next day she scouted the trail all the way to the village, and lay behind some palm fronds as she watched village life. She went there each day for three days, and discovered that the men and women were rounded up just before noon and marched off to the coconut plantings. Two of the pirates always went with them. One of them was the bearded blond one whom she had seen drunk. He had made a cat-o'nine-tails whip and used it quickly on anyone who did not move fast enough.

Martha wept as she saw Tero whipped. She moved closer to the palace and saw Navarre come out, stretch and then go back inside.

Daily now she practiced with her bow and arrow, realizing it was the only distance weapon she had. She became better and better with it and asked Tero to fashion arrowheads she could bind onto the tips of the arrows. She dug roots, picked fruit, and now and then shot a small rabbit-like animal and cooked the meat.

Many days she went to the village, and on the way there and back she worked on her half-way camp of lean-to, fire ring and spring until she had two complete homes.

That night she crept into the village long after midnight. She suspected that she would be attacked at any moment, but she had two sharp knives to defend herself. She looked at the blond pirate's hut first and found him holding a bottle again, evidently passed out with drink. She slid quietly inside the hut and found his pistol, a six-gun much like Peter had owned, and also took a small box filled with cartridges for it. She wasn't sure how to work it except to cock it and pull the trigger. Martha took the two items, as well as three cans of salt pork and ham, and faded back into the trees. She hurried back to her mountain camp and wrapped the six-gun and the cartridges carefully in a pair of her bloomers and hid the package in a safe, dry place under a fallen tree.

Before dawn she was up and moving again. She took six arrows and her best bow and hurried back to her observation post near the village. She was just a hundred feet from the spot where the daily formation of workers was made. She expected some trouble as soon as the theft of the gun was discovered, and she hoped that she could confuse the matter even more.

Just after daylight she heard a roar from

the hut used by the blond pirate. He came storming into the open wearing his boots and cut-off pants.

"Thief! Some dirty native done stole my pistol. Who the hell's got my six-gun?"

No one responded from the huts where most of the natives were still sleeping. The pirate stormed up the hill to the palace and moments later Navarre came into view, strapping on both his pistols. The blond pirate had two of the dreaded cat-o'-nine-tails whips.

Navarre stopped in the middle of the open space less than a hundred feet from Martha. His roar could be heard all over the village.

"Everyone out, you sons of bitches! We're gonna stop this stealing before it damn well gets started. Out, out!"

Slowly the natives came, not understanding why, but lining up as they did for work, surprised at the early hour.

Navarre harangued them in French for five minutes. Tapo did what he could to translate as Navarre screeched. Most of the men and women didn't understand. They only reacted to the anger with fear.

Navarre screamed at them again, telling them in French that he had warned them about stealing anything the masters owned.

A stolen gun was a hanging crime. When they found out who took it, the thief would die. Anyone shielding that person would also die. He said that someone must know who the culprit was. All they had to do was point out the guilty man and they could go back to their huts.

No one moved. Navarre ordered each of the men to be given three lashes. The other two pirates came out to watch the show. Navarre ordered the native men to turn with their backs to the blond pirate with the whip.

Martha bit her lip as the whip whistled through the air and cut into the first man. After three lashes he went to his knees. Martha was sobbing now. She could not let them be punished. Quickly she fitted her best arrow into the bow, moved the foliage aside and sighted in on the blond pirate with the deadly whip.

She pulled, sighted again and let the arrow fly. As if she were watching someone else's work, her eye tracked the arrow as it sped through the quiet tropical air. It ran straight and true. The pirate had just swung and brought the whip back to hit the second man the second time. The arrow slammed into his back and just below his right shoulder, and he crashed forward into the man he had been whipping. The pirate hit the dirt screaming in pain. His hands dropped the whip and splayed out in front of him.

There wasn't a sound in the compound except for the wailing pirate. Navarre turned toward the jungle. He knew the arrow had to come from behind them. He emptied one of his six-guns into the foliage, but Martha was low to the ground behind a fallen coconut palm log.

When the sound of the shots died, Martha called to him.

"Marcel Navarre, you murdering monster of an animal! The natives didn't steal the gun. I did. You touch another person out there and I'll put an arrow through your black heart. These are human beings, not cattle. You treat them humanely or I'll come down on you with a vengeance that will make you scream in terror."

"Martha?" Navarre yelled. "Martha, is that you, you wonderful whore? I'm coming to get you."

As she spoke Martha had nocked another arrow. When Navarre charged toward her she hurried her shot and saw the arrow only graze his leg. She raced into the thick brush and jungle growth, not afraid of all three of the pirates thrashing around in the jungle after her. She was at home there now and could lose them easily. She ran lightly for a hundred hards and slid into a thick maze of thorn-covered brush, wiggling below it, and came up in the hollow center of the bushes where she could see out but not be seen.

Navarre and his two pirates searched for Martha until noon, then gave up. As they went back toward the village, she followed them, and when she came to the edge of the jungle she called out to Navarre again.

"What's the matter, Navarre, don't you like playing hide and seek? Remember, any more mistreatment of the villagers and I'll come back and hound you to death. That's what I promised you anyway, remember?"

This time all three frustrated pirates fired their pistols into the jungle. When the sounds died down, Martha laughed.

"You're a very bad shot, Marcel," she said, and listened to his curses.

She left then, running the trails and through the jungle to her first camp, where she ate fruit and the rest of a fish she had baked the night before. The more she thought about her attack on Navarre and his crew, the more she decided she should continue it. With a little luck and some good shooting she could make life so uncomfortable on the island that he would want to leave. As she walked back to her hilltop camp she tried to think of more ways she could cause Navarre great suffering and pain — at the least risk to herself.

Late that afternoon, Tero came and said he could stay only a few minutes. The whole village thanked her for defending them. The pirate with the arrow wound in his back was furious, but he would live. No one had to work copra that day, but they would the next day. He cautioned her not to expose herself. He said they could defend themselves. She knew he meant it, but they had become a passive people. She told Tero she wanted to talk to Tapo. Could he come to the children's swimming place the next day in the late afternoon? Tero said he was sure Tapo would want to talk with her.

Before dark, Martha went down the far side of her hill and shot the six rounds from the big handgun. She had to hold it with both hands to fire. She couldn't even hit a tree from twenty feet away.

Martha didn't know how to take out the spent shells and put new ones in. She walked back to her hut and sat on the mat trying to figure it out. At last she gave up, hid the gun and shells and practiced with her bow and arrow until dark. If she had time and a dozen boxes of cartridges, she could learn to be an expert shot, but there was no time. She was sure that Navarre would lay a trap for her to try to capture her in some way. He would try soon, and with all of his men and arms. She would use the bow and arrow for her long-range weapon. In the past few weeks she had practiced shooting with the bow at least a thousand times.

She stretched out on the mat. Tomorrow she would work on a plan for a series of attacks against Navarre. She was confident that he would not find her hiding place here, especially at night. She closed her eyes and was sleeping at once.

When daylight came, Martha checked her supplies and weapons. She had one sennit belt Tero had made for her that contained all three of her knives in scabbards of palm fronds.

There were fifteen arrows, but three of them were not the best. They would have to do. She had still not devised her master attack plan. She decided generally to remove the comforts of life on Rapango for the pirates. This involved first destroying the food supply they had brought from the ship. The tins of food, barrels of crackers and the salt pork. She was sure the firearms would be closely guarded from now on. Martha decided she would attack quietly at night, or during the day if possible. Now she prepared to travel. Martha took the stronger of the two bows Tero had made for her, and six arrows, two of her knives and one can of baked beans she had stolen from the ship. Two days before she had dyed the short blouse, turning it a mottled brown and green color so she would blend into the jungle foliage better. Now she was ready to go.

She walked toward her half-way hut before the sun was an hour into the sky. While she was a quarter of a mile away she saw smoke coming from the jungle where her hut should be. Martha stopped, left the trail and approached the lean-to from the denser jungle side. She made no sound as she worked through the big trees, heavy growth, plants and giant tree ferns. When she was within a hundred yards of her hut, she stopped and listened. She waited for ten minutes, but heard and saw nothing un-usual. She moved ahead cautiously. What Martha saw made her want to scream in terror, leap up and rush into her small clear-ing. She sobbed noiselessly, and looked again. Yes it was Tero. He had been tied to a tree with his head down. From that distance she couldn't tell if he was dead or alive.

CHAPTER TEN

Stop! Martha told herself. It was obviously a trap baited with her good friend. Her first urge had been to rush into the clearing and cut him down, but she overcame the tremendous desire to run to him. She held her lips tightly closed to keep in her scream of anger and shock. Martha looked at the rest of the compound. Her lean-to had been burned to the ground. That was what had made the smoke she had seen, and it must have been designed to lure her into the trap. The other improvements in the camp were also destroyed. There was no one in sight except Tero, but she was positive someone was near by.

Martha took a deep breath, then examined the area around the camp she could see. She evaluated each branch, each clump of brush, each tree fern and shrub. Was anything out of place? Did any foliage look disturbed or unnatural?

She couldn't find a thing wrong. Stealthily, without a sound, she moved ten yards to her right and again evaluated every square foot of the jungle within sight. By now she had worked out the strategy. Navarre or one of his men was awaiting her with his six-gun or a rifle ready to kill both her and Tero as soon as she showed up. If so, the pirate would not be able to stay concealed long. He would get restless, clear his throat, need to have a drink of water, his legs would cramp or he would want to smoke.

Martha moved another ten yards, checking each area as she came to it. She was on the fourth sector when she heard the slightest clearing of a throat. It came from directly ahead of her, no more than fifteen yards away. Martha stared at the suspected area and waited. Five minutes later she caught a grunt and the movement of a palm frond. Now she realized the frond was too green to be so low to the ground. It was out of place. A man was hiding behind it.

With a target in mind, she moved to her right again and went deeper into the jungle, so she could get behind the ambusher. She made no sound. Once more she heard the grunt as the man adjusted his position. Martha hoped it would be Navarre, but she couldn't be sure. She had either to kill the man or capture him silently. There might be two ambushers at this one spot.

Fifteen minutes later she was in position. Martha had spotted the man lying on his stomach, a rifle by his side already aimed at the upside-down Tero. Martha had checked when she was closest to the tied-down native, and saw that he was still breathing. She knew she could do nothing for him yet.

Now she stared at the pirate. He was not the blond one, and he was remarkably good at his ambush work. She was now within fifteen feet of him and he could see her if he turned, but she knew he would not.

Martha evaluated the ground between herself and the pirate. It was wet and marshy, with a skimming of water on it. There was no way she could walk across it without making noise. She had no desire to shoot the pirate in the back, even though she knew he would gladly have done so to her. She took out her best arrow, nocked it and drew the sennit string.

"Put down your rifle and sit up," she said quietly, but loud enough so the pirate could hear. He seemed to jump, then freeze in place, then swiftly he sprang to his knees and turned a six-gun in his hand.

Martha had released her arrow just as he established his new position, and as she saw the gleam of metal coming.

Before he could bring the gun up to fire, the arrow caught him in the chest, drove through his lung, then into his heart, and continued until the tip extended out his back. The pirate's hand relaxed first, the gun dropped to his side, then the eyes stared straight at her without seeing and he tumbled slowly into the jungle floor.

Martha did not move for five minutes. She heard no more sounds around her. Slowly she continued her inspection tour around the outside of her second camp, leaving the dead man where he had fallen. When she was sure there had been only one pirate watching, she ran into the cleared area and cut Tero's bonds, caught him and lowered him carefully to the ground. He was still alive and didn't look hurt. It was a few moments before he could talk. She rubbed his wrists and ankles where he had been tied, and ten minutes later they hobbled together into the protection of the dense jungle growth.

Tero stopped and put his arms around her in a hug. In the few English words he knew, he told her what happened to him, and that they had captured Mirani as well. He would help Martha, because now he too was an outcast and would be shot on sight. Navarre had said that Tero was to be killed as soon as Martha had been captured.

Martha stopped and told Tero to wait. She ran back to the pirate's body and took the six-gun and rifle. In his pockets she found more shells for each weapon, and took those with her as well. It would give Navarre something else to worry about.

When she got back to Tero, he was almost normal. He walked with only a slight limp as he led her down a new trail and into what was unknown territory to her.

Later he stopped and they rested near a banana tree and ate some of the fruit. He said he did not know where they had taken Mirani, but he guessed she was still in the village, so if Martha did not stop at her first camp, she might find Mirani held prisoner in the village.

Now Martha knew where they were going, toward the children's swimming lagoon. Perhaps Tapo would be there. They found the old priest watching the children swim. He vanished into the jungle with them, and in the heavy growth, they talked.

Tapo knelt in front of Martha and kissed her hand.

"All the people on the Island of a Thousand Breadfruit honor you, Mrs. Dyke, and give you the blessings of all the great gods of our island including the mighty Kilu. We are forever grateful to you for your powerful attack on our enemy, and we are ashamed that a stranger had to show us how to defend ourselves and to stand up to such a mighty enemy."

"Tapo, great priest, it is your people who have saved my life. Tero and Mirani have done much more for me than I could ever do to repay them. Now tell us, where is Mirani?"

Tapo's face turned sad. "She is in the temple."

Tero wailed in anguish.

"No, no, Tero, she is not dead. The evil ones desecrated the holy place, brought shame and disgrace upon our people, and have released the anger and wrath of all our gods for a thousand years. Navarre forced Mirani to couple with him in the temple and made all the women in the village watch. Then he let his two crewmen force her into strange acts never before seen in our land. We are shamed for a hundred rainy seasons."

Tero moved away from them.

"Tero, it is better that we work together. They have the fire sticks and can shoot them well. We must use our wits to overpower them, or many of our brothers will die."

Sweat poured down Tero's face. His expression was vicious, unlike anything Martha had ever seen from him.

"Can you get the pirates outside the temple?" Martha asked Tapo.

"I think I can."

"Give us twice the time needed to walk to the village from here, and then we will be ready. Try to make all three pirates leave the temple by the great door that faces the jungles."

Tapo nodded and went back near the trail where he could enjoy the antics of the children splashing in the lagoon.

Martha showed Tero how to use the rifle. She instructed him carefully as her father had shown her years before. This weapon had only one shot, but if he did it well it would suffice. Once he understood how to aim and to pull the trigger, he nodded. They ran together down the trail toward the village, then cut into the jungle and came on the settlement from the side as close to the temple as they could, and to the door that faced the undergrowth.

The holy place sat on a small mound that had been built up many rainy seasons ago. The structure was open to the wind on all sides, but the half-walls hid the interior. They were a hundred and fifty feet from the entrance when Martha found a place for the rifle. She positioned Tero behind a log and showed him how she had seen her father rest the rifle over the fallen tree for support. She told Tero to shoot either of the pirates who came out the door. Martha moved closer to the hundred foot distance and hid behind a large palm tree. She readied three arrows, holding them in her left hand with the bow. One arrow was set in the string. She waited.

Soon Tapo came along the trail from his hut going to the temple. He walked inside and Martha could hear angry voices. A minute later Tapo was carried out of the temple by the two pirate crewmen. They dropped him on the ground and even as they did Martha pulled her bow, aimed and loosened an arrow. It did not fly straight, but wavered to the left just enough to miss the first pirate and strike the second one in the throat, wounding him fatally.

Before he fell, the roar of the rifle sounded and Martha saw the second pirate stumble backward, a rifle bullet in his chest. Tapo crawled away, then ran for the jungle. From the edge of the doorway pistol shots exploded. Tapo dodged and leaped behind a tree. Martha had her second arrow in the string and let it fly at the door of the temple. The arrow struck the door frame and stuck there quivering. Tapo ran from tree to tree until he was in the jungle with them. When he got to Tero, he took the rifle and ejected the spent cartridge and put in new ones. Tapo used the rifle and sent shot after shot into the temple until all his bullets were gone.

Tero circled around the temple, drew no fire, and found an old woman in her hut who said the evil pirate had run away from the temple toward the palace.

Tero told Tapo, then ran to the village and rallied all of the men, telling them to bring their machetes and spears. Together they formed a defensive line around the palace, leaving one avenue open to the lagoon. The men were hidden behind trees and rocks for protection.

Tapo and Tero ran toward the palace now and shouted to Navarre from safe positions.

"You are surrounded, Navarre!" Tapo called. "Your men are all dead. You have only one escape route to the sea. You may go to the lagoon if you leave right now."

Navarre answered with six shots, but hit no one. It was still early in the afternoon.

Martha ran into the temple, thinking that

Mirani must still be there. She found the girl huddled in a corner, a foot-long knife in her hand with the point on her chest.

Mirani looked at Martha and burst into tears. "No come!" she said. She pointed at the knife. *"Mourir."*

Martha didn't know the French word, but the knife made the meaning plain. Mirani was shamed beyond all possible chance for a continued life in her village.

"No, no!" Martha said. "Navarre raped me, too. He violated me, and I didn't have to die. Don't you see? You helped us put an end to his evil ways. You are a heroine, so you must live."

Gradually Martha moved toward her, talking softly, knowing the girl could not understand most of the words. At last Martha sat beside Mirani and took her hands and let her head rest on her shoulder where she cradled the now sobbing woman. Carefully Martha took the knife and placed it out of reach. She kept on talking, telling her that she was a natural leader, that her people needed her now more than ever. Nearly half an hour later, she walked out of the temple with Mirani.

"Your mother was queen here, wasn't she, Mirani? *La reine?* Now you must be the queen. The king is dead. You are the next in line to be the leader, you are the new queen."

Mirani shook her head in disbelief. The idea must have got through. Martha had helped put on her *ti* leaf skirt and the short blouse, and now she walked toward her hut in the village. Martha made Mirani promise not to do anything until she came back. She said the new queen should think of the many ways she could help her people.

Martha ran to the palace and found where Tero and Tapo stood behind the coconut trees.

"The pirate has fired twenty times with his pistols," Tapo said. "He has no chance to escape. I have urged him to go to the lagoon."

"And let him get away?" asked Martha.

Tapo smiled, but did not reply.

The priest and Tero talked for a moment. They decided to wait out Navarre if necessary until the next morning. Martha did not understand what they were saying. She was thinking back to tales of the wild west and Indians in the dime novels. If they were Indians, right now they would set fire to the ranch house. Why not? The palace could be rebuilt in a few days. They could burn it down and force Navarre out.

"Tapo, we can drive him out by burning

244

down the building."

Tapo looked at her as if he had been slapped.

"The palace?"

"It's only a straw hut, Tapo. The men can rebuild one in two or three days. And with Mirani as your queen, her palace should be down among the people."

Tapo frowned, his mouth gaped open. "Mirani, *la reine?*"

"Yes, of course. She's the next in line."

"But the . . . the pirate . . ."

"She was not damaged. She will be the best queen this island has ever known."

Tapo smiled. "The new ways. I told Matono we must think about the new ways."

He turned to Tero and spoke quietly. Tero nodded, called two of the men, and they ran back to the village. When they came up the trail to the palace, each had two blazing sticks that burned with a fury much like the pitch torches Martha had seen back in San Francisco.

The men crawled up on two sides of the palace and threw the flaming torches at the thatched roof. One caught immediately, two others dropped below to the mat floor, and soon the structure was burning in three places.

A sudden burst of firing came from inside

the palace, and Martha saw one of the men hit and roll behind a log. The palace burned furiously, and five minutes later Navarre stumbled out the far door toward the lagoon. He fired at the natives who held back, then replied with a barrage of a hundred stones. Martha didn't understand as Navarre was slowly forced toward the lagoon.

"It's like the wild pig hunt," Tapo explained. "We form a line of beaters through the jungle and drive the pig we want in front of us. We are in a curved line, so we direct where he can run. He is very much afraid, and we drive the pig into the lagoon. The wild pig is a bad swimmer. We keep him in the water until he is too weak to resist. Then we capture him."

"That's why you haven't killed Navarre?"

Tero smiled. Tapo nodded. "Navarre will die, but it will be slow and painful, and he will have much time to think on his sins."

Navarre's bullets were gone. He threatened with the six-guns but he could not shoot, so the native men forced him closer to the lagoon. At last he threw his guns at the natives and screamed at them.

"I won't go in the lagoon! Not in the damned water!"

Tero ran up, his machete gleaming in the sunlight. There was a fierce desire on his young face. He swung the machete close to Navarre, who suddenly pulled a knife from his belt.

"Hey, you're the one I hung upside down as bait. You're supposed to be dead." Navarre lunged at Tero, who sidestepped and kicked him in the stomach. Then he whacked Navarre's right arm with the flat side of the machete. There was a sharp crack and Navarre screamed.

"You broke my arm, you son of a bitch!" The knife fell into the white sand, and Tero kicked it away.

Tero tossed his machete to a waiting hand and stormed forward, hitting Navarre in the chest, driving him backward into the water. As soon as Navarre hit the water, the native men surged forward, forming a line, each now with his own short knife, walking forward, pressing Navarre into the deep water. Soon Navarre had to swim. He kept trying to get back to shore, but the knives flashed and kept him away.

As Martha watched, she talked to Tapo. "Mirani must be your next queen, Tapo. She will be a good queen, a good leader for your people. She has been to Papeete to school. She knows the new ways. She will be a fine queen, and Tero will help her."

At last Tapo said they would consider it

further and went to Mirani's hut where he talked to her about the problems, and they weighed all the possibilities.

Navarre kept trying to get back to shore. The knives pricked him now and then, and once a slash was needed on his good arm to turn him back to the deep water. He tried to dive under the ring of swimmers, but they were better in the water, and dragged him back into the circle by his hair.

Slowly they moved their circle to the center of the lagoon. Navarre was so tired he could barely stay afloat. When he sank one of the natives lifted him to the surface. Tero watched closely from his position in the circle of swimmers, and when he was sure, he raised one hand in a silent signal.

The shouting and jeering by the men in the water ceased. Navarre looked at them and screamed in fury, but even as his words were formed, his face drifted under the water. This time no one went after him. Every man should have the right to die in peace and by himself.

Tero followed him silently as the currents carried his now lifeless body. When he had been under water for fifteen minutes, the divers left Navarre at the mercy of the lagoon. The warriors of Rapango swam silently back to shore.

Tero turned at once and ran to Mirani's hut.

CHAPTER ELEVEN

It was the sixth day since the pirates had been buried. The new queen's palace had been built in the very center of the village. It contained six big rooms, and was made off the ground but in the usual native open-air style.

Tapo had crowned Mirani as queen of Ra-pango, and fitted her with the royal robe and the scepter which Tero had carved from an *inawa* limb.

Now Martha sat in the palace talking with Tapo and Mirani. Together they agreed that something must have happened to the sloop with the crew of the *Pacific Gem.* Either the sloop had sunk, or it had somehow missed Tahiti and become lost. In either case, they decided a boat must be sent to Papeete, and Martha must be on it. Tapo had supervised the conversion of a work boat from the *Gem* into a sailing craft. He cut down a small tree from the jungle and fashioned it into a mast, then put together several layers of linens from aboard the *Gem* to make the sails. There was plenty of rope, and at last he had the sailing ship ready for trials in the lagoon. Tapo had not forgotten any of his sailing know-how, and he taught Tero and his two crewmen everything he knew.

The twenty-four foot work boat had been covered in the bow with a thatch to provide shelter for Martha. She, Tero and the two crewmen would make the trip. They would return with goods the island needed, establish credit in Tahiti and arrange for a new trade agreement with the Pacific Steamship and Trading Company.

Martha sat in the sand watching the sailboat work around the lagoon. Tapo was nearby, giving his charges their final testing. Earlier they had gone over the reef and into the sea and sailed all the way arond Rapango. Martha still wore her *ti* leaf skirt and the short blouse. She had spent two days on the *Pacific Gem* with Mirani. They ate canned goods, slept in the featherbed, and traded more words and dreams. Almost all of her clothes were still in the big closet, Martha discovered. She would have to pack two suitcases of them before she left for Papeete, but she didn't want to do that until the very last moment. She would give the rest to Mirani.

Mirani came to the beach and sat beside her. Tapo had the urge to turn sideways to show respect to royalty, but he did not. Mirani had changed all the old tabus about royalty. She was just the same as everyone else, she told them, only now she had the authority to govern, the right and the responsibility to help them do what was best for them as a whole people. She had plans to build a pier into the lagoon so the steamships and sailing ships could dock and unload their goods easily, the way they did in Papeete.

She would set up a trading company, and everyone who worked on the copra would be paid and receive goods for that work. She was going to open a school, so the children could learn to read and write. Soon some of the young people would want to go outside, and for them education would be a necessity.

Queen Mirani was full of plans. Tapo would continue as priest, and the old gods would be worshipped and respected, but there would be new gods as well.

Mirani and Tero were joined in Marriage in a great ceremony and feast the day before the sailboat was due to leave. It was a magnificent affair with everyone dressed in her best *ti*-leaf skirt and flowers in her hair and wearing a pure white blouse. The young girls sang the old songs and performed the ancient dances, and there had never been such a feast that anyone could remember. They had a dozen kinds of fish, shellfish of every description, roast pigs, fruits and berries from every vine and tree, breadfruit and taro.

That evening when the feasting still went on and the bottles of *tacora* were raised in celebration, and the happy couple went into the newly built wedding hut, Martha sat down for a long talk with Tapo. She cautioned him to let Queen Mirani go her own way, that she would do only good for her people. She reminded Tapo that Queen Mirani had been outside as well as he, and that she was prepared to lead and guide her people into the new world. Queen Mirani would not permit anything harmful to soil her beautiful island. She praised Mirani for her plans to open a school.

Martha reminded Tapo about property and property rights. She urged him to have the queen declare the whole island and the lagoon as being owned jointly by every man, woman and child now living there, and that no one not of full native Rapango blood could ever own any part of the island. This would protect the people from outside land speculators.

On and on they talked until the sun came up, and Tapo dropped off to sleep as he sat cross-legged on the hut's mat.

On the day of the sailing, Martha hugged Queen Mirani, and promised to send her new husband safely back to her. She would help arrange with the authorities to bring a new crew back to the *Pacific Gem* so she could continue her travels.

Tapo had visited the big ship and closed hatches and covers and greased everything that he thought needed it so no deterioration could take place.

When Martha stepped into the small sailboat, she wondered if it were big enough to travel the hundred miles to Tahiti, but Tero was confident. He had two compasses to use and he knew the stars at night. Tero predicted that they would sail directly through the reef and into Papeete without altering their course by even one degree. They had the charts and compass bearings from the bridge of the *Pacific Gem*, and Tapo was sure they would make the journey straight and true.

Martha stood in the warm sand hugging Queen Mirani. "I'll write letters to you, and send you things on the ships when they call, and Tapo can read the letters, and we'll still be best friends." Then Martha climbed into the boat and would not look at her friends any more. Instead she moved to the bow of the small craft where she slid under the low roof and lay on her mat. Martha did not like saying good bye to loved ones.

Three days later, in the early afternoon, they arrived at Papeete, and just as Tero had predicted, sailed directly through the reef opening and into the harbor. It had been a calm and uneventful crossing. Tero was amazed at the buildings, the houses and docks and ships. Almost everything was made of brick or stone, which the dampness could not decay.

Martha had worn her native costume until they saw the first of the islands. Then she changed into one of her best dresses with a high neck and long skirt, and when she stepped ashore at the dock she created a sensation.

Two minutes after docking, the port inspector was at the boat, bowing and smiling and asking her in English were she came from. Quietly she explained about the loss of the *Pacific Gem* and asked if any of her crew had reached Papeete in a sloop. The inspector said that no such vessel had docked there recently with any survivors of the *Pacific Gem.*

When she told him about the pirates, and the name of Navarre, the man trembled with rage. But as she indicated the pirates had all been killed, his face beamed with a smile and he escorted her quickly to a small office he commanded.

"Madam, I am most sorry, but there is nothing I can do about your ship. You will have to see the representative of Pacific Steamship, a fine gentleman, Mr. Stanley Fowler. I would be pleased to take you to him."

Stanley Fowler proved to be a thin, tall man with no sense of humor, but with a good enough memory to recognize the daughter of his employer. He listened sympathetically to her story and said he would take care of the salvage and recovery of the steamship. He arranged unlimited credit for her and asked her what plans she had.

"I wish to return to the United States on the first possible ship," she said. "It can be sail or steam, our company or another, just so it will get me across the water to San Francisco."

Martha spent two months in Tahiti before a ship arrived heading for San Francisco.

The day after she landed in Tahiti, she and Tero went on a tour of the island. Together they saw everything: schools, churches, business buildings, stores, shops, taverns and the docks. Tero made sketches on pads of paper, putting down everything he saw, especially the docks and buildings, so he would be able to help Mirani build similar ones when he returned.

Martha took Tero to see the French governor. She made it plain through an interpreter that Rapango was not in the French protectorate, that it was an independent island kingdom with Queen Mirani as its ruler. She introduced Tero as the Prime Minister and husband of the queen. She said the inhabitants were in no mood to see an influx of foreigners trying to ruin their land or steal their crops. She asked only that the governor offer help for the tiny kingdom in case of an attack by pirates or foreign mercenaries. The governor willingly agreed, hoping that he might have the honor of sharing a drink with the beautiful lady from the United States. It was arranged and that night they dined at the governor's mansion — both she and Tero, much to the governor's surprise.

Stanley Fowler began assembling a crew for the *Gem* the moment he knew where she was. The company had been asking him about her for months. He could find few men who knew anything about steam engines, and he realized that every day he waited was dangerous. Some other crew could move in and claim salvage, and his firm would lose the ship entirely. Fowler rented an inner island trader, a twin-master, and had it ready for a quick trip to Rapango — as soon as he could find a crew of stem men.

Martha spent all one day buying presents for Queen Mirani. She bought two hundred combs, and suggested that one be given to each woman and girl. Martha bought hand mirrors, bolts of cloth, cases of soap, and a dozen other items she thought the women would like. For the men she found six good rifles and five thousand rounds of ammunition, and asked Tero to have Tapo train six guards to use the rifles and keep them handy as a defense against pirates.

The work boat was loaded and ready to sail. Before it did, Stanley Fowler went to Martha's hotel to advise her that he was ready to go to Rapango to reclaim the *Gem.*

"I have bribed two steamship engineers who say they can fix any steam engine, and rounded up a dozen more dubious sailors."

Martha smiled. "Mr. Fowler, would you

have room to take the Queen's boat on board for the return trip? Then the Prime Minister would be in no danger of the sea."

Fowler scowled, but when he saw the pretty smile from Martha Pemberton, he knew he would do anything she asked. The schooner sailed the next morning with the work boat tied down on board and all her cargo intact. Martha hugged Tero and kissed him, then waved from the dock until the ship was out of sight.

Three months later Martha stood on the deck of a sailing ship and watched the hills of San Francisco rise out of the mists and fog of early morning. She shivered. It had been so long since she had been home. So much had happened. She had not even sent word to her parents that she was alive and safe, since this was the first boat bound for San Francisco.

Martha was so nervous she could hardly move as the ship sailed closer into the harbor and toward the long wharf. Soon she could discern the streets of the town as the morning fog burned away. Martha stood at the rail and watched the sailors throw lines to the dock. She saw the ship tied up, and the long gangplank lowered.

Suddenly she did not want to go ashore.

Below, someone carried her two suitcases and two trunks down the gangplank and stacked them on the dock. One of the crewmen looked at her questioningly.

"This is San Francisco, Ma'am. You're home."

Suddenly Martha ran for the gangplank, hurried down it, still unused to trying to run or move quickly in the confining shrouds of a long dress. There was no one there to meet her. How could there be? Nobody knew she was coming. No one could know for sure if she were alive or dead.

She hailed a passing hack and gave the address of Pacific Steamship and Trading Company's downtown office. That would be better — not such a shock to her mother.

She paid the driver in francs, noted his surprise, then hurried into the building, up the familiar steps to her father's big outer office. A startled youth sat behind a desk, but Martha brushed past him and burst through the door into her father's inner office.

Harold L. Pemberton sat behind his massive oak desk, and glanced up over half-glasses to see who had erupted into his lair.

"Martha!" he said, dropping his pencil, standing, then rushing around the desk his arms wide.

"Oh, Father!"

"We — we thought you and the boat were lost at sea."

They were both crying. He held her tight, then leaned back and looked at her. "My little girl has come home!"

She had so much to tell him. There were so many things to do that must be done. Arrangements . . .

"My little girl was lost, but now we've found her!"

Martha couldn't say a word. She held on to her father as if he were her salvation. Tears kept spilling down her cheeks, and still she could not talk. She was home. That was all her heart could understand, all her heart could hear.

She was home. Her father was holding her warm and safe.

She was home.

■ ■ ■ ■

BOOK TWO

■ ■ ■ ■

CHAPTER TWELVE:
THE MISGUIDED HEART

San Francisco, July, 1874.
Martha Pemberton Dyke relaxed in her living room on a big overstuffed chair and looked out over California Street at the bay beyond. She thought back over the year that had passed since that terrible and wonderful day she arrived at her father's office after the trip from Rapango and Tahiti. So much had happened since then — so many things had to be done and done quickly. The events spun through her mind as if she were thumbing the pages of a book.

Her father had taken her home, prepared her mother, then brought Martha inside for a tearful reunion. She had no idea how physically and mentally exhausted she had been. For two weeks she did little but sleep, eat, take hot baths, and luxuriate in her featherbed.

Her father took care of the legal details: declaring Peter Dyke legally deceased, discovering his estate and transferring all goods, property and monies to the name of Mrs. Martha Pemberton Dyke. She had been surprised when her father showed her this quaint little house on California Street and told her that Captain Dyke had bought it the day before they left on their honeymoon.

"Evidently it was to be a surprise for you on your return," her father said.

A surprise it was — all furnished, down to dishes and linens and a caretaker who kept everything in perfect condition "until the Dykes returned from their trip."

More unusual information came to light that first month home. Captain Dyke had very little money: one bank account showed forty-eight dollars in cash, and the other about fifteen hundred. A safe box in the same bank revealed that Captain Peter Dyke was supporting a son in San Diego, to whom he sent ten dollars every month. Martha instructed the bank at once to continue sending the drafts regularly.

It was not until her return that her father told Martha that on her eighteenth birthday she had become the legal owner of a trust fund of $250,000, a fortune such as she had never dreamed she might own. The money was invested through a trust fund, and there were certain restrictions about how much of it she could use. There was about twenty thousand a year available. After she was thirty-one, she would have outright control of the whole fund.

It was more than two months after she arrived back home before she permitted herself to think of Allen. She was a widow and her year of mourning was over. She could think about marriage again — if she wanted to. She hired an astute detective to find Allen Cornelius and discover what he was doing and where he was now living.

The detective had given her a complete report after only a week. Allen Cornelius still worked for her father's firm. He had asked to be transferred to shore duty, and was subsequently assigned to the Seattle office where he had quickly worked up in the management.

He had returned to San Francisco with the ship four months after putting to sea that July morning a year before. His ship came back for extensive repairs after a storm. Allen had gone directly to the Pemberton home, but was advised that Martha was married and on an extended honeymoon cruise. Very soon after that, Allen married and went to Seattle.

Martha shook herself out of her reverie

and tried to read the book in her lap. This Mark Twain was interesting, but not tonight. She laid it aside and tried some needlepoint, but that too did not interest her. She relaxed and thought back again.

When she discovered that Allen was married and gone, she knew she had to find some work to do or she would go mad. She went to her father and told him that more and more women were going to work those days, and that she wanted to find some useful job in his company.

"Father, I plan on starting to work under my married name in one of your retail stores, to learn the business from the bottom right on up. Some day I hope to be general manager of the whole thing. I'll give that brother of mine a run for his money."

Harold Pemberton had been surprised, but had finally agreed. He had thoroughly investigated the piracy at Rapango. One of his boats had called there before the *Pacific Gem* was reclaimed. The captain went ashore and talked with Tapo and Queen Mirani, who gave him a complete story about what Martha had done in the short time she was on the island. Pemberton was impressed with the way Martha had coped with the situation.

So he had agreed to let her go to work,

but assured her there would be no special favors. She would have to gain advancement on merit alone.

The third month after she was home she moved into the Dyke home on California Street and found a perfect companion-cook-housekeeper, Mrs. Larson, who was also a widow. Martha did a little rearranging, but nothing extensive. She lived frugally compared with her parents in their mansion on the hill.

At the store she plunged into the new venture with vigor, at first specializing in the gift items the ships brought back from the South Seas and the Far East. The items fascinated her, and she learned as much about them as possible. No one in the whole store worked as hard as she did. She often stayed after closing to work out new stock arrangements or displays, and to request orders of new and interesting merchandise.

No one at the store knew she was a Pemberton. She kept that a special secret.

Shortly after she arrived home a reporter from the San Francisco *Daily Press* heard about her adventure and talked to a seaman, then tried to see Martha. She was terrified. She had no wish for any of the story of Rapango to come to light in the San Francisco newspapers. She turned to her father, who quietly talked to the reporter, who suddenly quit his job and moved to a better one in Los Angeles, with a healthy bulge in his bank account as well.

Martha had been on the job at Pemberton's Mercantile for just over eight months when she became manager of the third floor. She now was in charge of the giftwares section, bedding and linens, dishes and housewares. It was a surprise, but the store manager called her in and explained that she simply knew the merchandise better than anyone else and the current floor manager was going to quit working and go to Arizona to live with his daughter. It meant almost double the wages, and she would have twelve clerks under her as well as the responsibility of ordering all the merchandise.

Monday morning Martha went to work as usual, arriving promptly at 7:30 a.m. The store opened for business at eight. She instructed a new clerk in the Pemberton way of doing things and made sure the girl was properly dressed.

Martha had just returned to her small stand-up desk at the far corner of the floor near the stairs when Hadley Garrison came down. Hadley was attractive, about twenty-eight and supremely confident, considering himself irresistible. He was the floor manager in men's clothing and shoes, and more than one woman clerk had requested a transfer from his area for what they described as personal reasons. Everyone knew the real reason was his repeated advances and ungentlemanly requests. Ever since Martha's promotion, he had been coming down at least twice a day to talk with her and casually to suggest some kind of an after-work meeting. She had always laughed it off, but Martha knew that such tactics would not work forever.

"Ah, Mrs. Dyke, the only lady in this erstwhile establishment with a bit of class. I ask you, how do you like the latest fashion direct from New York?" He spun around so she could see his clothes and his body, too, she guessed. He wore the usual stiff white celluloid collar, neckcloth tied with a small knot in front just showing over the very high jacket collar of his black and white checked cashmere light weave wool suit. The lapels were much smaller than any she had ever seen, no more than three inches long, with the first suit coat button within three inches of his necktie knot. Three more buttons fastened down the front, where it was cut away to the sides. Matching trousers completed the suit over his shiny patent leather black shoes.

"Well, well, what do you think?"

"It's much too conservative for me, Mr. Garrison. Besides, I don't think it would fit me across the shoulders."

"Seriously."

She frowned. "Seriously, I like the cut, but not that awful check pattern. And cashmere is good for spring and summer but too light for fall, so remember that means you have to have them all sold out before the end of August. I'd say not over four dozen in various sizes."

He came closer. "Mrs. Dyke, don't you ever think about anything but business?"

"Of course, but you were asking me a business question."

"All right. I'll ask you a non-business question. How about having dinner with me tonight?"

"No. You're a married man with three — no, *four* children."

"That's only because I appreciate a truly fine woman."

"Then you had best go home and appreciate your wife."

"Don't you miss anything about not having a husband, Mrs. Dyke?"

"Certainly. I miss having a husband I can admire and respect, which are two qualities that I don't find in you."

"You just need time to discover them." He moved closer to her so his knee touched her leg.

She smiled up at him. "Mr. Garrison, did I ever tell you that I have killed three men? The first was with an ivory-carved letter opener on a steamship in Tahiti. He was in my cabin standing close to me like this and I stabbed him in his chest just below his ribs. The blade slanted upward and . . ."

Garrison backed away, a strange look of disbelief mingled with worry on his face. He held up a hand in farewell. "Thank you very much, Mrs. Dyke, for your evaluation of the latest men's fashions. I certainly will consider all of your suggestions." He almost ran up the steps and back to the safety of the fourth floor men's department.

Martha watched him go with a touch of a smile. Sometimes a bit of the truth came out sounding very frightening. She doubted that she would have any more problems with Mr. Garrison. And she would be sure that he didn't bother any of the girls on the floor. She solved a minor problem with an unhappy customer, and went back to checking invoices and packing slips against merchandise that had been unboxed by the night crew. That had been her idea. Why have the stock people working during the day and getting in the way of the customers with their big boxes coming up the only stairway? She won permission to have her men work from closing time until midnight every day, unpacking and moving up the goods. It really did prove to have advantages.

For no reason she thought of Allen Cornelius. It had been a long time since he had thrust himself into her thoughts — perhaps an entire week. How would it have been if only she were strong and had waited just those four months for him? Would they be married now, with a baby, and he at work on the ship? Allen, dear, sweet Allen! Why hadn't she waited for him?

The realization that he was in Seattle, a short journey away, kept pricking at the back of her mind. Should she go to him? Why? What good would it do? He was married.

She stopped thinking about him. With a quiet ferocity that sometimes amazed her, she shut him out of her mind and attacked the work to be done on her desk.

Hadley Garrison was not the only man at Pemberton's to make a show of interest in Martha. Some were honest and forthright, some sly and nefarious. But all were turned away with the proper tone and style which she thought the interest deserved. Mr. Garrison had received by far the worst scare, so far. She would have to remember that one for future use, it really was quite effective on men who assumed she was merely a limpid, quaking flower, blossoming only for them.

Martha dressed well. In fact she spent more on clothes than she earned, but she was never overdressed. Hers was a quiet elegance that impressed men and women alike, and let those who knew understand that she realized the value of fine clothes. Those who had no idea what her clothes cost were impressed that she always looked lovely without appearing to be extravagant.

Wherever she went she attracted attention, and this sometimes led to problems. But when she wanted to attend the opera and her mother or father did not want to go, she took her housekeeper, Mrs. Larson. The lady was in her forties and Martha bought her a gown especially for the opera. Twice Mrs. Larson had been approached by interested men at intermissions. She had been thrilled and talked about it for weeks afterwards. Not that she was interested in men, but it was so delightful to be noticed and appreciated. Quickly Mrs. Larson became indispensable to Martha. The housekeeper would gladly have walked across flaming steel spikes for her lady.

One day in late July, Martha glanced up from her desk and saw a Negro man standing nearby. He smiled when she looked up and walked over, holding a straw hat in his two big hands. He was tall and well built and his skin was a light brown. For a moment she didn't remember him, then she did.

"Johnnie Laveau! It's good to see you again. How is everything at the shipyard?"

"Fine, *mon,* good and fine. This fella no work there no mo. Work with Mista' Pemberton *mon.*"

Martha liked the quality of his lilting voice. It sounded almost as if he were singing.

"With Mr. Pemberton? Well, you must have a very important job. Come into my stand-up office and tell me why you aren't launching ships any more."

They talked for half an hour about the shipyards, how he had gone back to sea again, then bowed to the wishes of Mr. Pemberton and went to work at the corporate headquarters, the big office as the employees called it. Johnnie Laveau had not bowed entirely to conventional clothes, she noticed. He wore a suit, but with no stiff

276

collar or tie, only a regular shirt open at the throat. For a moment she wanted to show Hadley Garrison the latest new fashion, but she didn't. Johnny held out an envelope.

"Mon says bring you back."

She read the scratching that she recognized as her father's handwriting.

"Martha. I have something important to talk to you about. Please come back with Johnnie right now if you can get away."

There was no signature.

"Let me tell my assistant a few things and then I'll be ready to go," she said.

Half an hour later she sipped at the light red wine her father offered her in his big office. He had a straight belt of whiskey and then watched her critically.

"Yes, I think it's time. I'm going to promote you to assistant store manager at the Mercantile."

"Assistant . . ." She took a deep breath. "Don't you think that's rushing matters a little?"

"No, not at all. You know more about that store than the manager does now. He's getting old. He's got another year before he says he wants out. Wants to do some fishing and just sit around and let his children support him for a while."

"Assistant manager, Father! I don't know."

She sipped the wine, thinking that if she did take it she would suddenly be Hadley Garrison's superior. Now, she did like that idea.

A month later, she liked the idea of being assistant manager even more. Most of the floor managers had taken her promotion well. One man quit, saying he wouldn't work in any store where he had to answer to a woman. Hadley Garrison swallowed hard a few times, then smiled and knuckled under. Martha and the other assistant manager, Josiah West, quickly accepted the other man's resignation and suggested to the store manager that the senior woman on that floor take over. The idea was approved.

Now Martha was up on the eighth floor, where the executive and business offices were. She and Josiah West had matching desks, one on each side of the room. They had been working together comfortably for almost three months. Josiah was a medium-sized man, about five-feet eight, who at thirty-five had developed a bit of a stomach, and his hairline was starting to creep back. He wore spectacles, had clean white teeth and a fine smile. Josiah had worked his way up quickly in the organization, having been with the store for only three years.

The work load was split between the two of them, each the direct responsibility of four departments in the store below. This was a management job in every sense of the word, and covered the ordering of goods, marking, shelving and selling. When sales were announced in the newspapers, the floor managers made suggestions, and the assistant managers blocked out the actual goods to be sold and the prices. All the personnel problems came under their hands as well.

Josiah and Martha worked closely together. If one of Josiah's female clerks had a problem, very often he'd let Martha handle it. They worked together, covering for each other at times, and keeping up a unified front when Mr. Jacobson swept down on them. He was the store manager, and a hard man to work for, most said. But Martha found him fair-minded, willing to listen to problems, but firm and rigid once a decision was made. He didn't make exceptions for anyone, and that included assistant store managers.

Martha often had lunch with Josiah. Sometimes they had lunch at the small cafes in the area, other times they had sandwiches and coffee sent up. It seemed that more and more now Martha relied on this man to assist her, to provide support when she had a question about some project or decision she had made. He was a fine merchandiser and seemed to know instinctively what would sell and what wouldn't.

One day she waved as Josiah left the office and she realized that she liked this man. He was a good worker. He was pleasant to be around. Slowly she realized that she hadn't been thinking of Allen as much as she had before. Dear, sweet Allen! He was a memory, a long-lost love, a dream only partially realized. She thought of Josiah and knew he wasn't nearly the man Allen was. He didn't have Allen's fresh good looks, his tall, slender body, his fine mind — but Josiah was *here.* He was working with her. If Josiah had started out earlier . . . Martha stopped. What was she doing? She was defending Josiah in a comparison with Allen.

"Hey there, assistant store manager Dyke. No sleeping at your post, or old General Jacobson will have you shot at dawn."

"Guilty," she said, laughing. Josiah had come back into the office, and she hadn't heard him. "In my own defense, I was thinking about the new sales campaign coming up next week. Will that be a good defense?"

Josiah still stood over her desk, his light blue eyes looking down into hers. "No, Mrs. Dyke, that's no defense. You had that sweet wistful smile that could only be for a secret lover, and you're thinking about meeting him in some dark little cafe for lunch."

"Now there is a good idea," she said, her eyebrows lifted in delight. Then her eyes clouded. "There's only one part missing, and it isn't the small dim cafe."

They both laughed and went back to work. That noon they arranged to go for lunch at the same time and ate around the corner in a little store that specialized in thin sliced ham sandwiches with sauerkraut, dill pickles and cheese. That, topped with a glass of apple cider, completed the menu.

"You were looking wistful this morning when I interrupted you. I shouldn't have said a word."

Instinctively she reached over and patted his hand. "Josiah, you are a nice man." She moved her hand, but realized that a tingle had shot through it. It was the first time she had ever touched him, and the contact startled her. He must have felt it too, for he looked up just as she looked away. This was not good. She was not going to become involved with anyone, especially not anyone at the store. It was ridiculous, and it simply must not happen. She rushed through the rest of her meal, said she had to get right back to the store and excused herself before he could get up. She left in a hurry and paused outside the little eatery. She took two deep breaths before she felt that she could walk back to her office.

Martha had told herself that she had no intentions of remarrying. She had told her mother, but the dear woman still set up occasional dinner parties with an eligible rich young bachelor seated beside Martha. She had been married, she had experienced the joys of sexual fulfillment — now she had other things to think of. Some nagging doubt lingered in the back of her mind, but she pushed it away and walked quickly back to the store and up to her office. She was a business executive. She had a responsible management position with fifty employees to consider, a huge inventory to handle and a budget that astounded her every time she looked at it. There simply was no time or place for any romance in her life. *Romance!* That was funny. She had no romantic feeling at all about Josiah. It was just that he was there. He was sympathetic and kind, and he supported her in her decisions. He was always there. Always waiting.

She knew that he was a widower. His wife

had died in a smallpox epidemic back east somewhere when she was with child. That was about all she did know about him, but it was enough. She was angry with herself now for thinking so much about it. There was nothing there, no chance that there ever would be, and it was simply a waste of valuable time to think in any manner about such a relationship. Besides he was so old — at least thirty-five!

She sat at her desk and looked at the stack of applications for work. She had to pick two new girls for housewares and one man for the hardware department. She might as well get started on it.

For an hour she went through the stack of papers and found the three people she wanted, then added a reserve for each department and had the clerical helper write letters to each one, asking them to come in for interviews. Next she flew into the job of finding ideas for the new advertising campaign. She wondered idly if she was doing too much. Perhaps it would be more efficient if they had a separate department to handle the people, and another one to specialize in the advertising and promotion. It was all a dream. She'd dreamed enough. Now she had to go to work.

That evening she and Mrs. Larson went

to the opening of the San Francisco Opera. They weren't doing complete productions, rather several arias from the *Marriage of Figaro*. She was entranced. The music was not the best, the costumes were obviously shoddy and much used and altered, but the rich voice, the contralto, more than made up for all the problems. She guessed that their little production in no way would meet the standards of eastern opera houses. But out here, in the uncultured west, it would simply have to do for now. For her, it was enough.

She came home feeling so high-spirited that she thought she might burst. The opera hadn't been *that* good. Then what had? She felt as if she wanted to run on rooftops, to pick a pocketful of stars, to race a whirlwind. She caught herself wondering what Josiah was doing.

"Ridiculous!" she said to the mirror over her dresser. The man was nothing to her at all, just someone she worked with. He wasn't the romantic type who would sweep her off her feet and rush off with her to the South Seas. He wasn't the kind of lover who would invite her to an upstairs room and quietly yet firmly seduce her into the ecstasy of loving tenderness. He wasn't the kind to tie her up and do what he pleased. He was simply Josiah, Josiah West, her co-worker at the store, at Pemberton's, one of the best mercantiles in the whole of San Francisco.

She remembered the sly grin he had, the infectious laughter, the gentle way he looked at her. Now that she thought about him a little more, it seemed almost as if he were waiting for *her* to make the first move. She pulled her gown off over her head and threw it on the bed.

"Well!" she said out loud again. If Josiah were waiting for her to invite him into her bedroom, he could wait a long time. She giggled just thinking what her father would say if he knew she even thought about this.

The next day, work went as usual. They were busy at lunch time and he went out without her. She went later, and when she came back, Josiah was up to his elbows in advertising proofs. An equal number were stacked on her desk.

"Oh, dear!"

"I agree. Start reading," Josiah said. "There should be a better way than this. They have to be checked and ready before we go home tonight."

Martha looked at him as he said it and went out the door and down to the fifth floor, where she found Priscilla Cole.

"Miss Cole, do I remember you said you

had been to school through the eleventh grade?"

"Yes, Mrs. Dyke," Priscilla said, so frightened to be talking to the assistant store manager that her eyes were threatening to overflow with tears.

Martha noticed, and smiled. "Please, Priscilla, you've done nothing wrong. Just relax. Are you a good speller?"

"The sisters said I was. I won the school spelling bee once. Of course, that was two years ago."

Martha made up her mind at once. "Tell your floor manager you'll be working in my office for the rest of the day."

The girl stood there.

"Yes, really, Miss Cole. Go tell her what I said. I'm sure there'll be no problem. I have some work that will be a little different for you."

Ten minutes later, upstairs, Martha found an empty office with a desk and spread the proof sheets on it. "These are the advertisements as I wrote them up. This other stack is how they look when the printer sets the type and puts the engravings in. All you have to do is be sure the printed part reads exactly like the part in pencil. Easy, right?"

Priscilla nodded.

"Well, not so easy, really. Read each word

by itself so you're sure it's spelled correctly, then check the price." Martha gave her a printed card. "This is a set of proofreader's marks our printer likes us to use. Now why don't you relax, look over the proofing marks a few times, then see how it goes. I'm sure you can do it, and it should be interesting." She smiled at the young girl and went back to her office.

While Josiah sweated over his proofs, Martha cleared up several small problems and then went back to see how Priscilla was doing. She was very good at it, in fact, much better and faster than Martha was herself.

That afternoon when the advertising man from the paper stopped by, Martha's pages were all done. Josiah was still working on his last two. Martha helped him. It was well past quitting time when the proofing was finished and the newspaper man left.

"How did you get yours done so fast?" Josiah asked.

Martha told him. "After all, we're managers. No rule says we can't use a clerk as a proofreader if it helps the company. Since she's paid less than we are, it costs the company less to have her do it, and we can be doing some more important work."

The other offices were dark. There was probably no one else in the building except a few night stockmen.

Josiah closed his desk and came toward hers.

"Ready to go? I'll walk down to the street with you."

She nodded and turned and he was so close to her that their arms touched. She wondered if he had planned it.

"Martha . . ."

"Yes, Josiah?"

"I just wanted to say that you're the most wonderful person I've ever known. Kind and warm, and so human and thoughtful. Like helping me with the proofs. Thank you." He reached out and kissed her cheek.

Martha was surprised, then at once pleased. She didn't pull back. His lips hung close to her face.

"Josiah, I enjoy working with you. But lots of times you help me, too, remember?" She reached out and kissed his cheek, and his arms came up and touched her shoulders.

"I promised myself I was never going to do this, Martha. Lord knows I've wanted to for so long." His arms came around her shoulders and pulled her gently toward him. She turned to look at him, and as she did he kissed her lips. Martha didn't try to pull away. It was a long kiss. At last Martha pulled back and their lips parted. Her hands had been at her sides, but now she brought them up to his waist and placed her cheek on his shoulder.

"That was nice, Josiah, very nice." She was feeling confident, happy, a warm, secure emotional response. For a moment she wondered how long it had been since a man had kissed her.

"Yes, Martha. It was beautiful, just like you." He bent down and kissed her cheek. Slowly her face turned to him and their lips met again, firmly, surely, honestly. He held her tight, her arms went around his back and their bodies pressed together. Far off in the twilight of her mind Martha realized she was not being rational, she was not thinking clearly. He was only an employee in one of her father's stores. But the warmth surged through her body, she felt his chest crushing her breasts, his lips were hot on hers and the tingle of anticipation danced along her nerve endings. This was totally impossible. It shouldn't be happening, but her heart was thumping so fast, so wildly, and deep within her she sensed a growing urgency.

His lips broke from hers. "Oh, Martha, I never intended to kiss you that way."

"Don't talk, please, Josiah. Don't say a word." She clung to him, reveling in the feel of his body hard against hers.

"Martha, let's sit down on the carpet, shall we?" Without waiting for an answer he unwound his arms from her, took her hand and helped her sit on the carpet. For once she was glad that the office did have the old rug. He moved quickly to the door and snapped the inside lock, then sat beside her. Josiah kissed her lips softly, then put his arm around her.

"Sweet, darling Martha."

"Oh, yes!" she said, reaching for his lips.

His hand brushed her breast, then touched it, and when there was no objection, he cupped the mound, rubbing tenderly.

The glow in her erupted into a blaze. Martha closed her eyes as he kissed her, and let her lips part the way Peter had shown her. She moaned softly as he held her and leaned her back until she lay on the carpet on their office floor.

She told herself this was idiotic. There was no reason, no logic — he was an employee! But the fire inside her burned brighter and brighter and when his hand worked through her dress and chemise and closer around her bare breast, she desperately wished that he would hurry.

CHAPTER THIRTEEN

Later, when he handed her the chemise, she realized that it had been almost two years since a man had watched her dress. That had been Marcel Navarre. She shivered. Martha slipped on the chemise, then arranged her dress so she could pull it on over her head.

They still sat on the floor. Josiah had pulled on his trousers but not his shirt. His body was firm, with a taut belly.

"Should we talk, Martha?"

"Yes. I . . . this does put something of a different slant on our relationship, I . . ."

"Martha, believe me, I never intended to . . . to do this. I did want to kiss you. It was a spur-of-the-moment thing, and you were so thoughtful and sweet to help me with the proofs."

"Josiah, I'm not blaming you. It just happened."

"I'm not saying, Martha, that I haven't

thought of trying to seduce you. I would wager that half the men in this building have had thoughts like that. A quiet dinner, wine, then a luxurious room somewhere with a hired violinist playing, low lights and a big soft bed."

"That would have been much better than the floor," she said, and they both laughed.

"Josiah, I am not an innocent child," she continued. "I knew what was happening after that second kiss, and it was up to me to stop it." She had her dress down over her head now, and peeked out at him. "Josiah, I guess I wanted it to happen. I wanted you."

He bent and kissed her again. She dropped the dress and put her arms around Josiah, letting him lean her slowly back to the floor. His kiss moved down from her lips to her throat, then to her chest, and at last centered on one of her warm, responding breasts. Martha couldn't stifle a moan of delight. Without taking their clothes off, they made love again, the passion exploding within them until they were limp and completely spent.

When they started to dress she made him go to his desk. She put her clothes on quickly, watching him finish, then met him at the desk.

"Now, we talk," she said, smiling.

"Martha, I've decided that I should come right out with it. I want to marry you. I'm not saying this just because we made love and I feel obligated. I love you, Martha. Ever since you first came to work here over a year ago. But I never dreamed . . ."

She took his hand and held it. "Marriage? Josiah, I promised myself that I would never marry again. Now, I don't know. I'm very fond of you, Josiah, we work well together, but is that enough to base a marriage on?" She watched him. "Josiah, let me think about it for a few days. In the meantime, you and I shall *not* work late any more, and we will *not* go to lunch together. Let me get my poor heart back to beating regularly and see what I can decide."

A week later Martha told Josiah that she had decided she should marry him. She told him not to be worried about her being pregnant, because she hadn't got pregnant when she was married. They wondered about a formal courting time, and decided that was not needed, since she was a widow and he a widower. That evening they went out to the Blue Peacock, one of the finest restaurants in San Francisco. That was where Martha revealed who she was. Josiah blinked as she told him, then reached for his wine glass and drained it.

"You mean you're the daughter of Harold Pemberton, *the* Harold Pemberton who owns the Mercantile, the ships, everything?"

"Yes, and I have money of my own, but we could still live entirely from your salary and mine at work, if you wish."

Josiah had another glass of wine. "You know what everyone is going to say. You know what the rest of them will think, even if they don't say it. And your father! Christ, how do I walk up to the president of the firm and say I'd like to marry his only daughter?"

"He's a very nice man. I happen to like him a lot. How do you know he's such a raging monster, ready to eat you alive?"

"He'll fire me. Send me packing. Maybe we better just stop this whole thing right now."

"No, Josiah. I'll talk to Father first, if you like. Then, when I have him all prepared, you can come in. We'll do it at a restaurant. Then you'll feel more at ease."

They talked about it for half an hour. Dinner was a total disaster. He was still convinced there was no chance he could ever marry her, and wanted to stop everything right then. At last she got him to admit that he would not panic yet, that he would take some time to think about it and they both could do some thinking.

When they got into a hack to take her home, she kissed him.

"Josiah, I've sent my housekeeper to her sister's. I want you to stay with me at my home tonight."

During that long, remarkable night of love-making, Martha convinced Josiah that in a month or two he should meet her father and talk with him about their future together. There was no hurry, no rush.

After that they went out two or three nights a week, always to dinner, then sometimes to a stage revue or to a new production of the opera. Whenever he suggested that she come up to his small apartment, she shook her head.

"We'll have years and years for that. Why use it all up now? And we don't want to cause gossip or a scandal. Already there have been items in the newspaper. Did you see the story in the *Daily Press?*"

"No."

"It was in one of those columns where they say all sorts of things about all kinds of people. Nothing to worry about."

They planned on announcing their engagement in September, and would be married before Christmas — perhaps.

"Of course you won't be working after that," he said.

"Why not? I love my work, I want to go right on working."

"A married woman, working? It isn't right. And it isn't the right thing for a society lady like you to do."

Martha laughed. "I don't care what the society gossips say. I do what I please, not to please a bunch of old ladies."

"Yes, I remember, but you haven't lately. I could lock the office door again."

"Oh, you could, but you don't have the only key, not any more."

That night they had dinner, then took a carriage ride around the shoreline of San Francisco Bay. There were more and more gaslights burning these nights, and it made the whole area look like a fairyland.

The next morning her father called her to his office. Harold Pemberton poured his daughter a glass of rose wine and smiled at her.

"This is not a business meeting, Martha. Your work in the Mercantile is going very well, remarkably well. There were some persons who advised against letting a woman be a manager. But you have certainly proved them to be entirely wrong." He paused and sipped at the wine in his glass. "My query is purely personal, and I know that I have no right to ask. However, you can probably imagine how a parent worries about his children. Is it true what I've been reading in the newspapers about you and one Josiah West?"

"Yes, Father. I've been seeing him socially. We go to the opera and to dinner. We work together at the Mercantile, and I enjoy his company very much."

"I see." He stared into his wine, then went on. "Do you have any more serious intentions toward this man?"

Martha giggled. "Do you mean, are my intentions honorable?"

Her father laughed too now, glad that the serious aspects of the talk were over. He had always been reluctant to enter into any personal discussion with his children, and it was no easier as they grew older.

"Father, I like Josiah very much. He's a widower with no children, and we enjoy each other's company. Really, I think it's much too early to talk about the possibility of marriage. Do you object to Mr. West?"

"No, no. I know so little about him. I'm just concerned whenever you might be considering marriage. There is always the possibility . . ."

Martha giggled again. "Daddy, let me tell

you what Josiah did when I told him that you were my father. At first he absolutely refused to see me any more. He was so frightened that he shook. He trembled. He said he knew he would be branded as a fortune hunter and before he knew it he would have lost his job and probably be run out of town or shanghied on board one of your ships for China. He was petrified. It took me a week to calm him down."

Harold Pemberton listened and entered the information in his mental file about Josiah West. Then he stood. "I have a meeting shortly, Martha. I just wanted to caution you and hear what you felt about this young man."

Martha knew when she had been dismissed. She ran around the desk, gave her father a big kiss and hurried to the door. "I'll be sure to let you know if we do decide to get engaged. Now I think I better get back to work before I am discharged!"

When she left, Mr. Pemberton pulled a cord on his desk. It went through a tube to the ceiling and into the front office, where it rang a small bell. Jenkins, his front office assistant, came in.

"Yes, Mr. Pemberton?"

"Have that man come in who has been waiting. And don't disturb us."

"Yes, sir."

The man who walked into the office a moment later was tall and thin, with sunken eyes, a sharp nose and a mouth with lips like two hard lines. He sat down when motioned to. Harold Pemberton sat looking over a sheaf of papers. They had just arrived that morning from the files downstairs. He had read them at once and found nothing irregular, no surprises or anything to alert him about the background or record of one Josiah West, assistant manager of the Mercantile.

Mr. Pemberton gave the papers to the man across his desk.

"This is all the information we have about one of our employees whom we are considering for promotion. There seem to be only sketchy details about a five- or six-year period that we need to have checked out, especially between the years of 1865 to 1870. We'll require a complete investigation including travel for on-the-spot questioning of friends and employers. This must have immediate, rush priority. Are there any questions?"

The man shook his head. "None, sir. We'll copy these documents and have them returned to you today."

"Anything else?"

"Time, sir. How much time do we have?"

"I wish I knew. I'd say anything you can do in two weeks should be in a report on my desk at that time. If it isn't complete by then, finish it as quickly as possible."

"The fee will be rather high."

"No matter. It could prove to be well worth it."

On Sunday, Martha and Josiah went for a picnic along the bay, driving a rig down the peninsula, at last chosing the Pacific side and finding a secluded little beach where they could eat their sandwiches and fried chicken and a warm bottle of wine. It was a perfect day.

"So you do like fried chicken, even cold," Martha said. "I was hoping you did. There's so much a girl should know about a man before she thinks about marriage."

"Besides how well he makes love?"

Martha blushed. "Now, Josiah, we agreed. That was something we did need to find out, and now we know, and we're going to be very proper from here on. If we do decide to get engaged and married, we'll have plenty of time for that."

"You were remarkable in that featherbed," he said.

"Well, Josiah, we have both been married before. It wasn't as if it was our first romp, now was it? All right. Let's talk about something else. Literature. Have you ever read any Shakespeare?"

"*Hamlet, Macbeth, Othello* — but they help me very little in my work at the store."

They talked about Hamlet and his madness. When the sun began to sink into the fog bank at the edge of the water they got ready to leave. Josiah suddenly caught her and kissed her lips. They rolled on the blanket and he lay on top of her at last, kissing her eagerly.

"Josiah, we agreed to wait for a while, remember?"

"Yes, but I wish I hadn't." He rubbed both of her breasts, kissed them through her dress and got up and helped her to her feet. "Should we talk again about that engagement?"

"First I want to bring you to the house to dinner. How would next Sunday night be? You can meet my mother and father and my younger brother and sister at the same time."

"Must I really?"

"Yes."

The dinner was not a smashing success. Martha's mother had been shocked at first by the suggestion that her daughter was even interested in this man. He was so plain.

He had no family, no social background, not even any money.

"Mother, don't be shameful. Josiah is a very nice man, and I enjoy his company. That should be enough for you."

The conversation had taken place in the upstairs hall before their guest arrived. During the evening there was a slight overtone of tension in the room. They escaped early in the evening for a ride around town to look at the gas lights, and Josiah was most grateful.

"Your mother does not like me," he said with accuracy.

Martha shook her head. "It's just that you're not the type of man she had picked out for me. She's an unstoppable matchmaker, but we don't have to worry about her. Father is the important one, and he was rather pleasant, I thought."

Their engagement was to be announced for the following weekend with a grand ball in one of the biggest hotels, the Manor. Two hundred friends were invited for a "special occasion," which was the current way to let everyone know that it was to be an engagement party.

Mrs. Pemberton made the arrangements, not without a little reluctance. She hired a small orchestra, some entertainment and the big ballroom for dancing.

Martha did not go to work the Friday of the party. She slept late, then took a long bath and had a hairdresser come to fix her hair exactly right.

By mid-afternoon she was a nervous disaster. There was no place she wanted to sit down. She was tired of walking. Why was she so worried? Mrs. Larson had told her a dozen times that everything would be fine. She had only to wait until it was time to go to the hotel. Before the carriage came to pick her up, Martha wished desperately that she had worked that day.

In his office, Harold Pemberton looked over the report he had received from the detective firm a week ago. There was nothing in the early life of Josiah West to suggest anything other than honesty and straightforwardness. The report covered his early employment in various retail firms in San Francisco. It was complete up to 1865, when the last employer said West went to Seattle to work. Pemberton put the report down and paced his office, his pipe spouting puff after puff of blue smoke. Somehow he had a bad feeling about Mr. West. Yet the professional investigators had failed to find even a hint of anything wrong. Was he going to experience this kind of trouble with each man Martha was interested in? Was he being overly protective?

He had not worried about Peter Dyke. He knew the man was a real man who had sown his wild oats in the past, and who was not rich — but a man who might become so on his own. Dyke was a mid-range opportunist, but he admitted it, and Harold Pemberton had liked that trait in the man, had been charmed by him.

But Josiah West . . . somehow he just didn't come clean in the wash. After tonight, it wouldn't matter what the detectives found out. There would be too much talk if the engagement had to be broken. Still . . .

The ball was a huge success. Over a hundred and fifty of the best names in San Francisco crowded the dance floor waiting for the announcement they guessed was the engagement of the widow, Mrs. Martha Pemberton Dyke. It was past ten o'clock, the traditional time for such announcements. A fresh table of champagne rolled out and the guests clustered around it, some wondering about the dalay.

Harold Pemberton sat in a room on the third floor of the hotel grasping a sheaf of papers and scowling at the same thin-faced man who had taken the detective assignment weeks before.

"Why couldn't you have sent word to me earlier?"

"There was no way, sir. I took the first steamer I could get, and this was absolutely the first chance to arrive."

Neither Martha or Josiah had put in an appearance at the ball yet. They were being saved for a grand entrance and the big announcement.

Now they were both summoned to the third-floor room and arrived somewhat breathless and expectant. Martha wore a striking blue silk gown with a short train, cut low to show some cleavage. Her hair was piled high on her head and her smile was radiant.

She came into the room and at once caught her father's ugly mood, his angry face. Josiah cringed as he went past the door, but saw that it was too late to retreat.

"Sit down, both of you," Mr. Pemberton said. They sank into chairs, Martha's spirits dropping at the same time. Her father turned to Josiah.

"Mr. West, have you ever lived in Seattle?"

"No, I was in Los Angeles for a while, and Portland."

"Mr. West, I have a report that says you spent over five years in Seattle, from 1865 to 1870, in fact."

"No, it must be someone else." Sweat beaded his forehead.

"Father, what is this all about?" Martha demanded.

"It's about you and this man. Josiah West is indeed his legal name. I'm surprised he didn't change it. Mr. West is a liar, a cheat, a deserter. He is married and has three children and a wife now living in Seattle in the very worst poverty imaginable."

Martha jolted to her feet. "Tell me it's not true, Josiah!"

He frowned and turned away.

"Tell me it isn't true!" Martha screamed at him.

"I'm afraid your father can tell you better than I can. I've always tried to escape facts whenever possible, especially when they are unfavorable, and about myself." He stood. "I understand I'm no longer employed by Pemberton's Mercantile?"

"That is correct, sir," Mr. Pemberton said. "And you won't find worthwhile employment anywhere in this city."

"Are there any legal charges you are bringing against me?"

"No, you know there can't be. I only wish there were — fraud at the very least. And since there was no legal engagement, there are no grounds for a breach of contract suit."

Josiah turned back to Martha. "Martha, I assure you . . ."

She flew at him, her fingers trying to dig into his face. He grabbed her hands and held them. "At first I didn't know who you were, and I was attracted to you . . ."

"When did you know who I was?"

"From the second day after you were promoted to floor manager. It was too fast. It wasn't hard to discover who Martha Dyke was. I'm surprised no one else even tried to find out."

"Get out!"

Martha collapsed in a chair.

Her father helped her back to the room where she had been waiting for the ball to start. She lay down on the bed, ready to cry.

He watched her for a moment. "Martha, it's time for me to go down to the party and announce that this is your mother's and my twenty-second wedding anniversary."

Martha only nodded and watched him leave. Josiah had known all the time. That was what hurt so much. He didn't ever like her as a person, he was always thinking . . . Josiah had worked on her, he was nice to her, made her feel wanted and respected and loved. Then when he saw that she was not going to suggest that they be more than just friends, he seduced her. That late-night work had not been planned, but he had decided on what circumstances he needed, something natural so that they would be working late. He waited, knowing that he could seduce her, knowing that she must be yearning for a man's body again whether she realized it or not. He had used her. He had plotted and lied and put on a good acting job when she told him who she was. He must have sweated, playing it so close, telling her he couldn't ever see her again. Oh, but he was good at the game.

Martha lay on the bed and heard her father close the door. Then the tears came in surging streams and she rolled over and sobbed into the pillow. Why? Why did it have to happen? Half an hour later her mother came in.

"Oh, you poor baby! Your father told me all about it. That is just dreadful. I never liked that man, from the first day I heard about him. It just goes to show that Mother knows best. Well, he's taken care of. That Josiah what's-his-name will never get another decent job in this town again. Your father will take care of that through the Merchants' Association. Just don't you worry about that." Her mother stopped.

"Dear, I know how you must feel. This is exactly what we were trying so hard to prevent. And he is already married! A bigamist. He was going to commit bigamy. Abandoned his wife and three children in Seattle — shameful, scandalous. He left them without a thing to live on and they've been begging from relatives. It's just a miracle that Harold found out in time. If he hadn't hired that good detective to work on the man as soon as you seemed serious about him . . . well, we would never have known. We've sent word to Mrs. Larson, and we're going to bundle you up in a carriage and send you home for a long hot bath and then get you tucked into bed."

Martha put her head down on her mother's lap and cried.

The morning after, Martha went back to work. She knew that the store would be short one assistant manager. It couldn't function without both. She told Mrs. Larson to go on as if nothing had happened. "Mrs. Larson, I am an adult, I went into that with my complete senses, and I can withstand a little bit of disappointment."

But all day long she swore to herself that she would never trust another man as long as she lived. She would see that everything was checked and proved and then double-checked and honest before she believed it. Her innocent, trusting days were over.

The store was alive with rumors and stories about why Mr. West was not there any more. A few of them came too close for comfort. She evaluated her own work duties, did those things that had to be done quickly and checked on Mr. West's desk. She handled the approval of certain orders that should be sent out, then selected a new employee who was due to be interviewed and had the rest of the necessary items taken care of just before the store closed.

Just before she was ready to leave, a messenger told her that the store manager, Mr. Jacobson, wanted to see her in his office.

Jacobson was a slight man with pure white hair and a white moustache, a nimble mind and an affinity for gambling which he kept closely in check.

His eyes were dark brown and he peaked his hands now as he sat in his swivel chair and watched her.

"Mrs. Dyke, I understand that you have handled all the required work due out today from Mr. West's desk."

"Yes, sir, I thought it best to do it."

"Do you think you can continue to handle

your duties and those of Mr. West as well?"

Martha had not even considered it. She thought over the workload for a moment. "Yes, sir, I can. I would need to have a full-time assistant or secretary, who would be on a much lower pay scale of course."

"Would you like the responsibility of being the only assistant manager?"

"Only if I were to receive half of the salary that Mr. West earned in addition to my present pay."

"What?" Mr. Jacobson asked. Then he frowned at her, but his expression of surprise evaporated and he chuckled. "You know, Mrs. Dyke, when I first hired you on here, I was told who you were and instructed not to give you any special privileges or advantages. You won your first promotion by your excellence on the floor. Your move to assistant manager was not my choice, but I soon found it was justified. Now I believe that you will be the right person to take over my office late next year, when I retire."

He stood and walked around his desk and watched her. "I am sorry about the episode with Mr. West. It reflects on my judgement for not spotting the man as a rogue from the first. I didn't check his references well enough. But all that is behind us now. About

311

having one assistant manager — it sounds reasonable. I'll have to check with my superiors, of course." He stood and held out his hand. "Mrs. Dyke, it has been good working with you, and I hope you'll stay with us for a long time. If you do, I'll feel better about giving up my position here."

Martha smiled, thanked him and went back to her desk. She would move the other big desk out and have a smaller one put against the far wall. Perhaps Priscilla could be her secretary and assistant.

Martha closed up her office and walked down the steps. She was still not sure exactly how she felt. Her heart had been smashed into a hundred pieces when she heard the awful truth about Josiah. She had been shaken, emotionally and intellectually, because she had trusted Josiah. Now she was still a little . . . what . . . numb, she decided. Numb, and still angry, and confused. Could she ever trust another man again?

Instead of going home, Martha walked to the docks and along the places and streets where she and Allen used to stroll. It had been so long ago. The streets were no safer now, but there were two hours yet until dark.

As she turned a corner she noticed someone behind her. It was the same tall man she had seen before. She almost ran, then she looked again and realized that the man was Johnnie Laveau. She called to him and he walked up to her.

"Begging pardon, *mon,* you not supposed I to see."

"Did father send you to be my watch dog?"

"He say me watch you home go, then watch to work go."

"I'm perfectly fine, Johnnie, but I thank you. I just had a disappointment, and I'm trying to get over it."

"This no place young girl walk."

She looked around, remembered the wharf rats and the man with the peg-leg and knew Johnnie was right. Her father really knew her well.

"Would you come home with me and have dinner with Mrs. Larson and me? We'd love to have you."

He shook his head. "Just get you home, *mon,* that all."

CHAPTER FOURTEEN

Every night after work for a month, Martha walked along the docks and the waterfront where she had been so happy with Allen. She didn't dare think of him. At first she decided she had to change her whole way of life. It had been a mistake to go into the store, to try to work at a job. Perhaps she should go into some kind of charitable work, to help her fellow man. But a few days later her thinking changed, and she came to realize that she had not been the cause of the problem. It had been a very human, natural error in judgement. How could she know that the man was so underhanded, so sneaking and devious that he would spend half a year in a plot to win her hand in marriage? He was merely an opportunist.

For a week she worried about his family. That was one small beneficial work she could do. She located the detective agency and the man who had tracked down Josiah.

She summoned the same thin-faced man to her office the following day.

"Can you travel to Seattle?" she asked the man.

He nodded.

"Can you guarantee delivery on a package of cash?"

"We are not a delivery service, Mrs. Dyke."

"I understand that. I'll pay your regular costs for travel to and from Seattle and whatever other costs you have, plus your usual investigating fees. It is important to me that this delivery be made correctly and that the money reaches the right hands."

The man said he understood, and that they would accept the job.

"I want you to deliver a small pouch containing five thousand dollars to a woman in Seattle and obtain her signature on a receipt."

"That's all?"

"Yes. The name is Mrs. Josiah West. I believe you know the address."

The thin-faced man's eyes sparkled for a moment, then his face returned to its previous blandness.

"Yes, it's in the files. You'll have the delivery signature within a week."

She handed him a sheet of paper. "Here's

a draft for your expenses and an advance. Please bill me personally for any additional costs."

He looked at the draft amount, nodded and left.

Martha sighed. Josiah would probably get most of the money if he were back in Seattle, but at least this was one small effort she could make to right a wrong that she may have had some hand in continuing. She looked down at her list of jobs to be done today, made a heavy black line through "Seattle," and dismissed it from her mind. It was done, over with, and now she would not think of it again. There were so many other projects that needed her attention.

That afternoon after work, she walked along the docks again. She knew that Johnnie Laveau was somewhere behind her, watching, waiting. No one bothered her. She walked and dreamed, and just before dark, Johnnie stopped his carriage in front of her. She got in and he drove her home. Lately they hadn't been speaking. Instead they smiled and waved and he went back to his other duties, whatever they might be.

The next morning at her desk, she called softly and the pretty young girl who had helped her on the advertising proofs several weeks ago came in.

"Yes, Mrs. Dyke?"

"Priscilla, would you tell the floor managers that I'd like to see them for a ten-minute meeting right after closing time? It won't take long, but it is important."

Priscilla said she would, and left, allowing the connecting door to remain open a few inches so she could hear if Mrs. Dyke called.

The store meetings had been Martha's idea, instead of sending cold written messages, and it had worked well. Small complaints from the lower management level could be caught early and worked out, often with beneficial results.

Martha stared down at her job list. She had decided that she wanted to stay in the store, that she could contribute in some way here. She knew she could always quit, go home and wait for some man to marry her. She did not deny that there would be someone. Men found her attractive, evidently interesting to be with, and her mother would see that there was a steady stream of beaux. Did she want that? Were marriage and a family so very important to her? It was a constant question. She would always be asking herself about it, and she would never know how to answer.

She looked at the list again, then went to her drawer of applications for employment and checked on six, selecting the two whom she wanted to talk with and asked Priscilla to write short notes to them, asking them to come in for interviews.

While she was thinking about it she walked to Mr. Jacobson's office. His secretary smiled and said she could go right in. The store manager was looking over a page of closely spaced figures.

He glanced up and smiled. "Ah, my replacement. You're early today."

She laughed, knowing that he enjoyed this gentle teasing of her. At one time he had told her he only teased people he liked. She sat down across from him.

"Mr. Jacobson, you know that suggestion I sent to you last week about setting up a personnel department? Have you had a chance to look at it yet?"

"Yes, Martha, I have. And it's a good idea. But I just don't see how we can work it into our organization. Are we talking about two more people on the payroll? Now, where are we going to put them on the chart? What pot of money is their salary going to come from? Whom do they report to?" He smiled. "We could always put them under your direct command and take their pay out of your salary."

Martha smiled. "If you think it's a good idea. I'll do some thinking, and see what I can suggest about the pay. I have an idea about coming up with some money."

"You do that, young lady. You just do that. And all the time I'll be thinking about how I'm going to be tying those flies in the field to take advantage of a new hatch of black gnats, say, and I'll be pulling in more of those rainbow trout than I can eat. Did I tell you about the last time I was over there in Arizona?"

Martha shook her head.

"It was last fall, and I was up in the hills aways along this just great little trout stream, and . . ." Mr. Jacobson stopped talking. Martha looked up and saw his eyes go wide, his hands grasping at his chest. Suddenly he began to gasp for breath. Before she could react, he slid down in his big chair and fell to the floor behind his desk.

Martha screamed for his secretary and rushed around the desk. She pushed back the chair, and saw his hands still at his chest. He struggled for breath. He looked up at her as she pulled his shoulder away from the leg of the desk and pushed the chair back so he could lay out flat on the carpeted floor.

"Hurts!" he whispered. "Damnit to hell,

but it hurts!"

His secretary, Mrs. Aldrich, took one look at him and hurried out of the room. His doctor's office was just across the street. She ran all the way to bring the medical man.

Martha held Mr. Jacobson's head in her lap, wiping sweat from his face, which was still distorted with the terrible pain.

"Hurts . . . so . . . bad . . . Martha," he said. She hoped Mrs. Aldrich would bring help soon. There was nothing she could do. His breathing had steadied. She wasn't sure she knew how to feel for his pulse, so she didn't try.

Mr. Jacobson lay there trying to gain strength. At last he looked up at her.

"Take . . . care of . . . care . . . of . . . the . . . store." He finished the last word, and his eyes fluttered then closed. For a few moments he lay quietly, then his whole body shuddered, his hands caught at his chest again and a scream of total agony came from his lips. The sound faded, his hands relaxed at his chest and his head turned slowly to one side. His eyes were wide open.

Martha watched him, tears spilling down her cheeks. Mr. Jacobson didn't move — not a twitch, not a sound. Then a gushing of his last breath came from his lungs and

Martha knew what they meant by a death rattle. She hated the sound at once. Martha touched his temple, but could find no pulse. Tears worked down her cheeks. Mr. Jacobson was gone. Just a few moments before he had been joking, laughing, telling her about his first love, trout fishing. She held his head in her lap and let the tears come. It wouldn't do any good now if Mrs. Aldrich did come back with a doctor.

The store was closed the next day in honor of Mr. Jacobson, and for his funeral. Martha was still numb. Too much had happened too quickly again. She sat through the church service, not hearing a thing. Then the slow ride in the carriage to the cemetery and another few words. She couldn't bring herself to drop any earth on the casket. It seemed so final. Mr. Jacobson would never get back to Arizona to fish, would never make those lures to catch the trout. On the way home, she began to cry again. Why did people have to die?

That evening she and Mrs. Larson sat in the parlor reading. Martha realized she knew little about death, had not been touched by it often; perhaps that was why she had been so shaken when she held Mr. Jacobson's head in her lap as he died. She tried not to think at all about the store, and went back to her book.

The next day she sat in her office, suddenly overwhelmed by the huge amount of work to get done. She was asking Priscilla to do more and more of it. The girl was intelligent, learned quickly, and had a tough-mindedness about her that Martha liked.

Martha was totally surprised when her father walked into her office just after midday.

"Father, I'm so sorry about Mr. Jacobson. I know you had been good friends for years."

"Yes, almost forty years." He sat and watched her. "Did John ever talk about retiring?"

"Yes, many times. Fishing in Arizona."

"And did he say you should become manager here when he stepped down?"

"Yes." She stopped. "Oh, oh, land sakes! I mean . . . I simply hadn't even thought about that. There's been so much to do."

Harold Pemberton studied his daughter. He was sure she hadn't even considered it. She was hard at work, trying to get a job done that needed doing. It was so like her.

"Do you want the position, Martha, as manager of the Pemberton Mercantile?"

"Oh . . . oh, my goodness." She looked up

at him. "Sometimes we just can't plan out our lives very well, can we? Circumstances seem to sweep along and change our best plans." She stared out her window for a moment before she looked back at the president of the corporation's board of directors and general director.

"Yes, Mr. Pemberton, I would like to be manager here. I totally enjoy the work, and I think I'm good at it." She paused. "And I expect I want to show some people that I can do the job here, even if I am a woman."

Her father chuckled. "You're a regular Susan B. Anthony. Next thing you'll want is to be able to vote and smoke little black cigars."

She jumped up and ran to him and kissed his cheek. "No, Daddy, I'll never want to smoke. I tried it, and it's just dreadful. Voting might be another matter." She sobered. "Do I get the job?"

"If you want it, it's yours. I don't know anyone else who could do anywhere near as good a job as you will."

She went to the window and looked out. She could see the masts of some ships in the harbor, the blue expanse of water and the hills beyond. Tears brimmed her eyes.

"What else is involved besides the store?"

"There will be some corporate board

meetings to attend. You won't be on the board, but you'll report to it on your store. A dozen or so meetings a year should take care of it."

"Father, I'll do the very best that I can. If that isn't good enough, you be sure to fire me."

Harold Pemberton had never been more proud in his life. A strange little shiver ran down his spine, and he wondered if some day this small lady would be running the whole corporation.

"You can be sure I'll cashier you in a second if you don't do your job," he said. "Now, I think we should celebrate and go out for a very special lunch."

Two weeks later Martha had the store whipped back into shape. She promoted Hadley Garrison to one of the two assistant store managers. Priscilla Cole was named the other assistant manager, much to the surprise and chagrin of Garrison. Martha had a two-hour conference with Hadley before naming him to the post. She told him frankly that he had a reputation as a cad and a bounder who took advantage of women. She said if he so much as touched one of the clerks or floor managers he'd be out of a job and walking the streets looking

for work. He was a good retail man. All he
had to do was learn to keep his hands to
himself. His roving days were over if he
wanted to keep his job.

"Priscilla can help you a lot. She's been
nearly doing the work for the past few
months."

Garrison nodded, his usual smirk gone.
"Yes, I understand."

Martha quickly set up a personnel department with one man to look for applicants,
screen them and suggest those best suited
for employment. Another one-person department was established for advertising.
She hired a layout advertising salesman art-
ist from the newspaper and put him in
charge of the entire advertising approach
and content. He would consult with floor
managers and get approval from his office.
Soon he needed two helpers.

Martha talked long and hard with her
father, and at last won permission to ask
Johnnie Laveau if he would come into the
Mercantile as her special assistant. He
would still function as her bodyguard and
screen visitors, as well as act as liaison
between her and the president's office. It
was an unusual position, and often Johnnie
had little to do, but Martha felt more secure
knowing he was in the outer office. He was

his usual strong, confident self, but never intruded into her personal life. Ritualistically he called for her in a carriage each morning at home, drove her to work, put the rig in a livery and came into his office. At night he returned her to her home. Many times at noon he accompanied her to lunch.

Each morning on the way to work a small gray mongrel dog rushed out at the carriage yapping and barking furiously as they drove past. Johnnie knew that the dog upset Martha. One morning she mentioned it.

"I wish he wouldn't do that," she said. "He might run under the wheels and get hurt."

Johnnie nodded. "Time maybe come, I have talk with dog."

Martha laughed about it. She was thinking about the new advertising campaign she had to approve that morning. Something was wrong about it, and she didn't know what. She'd ask Hadley what he thought. With all his faults, his was the best retail mind in the store. And he *had* been behaving himself lately.

The next morning Johnnie picked Martha up as usual, and when they passed Third Street, the small gray dog came charging out from the sidewalk right on schedule, but when he saw Johnnie in the buggy he stopped suddenly, his tail whipped between his legs, and he ran for the fence whining and yelping as if he had been kicked.

Martha noticed the strange reaction and asked Johnnie about it. He shrugged.

"Dog, he funny. Maybe bite carriage, it bite back."

It was the first occurrence of a regular morning event. The little dog attacked every wheeled rig that rolled past its favorite corner, but only until Johnnie Laveau drove by. Then the dog whined, tucked in its tail and ran for the safety of its own fence. Martha wondered about it, but soon forgot about the little dog.

There were other small problems to keep her involved. The office ones she took care of neatly and quickly, but another one near where she lived continued to vex her. One morning she was so angry she spilled over when Johnnie picked her up.

"That crotchety old Mrs. Mahon has been at it again, Johnnie. She lives right beside me and this morning she somehow got a policeman to come out at six-thirty. I like to play my piano at that hour, and she had complained, saying it was too loud and disturbed her sleep. Can you imagine anything so petty? That old lady simply caused the whole nasty problem," Martha went on.

"Oh, the policeman was polite, but he said it might be better if I played a little more softly before eight in the morning. Can you imagine that? It isn't the first time that old maid has bothered me and others in the neighborhood."

Martha laughed and shook her head in surprise. "I'm sorry, Johnnie, it wasn't that important. But every time I think about it I get angry. I was furious at the time. But I guess . . . Well, that poor old soul probably has nothing else to do. I should be a little more charitable."

Martha put it out of her mind and tried to concentrate on what she had to do the rest of the day. She was trying to think four months ahead of the seasons so she could be sure all the ordering was done for the spring clothes.

A week later, Martha heard that Mrs. Mahon was ill. That was not out of the ordinary. She had had sick spells now and then for years. Martha asked Mrs. Larson to take over a fresh-baked apple pie and offer her condolences. This too had been something of a ritual during the past months. That night Mrs. Larson came back with a strange story.

"She can't talk," Mrs. Larson said. "Mrs. Mahon is in fine spirits, and she's as spry as ever, but she seems to have lost her voice completely. The doctor doesn't know what to make of it, but he decided if it came without any cause, it should go away in the same way." Mrs. Larson said the more she talked with the housekeeper, the more interesting it became.

Mrs. Levens, the old lady's housekeeper, had found the family cat about a week ago in the front lawn, all cut to pieces and dead. It was staked out in the front yard and deliberately killed.

"Mrs. Mahon loved that cat, so she buried it herself in the back yard," Mrs. Larson said. "After that she started to lose her voice, and now it's gone entirely."

Martha was getting ready to go to a concert. Mrs. Larson had begged off, and her mother and father were not going, so she asked Johnnie if he would go with her. He said of course, and picked her up promptly at eight. The singing had been less than good that night, even though two new voices were used. The soloists had just arrived from St. Louis. The general opinion was that they had either been still getting used to the change in the climate, or they were both half drunk. The consensus favored the latter.

Johnnie drove Martha back to her California Street home and saw her safely inside the door. When he heard the bolt slide into place he left and drove on California Street until he came to the edge of town, where a small two-room building stood. He put the carriage in back, unhitched the bay and hobbled her where there were still a few shoots of green, and went in the back door of the building.

It was dark inside, but the familiar odor of the incense he had left smoldering in a nearly closed tin box permeated the room. He moved carefully to the side, found a round of sulphur matches and tore one off, lit it and put the flame to a small coal oil lamp wick. When he saw that it was lighted, he set the glass chimney in place. As the faint light seeped into the dark corners of the room, Johnnie saw that nothing had been disturbed. He never used a lock on his door, but no one ever came into his rooms.

The doll lay where he had left it, with the head slightly below the level of the body, and with the silk thread bound securely around the neck at precisely the correct spot. The doll was about six inches long and carefully crafted.

Johnnie dropped more incense in the tin and sniffed in satisfaction. Then he moved to a cabinet with open shelves that were filled with small jars, many of them containing powders of a dozen different colors and consistencies. There were roots and herbs, vials filled with colored liquids and tins of salves and creams. He took out one vial of red fluid and let one drop fall on the doll. The splotch touched the face and head and soon the whole upper half turned a dark red. He watched for a moment, smiled and returned the vial to the shelf.

On the other side of the room sat a sturdy table built of scrap lumber. On the table lay a foot-wide board two feet long. A cat lay on the board, spread-eagled on its stomach its face toward him. The cat was alive. Its loose skin had been stretched out on each side as if it were a pelt drying, then the skin had been nailed to the board. Johnnie took a knife from his pocket, opened the sharp blade and made one long, delicate incision down the cat's back, cutting only through the skin, carefully avoiding any tissue below.

The cat screeched and yowled in pain and anger, but Johnny Laveau hardly noticed. He was busy catching the small quantity of blood that came from the incision. When the bleeding stopped, the cat still screeched. Johnnie stepped back and stared hard into the cat's eyes.

He said a few words in some sort of a

chant, then again gazed into the eyes of the tortured animal.

"Eh! Eh! Bomab hen hen!
  Canga Bafie te
Danga moune de te
Canga do ki li!"

Johnnie Laveau went back to the small doll and watched it for a moment. Then he held up the vial of blood he had caught from the cat and drank it.

CHAPTER FIFTEEN

Martha sat in her big manager's office and looked around. She had made many changes since she had moved in. There was a new carpet on the floor, and two more chairs. The brass spittoon in the corner was gone. A small conference table sat near the windows with six chairs around it. The wooden shutters were replaced with softer, more pleasing light green drapes. The desk now faced the door, and the side chair was soft and upholstered, inviting longer sessions with guests, employees and business people. The fishing trophies and mounted fish on the wall had been replaced with four fine oil paintings of pleasant country scenes.

The door opened and Johnnie Laveau stood there, silent and serious, letting her know he was at his desk after putting the rig away. He turned and closed the door.

Martha lifted her brows to avoid wrinkling the soft skin around her eyes. She had started to frown. Quite suddenly, and as a complete surprise, Martha realized that she was beginning to rely too much on Johnnie Laveau. It was almost as if he were a substitute husband. He took her to social events, drove her carriage, took her to and from work, protected her when she wanted to walk along the docks, helped her in the business.

Two weeks ago the red-shirted teamsters had demanded more money, and said they wouldn't deliver Martha's goods from the docks unless she increased their wages. Johnnie had been there. She listened to their complaint and had Johnnie investigate it. He discovered that some self-appointed "superintendent" at the docks was taking one-quarter of the men's wages. Johnnie talked with the teamsters and they agreed to his plan. Later that day the "superintendent" of loading at the docks found himself shanghaied as a crewman on a sailing ship headed around the Horn. Once again the teamsters were getting their full pay.

Yes, Johnnie was becoming much more than just a worker, a "convenience." He was working himself into the whole way she was operating. He was almost like a husband, except sexually. She paused. For the first time she realized that she never thought about Johnnie Laveau sexually. Would he be a good lover? She hurried on to assure herself that she had no intention of ever finding out, but it did seem unusual to her that after working with him so closely for so long, the idea had never crossed her mind before. She called him in and gave him a thin envelope that needed to be taken to her father's office. As he reached for the envelope, she held it a moment and looked into his eyes when he glanced down at her.

"Johnnie, I'm not very good at saying 'thank you,' and for that I apologize. It's long overdue. You are becoming my good right hand around here. I don't think I could get along without you now."

She caught the trace of a frown on his frankly open brown face. She had never seen him uncertain or confused before, but the slightest hesitation gave her that idea now. She hurried on. "I'm giving you a raise in pay — now I know you've said that how much you get paid doesn't matter to you, but it does to me. You earn it, and I want you to have it. Put it in the bank, use it to feed the pigeons, sent it back to Jamaica. It's yours. Thank you again, Johnnie Laveau."

He nodded, and walked out on his way to the corporate headquarters building.

That noon, Martha took Priscilla Cole to lunch. It had been over a week since they had eaten together. Martha picked a small restaurant where they could have some French food. They both stuffed themselves, and celebrated the lunch with wine. After the second glass, Priscilla looked at her employer.

"Martha, do you realize there's been some talk around the store that isn't very nice?"

"The rumor mills, the gossip mongers are at it again? What about?"

"Martha, can I be frank?"

She frowned. She had taken Priscilla into her confidence many times, and they were good friends, but such a question put her on the defensive now.

"Of course, Priscilla. We're good friends and we shouldn't hold anything back."

"Well," she paused and looked away. "I really don't know how to say this politely. The point is, quite a few of our own people are starting to talk and wonder about you and Johnnie Laveau."

"They are, are they?" Martha sipped her wine. She should have expected it sooner than this. He'd been in the next office for six months, he was remarkably attractive, and single.

"I should have guessed. Johnnie is only a

good friend and a valuable employee. He's helped me in many ways. I've known him since I was seventeen."

"Everyone knows that. What the gossips are saying is that sometimes you work late here, and so does he . . ."

"And they think we're having an — an affair?"

"Yes. I don't think I should have mentioned it."

"You're right in telling me, Priscilla. I can take some precautions so there's no more suspicion."

"He is terribly handsome, don't you think? I mean, he's tall, wide shoulders, his face is so lean and forceful."

Martha watched Priscilla with surprise, but in a moment she knew. "How long have you felt this way about Johnnie, Priscilla?"

"What? Felt what way?" she asked too quickly.

Martha giggled. "You're half in love with him already, aren't you, Priscilla? Admit it."

Priscilla set her lips firmly. "He seems like a very nice man, and I do like his looks . . ."

"But Priscilla, he's a black man, he's a Negro. There would be no way . . . I mean no chance of anything like a normal life for a black/white marriage in this town."

"Society can go fly a kite!" Priscilla said.

"What do I care how they think?"

Martha smiled again. "Has he ever — ever encouraged you — you know."

"No, not a word. And of course I could never . . . make any kind of advance."

"I think that's the best plan. Do you want my advice?"

"Desperately!"

"Concentrate on someone else — that third-floor manager, for example. He's not married, and he always makes excuses to come up to your office. Right?"

"Honestly, Martha. I'm not *that* desperate. He must be all of twenty-two, and he doesn't even shave right. I have some pride, after all."

Martha smiled. Matchmaking just wasn't her forte. "Well, then, concentrate your charm and wit on somebody else, and quit thinking about Johnnie."

They paid their bill and walked two blocks back to the store. Martha saw Priscilla look at the big clock in a jewelry store window.

"Don't worry about the time, you're out with the boss." They both laughed. They were half an hour late getting back to work.

Martha sat at her desk digesting what Priscilla had told her. It only reinforced what she had briefly thought about this morning: that Johnnie Laveau was an extremely attractive man. But that was as far as it could ever go. She smiled, thinking of what Priscilla had said about society. Her assistant store manager wouldn't care what anyone else thought if such a match would please her. She was a rebel, but something of a timid one. Martha pulled out her pad and looked at her job list for the afternoon.

Twice during the next month, Martha was invited out to social evenings. The first was the opening night at the opera, an important social occasion. Her escort was from the corporate office staff. She had seen him occasionally, and had known him for four years, but he was ten years older than she. He had been widowed about a year before. It was the most boring evening she had ever spent, and besides that, the opera was not very good at all.

The second man was about her age, a bachelor who worked in the shipping end of the company. Her mother had matched her with him at one of her dinner parties. He was blond, had a high, nervous laugh which she charged up to the fact that he was dining at the big boss's table and matched with his daughter. Ronald was four inches taller than she, thin as a flagpole, and a social snob of the worst kind.

Martha sat in her office now, ready to go

home, but not wanting to pull the small cord at the side of her desk which would summon Johnnie.

Why did she still do it? Every man she met, every eligible male who was thrust at her, even men she saw in the street all had an impossible goal to meet: they had to be as good as or better than Allen Cornelius. The thought of his name brought a stab of anguish into her soul. That afternoon so long ago came surging back as if it were yesterday. She was in that bare little room again where she had known her first true love. The joy, the thrill of it all — where had it gone? Why did it have to be so difficult? Why did every man have to measure up to Allen? Was she simply refusing them all because Allen had not been the dramatic wonder she now remembered? Her image of Allen had been heightened, built up, blown all out of proportion to reality. She knew this, but still she played the game, a game that no man except Allen himself could ever win.

She pulled the call cord, and a moment later, Johnnie came throgh the door.

"Ready, Miss?" he asked in his lilting voice.

Martha said she was and they walked to the carriage. *Was she ready,* he had asked.

Now that was an open-ended question. Ready for what? She seemed ready for a lot of things, but was she ready for romance again? To be courted? To be loved? She refused to think about it. Maybe later — much later.

For a moment she wondered how Allen was doing, how his family was, what he was doing in the business. She knew that he had been promoted and was now the manager of company operations in Seattle. That wasn't the biggest job in the firm, but it was a good start. *Allen, Allen, Allen!* Why couldn't she get him out of her mind? Tomorrow she would check with the people at the corporate headquarters and see what information they had in his file. She was sure they would have an executive record on Allen by now.

When she got the file the following afternoon at the headquarters building, she went through it quickly. There was a brown-toned portrait of Allen standing beside his desk, very formal, painfully stiff. Allen looked older. He had a few lines in his face now, replacing the round youthful cheeks she remembered. But he was still handsome, the best-looking man she had ever known. She slid the photograph into her purse and put the rest of the folder back in the file. All the rest of the afternoon, she sat in her office staring out her window toward the north and thought about Allen. Some day she would go to Seattle and visit him. She would be strong and firm and polite, and not be affected by his good looks and his charm.

That night her mother had invited her to another dinner party, a Friday night affair. They would have dinner and then dance to a small orchestra in the large parlor and dining room in their home. It wasn't a ballroom but the two areas with the arch opened between them would be eighty feet long. It wasn't until late that afternoon that she had the idea. She called in Johnnie and explained it to him. For a moment he laughed, then he shook his head.

"You mama no like. She boot me Johnnie right out on ear. Johnnie go poof! back on small ship."

"Not at all, Johnnie. I'll defend you every way, nothing bad can happen to you. They might be angry with me, but you they can't touch. Hurry, now, and get the suit, and be back here to pick me up at six."

Johnnie shook his head laughing. "You crazy woman," he said as she shooed him into the hall.

That night when the dinner guests had all arrived in the big mansion on the hill, there was still one empty chair. A nervous young man sitting beside the vacant place stood and began pacing and watching the door.

"She should be right down, Donald. She's probably just fussing," Mrs. Pemberton said.

A few minutes later Martha walked into the dining room. On her arm was a tall, distinguished-looking Negro man dressed immaculately in a formal dinner suit and black tie. A murmur of surprise slashed around the table set for twenty. Harold Pemberton rose first, followed quickly by the ten other men.

"Ah, Martha, we thought you might not be hungry tonight. And Mr. Laveau, it's good to see you again." He snapped his fingers at the maid, who quickly brought in another chair and a table setting.

The eyebrows of every woman in the room arched an inch high as the females examined the colored man who was evidently escorting Martha Pemberton Dyke. Unheard-of. Proposterous! Outrageous!

The whispers began.

"She certainly isn't going to *sit beside him,* is she?"

"Where in the world did he come from?"

"Oh, he's the black who works for her at the Mercantile."

"I never thought she should have been *al-*

lowed to work downtown, anyway. Now look."

"Just goes to show you that class and breeding simply do not always pass on to the children."

"Well, if she thinks *I'm* going to dance with him . . ."

"He does have a striking profile, though, don't you think?"

"Poor Abigail. She looks like she wishes she were sick upstairs."

"Another half-hour and she will be."

Dinner came then and the chatter resumed around the table. Donald, on Martha's left, was struck absolutely dumb. He said not more than three words during the whole six-course meal. Not even Mrs. Pemberton on his left could get him to open his mouth when his fork wasn't in it. Just before dessert he excused himself and fled out the front door, not even fetching his top hat and gloves.

Martha wanted to giggle. Under the table she poked Johnnie in the leg and grinned. He smiled back, enjoying himself although he knew he should not. It was one grand joke on Mrs. Pemberton. He knew this would be the last time Martha's mother asked her to come to a dinner party without allowing her to bring her own escort. His grin broadened as he heard whispers down the table. He could imagine what they were saying. Then in the far end of the room the musicians gathered, with two violins, a piano and a huge string bass. Chairs scraped as the diners began to ease away from the table.

Before either her father or mother could approach her, Martha caught Johnnie's hand and they walked out of the house, got into the carriage and drove away.

Martha was concerned now about what she had done. "Johnnie, I didn't do this to embarrass you in any way. To me, you're much too important — more of a man than anyone in that room tonight, except my father. I wanted to remind my mother gently that I can choose my own friends, that she does not continually have to provide me with dinner partners. And I wanted to tell them that Johnnie Laveau is just as good as any of them, and probably one hell of a lot better than most."

"You believe, *mon?*"

"Absolutely."

He stopped the rig. A gas street lamp glowed faintly half a block down. Johnnie looked at her seriously. "Then you say Johnnie good as any those. Then Johnnie should be able . . . Then can Johnnie . . ."

He bent and kissed her cheek, then his lips touched her nose. His arms came around her and this time his lips met hers and clung there, hot and wanting.

For Martha it felt like her very first kiss. It had been so long since a man had embraced her. She clung to him, felt his tongue press against her lips, knew the pressure was building inside of her and relished the surging of her heart as it raced her blood faster and faster through her body.

His lips left hers and she tried to see his face, but it was too dark.

"Johnnie, I liked that," she said in a soft, small voice.

He didn't ask her, but simply kissed her again, more gently this time, only his lips touching her, thrilling her with fire and the passion that she had thought had burned out a year ago.

Johnnie broke it off, took the reins and drove to her house on California Street. He sat there the reins in his hands. She took the leathers from him, tied them and began to get out of the rig.

Johnnie saw her to the door as usual, but there the pattern changed.

"Johnnie, please come inside," she said.

He did. There were no lights on, since it was Mrs. Larson's regular Friday night visit to her sister. Martha found a "stinker," a sulphur match that came pasted together in a round package, and lit one, went to a lamp and lighted it. The shades were already down.

"Johnnie, will you kiss me again?" It was not real. This was all a dream, a fantasy. It had to be an illusion. But with her eyes closed, it was hard to tell that it was not real. She couldn't even tell who was kissing her. Quickly she remembered her talk with Priscilla. Such a pairing would never work for either of them. Had Priscilla's words opened her eyes to what a physically attractive man Johnnie Laveau really was? Probably. If Johnnie had said anything, or did anything else right at that second, she would have been strong enough to tell him he should leave. He didn't. It was a long kiss, and when it ended he waited. She sighed, flashed a smile at him, and caught his hand. In her other hand she picked up the lamp and carried it into the first floor bedroom. She was embarrassed for only a moment. One of her petticoats lay on the bed. She pushed it aside, put the lamp on the stand, and sat on the edge of the big bed.

"You sure?" he said.

"Yes, Johnnie. Yes, I'm sure."

He sat beside her, kissed her again, then

bent and kissed the swell of each breast where it surged past the sides of the dress's keep neckline. Martha gasped then slowly leaned backward on the bed. She wasn't sure where she was going or what was going to happen, but she knew for certain that Johnnie Laveau wold be a considerate and gentle lover. She had waited so long for this to happen, she knew it would be good.

In the early morning hours they talked.

"Johnnie, you have had many girls, right?"

He nodded.

"Did you love any of them?" She continued quickly before he could reply: "I've been married, and I loved my husband, but he's gone, and now I have no one. I'm not asking you to love me, Johnnie. I'm not saying I want you to marry me. We both know that it might work in Jamaica, but here it never would. Maybe in a hundred years from now, but not today. I'm sorry I made you uncomfortable at dinner. I shouldn't have done that."

He bent and kissed her bare breast. She went on.

"I'm still in love, Johnnie, with Allen Cornelius. You probably never met him. I was almost eighteen and I adored him. We made love just once, and that same night he sailed away before we could marry. I was heartbroken. I wanted to die. But of course I didn't. Then I married Captain Dyke, because my mother wanted me to."

His lips moved to her other breast, and Martha moaned softly.

"Oh, that is nice, Johnnie. So sweet." Her hands stroked his black hair. "You knew the rest. I lost my husband to a pirate and eventually came back home. Allen came home while I was gone, heard I had married, so he married, too. Now he's in Seattle working for the company. I still love him, Johnnie. What can I do? Tell me, what I can do?"

Johnnie Laveau comforted her the only way he knew how, driving her desire higher and higher and then helping her to release her tensions and passion in a shattering explosion of joy and triumph and trembling.

Later he left the bed, pushed the comforters over her and dressed quickly. It was still dark, but dawn would be coming within two hours. Johnnie Laveau knew that he had been used by Martha Dyke tonight. But she had more than repaid him for his embarrassment at the dinner.

By doing so, she had given him another clue, perhaps another way that he might be able to serve his mistress. He understood now how she felt. There was a man — this

Allen Cornelius in Seattle. He would see what he could find out about the man.

Johnnie knew that this night had been a one-time passionate explosion which would never be repeated or referred to. But he had gained more knowledge about his charge, and perhaps some day he could help her find the true happiness that she longed for.

He drove his rig away quietly, and at his own small house, checked the condition of his storeroom. Everything was exactly as he had left it. He loosened the silk thread around the doll, but still left it tight enough to be effective.

He only had time to prepare a quick breakfast and change out of his formal evening clothes before it was time to drive to Mrs. Dyke's house. If she wasn't ready, he would wait for her.

CHAPTER SIXTEEN

Martha had awakened at six o'clock and drifted back to sleep. She came awake half an hour later when Mrs. Larson banged pans in the kitchen. Usually Mrs. Larson was as quiet as a soft padded cat. It was past the time Martha should be up and moving. The whole thundering force of what she did last night came pounding down on her. She had made love to Johnnie Laveau! She could barely stand to think of it — not because he was a Negro, not because he was her employee — but just because she had let down, relaxed, given in so easily. And it all had been her idea. She was not used to casual sex, and it offended her now, just thinking about it. Her mother would simply faint dead away if she ever suspected.

Poor Mother! She was probably upset enough about last night, when Martha had violated one of the unwritten rules of San Francisco high society by entertaining a

Negro at a social event. Her father would probably chuckle at her boldness, at her slap in the face of high society, but he wasn't wrapped up in it the way her mother was. He would understand that she was trying to cut the apron strings, to tell her mother that she wanted to run her own life and pick her own friends.

She was sure the "nice" people of San Francisco wold now forever consider her just a little wild, a bit strange and unconventional, to say the least. But she didn't care about them. Maybe Priscilla had the right idea, after all.

What now? Sleep until noon? Avoid Johnnie?

She bounced out of bed, dressed quickly and didn't stop for breakfast. "I overslept," she called to Mrs. Larson. "I'll have some food sent in at the office." When she looked out the front door she saw Johnnie waiting with the rig. She was about twenty minutes late.

Martha stopped before opening the door. Oh, dear! How could she greet Johnnie this morning, what could she say? How should she act? Her tone? Her bearing? Each time she moved now she felt a slight strain on parts of her body that hadn't been active

lately, a constant reminder of the night before.

Martha pulled the door open and walked
down the steps. She waved at Johnnie as
she always did. Act naturally, she told
herself, like any morning. Never look back.
Act as if nothing happened last night.

When she got to the carriage, Johnnie was
there as usual, helping her step into the rig.
Then he climbed up himself. He was the
same as always, polite, reserved, proper,
friendly. If he had sniggered or laughed,
even grinned knowingly, she would have
died. She could read nothing in his bland
face.

Now what should she say? The seconds
ticked past. He started the rig and they
moved toward downtown.

"Did you get moved into your new office
yesterday?" she asked at last, finding a safe
subject.

"Yes, Ma'am. Too big, one guy me."

"It's right for you, Johnnie. Remember,
you're an executive."

There, it was done, the first words, now
the rest would be easy. Natural, keep it all
natural. But she shouldn't chatter like a
blackbird. Easy but not nervous.

At the office there were a thousand things
to do. She realized that she was crowding in

on the proper duties of her two assistant managers. She called them both into her office and told them so.

"I'm sorry, but I've been interfering, getting into your areas of responsibility. Why should I do it, when I hire you to do the job? Now I'll check closer on how your jobs are progressing. But any time I don't think it's going the way it should, I'll drag you both on the carpet. That means you help out each other, make suggestions, work together. Hadley, I'm going to put the advertising department under your control. You'll come to me only for broad campaign direction, timing and general approach approval. Priscilla, you'll have personnel answer to you. Establish general policy and maintain your supervision there." She smiled. "I'm trying to get this old ship sailing so well that I can take a week's vacation."

She had said it on a whim, not really sure that she meant it or why she had let it out. True, she had been thinking about taking some time off.

Last night's experience had left a mark, opened old desires and passions that she knew now she could not bury forever. But the central force behind them was not Johnnie. She knew that she had used him again, this time used his powerful body to bring her pleasure, to ignite the smoldering coals of her own desires. She simply was not designed to be a widow — at least not for long.

She sat at her desk and looked out past the open green drapes to the north. Allen was up there. Allen was married. But he was her one true love. Perhaps she could take a vacation to Seattle and go to the company offices and just watch him without making contact. She could observe him without letting him know who she was. It sounded exciting, but she realized at once that it would be impractical. How could she do that? Snatch glimpses of him from across the street as he arrived for work? Go into his office, apparently by mistake, and then rush out? Maybe follow him to a restaurant in the evening when he ate out? No, no — they were all impractical ideas.

If she went to Seattle, she would have to see him. She could meet him and tell him she worked for the same firm, in the Pemberton Mercantile, and was on holiday. Yes, that might work. But would he recognize her? He might not. But then she remembered that torrid night of love-making and knew that he would know who she was in an instant. She hadn't changed that much in three years. No he would recognize her, he would be unmoved, and she would break down and cry and beg him to . . .

Martha shook her head and looked down at her desk. She had more than a day's work to do, but somehow it wasn't getting done. She called in Johnnie and asked him to have someone get the company coastwise steamer schedule for the whole area from San Diego up to Seattle. He left without a change of expression.

If there were only somebody she could talk to about it. She looked at Priscilla's door. That noon they went to lunch together. The women talked for two hours. Martha laid out the whole situation honestly. Priscilla thought about it for only a minute.

"Martha, I can't advise you what you should do. All I can do is say what I would do if it were me in the same situation. If I were you, I'd have my bags packed before dinner and be off for Seattle on the morning boat. Why fool around? You've admitted that he's your first true love, and that you still feel for him whenever you think about him. You're still in love with him, that's easy to see. He might not even have that wife any more, for all you know. One of those Washington lumberjacks might have run off with her."

"But if he *is* still married . . ."

"Take the tough problems one at a time, Martha. You don't even know how he feels. Maybe he's just as much in love with you as you are with him. Who knows what might happen? We can run things for a while at the store. Go."

Back at the office, Martha made up her mind. She had to go to Seattle. She had to find out how Allen felt about her, one way or the other. If he were still happily married, if he had a family and was content, she would come back to town and try to put her life back together, and go on without him. But if he still loved her . . .

Martha let all emotion drain from her. She looked out the window, then walked calmly back to her desk. She would need two weeks to put everything together here and get the store running smoothly. Until then, she would not think about Seattle or Allen. She had a thousand jobs to do, and they must be done correctly, and soon.

In the next two weeks, Martha worked feverishly. She put the store into shape so it would run without her for a time, then told her father that she was going to Seattle for a two-week vacation.

"Excellent idea, Martha. You need a good

vacation. And while you're there, you can take a look at our firm's facilities and operations. Seattle's still a small village, but it has a great growth potential as a seaport and as the major city in the territory of Washington."

Martha said she would bring back a report.

Johnnie obtained passes for them both on the coastal steamer *Astoria,* and they were ready to go. It had been taken as a matter of course that Johnnie would go along as her bodyguard. Priscilla took Martha to lunch the day before she sailed.

"I'm so glad you're going," Priscilla said. "You have every right to see him, to find out if you still love him. He may be a very different person now. You never can tell."

Martha smiled. "I knew Allen for only a few months, but I'm sure he'll be the same man I fell in love with. He's . . . I don't know how to describe it . . . he's *quality* . . . a gentleman . . . *educated.* Do you know what I mean?"

Priscilla laughed. "I know a girl in love when I hear her chattering away about a man." Priscilla squeezed her hand. "I'm sure everything is going to work out just beautifully. Don't worry about a thing."

■ ■ ■ ■

The next morning the boat left promptly at ten. She was a new boat, tested and proved and heading for Seattle non-stop. The ship was designed to carry over a hundred passengers as well as its huge holds full of freight. The steamer had quickly become the fastest method of transportation along the coast. Martha had no idea how long it would take to go to Seattle. She was in the "CC" stateroom, which she found out was the "Company Class" cabin, reserved for high officials in the Pacific Steamship company. The cabin was almost ten feet square, luxurious compared to the normal cabins. She read steadily for three days, then slept, and was anxious when the big boat turned into the Strait of Juan De Fuca early one morning, and then threaded its way south through Puget Sound past dozens of islands to the port of Seattle.

Martha wasn't sure if there would be a reception committee or not and was relieved when she found none. She was somewhat disappointed at the size of the town, but the miles and miles of evergreen-covered islands and hills on the mainland fascinated her. She had no idea so many trees existed anywhere on earth. There were many more trees within the city than there were people. About five thousand souls, her father had told her, a kind of small frontier town that was just starting to think about growing up, with lumber as the backbone of the economy.

Johnnie walked behind her down the gangplank to the dock where he had already put their luggage into a short wagon with two seats. There were no regular hacks in sight. They had reserved rooms at the Evergreen Hotel in a letter on the last steamboat, and their rooms were ready.

The ship had arrived off Juan de Fuca a little before daylight, and had waited until dawn to work its way through the islands and down to Seattle. Now the time was just after noon, so Martha asked Johnnie if he would meet her in the dining room. He shook his head.

"No ma'am, would not like. Me fella stay away. You not even see, *mon,* but fella watch you."

With that he walked down the steps and left her. Martha had a momentary feeling that she had been abandoned, but she knew he would be around the instant she really needed him. She also knew that many hotel dining rooms had signs that indicated no

Indians, Negroes or Chinamen were admitted. Martha had a quick lunch, then found a weatherbeaten cab in front of the hotel and asked to be taken to the Pacific Steamship and Trading Company office on Fir Street.

The address proved to be that of a plain two-story wooden building a block from the waterfront. The lower story had been recently painted and it had the looks of a bridegroom in very grubby company. She stepped down from the hack, gave the driver a quarter, and walked into the building. The interior was immaculate. Floors freshly varnished and polished, the woodwork well painted and cared for. She found herself in a lobby with a desk and a pleasant young woman greeting her.

"Yes, ma'am. How may I help you?"

Her manner was proper, friendly, yet businesslike.

"I'd like to see Mr. Cornelius."

Her smile brightened. "You must be Mrs. Dyke."

Martha nodded.

"Mr. Cornelius said you might be coming in today. He told us you're a very important person and that we should take good care of you." She rang a bell and a boy of about twelve came from a door to the right.

"Henry, please take Mrs. Dyke up to Mr. Cornelius' office." She turned back to Martha. "Welcome to Seattle, Mrs. Dyke. We hope you like our friendly little town."

Martha said she hoped so too and followed the boy up stairs that had been hidden behind the doors to the left. The steps were wooden, well varnished and waxed, and had a strip of carpet up the center. On the second floor the same well-kept condition of the building prevailed. The boy stopped in front of large double doors with the Pacific Steamship and Trading Company crest carved in them in deep relief. The boy held open one door and indicated she should go inside.

Martha hesitated. What in the world was she doing? Then she heard someone move inside and she walked quickly through the opening trying to look very much like a businesswoman dressed in her conservative clothes and ready for a conference.

Inside the room, she found a woman seated at a small desk, where she worked on a set of books. The attractive girl looked up and smiled.

"Mrs. Dyke?" When Martha nodded, the woman rose and led her to the far door, which she opened, and let Martha walk into the inner office. She stared across the open space to the desk. Standing behind it was Allen. She wanted to cry out and run to him with her arms wide, but she held back.

"Mr. Cornelius. It's been a long time."

He smiled and the memories flooded back over her, draining her resolve, turning her legs into soft sticks of clay. She had no idea how she kept standing. He laughed softly, the way she remembered he used to do.

"Yes, Martha — Mrs. Dyke — it has been a long time." He looked at the girl near the door. "Thank you, Miss Renne." The woman retreated and closed the office door.

Martha hadn't moved since she had first seen him. He walked around the desk and motioned to a soft leather couch at the side of the office where a window opened. It had a view of the docks and the port beyond.

"Martha, please sit down. We have a lot to catch up on."

"Yes, we do. So much. I don't know where to start." She made it to the couch and sank onto it gratefully.

"You haven't changed a bit, Martha, except you're even more beautiful now than you were, if that's possible." A change came over his face. "Martha, I was so angry when my ship sailed that night. They woke me at three a.m. I had four hours of work before sailing with the tide. There were a thousand little jobs to get done, and I had to do them, see that we had full kegs of water, check the rations — vital duties. I simply had no time to get word to you, and I couldn't leave the ship. I didn't desert you, Martha. I swear to God. I wanted to come back to you that morning almost more than I wanted life itself. I should have left the ship, jumped overboard and swum for shore!"

"Oh, no!"

"Yes, I should have. But I wasn't as strong as I wanted to be. So I did my jobs, and hoped there would be time to get ashore. Then the anchor was coming up and we were moving. After Hawaii we were hit with a battering storm and had to turn back, then come on back to San Francisco for repairs. It had been only four months or so, and you were gone — married and gone. My heart broke again that day when I found out. I roamed the streets for a week. I was drunk and robbed, my shoes stolen. I just didn't care. My captain found me and locked me in the brig until I sobered up, then he made me see that by killing myself I would lose any chance of ever knowing you again.

"At last I realized that he was right. I transferred to shore duty and came here to Seattle. But I never could forget about you,

Martha. Then a year ago I heard that you were home and safe and . . . a widow. But by that time I was married and had a son."

She leaned toward him. He sat on the couch and moved toward her. Allen reached out and touched her cheek, then her chin. She felt fire at each contact.

"The most beautiful girl in the world. I must have been out of my mind not to jump that ship as soon as I knew we were moving!"

Then they were in each other's arms, clinging to each other, bodies pressed tightly. He turned his head, found her lips and the kiss was a joy like she had never known before, pure and true, with the promise of unending bliss. She treasured the moments and at last he eased away from her and dropped his arms.

"I'm sorry. I shouldn't have done that."

"Oh, yes! I'm glad you did."

"But you're forgetting, Martha. I'm married, I have a wife and two small children. We can't go back to the way it was. We never can! Martha, when I asked to come to Seattle I talked to your father. He knows my father in Boston. The family sent me out here for punishment. I told your father the whole incident and he chuckled and understood. I told him that I had worshipped you and hoped to court you, but that now there was no chance. I wanted either to go back to Boston or to get away from San Francisco. So he sent me up here to Seattle, where I could build up the company's operations, establish a new shipping point, and where I'd be well away from you when you came back.

"I'd been here only a few months when I first met Linda Sue. I was in the Falling Axe bar for a drink when a young girl came in and marched right up to the barkeep and asked if Mr. Milligan Cogson was there. The barman didn't know the name, so he bellowed for quiet and asked if anyone knew the man. A deputy sheriff said he knew him, he had helped bury him a week before, after he was killed in a knife fight. The girl fainted. Nobody would touch her. So at last I picked her up and took her over to Doc Warnick's office.

"Doc kept her for a few days, but said there wasn't anything the matter with her, just shock at hearing about her father's death. Besides that she didn't have any money, no relatives in town, and no way to get back to New Orleans, where she had lived."

Allen looked away. He knew he wasn't telling this the way he wanted to. She had to understand exactly what happened.

"Well, one thing led to another, and I got her a job working at a little cafe down the street. She was grateful, and two months later we were married. By then everyone said you and the *Pacific Gem* had been lost at sea. I didn't think I'd ever see you again."

He reached out and kissed her lips tenderly, then pulled back.

"I still can't believe you're here. Do you ever think about that last afternoon we spent together in that little rented room? I do, often, and dream about what it might have been like if only . . ."

"Oh, yes, Allen, yes. I have remembered that afternoon dozens of times, and I shall for the rest of my life! It's what helps me keep going sometimes when things are really bad. It helps me when I want to have you with me, with your arms around me."

He moved back a little, surprised at the intensity of her reaction. "Martha, we just can't talk this way, can't even think this way. Linda Sue is a kind, gentle woman. She's a southern girl, and while she hasn't had a lot of education, she's bright and happy all the time. I'm very fond of her, and of course, there are the children to consider."

"Do you love Linda Sue, Allen?"

"She's my wife. My *wife.* You have no right

to ask that question, Martha. Not even you have that right."

"But I would have been your wife, if that boat hadn't sailed that morning. It would have been *me* loving you and taking care of you and giving you children."

He shook his head, his face more stern than she had ever seen it. "But it *isn't you.* It's Linda Sue. We were married and we've lived here in Seattle, where I'm now the manager of our operation. I've been instructed to give you the grand tour of our facilities, such as they are."

"But, Allen, what about us? What about you and me and our love for each other?"

Allen scowled, stood and paced to the window and back. "Us? You and me? Mrs. Dyke, we have no joint future. There is no *us.* We can be friends. We can respect each other. We can be business associates — but that is all. The gods have decreed that we shall be separated, so we shall be! Why else should the ship sail so quickly without warning? Why else would a waif be thrown in front of me and win my protection and my love? It's a plan, a master plan that we dare not challenge."

Martha felt her whole being torn apart by his words. It was as if she had no reason for living. Without Allen, now that she had found him, now that she had kissed him again . . . no, there must be some middle ground, some alternative course.

"Allen, do you really believe all those things?"

He walked to his desk, then to the window, before he came back, standing over her. "Does it really matter, Martha? I'm married. I have legal and moral responsibilities, and a duty to the company. Do you think your father would permit me to remain in my capacity with the company? Do you think he would permit me to have any contact with you if I deserted my family? You know he wouldn't. He could ruin me in a dozen ways. Your father is an extremely powerful man. There is no circumstance that will cause me to leave my family. So there is nothing we can do. There is simply no *us*. Perhaps the fates . . ."

"But, Allen, I still love you with all my heart. I was married, too. It didn't dilute my love for you. I've come back to you, Allen, to beg you, to plead with you —"

"Martha!" he said sharply, and caught her hands. "Martha, there is simply nothing either of us can do. Believe me, I've been over the situation a hundred times. There is *absolutely* no other solution than the one we have right now. You must stay in San

Francisco, and I must stay here." He walked back to the window, then went to the connecting door and opened it.

"Miss Renne, will you send a messenger to my home and tell my wife that Mrs. Dyke did come, and that my assistant manager and myself will be having dinner with her tonight."

He closed the door and went back to his desk where he picked up a letter.

"Allen, I didn't come up here to meet your office staff or take a tour of your buildings."

"But you will have one. You must understand, Martha. We're not quite on the same level we were three years ago. I'm no longer a junior officer on board one of your father's boats. I'm now the general manager of Pacific Steamship operations in Seattle. We both have certain responsibilities to the company. And when the president of the corporation sends me a letter instructing me to give a complete tour of my facilities, I damn well am going to do just that. Besides the tours, I'm sure we'll have lots of time for reminiscing. Later tonight I'd like you to come to my home and meet my family."

"No! I'm afraid I wouldn't like that, Allen.

No, I won't meet your wife or your children."

He shrugged. "All right. I think I understand. But I hope you can see that this must be a totally business relationship. There is no chance that under the present situation there can be anything more than friendship between us. Do you understand?"

Martha stood, her head spinning with arguments, with anger, with the terrible guilty feeling that she was throwing herself at this man and he was rejecting her totally.

"Allen, I understand that the fates have dealt unfairly with us, and now is our chance to even the score. I understand that you are respectful of my father's power, and that you are also afraid of his money. But I have enough money for both of us to live on — here, in Boston, in New York — for the rest of our lives! Money can solve almost any problem, Allen."

"No, Martha! Could your money give me back my self-respect if I deserted my wife and family? Could money help my conscience any? Could money and security give me a sense of accomplishment, knowing that I was successful on my own talents? Martha, there is a great deal that money can't buy, that property and power and a bank account will never help a person to attain. And I think you know that. Let's have our meeting, remember what our tender moments were like, and even think of what might have been. But that's all we can do. I'll take you on the complete tour, and I mean from every ship's locker and warehouse to our sawmill. Then you'll sail for home with your heart free of me, and I pray to all the gods that you will find a happy and fulfilled life."

Martha turned away from his honest, righteous stare. "Allen, I'm not used to being told 'no' to an order. But if I had thought it through, this is how I should have expected you to act. You've been a dream, a vision of perfection to me, for three years. How else is a dream supposed to act but courageously, strongly, perfectly? Yes, I should have known. I'll be proud to go along on your guided tours, only because you will be there, and it will give me a few more moments to be near you. After the tours are over, we'll see. We'll have to live it one day at a time. Who knows? The gods may not be through meddling in our lives yet."

He smiled, knowing that he had won, at least for now. The final arguments would come later, and he was not so certain about them. God, but she was beautiful — so ap-

372

pealing. She had been marvelous at making love, even the first time. No! He couldn't go on thinking that way. He had responsibilities.

"Well, now that our little problem is settled, let's get your tour started with our office building. You may have noticed that we have more improvements done on the inside so far than on the outside. But we're working on that, too. We have a definite budgeted amount of money each month for building improvements, and we use every penny."

The tour continued, with Allen explaining where each department was, what it did, and how they were combining services for each of the divisions under one roof. For example, bookkeeping had been centralized for all of the operations, and in doing so, Allen estimated that he was saving over five thousand dollars a year.

Martha listened, but mostly she watched Allen, marveling at how little he had changed. She memorized his face again, each line and shape, each smile. His hair was combed differently now, more controlled. There was nothing that would change his good smile — so open, so concerned, so intense. His face displayed his complete range of feelings as if it were a showcard.

Just after five, they came back to Allen's office, where his second in command waited. Caleb Jones stood quickly as they entered and Allen introduced them. Caleb was about forty, had a paunch, and his hair was creeping away from his forehead.

"It's an honor to meet you, Mrs. Dyke. We hear a lot of good things that you have been doing with the Mercantile. Perhaps you could give us some suggestions while you're here."

She thanked the man, and noted that he was sincere in his compliment. She made a note to remember his name.

For dinner they went to a small seafood cafe which had a long table loaded with every kind of cooked seafood available in the ocean and rivers for fifty miles around. There was giant crab, a dozen kind of filleted fish, clams, oysters, prawns, and in the center of the table a freshly caught and baked forty-pound salmon. Martha had never eaten so much seafood at once in her life, and it was delicious.

After the meal, Caleb excused himself, and Allen drove Martha back to the Evergreen Hotel. They sat in the buggy for a moment, looking at each other.

"Would you like to come up to my room

for a minute?"

"I'll see you safely to your door," he said, tying the reins and helping her down. The room was on the second floor and he walked beside her, at ease, as if he met old lovers every day. In truth he was in turmoil inside. He had to maintain his composure at all costs. He had to be the controlling factor.

At her door she unlocked it and pushed it open.

"Would you like to come in for another short minute?"

Allen shook his head. "No, I don't think that would be wise." He bent and kissed her cheek, and straightened quickly. "I think that had better do for tonight. I'll have a carriage here for you at nine in the morning. Tomorrow we take a tour of the docks, the ships and our lumber warehouses."

Before she could reply, he said good night and walked away from her down the hall.

Neither Martha nor Allen saw Johnnie Laveau standing on the back steps watching the procedure. He had kept her in sight as soon as she left the Steamship offices, through the dinner and the trip home.

Johnnie grinned as he saw Allen Cornelius walking down the main stairway. Now, there was one smart man, Johnnie decided.

In her room, Martha closed the door and

locked it, leaving the skeleton key in the lock and partly turned so no one could push the key out of the lock and open the door. She knew that two or three keys would probably open all the locks in the hotel.

She walked to her bed and sat down, unsure of her reaction to Allen's walking away from her. He had not trusted himself to come into her hotel room, or even to look at the bed. Martha sensed that it was a contest she was in, a battle over Allen Cornelius with a woman she had never even met. But how could she compete for another woman's husband? She didn't know. She hoped she could be alone with Allen. She knew that if she could be in his arms for just a few minutes the old desire would swell up in him too. She knew she shouldn't be thinking this way. It was wicked and evil. But how else could she think? What other weapons did she have to use? Certainly she had no marriage vows and no children.

She wondered just what tomorrow would bring. More touring, more inspections, more reports she would need to give to her father when she got home. But what about the important part? Tomorrow would Allen show any signs of weakening?

CHAPTER SEVENTEEN

Martha woke early the next morning, lay in her bed wide awake and watched the dawn. She had no idea what time it was, nor did she care. The sky through her window looked dull and gray, and when at last she got up she saw that a chill soft rain was falling, almost a mist, it was so fine. The eaves dripped, the dirt street below had changed overnight into a three-inch deep avenue of mud. Horses splashed and slipped as they drew wagons and carriages through the streets.

Martha went back to bed. She had made up her mind that she would not go on any tour today. She would stay in bed and admit no one to her room. If Allen came at nine or nine-thirty, he would find her undressed and absolutely not going on any tour. Then she decided that this might not be the best tactic. No, it would never do. She had been totally rejected by Allen, so she would get dressed, pack, and steal away, take the next ship, of whatever company, that was headed for San Francisco. There must surely be something floating that would be leaving today. She would be on it.

Slowly she got up again, and realized the room was very damp. She saw that the window was open an inch, and quickly closed it. She was shivering, so she got back under the covers. She would get warm first, then she would decide about going home. It would serve him right if she hurried home and told her father what a terrible job Allen was doing up here. Yes, that would serve him right.

No. Then her father would find out that he was doing a remarkable job, and he would remember that Allen had talked to him about her. Her father would mark it up to an emotional outburst by an unstable woman, and decide that she certainly shouldn't be running the mercantile. She could lose her position.

Well, what *was* she going to do? If he would only listen to reason. He had married that girl just to help her out, so why couldn't he unmarry her? There should be such a thing as prior claim. She had seen Allen first. She had been courted first. She had made love with him first.

Silently, Martha Pemberton Dyke began to cry. The tears came, spilling down her cheeks, dripping onto the comforters. It was simply not fair! How could that poor southern white girl come up here and steal away Allen? It was outrageous!

She was still sobbing five minutes later when a knock sounded on her door.

"Go away! I'm sleeping," she called loudly. The knock came again. Martha screeched out the message twice again before she threw back the covers and ran to the door.

"Go away. I'm not going on any tour in the rain!"

"Shore, *mon.* This fella no tour. This fella bring you some hot breakfast."

It was Johnnie. She unlocked the door.

"Johnnie, now you wait until I'm back in bed, all right?"

"Shore, *mon.*"

She called a moment later and he came in with an enormous breakfast, three hot cakes with two sunny-side-up eggs on top, six strips of thick cut bacon and three rounds of sausage, hot butter and syrup, scalding hot coffee and three pieces of toast with a scoop of blackberry jam.

Martha sat up in bed, surprised by all the food.

"Cook, he say, lady keep up strength,"

Johnnie said as he put the tray in front of her. From a pocket he took out silverware and a cup. She spread the butter, poured on the syrup, filled her coffee cup from the pot and began to eat.

Between sips of hot coffee she frowned at him. "You go right over to that Allen Cornelius, and tell him I said I'm not going on any guided tour in this terrible rain."

Johnnie nodded and walked to the door.

"No, wait, Johnnie, that might not sound right. Tell him I'll go on the tour the minute the rain stops."

Johnnie put his hand on the door knob.

"No, not that, either."

Johnnie stopped, leaned against the wall with his arms crossed over his chest.

"Tell him I've got to go home on the noon boat. Then find out if there is a noon boat and if we can get on board."

Johnnie watched her. "Sure?"

She shook her head. "No, no, Johnnie, I'm not sure of anything. It's just that damn wife of his. If only he wasn't married and everything, it would be perfect. She's just some little trash he picked up off a barroom floor. Oh, damn, I wish he had never married her! It would have been so good. Johnnie, you must know by now that I love this man with all my heart. I just don't know what to do.

Maybe I should go have a talk with her and order her to take her two brats and run back to Louisiana where she belongs. She's just some trashy little gutter maid, and she stole my love."

Johnnie looked at her, frowning, unable to offer her any help.

"Johnnie, sometimes I wish she would just wither up and blow away in a puff of dust. Wouldn't that be grand? Wouldn't that solve all my problems?" She laughed and shook her head. "But it isn't every day that a miracle happens. Allen and his gods have really complicated my life this time. So you suppose there are a whole group of super beings up in the sky somewhere, playing with our lives, moving us around like puppets on a string and making us do anything they want us to?"

He didn't answer, just watched her with his big black eyes.

Martha took a deep breath, realizing too late that it brought her breasts up pressing tightly against the thin flannel nightgown.

"I just don't know what I'm going to do, Johnnie. I'm so confused and mixed up." She chewed on a strip of bacon and shook her head. Then she looked up at him. "Did you have breakfast?"

He nodded.

"Like this?"

"Two like this."

She laughed and went on eating. At last a plausible plan formed in her mind without any scatter-brained emotional outbursts.

"Johnnie, go see Mr. Cornelius and tell him I have a bad cold and I don't think I should be out in the rain today. Tell him to come to the hotel and maybe we could talk in the lobby or in front of the big fireplace."

Johnnie didn't wait this time. He turned and was through the door before she could countermand it. She thought of going over and locking the door behind him, but she didn't, and smiled instead, hoping. She checked her pure white flannel nightgown to be sure the neck was buttoned and both sleeves were neat. Then she finished as much of her breakfast as she could. It was twice what she could eat. She put the tray on a small night stand and snuggled down in the bed, feeling warmer now from the coffee and the hot cakes, and because she knew that Allen would surely be coming over and knocking on her door.

Johnnie ran lightly down the hall to the stairs after leaving Mrs. Dyke's door. He walked out of the hotel and to the Pacific Steamship office through the light rain. There he gave the message to Mr. Cornelius's secretary, who said she would take it right in to him.

Outside the building, Johnnie paused, thinking. His mistress was unhappy. He didn't like to see her that way. It was his responsibility to help her stay happy. The more he thought of it, the more he concentrated on the one major problem. But he had brought nothing with him, only a small leather case filled with certain essentials for defensive uses. That would not help.

He ran back to an alley across from the Evergreen Hotel and leaned back out of the rain in an overhang. There was much he could do — a great deal he could do. If one person was unhappy, why not make another person unhappy?

He had seen a general store and an apothecary shop. What he needed was a good herb store, but he knew there were none in Seattle. He thought and planned as he waited. There should be some simple substitutes he could use. The potency was not the important element now. It would only be a gentle warning, and if she were from New Orleans it would fit perfectly.

Johnnie leaned back out of the rain. He was cold, but he had been cold ever since he sailed from Jamaica. Ten minutes later a carriage pulled up at the Evergreen and

Allen Cornelius got out and went inside. Someone followed him with yellow slickers and rain boots. Johnnie grinned. Mrs. Dyke would be going on that tour after all. She would be in good hands for several hours. Plenty of time. He only needed an hour or two. Johnnie grinned and ran toward the general store, heedless of the light drizzle.

It was twenty minutes after Johnnie had left her hotel room before Martha heard a knock on her door.

"Yes, who is it?" she called.

"Allen."

"Come right in."

He walked in and started to close the door, then saw that she was still in bed and left it open.

"Oh, I thought you would be dressed."

"I'm completely covered," she said, sitting up in bed. "You didn't really mean we'd take the tour in this rain?"

"We don't let a little dampness bother us up here," he said. "Sometimes it rains during some part of 250 days a year."

"Really? Is that why the trees grow so well?"

"Yes. I really shouldn't be here, you know."

"Why not?"

"Because you're . . ."

"I'm ill in bed with a cold."

"It must have been a sudden cold."

"Yes. With a sick headache, upset stomach and stuffy nose."

"And no appetite, I would guess, after you just ate most of the logger's special breakfast." Allen couldn't help but laugh. "Martha, it won't work on me. I remember a few of your little tricks, remember? Now you have exactly twenty minutes to get dressed ready for the street. I have a raincoat and galoshes for you, and a rainhat. You won't get a drop of rain on you. I'll meet you in the lobby in exactly twenty minutes. *And you be there!*"

He walked to the door, went out and closed it.

Martha threw a pillow at the door. She fumed for ten seconds, then got up and dressed quickly, putting on a heavier dress than she had worn yesterday, one with a shorter skirt that didn't quite drag the floor, and sturdy shoes. Then she chose a short brown brocaded satin cape that was trimmed with satin ribbon ruching and fine gauze on the shoulders. It had a high decorated collar with a black satin ribbon bow in front.

Martha added a plumed hat in matching color and marched down the hall to the stairs and the lobby. Allen met her at the bottom of the steps grinning, and led her to the side where they traded her plumed hat for an oil slicker hat and a brown oiled slicker poncho and rubber overshoes too big for her.

"Now you could walk to Portland and not get a drop of rain on you," Allen said. She had not spoken since she came down, only watched him as he tended to her wet weather needs, and at once she was glad she had capitulated. At least she would be with him all day.

The tour was one dreary group of buildings and ships and docks after another. Allen had set up one division to buy, hold and ship lumber from the sawmills to various lumber-hungry towns along the coast. Four of the company's cargo ships were doing nothing but hauling lumber. There was little return cargo, because Seattle was so small and needed little goods. He told Martha that five years before there had been only 1,107 persons living in the whole town of Seattle. If they could gain two thousand persons a year, they would have over eighty thousand persons living in the town by the year 1900.

"Think of it, eighty thousand people! I know that's not as many as San Francisco has in one little section of town, but it would be a tremendous growth for us here."

The rain stopped at noon. They had lunch in a small cafe, and Martha found the food hardly worth eating. In the afternoon, the tour ended at the wharf where the ships were being loaded with raw lumber fresh from the mills which dotted the valleys behind Seattle. In almost every ravine she could see a column of smoke that came from what Allen called the "burn pile."

"There has always been a high need for first-class lumber in the West," Allen said. "To help supply that, we've bought one of the better sawmills, and Pacific Steamship is now producing lumber out there for our own ships to haul. It's a new venture, and we're all mighty proud of it. If you have no objections, I'd like to show the mill to you."

"I don't want to see anything else, Allen. I'm cold and I'm wet and I'm tired. Please take me back to my hotel."

"Then how can you give your father a complete report? This is the last of it. Just a half-hour's ride out to the mill, and a quick look around. I'll have you home for a change and then a big steak dinner before eight."

"Allen, I never could win arguments with you. I especially didn't win that last afternoon in San Francisco. You really raped me that day! Did you realize that?"

"Then it was the quietest and most co-operative rape in history. For a while I thought *I* was the one being forced." He frowned. "Let's not talk about that, thrilling as it was. This is business time, all business, right?"

"Anything you say, Allen. Just anything. See how easy I am to get along with?" She wanted to push over beside him in the little covered carriage, to snuggle closer and hope that he would put his arms around her, but it didn't happen.

All day she had been hoping for some break, for some change in Allen's attitude, but there was none. No hug, no quick kiss, no intimate or personal talk. Only business, business and more business. She was so sick of docks and buildings and ships that she wanted to scream. But she didn't.

Allen whacked the reins on the black and they speeded up, rolling down Fir, then onto Front and at last another street that had no name and quickly became a lane that headed south out of town and along the shores of Lake Washington. The country became heavily wooded, the road little more than a one-buggy trail as they wound farther into the woods. Two miles down the road, they rounded the bottom of the lake and turned inland, where they came to a fork in the trail. The one to the left seemed to be the better traveled. Lumber wagons had to come from the mill. But as Allen remembered they had turned to the right at this point. He slanted the carriage to the right.

"Now, we have just two miles more up this road and we should be at the mill. I came out here about a month ago, and I'm anxious to see the progress." He sniffed. "I can even smell the burner smoke. We should see it before long."

They drove through the heavy fir and hemlock forest. At some points the trees touched the top of the buggy. The trail suddenly changed, becoming less traveled-looking. Allen worried about it for a moment, then shrugged. This had to be the way. A cloud blew over, dropping a little more rain on them, then it was gone and the sun came out again, but low in the sky. Martha guessed it must be nearly four o'clock. It had been a long and exhausting day. She would not have any trouble sleeping that night, she was sure.

Allen looked concerned. "I don't remember it being quite this far," he said. "There should have been some kind of old building along here somewhere. These damn little trails all look so much alike, out here."

They drove another five minutes, then Allen stopped the buggy and looked around. Everywhere was virgin timber, Douglas fir, a few red and Port Orford cedar, lots of hemlock and an occasional stand of noble fir with their pine cones standing straight up on the tips of the branches like lookouts.

"Another half-mile," Allen said. "Then, if we don't come to that old building, we'll turn back. I could have sworn this was the right trail."

They continued, and the forest closed in on them more. At last they saw a building ahead and Allen sighed with relief. It was a two-story house, but it hadn't been used for a long time. Half the windows were broken out.

"Dammit!" Allen exploded. "This is the wrong road! Now we'll have to go all the way back."

He began to turn the rig around in the front yard that had grown up with ferns and small trees. Martha yelped when she saw a rifle barrel extend through one of the broken windows. At the far end of the house another long gun pointed at them. Directly in front of the horse a man jumped out waving a double-barreled shotgun.

"Hold it right there," the man with the

scattergun barked. He was big, bearded, roughly dressed, and a cigar stuck out from his clenched teeth.

Allen swore under his breath.

"Look, sorry, we got on the wrong road. We are looking for the new Pemberton mill. I'll just turn around and leave you alone."

"I said hold it, goddammit! Now get down from that rig!"

"What? We're just lost, that's all."

"Loudmouth, you want two loads of buckshot messing up your fancy suit? Get out of there right now!"

Allen's face whitened, but he stepped down from the buggy, motioning for Martha to stay where she was.

"I don't see the problem," Allen said. "We're looking for the Pemberton sawmill, and we simply took the wrong turn."

"Yeah, probably. Get the lady down, too. Need to take a gander at her." The cigar tilted upward and Allen stepped back to the carriage and reached up to help Martha down. She had taken off the slicker, and when she stepped down, the short brocaded cape seemed entirely out of place in the rugged outdoor setting.

The big man with the cigar laughed when he saw Martha.

"Yeah, oh, yeah. I think you two better

stay with us."

Martha wanted to scream. The pattern seemed all too familiar, like she was reliving her experiences on Rapango. She decided that a strong vocal attack couldn't hurt anything.

"Who is in charge here?" she demanded loudly, her voice loaded with authority.

The cigar drooped, the big man walked up in front of her and lifted her chin with a grubby finger. Her hand flew out, slapping his face before he could stop it. He started to slap her back, then held up, his face boiling with anger.

"I'm the boss. What the hell you care?"

"Because I'm prepared to do business. You're obviously outlaws coming to or going from a holdup of some kind. I'll simply make a better bid, offer you more money. That is what you're after. I'll pay you five thousand dollars to put your guns away and let us drive out of here."

"Five *thousand*?" The big man pulled off a battered brown hat and scratched his matted hair. "You crazy? Nobody got that kind of money." He scratched his crotch, and Martha pretended not to notice. "Five thousand! 'Course you is all spiffed up fancy, and this guy is driving you around." He worried it, walking around them. No one else had showed himself, but the weapons were still trained on them.

"Even if I did let you go, how I know you wouldn't bring back a sheriff? How could I pick up the money? You ain't got that much with you."

"No, of course not. If I give you my word that I'll bring the money, it will be delivered, with no word to the sheriff."

"Lady, I don't trust you, 'cause I learned the hard way not to trust nobody." He held up his left hand, which had the thumb gone, the fingers twisted. "See that? I trusted a man once and he tried to kill me five minutes later. Left me for dead, he did, and took the money and the horses. No, ma'am, I don't trust no man, woman, child or horse. Now, who the hell is this gent?"

"This is Mr. Allen Cornelius, general manager of Pacific Steamship and Trading Company operations in Seattle. He's an important man in town, and if he doesn't get back to his office before dark there will be search parties out. We told his office we were going to the mill. Before morning there will be two hundred sailors, longshoremen and loggers swarming all over these hills, hunting us."

"Big moose fat chance. Can't he talk for hisself?"

"I most certainly *can* talk. And the lady is right. Your best bet is to take the money and move on. You couldn't rob anything in town and get that much money, not even both banks."

The man with the shotgun jumped, stared at Allen, then motioned with the shotgun.

"Okay, too damn much talk. Billy! Come out and get these two and check 'em for guns, then put 'em in that upstairs lock room. I got me some thinking to do."

Billy came up behind them, opened Allen's coat and took a Derringer from his waistband, then patted his trouser legs but found nothing more. Billy stood in front of Martha and grinned. He was about nineteen, with a thick black moustache and coal-black hair. He was Mexican.

"Senora, you have a gun under all those fancy clothes, yes?"

"No, of course not."

"Then Billy won't have to look." He held a .44 six-gun in his left hand and motioned them to walk ahead of him into the run-down remains of the frame house.

"Save very nice room, best in whole cantina, just for the senora." He never let the muzzle of the pistol wander far from them as he ordered them up the rickety stairs to the second floor and to the middle room.

The door was solid. Billy pushed it open and motioned them inside. The window was intact, nailed shut. There was a striped ticking in one corner filled with straw for a mattress, but no other furniture in the room.

"Amigos, you have a nice stay," Billy said, and closed the door, locking it with as much noise as he could.

Martha looked at Allen, her chin starting to tremble. "Allen, what can we do?"

He shook his head. "I don't know. I'm furious that I didn't stop when I thought we were on the wrong road. I hoped that after just another half-mile we'd be there. It's all my fault, absolutely my fault."

Martha frowned. "We're not assigning the blame, Allen. We have to figure out how to get out of here, how to get free and back to Seattle without being shot full of holes."

"Yes, right." He went to the window and tried it, then saw the nails in the frame. He could break the glass, but that would mean too much noise. The windowsill itself might be less solid.

Martha was testing the door and the walls. In some of the rooms she had seen gaping holes, but these walls were solid. The gang must have kept other prisoners in this room.

"Who are they?" asked Martha.

"We've heard that there was some kind of

gang up north farther, but we've never seen them in Seattle. The banks must be what they'll go for."

Half an hour later they sat on the mattress. There was no possible way out of the room except through the window glass or the door. Everything else was solid, tight, too strong for their bare hands.

"Martha, I can't tell you how sorry I am that I got you into this mess."

"Perhaps your fates are still at work," she said. "Only this afternoon my situation looked hopeless. This at least means we can be together for a while longer. Would you hold me, Allen? I'm starting to get cold and frightened."

He moved beside her, put his arms around her and held her close to him. She tried to relax against him.

"They can't afford to stay around this country very long. What they might do is ride off in the night, rob the bank in the morning and then ride off and leave us here. By the time we can break our way out and get into town they would be halfway to Portland."

"No, I don't think they'll do that, Allen. We saw them. We can both identify two of the gang. They can't just leave us here alive. It's too risky for them."

Allen winced and wanted to scream. How had he got them into this disaster? He had wanted to show the big boss how well he was doing. Damn. He was showing off to a girl, something he hadn't done since he had broken his arm in the fifth grade in Boston. Well, wait until she reported on this one! If either of them were still alive to report anything. He'd be lucky to get a sweeping job in Martha's big store.

They heard horses in the yard below and both ran to the window. All they saw in the fading light were the rumps of four horses riding off into the darkness.

"Have they all left?" asked Martha.

"We could find out." Allen began pounding on the door, then called out loudly. He repeated the pattern four times, and suddenly a voice answered, close to the outside door.

"What the hell's the matter with you?"

"We're hungry. And we need some water. Mrs. Dyke isn't feeling well. Could you bring us some drinking water?"

"I ain't no servant . . . Aw, hell. I guess I can see if there's any left."

A few minutes later, another voice penetrated the door.

"Both of you get on the far side of the room and tap on the window glass. Do you hear me?"

They moved to the window and tapped. "We're both over here," said Allen.

The door lock rattled, then the partition opened, and Billy stood grinning at them, the .44 six-gun in his hand. Behind him came a slender youth with sunken eyes and almost no hair. He laughed and watched them both, then ran toward them. Allen pulled back defensively, ready to do battle.

"Hold it, big man," Billy said, the .44 sighting in on the manager's chest. "Just hold still while Junior here ties your hands behind your back."

"Tie my . . . why?"

"No questions, else you want a chunk of lead in your body."

"Why are you tying him up? He can't get out of this room," Martha said.

Billy turned to her. "Just so we know fer dead rights that he's not trying to go anywhere." Billy frowned in the dim light of the lantern. "Hey, pretty, you part Mexican?"

"Of course not."

"Sure look like it, beautiful."

Junior tied Allen's wrists, then pushed him on the floor and tied his ankles tightly. When that was done, Billy holstered his pistol and walked up to Martha.

"You and me, pretty little chili pepper, we gonna have ourselves a long talk. The honcho done went to look over the lay of the land around those banks, but he didn't say nothing about what to do with you. So you come along now and be a nice little bird."

Junior laughed and pushed Martha toward the door. Billy slapped Junior across the mouth and the slim man with the wild eyes backed off, and let Billy guide Martha down the hall to the next room where a lamp burned. This room had a bed, two chairs, even a dresser. Inside the room Billy pointed to the bed.

"Sit down, pretty lady. You and me gonna have ourselves one fine little party before our great leader returns." He unbuckled his six gun and slid the belt and holster well under the bed and out of reach. Then he pushed the door shut and threw a three inch iron bolt into place.

He peeled out of one shirt, only to show another one under it. Billy walked toward her, his hands pushing the short cape roughly aside.

"Now, pretty senorita, let's see what you've got wrapped up inside all of them expensive clothes."

CHAPTER EIGHTEEN

Martha shrank back, trying to avoid Billy's hands. He was serious. Allen was tied up, the gang's boss was gone, there was no one to stop him. Nobody except her.

"Do you do this often?"

"Do what?" he said grinning, touching her breast until she pulled away.

"Go around robbing people, kidnapping them, pointing guns at them, raping women."

"Shit, I do them things all the time."

"How old are you, Billy?"

"Plenty damn old enough for you. Most twenty, now. Me, I pulled down a girl's bloomers first time when I was fourteen."

His arm curled around her shoulder as he sat beside her on the bed. She could feel his leg hard against hers. His hand pushed under her cape and touched her breast.

Martha faced the situation. She could not prevent him from taking her, he was too strong. So what was left? Could she bargain? Was there anyway she could use him, use herself to help them out of this problem?

"Billy, how about a bargain, a trade?"

"What you got under them clothes that I can't take for free?"

"Cooperation. I can show you some tricks you haven't even heard about. French tricks, I was in Tahiti and some of those natives are fantastic, and the sailors too."

He was cautious. His hand went over her breast, and she didn't shake it away this time. He grinned and began rubbing her gently.

"What you want that I should do in trade?"

"Let us escape. Late tonight, some time after the boss gets back. Leave the door unlocked, or let us go out the window. Anything. We won't do a thing to upset your plans. Just let us get away and back to town. I don't want to die, Billy."

"Hell, you won't die. I let you go, old — the boss would scalp me."

"He doesn't have to know," Martha said. He squeezed her breast hard, but she didn't cry out. "The boss would never know, Billy. If he did, you could put the blame on Junior. He isn't quite right in the head, is he? The boss wouldn't hurt Junior."

"I don't know. Dammit to hell, I just don't know."

Her hand moved over to his inner thigh and began rubbing, then moved higher. He looked down, grinned at her and bent to kiss her. She turned away.

"First our bargain, Billy."

"I don't know. Damn risky." Then he lifted his brows. "It might work if we let Junior have a turn with you, too. He don't get a girl very often."

The thought of it made Martha want to vomit. That crazy man? She turned away gasping for air.

"Hey, he ain't so bad. We can have the lamp down low." His hand penetrated her dress buttons and past two other cloth layers and now lay quietly on the bare flesh of her right breast.

Martha knew her breathing had quickened. She had to make the bargain. It was their only hope. She lifted her hand higher on his thigh until she felt the bulge at his crotch.

"Oh, lordy! Goddamn!" Billy said. He was breathing hard now too. At last he nodded. "All right. It's a bargain. But for both of us."

"Yes, Billy. Both. It's a deal." As she said it she leaned back on the bed and Billy followed her.

Martha tried not to remember what happened next. Her body responded to the man's caresses, to the age-old drives and urgings that the mind had absolutely nothing to do with.

Much later, Billy lay panting and laughing. "Hot damn, never in my life . . . I mean, Jesus, that's about the wildest . . . I didn't know a body would bend that way . . ."

Martha lay there, pulling the dirty comforter over her, suddenly embarrassed. Billy shook his head and pushed it back so he could see her naked.

"I ain't never had one built like you are," Billy said. He bent and nuzzled her breasts with his face. "This is one day I ain't never gonna forget."

Then he dropped down on her and used her body again before he rolled away and dressed. He opened the door bolt and called to Junior. The man came in, his sunken eyes wide in anticipation. When he saw the naked woman lying on the bed, he yelped and dove for her. Billy stopped him and made him strip off his pants first.

Martha had closed her eyes as soon as Junior came in. His bald head and browless eyes terrified her. She turned away and knew he was near her. Then his hands pawed at her body, and she tried to think about pleasant things, about anything but this. She wished she hadn't agreed to the bargain, and for a moment she wanted to scream and throw him off and fight him. Then she remembered that there was no other way. It was this . . . or death. No alternative. She had to do it to save Allen. To save herself.

Vaguely she realized he was lying on her, and that he was taking her. It was a bad dream, only a dream she wouldn't remember. She would let none of it register on her consciousness. She drifted off into another world, where everything was pleasant and pure, everyone was loving and kind, and no one ever hurt another person — or even an animal.

She was barely aware when he screamed and began crying all at once. She knew then that he was through. She remembered Billy pulling Junior off her and pushing him out the door.

She tried to sit up, but couldn't. Billy lifted her. He helped her dress, and she wasn't even sure who he was. He must be Billy. Gradually Martha let her mind come back to a semblance of reality. By the time she was dressed, she blinked and could understand.

Martha looked at him and Billy came into focus. "Now you remember our bargain. Give me a hammer or a bar so we can loosen the window frame."

"Yeah, I'll bring it up later."

"Now, Billy, you made a contract with me. I paid my fee — I paid twice over. Now it's your turn."

He growled, went downstairs and found a hammer, then came up and gave it to her. He took her down the hall and into the dark room where she had been before and locked the door. Billy was grinning. Hell, he'd have some wild tales to tell around the campfire now.

Martha stumbled into the room and almost fell.

"Martha, is that you?"

"Yes."

"Are you all right? Did he hurt you?"

"No, he didn't hurt me, Allen." She knew she should be doing something. What? What should she get started on? Then she remembered the hammer. They had to get the window loose before the others came back, and get away while it was still dark.

"Martha, did he make advances to you, try to kiss you?"

"Allen, I'm all right. Are your hands still tied?"

"Yes. I couldn't get them undone."

"Where are you? Let me work on the ropes." She found him on the mattress and pulled at the knots. She had to do it by feel, and it took a half-hour before she had them loose enough so he could wiggle his hands free. Then he untied his feet. She put the hammer in his hands.

"Look, I talked him into giving me this hammer. All we have to do is use it now to get the nails out of the window, or take off the window frame so we can get the window out and get to the ground and away before the gang gets back."

"How did you get the hammer, Martha?"

"I asked him for it. Now don't ask any more questions, and help me work on this window."

"He did make some advances, didn't he? I knew he would. I'll kill him!"

"Now is a fine time to worry about my honor and my virtue. Aren't you a little bit late?" Martha wished she could see Allen's face. She gave him the hammer, then turned and felt her way to the window. Carefully they worked on the frame, hoping they could loosen it from the inside and take the whole window out of the slot. There was simply no way to find the nails which held the window in place, and they couldn't risk the noise of breaking out the glass.

"If we can get out now, we'll leave before Billy and the other one know what's happening," Martha said. "There must be two more horses out there somewhere."

"Won't they be watching?"

"I don't know. Let's get the thing open first!"

They worked for an hour, but there wasn't enough light to let them figure out what they were doing or what needed to be done. At last they gave up and fell onto the mattress, exhausted.

Martha wondered if Allen would move closer to her, wondered if he would kiss her, even try to caress her. But before she could think about it a second time, she fell asleep. When she woke it was almost morning and she was stiff and sore from the lumpy, hard packed ticking mattress.

With the first light of dawn she was up working on the window frame. One board came off easily now that she could see what she was doing. There was no way she could dig out the nails that held the window to the lower sill. They would simply take the sill out with the window. She took the board off the side and saw that it could be quickly put back in position.

As she worked on the other side, Allen

woke and came to help. His muscle came to the fore and the other side of the window began to loosen. As it got lighter, they saw some of the gang members moving around below. That made their work more difficult. They could pull at the frame board only when no one was in the yard. The window looked down on the front of the yard. Martha counted six men. By mid-morning Allen had the second side of the window frame loose. Now all they had to do was pick the frame and window out in one chunk. They set it all back together so it looked normal, and waited.

Junior brought them food about eleven — beans, venison, stale bread and coffee. They were both so hungry they ate every scrap.

In the afternoon they waited, hoping they would have a chance to slip away to the ground. But how? Martha hadn't thought about that. She looked out the window. It was ten feet to the ground. They could hang by their hands on the window ledge and still be almost six feet to the ground. A fine way to break an ankle. What else? She looked around the room and saw the ticking. If they tore the material in half and knotted it . . . yes. Just before they went out, they would do that. It would make a rope about ten feet long and get them safely to the ground.

Now all they needed was the right time to go out.

Billy came to the door, knocked, and told them in whispers that they would all be there that night — something about a payroll coming into Seattle from Portland on the morning boat.

Martha sat against the outer wall near the window. Allen came and sat beside her.

"Allen — I don't see how this makes any difference at all, but I do feel better. It's as if being in danger together has made you closer to me."

Allen brushed tears from his eyes. "Martha, I realize now what you did for both of us last night. I realize the only thing that young outlaw wanted was you, and to get that hammer you must have let him rape you." He wiped his hand across his eyes. "You bargained with yourself, and that just might save our lives. I have a very heavy debt to repay to you if we ever get out of here."

She wanted to tell him he could start repaying right then, that he could at least kiss her. And then he did. He moved closer and kissed her lips, then put his arms around her and the flames gushed up as his kiss consumed her in a towering fire storm. They pressed against one another, lips on fire still, and Martha could only murmur her approval.

"Darling Allen, I love you so!"

He stared at her, then kissed her again. She willed him to go on, to continue to make love to her.

Gently she took his hand and pushed it past the buttons of her dress and felt its warmth as his fingers covered her breast.

The knock on the door broke them apart, and they stood quickly as the lock rattled and the door came open. Martha glanced at the window, but saw that it was all back together and the hammer was hidden under the mattress. It was the boss himself, complete with battered brown hat and cigar. Martha saw that the cigar was not lighted.

"Damn, but you are a pretty one," the outlaw leader said. "Just wanted to tell you that I'm gonna take you up on your offer. Only first we hit the bank, then you give me your cash. If you ain't got it with you, we'll wait. We'll get the bank first thing in the morning, then come out this way, pick you up and take you with us to Portland. Along the way I intend to make good use of that body of yours. Then in Portland you can get the money."

"That wasn't the offer I made to you."

"Tough. That's the way it's gonna be, unless you'd rather take the wrong end of a shotgun blast at six feet."

She shook her head.

"Then just forget your high and mighty. You be ready to travel tomorrow at dawn."

He went out, slammed the door, and locked it.

She turned to Allen. The mood was broken. Now they had a new problem to worry about. There had been no mention of taking Allen along. She realized that they didn't need him. They seemed like the kind of men who would shoot Allen simply to get rid of him and avoid leaving witnesses.

She tried to keep busy. They tore half of the cotton ticking material off the straw, leaving the top of the cloth in place, and tied knots in the other half. The rope would be strong enough to support their weight. Just before they went out the window, they would fix the rest of the ticking rope. Allen found a place on the window frame where they could tie the cloth.

Then they waited. It was growing dark again. Martha talked about the old days, about the walks they had taken in San Francisco.

"I loved you from the first time I saw you come on board the *Star of the Sea* to play Mah-Jongg with Captain Swartout. From that first day, I worked out scheme after scheme to meet you." He reached over and kissed her cheek, then drew back. "Those were exciting times."

Martha watched him. He was fighting himself, trying to say to himself that it was all right, that he could let go, that they should make love right now before it was too late. At any moment the outlaws could charge through the door and kill them both. They talked about everything except what they wanted to. Never did they mention divorce. No divorced person worked for Pacific Steamship. It was company policy, and was strictly followed. Divorce was officially a cause for dismissal of even the highest officer. It had kept three marriages together in the top ranks of management that Martha knew of, and in the process turned all six of the people concerned into angry, unhappy, unfaithful individuals. There was no point in discussing divorce if either of them wanted to stay with the company.

Night dropped suddenly over them, and Martha positioned herself at the window to watch the movement outside. She spotted the outside guard at once. He was smoking, and sat on an upturned bucket just past the edge of the old barn, where he had a commanding view of the house and the lane leading up to the buildings. He sat there for an hour, then stretched his legs, walked around the barn and came back. She wondered how long he would be on duty.

At ten o'clock the guard changed. They had planned to make their try at escaping about midnight. It might give them a few minutes more head start. The new guard who came on sat on the same bucket. At the end of the hour he made a circuit around the barn. Martha guessed that the horses must be in back, and the guards were checking on them as they stretched their legs. That meant the best time to go out of the window would be as soon as the guard started around the barn. They wouldn't have much time.

Now they removed the boards from the window, pulled the window out and set it by the wall. Allen tied the cloth rope to the window frame. Martha had torn the other part of the ticking cover in half and had it tied into the second part of the cloth rope, which Allen tied to the first part. They were ready.

The next time the guard took his stroll around the barn, Martha moved up and sat in the open window. Her skirts got in her way, but she pushed them through. As soon as the guard vanished, Martha dropped the rope, and using her hands and feet on it, she let herself down. When she was safe, Allen went down the rope quickly, the hammer stuck in his belt.

On the ground he tried to tear the rope free, but it wouldn't come. He balled the cloth up, and on the second throw, pitched it back through the open window. They kept the hammer and ran into the woods.

After only a few minutes they heard shouts from the main house and yells that the prisoners had escaped. Allen and Martha crept back into the woods, now unable to go around the barn to steal a pair of horses. Instead they moved silently into the brush and settled down to wait.

Martha kept wondering how they could defend themselves. She wished she had time to make a bow and arrow, that would be a good silent weapon. They didn't even have a knife. She asked Allen if he had a pocket knife and he took out a small folding knife with a two-inch blade. He gave it to her and hefted the hammer himself. They each found a sturdy stick to use as a club. They saw searchers through the screen of trees near the house. Some had lanterns. At least one mounted up and rode down the trail to town to cut off any exit that way.

"Remember, we can't charge out into the woods, or we'll get lost and never find our way out. It's forty miles if we head in the wrong direction. That means we have to stick close to the trail, which they will keep well guarded."

"So we have to attack them," said Martha.

"Attack? With what?"

"What we have — the hammer, your knife, and our clubs."

As they whispered, a man with a lantern came swinging around the back of the house and peered into the brush. He would have been an easy target for a handgun shot. Allen hefted the hammer, wishing he was within swinging distance. He decided that he couldn't throw the hammer accurately enough to do any good. The hunter worked toward them cautiously, coming to the very edge of the woods. Martha lifted the pocket knife, holding it by the blade. She reversed it and held it by the handle. There would be less chance that it would close that way. She might have a chance of throwing the little knife if the man came close enough. She indicated this idea to Allen, who shook his head. She affirmed the idea and began moving toward the oncoming man. She walked through the woods so silently not even Allen could hear her.

Martha used her Rapango skills and moved another six feet toward the searching man with the lantern. Her target was perfectly outlined by the light. She moved behind a two-foot thick Douglas fir tree and waited. The searcher came closer. When he was fifteen feet away, and the dim rays of the lantern were touching the fir tree Martha stood behind, she got ready.

The outlaw lifted the lantern to eye level and swung it back and forth, then dropped it near the ground and repeated the maneuver. This time, when he raised the lantern, Martha threw. She aimed just over the hand holding the light and in the center of the man's chest. She couldn't tell how the knife flew. All she heard was a surprised grunt, then the man went down in a jumble of arms and legs, and rolled onto his back. The lantern hit the ground and fell over, but kept burning for a moment, then went out.

Martha watched the man for a full minute. He never moved. She ran lightly to him and looked down. She shuddered as she saw the handle of the small pocket knife extending from the man's chest. He was dead. She tugged the knife from him, and checked where his six-gun had fallen. She found the weapon and picked it up, hoping that it was fully loaded.

A second later Allen stood beside her, saw the body in the faint moonlight and unbuckled the outlaw's gun belt and strapped it around his own waist.

He motioned that they should move farther into the woods, then to the right toward the road to town.

"We've got to keep that lane in sight or we'll be lost in here for a week," he whispered. They came out on the lane a few strides later, and almost at once saw the rider in front of them. He yelled and rode hard at them.

Allen lifted the six-gun and aimed carefully, did not let a wild shot from the gunman distract him, and fired one shot. The rider pitched off the horse, but as Allen ran to catch the animal, it bolted from him and ran at full gallop back toward the buildings.

"The others will be coming because of the shots," Allen said. "Let's see if we can find his gun." They looked for a few moments, heard the downed man moan, and gave up, running along the road toward town until they heard hoofbeats behind them. At that point they ran into the woods and knelt down, hoping the riders would go on past. One did. The other stopped a little behind them. They were trapped. There was no direction they could run.

"We need a horse," Martha said. "Preferably two, and without the others knowing we have them." She looked through the moonlight at the rider fifty yards away. "Do you have a belt?"

Allen said he did. She looked around the thick forest for what she needed. In the gloom she picked out a fir tree fifteen feet tall.

"Climb it, Allen, and see if you can grab it near the top and bend it down to the ground."

He did so, and the small tree bent dramatically. Using his belt, she fastened the top of the tree to the trunk of a nearby fir and looked around the woods.

"We need a big rock, a stump — something heavy."

Allen was getting the idea. He found a rock that weighed about twenty pounds, and with strips torn from her petticoat, they tied the rock to the bent-over fir about two feet from the top.

"Primitive yet effective," Martha said. "I learned this little trick on Rapango." She stood behind the fir where the bent-over tree was fastened, judged the distance, the arc the tree top would make, and picked out her target spot. She figured a quick way to release the belt and told Allen exactly what to do. He understood where he had to go and where he had to lead the searcher.

Allen began making small noises in the brush, trying to attract the attention of the man on horseback. The woods were too thick there for the horse. The man would have to dismount. Allen heard a low whistle answered by another one. A few seconds later the man from the lane was creeping slowly into the woods. Allen stumbled and moved on, stumbled and fell, but stayed out of the gunsights of the outlaw. The chaser moved more quickly and Allen surged across the point on the ground which Martha had picked as her target. Allen ran faster then, and vanished into the thick brush a few yards away. The man with the gun came cautiously. He had the pistol out and cocked. She watched him move toward her target spot on the ground.

Ten feet away, she held her breath. Six feet away. He stopped. Allen had been deathly still, but now he groaned, and the outlaw came another two steps. *Now!*

Martha loosened the belt and the bent-over tree followed nature's demands and began straightening itself quickly. The straining fir trunk snapped forward, carrying the twenty-pound rock with it, and smashed into the surprised outlaw.

It happened so fast that the man didn't even have time to cry out. His hand flashed up in a reflexive defense, but the rock broke his wrist as it rammed past, hit his chest, smashing him backward. His chest caved in, three ribs splintered into his heart. His gun was still clutched in his dead hand.

After the soft swish of the tree, the forest was quiet again. Martha sat and looked at the man, awed that the trap had worked so well. Tero had shown her how to make the device, but she had never used it on a man before.

Allen hurried back, picked up the gun, checked its loads, then grabbed Martha's hand.

"I'm continually amazed at you. Isn't there anything you don't know how to do? Now let's go find his horse." They walked to the edge of the woods and crept along the side of the road to where the horse had been tied.

"Can you ride, too?"

She nodded. He helped her up, then swung up behind her and began walking the horse toward town. There was still one mounted man ahead of them.

They rode a quarter of a mile before they saw the other horse. The rider had just lit a cigarette. Allen came almost up to the outlaw before he discovered his buddy wasn't on the roan. "Hands up," Allen said, leveling a six-gun at the small rider in a white hat. "Off the nag on this side, and easy, or you're dead."

The man slid off, his hands well away from his gun.

"Now, with your left hand, take out that pistol and toss it to me nice and easy. You understand? I'd just as soon put six slugs in your hide as stare at you, but I don't want to upset the lady."

The man did as he was told. While Allen caught the other's pistol, the outlaw slapped his mount on the flank, sending it shying and running down the road toward town. Allen bent and slashed his gun barrel across the outlaw's head, dropping him to the ground.

Then they rode hard and caught up with the black half a mile down the road where it stood, winded but calm. Allen got down, caught the horse and mounted it, then they galloped for a mile until they found the junction with the main road and the way back to town. Now they were along the lake and there was no way the other riders could go cross-country and cut them off.

They slowed to a walk and let the horses

rest, then picked up the pace. Neither spoke. Too much had happened. Martha felt a sickness rising in her. Two more, maybe three more men had died. She remembered the sickening, crushing sound as the rock hit the man and she stopped her horse. She leaned over the side and retched. She vomited until nothing more would come up, then wiped her mouth and shook her head. They rode slowly on.

They got back to the Evergreen Hotel some time before dawn. Martha tied the horse at the rail in front of the hotel and told Allen he should see the sheriff. She would talk to Allen later.

When Martha wearily climbed the steps to the hotel's second floor, she saw someone sitting cross-legged in front of her door. She thought of running, then at the sound of her footsteps the man's head lifted and she saw it was Johnnie Laveau. He stood gracefully, a smile on his face.

"Good have you home, *mon.* Much worry. Mr. Cornelius home, too? Much worry."

"We're both safe, Johnnie, thank you. I'll tell you about it tomorrow. Right now all I want to do is take a long, long sleep, maybe for a year!"

CHAPTER NINETEEN

Allen Cornelius sat on the horse and watched Martha slide down from her mount in front of the hotel. He knew he should have jumped off and helped her, and seen her safely to her hotel door, but somehow after the imminent threat of death that had hovered over them for so many hours, the street in front of the Evergreen Hotel, even at night, seemed like the safest spot in the world.

He waved at her and realized that he should warn the sheriff about the gang's plans to rob the payroll the next day — no, this day. He had no idea who would be on duty. The sheriff had recently been elected, and was not a lawman by any stretch of the definition. He had run for the office so he wouldn't have to work in the woods or the mills, and he had won. He hired one deputy who had been a lawman before in Oregon. The sheriff's office consisted of two small rooms in front of the two-cell jail. Allen wondered if he should get off his horse or just yell for the deputy. Chances were the man would be sleeping, since there was little trouble around Seattle once the saloons closed. At last Allen made up his exhausted mind to get down, but instead of swinging his leg over the back of the horse, he curled it over the saddle and slid down the side of the mount. His knees almost folded when he hit the ground.

The sheriff's door was locked. Allen knocked with his fist, then made sure the hammer wasn't on a live round and rapped on the solid door with the butt of his borrowed pistol.

"Yeah, hold on!" a voice called from inside. A minute later, a man opened the door. He wore long johns and a Stetson, and carried a shotgun in his hands. A lamp gave off a feeble light behind him.

"Oh, Mr. Cornelius," the deputy said. "We been huntin' all over creation for you!"

"Yes, Irvin, I imagine you have. I was kidnapped by a gang of men who say they want to rob the payroll shipment coming in on the noon boat today. You've got to stop them. Should only be four of them — maybe three."

Allen told him what he knew and the

deputy impatiently tried to break in. When Irvin finally got to talk, he made it simple.

"Mr. Cornelius, we'll watch the bank. Now you get yourself over to your house fast. Doc Warnick is there with your wife and she's mighty sick. We been trying to find you to tell you."

"Sick? With what?"

"Doc says he don't rightly know, but she's bad off. You get on home. Sheriff'n me'll take care of that bunch trying for the payroll." He found out where Allen had last seen them, and sent Allen on his way.

No longer was Allen bone-tired. Linda Sue sick! How? She was always in the best of health, never even caught colds. He couldn't understand it. And what did the deputy mean — Doc Warnick didn't know what was the matter with her? He was a doctor, wasn't he?

Allen rode hard the five blocks to his home, tied up the horse to the gate and ran up to the door. Inside he found Doc Warnick sitting in the big rocker, sleeping. He shook the doctor's arm until he woke.

"Huh, what? Who? Oh, Al! Glad you got back. Where the hell you been? We've been looking all over town for you." He got up and motioned for Allen to follow him into the first-floor bedroom.

425

"Danged if I can figure this out. She's sick, that's all I can say. Don't know what with, or from what, or why. She's just sick. One minute she's unconscious and I just don't know what happened. She gets a chill, then an hour later she's got a high fever. Keeps mumbling and sometimes shouts some strange words. I just don't know what to do — how to treat her."

Allen looked down at his wife, lying on the bed, so pale in the faint lamp light, her brown hair falling over one eye, damp from sweat. He pushed it back. Her breathing was regular. Doc Warnick put his hand to her forehead and motioned Allen out the door.

"Now do you know any reason why she should be this way? Has she been complaining? Does she faint a lot? Is she pregnant? Has she been taking any medicine?"

"Nothing, Doc. She's been healthy as a horse. Not even a cold. I can't think of a thing."

Warnick rubbed his hand over his head. "Damnit, I was afraid that was what you'd say. We just don't have anything to work with. Not a clue."

"How long has she been this way?"

"Over twenty-four hours that I know about. Out of her head all that time, talking crazy. But she didn't have a fever at first.

That's what puzzles me. A straight fever I can fight, but this comes and goes. I don't know what to do."

"Not any disease you heard of?"

"None. I thought and thought. Just don't match up with nothing I know about. We need to get her to eat, some soup, broth, anything she'll take. She's got to eat to keep up her strength."

"I'll stay with her the rest of the night, Doc. You go on home and get some sleep yourself. I appreciate what you're doing."

Doc Warnick looked at Allen, then nodded. "Where you been?"

Allen told him briefly about the wrong turn, the bandits and the kidnapping.

The doctor closed up a leather bag and headed for the door.

"Al, you try to get her to eat that broth. She can swallow all right. Force her somehow. It ain't like she was unconscious. Make her eat."

"Right, Doc. And thanks."

When the doctor left by the front door, Allen went back to the bedroom. He didn't think about the children until then. They were probably at the neighbor's house next door, with Mrs. Jenkins. He had to worry about Linda Sue. He sat watching her for a few minutes. She frowned, cried out and then said something. He wasn't sure what it was.

"Ya, ye, ye, li konin tou, gris-gris;
Li te kouri likal, aver vieux kokodril,
Oh, ouzi, ye!"

Allen leaned back in surprise. Then she said it again, and again. It became a soft chant. He shook her shoulders, tried to wake her up. He talked to her, but she wouldn't respond in any way.

The mumblings came softer and softer until she seemed to be sleeping again. Allen went to the kitchen, found a fire banked in the cookstove and a pot of turkey broth bubbling slowly. He took some in a cup and with a spoon tried to feed the liquid to his wife.

Linda Sue accepted a few spoonfuls of it quietly, then without warning she screamed. When the sound ended she was saying the words again: "Ya, ye, ye, li konin tou, gris-gris."

Allen had no idea what it meant. Some of it sounded French, but he wasn't sure. What in the world could have caused this? As he stood near the stove he went to sleep. Allen caught himself from falling, and went back to the chair by his wife's bed. He had a feeling she would be better by morning. The fever or the seizure should be over by then. There was nothing he could do now but watch. He would not go to sleep.

Allen sat down in the chair and at once nodded off. He caught himself and sat upright, watching his wife, trying to get her to take more soup. The spoon dropped from his fingers. He sat stiffly forward, straining his muscles, willing himself to stay awake. Allen put down the cup of soup and the spoon, then just for a moment he relaxed.

He woke with a start two hours later and checked his pocket watch. Five o'clock. Now he must stay awake. He heated the soup after building up the fire, and got a few more spoonfuls of it down her throat.

He tried again, every half hour until daylight. He was stiff and tired from sitting in the chair for so long. He took a walk around the house to get warm, built up the fire again, and then checked Linda Sue. She had thrown off the blanket, so he draped it over her again and added another. Her skin was cold. That startled him, but it was not a death cold, only a chill. Again he built up the kitchen fire and reheated the soup. This time she ate more of it, eagerly, then suddenly stopped, mumbled something, and turned her head.

He shook her gently, then again, but she wouldn't waken. A knock sounded on the front door, but before he could get there, it opened and Doc Warnick hurried in. He took off his hat, nodded at Allen, and touched Linda Sue.

"Cold. Amazing. I just can't understand this." He felt for her pulse. "Has she eaten anything?"

Allen told him about the broth. "Good. Every little bit helps. I've got a powder here that is supposed to get her whole body working faster. Let's dissolve it in a spoonful of that broth."

Allen brought the cup and they tried it. She accepted half of it, then refused the rest, with her eyes still closed.

"The children?" Allen asked.

Doc Warnick pointed. "Next door. Mrs. Jenkins said she'd keep them until we get this cleared up. We don't know — it might be as contagious as the pox."

Allen looked at the clock on the dresser. The hands showed that it was not quite eight.

"I should get over to the office for a few minutes and let them know I'm still alive. Can you stay for a half hour until I ride down there and come back?"

The doctor said he was going to stay

anyway. He stared at the pale woman on the bed. He was fascinated, and at the same time worried and fearful that nothing in his skills or understanding could save this woman from death.

Allen was gone an hour. He straightened out one major problem, accepted many expressions of sympathy, then left the operations in control of Caleb Jones. Before he rode the borrowed horse back to his home, Allen had a note sent to Martha's hotel room, explaining where he was and why.

All morning he sat at his wife's bedside. The doctor was in and out. There was no change. They tried one more powder dissolved in soup, but she would not drink it.

Dr. Warnick rubbed his chin, his face showing his frustration now. "It isn't the mumps or measles, the whooping cough, or any kind of fever I've ever seen. It sure isn't the pox, the plague, consumption, or bad bowels, and her heart sounds good. I can't hear any change in her lungs, best I can tell. Must be something I don't know about yet, Al. Wish to hell I did. Then I could figure out how to help her."

Just after noon Martha knocked on the front door.

"Oh, Allen, I just heard. I'm so sorry! Is there anything I can do?"

"I don't know, Martha. The doctor is puzzled. Says he's never seen anything like this before. I just don't know what to tell you."

"For you, then. Have you had any breakfast . . . or lunch?"

Allen shook his head.

Martha went straight to the kitchen, put the turkey soup on the warming part of the eight-lid kitchen range, and built up the fire. She checked the cupboard and found it nearly empty. Outside, where Johnnie sat in the carriage, she told him to go to the general store and the butcher shop. When he came back he had two big beef steaks and a small box of groceries. An hour later Martha sat Doctor Warnick and Allen down at the kitchen table for a steak dinner, with mashed potatoes, gravy, carrots and squash, and an apple cobbler. She made a big pot of coffee as well, and both men ate as if they had forgotten what food looked like.

Martha sat with Linda Sue as the men ate, and she worried. This woman, whom she had hated without ever meeting, now seemed an important part of her life.

Dr. Warnick gave Martha the names of two women who were practical nurses, who would sit with the sick. She sent Johnnie after one of them, giving him a ten-dollar bill in advance payment on her wages. The robust widow was there in half an hour ready to stay as long as needed. Martha relaxed. Now at least Allen could get some sleep instead of sitting up with Linda Sue around the clock. She instructed the widow what to do, and to be sure to cook for the three of them.

After Martha went back to the hotel, she had Johnnie buy more groceries and take them to the Cornelius home. Then she had a large lunch at the dining room.

Upstairs she arranged to have a bath. She asked that the portable bathtub be brought to her room, with six big buckets of hot water. She would take a two-hour bath, as long as the water stayed hot. Martha had not felt so grubby for three years, not since Rapango.

Rapango! That had been a million years ago. She wondered about Tero, about Mirani. She would have to send Mirani a present on the next ship to go there from the company. Martha settled back in the warm water and soaked away the aches and pains of the last day. It felt so good to be in a hot tub again!

For a moment, she thought about Allen's wife. It was some strange sickness, and the local doctor had no idea what it could be.

She stopped thinking about it. Allen's wife would be well in a few days, and then Martha would get on the boat with Johnnie and go back to San Francisco, and it would all be exactly the same.

She wondered about what might have been. What would it have been like to live with Allen all this time, as his wife? To cook for him, take care of him, to lie in bed beside him? She sighed, and turned to look out the window. The sun was out. It was a beautiful day, and she hadn't even noticed.

After her long bath, she went to her door and saw Johnnie down the hall. She called to him. Now she told him what had happened on the trip to the sawmill, leaving out some of the more gruesome parts.

"We got away at last and came back to town. I'm sorry it caused you so much trouble."

"No trouble, *mon.* Big man's lady sick?"

"Yes, Johnnie. The doctor can't figure out what's wrong with her. I don't feel that we should just pick up and leave while she's so bad. We better put off going back for a few days. Would you mind?"

"No mind. You want Johnnie, carriage tonight, go see sick lady?"

"Yes, Johnnie, that's thoughtful of you. Why don't we go by about seven."

He stood and went to the door smiling broadly. "Plenty soon troubles all over!" he said, smiled again and went out.

Martha cocked her head in surprise. Now whatever could he have meant by that? She didn't always understand Johnnie, but she knew her father had insisted that he be with her. She wasn't going to worry about it. She wished he had been along on that ride to the mill. It would have been a much less harrowing experience, she was sure.

That night after dinner, Johnnie arrived with the carriage at the front door of the Evergreen Hotel and handed her up. They quickly arrived at the frame house where Allen lived and Johnnie helped her down but stayed in the carriage as she went to the door.

Allen answered her knock, his face drawn and pale. His hair was rumpled and un-combed. He wore the same clothes he had when they had been at the outlaw's hideout. His beard was now showing plainly. For a second, she thought he was going to cry.

"How is she, Allen?"

"Worse. Pneumonia," he said. "Doc has been worried about it, because of the way she's been breathing. Now he says it's for sure. She's got pneumonia, and he says that it's . . ." Allen turned and walked away from

435

her. He went to the parlor and slumped in a chair.

Martha went to the sickroom and saw Dr. Warnick bending over the silent form. He straightened.

"Mrs. Dyke, did he tell you?"

"Yes, but isn't there something we can do? Some medicine? Isn't there any way to fight back?"

"Not now. We don't have a medicine. A hundred years from now they may know how to fight it, cure it. But now, once a person has pneumonia . . . well, it kills so quickly that we hardly have any time. Her temperature is so high it scares me. Her heart is pumping at 120 times a minute. She's developed a cough that is shaking her to pieces. And her breathing has quickened considerably. There is simply nothing I can do, Mrs. Dyke."

"I understand." She turned.

"Hope and pray, Mrs. Dyke. That's about all that's left."

Martha walked back to the parlor. She had to say something. But what did she know about comforting the loved ones of a sick person?

She sat down beside Allen and took his hand. "Allen, there is always hope. I've known two persons who had pneumonia and came through it. There's always hope, Allen — hope and prayer."

She sat with him for a moment longer. He didn't speak. She stood, patted his shoulder and looked down. "Allen, I'll be in the hotel if I can do anything. Just let me know. Take all the time from work that you need to, no problem about that. Send for me if Johnnie or I can be of any help."

He looked up, and nodded his thanks. She could see that he had been crying.

That night in her hotel room, Martha tried to read. She put away the leather-bound volume of *Macbeth*. The long-ago political maneuverings and dealings did not interest her tonight. There was a real life-and-death struggle going on in the small frame house up the street, yet there wasn't a thing she could do about it.

Martha slept poorly that night.

When she woke the next morning she saw a paper near the door. She picked it up and guessed it had been slid under her door some time during the night. The message read in a careful hand:

"Linda Sue Cornelius died of pneumonia complications shortly after two a.m." It was signed, *"B. Warnick."*

Martha went to the bed and sat down, still in her long cotton nightshirt. The poor girl was dead. So sudden, so quick. *Linda Sue was dead.* For a brief moment a surge of tremendous joy lifted her. Linda Sue was gone. She no longer stood in the way. Allen was a widower!

For a few seconds the realization of this fact made her head spin. She fell back on the bed trying to imagine what those four words now meant. But at once she was ashamed of herself. A girl had died tragically, such a young woman, and the mother of two. Terrible!

But think what it meant to Martha Pemberton Dyke!

Martha lay there for fifteen minutes, no longer able to deny that the girl's death would mean a dramatic change in her life. It would be wonderful — fantastic. She let the dreams and fantasies of what it might be like wash over her.

Then she stood, calm and controlled, washed her face in the china bowl on the stand, and dressed. She put on the oldest and least revealing dress she had brought with her. The night before, she had washed her hair, and now it was straight and hardly becoming. Good. She brushed it out, then wrapped it in a bun at the back of her head and hid it under a scarf. Just before nine o'clock she went downstairs and had breakfast. Later, when she stepped into the lobby, Johnnie appeared at her side.

"Johnnie, did you hear about Mrs. Cornelius?" He looked at her and shook his head. "She died last night of pneumonia. Do you think it's too early in the day to call on Mr. Cornelius and offer our help?"

Johnnie shook his head, and led her outside to the carriage. She knew it was too early. She was not family, but then, he had no family here. Neither did Allen's dead wife. She was his friend, and she *should* go to help Allen and comfort him. She was the closest person he had. With these ideas firmly in her mind, she still hesitated when she stepped up to the door of the small frame house. Then she lifted her chin and knocked hard three times.

There was no answer. She knocked again. After a short wait she heard movement inside, and the door opened.

"Yes?" said Allen.

He had opened the door only a few inches. His hair was not combed, his beard was much longer now, his clothes rumpled.

"Allen, I've come to help you. Please let me in."

He held the door in the same position and stared at her.

"Allen, I want to help you. You need

someone to help you. I'm the nearest thing to family you have out here, Allen. Now open the door so I can get you some breakfast."

Slowly he let her push the door inward. She had never seen him so crushed, so mute, so depressed. The parlor was a jumble of clothes, papers, a chair tipped over.

Allen sank into a chair and closed his eyes.

"Allen, have you had any breakfast?"

He shook his head.

She went into the kitchen, picking up things on the way. The kitchen was clean, the dishes done and put away. It looked as if the nurse/housekeeper had just left. Martha found a good stock of food Johnnie had brought the night before. She built a fire and made some coffee, then began cooking breakfast. She took Allen some coffee and soon brought him a plate of eggs and flapjacks. He ate listlessly.

She cleaned up the living room, talking to him all the time, but he never replied. When she had the parlor clean, she went toward the downstairs bedroom. She stepped inside. The bed had not been made. Everything was the same, she guessed, as it had been just after they took Linda Sue away. She left quickly.

Back in the parlor she talked to Allen. She

mentioned how much she liked the Seattle area, the fabulous mountains and the unending stretches of evergreen trees. The lakes and the ocean were wonderful, too. She had no idea if he heard what she said. He didn't respond, only sat with his eyes closed. There was nothing she could do until he came out of his grief. She watched him for a few more minutes, took away the dishes and refilled his coffee cup at his elbow. Then she went into the kitchen to wash the dishes and put things away.

Allen knew that Martha was there. He simply didn't want to talk to her or to anyone. Linda Sue was dead, and it was his fault. If he hadn't been trying to show off to the president's daughter so he would get a good report . . . if only he had been here, he would have caught her sickness at the very start and would have taken care of her so it couldn't have turned into pneumonia. It was plainly his fault, and he would have to live with that fact for the rest of his life. For a time he even questioned how long the rest of his life should be. Did he have a right to continue living when he had taken a life? But he thought back and realized he had clubbed a man and probably killed him only the day before, and he had reacted to it as if he had swatted a particularly vicious bumblebee threatening him. This was different. She was his wife. He had sworn to protect her, in sickness . . .

He bent and held his head in his hands. Yes, he should live, but her death would weigh him down forever.

Then quickly the conflict slammed into his mind. Now he was free to marry his first true love. Had he in any way . . . had he in any manner *wanted* Linda Sue . . . Allen shook his head, but the thought simply wouldn't go away. It paralyzed him. The very thought that he would even consider doing such a thing . . . even the idea that his subconscious could devise such a monstrous idea . . . but he had had nothing to do with her illness. And when he got back he had seen that everything possible was done.

Doc Warnick said that once pneumonia took hold of a victim there was nothing medicine could do. Some died, some lived.

But why Linda Sue?

He lay on the couch now, his hand over his eyes. He heard the door open, knew Martha was still there, and he guessed that she was cooking something. He wasn't hungry. He hadn't eaten since the previous night, or was it the morning before — he couldn't remember. Why should he eat? He

442

had decided that he should continue to live, so he would *have* to eat.

He realized numbly that he should be making some arrangements for her burial. Tomorrow. Or had Doc Warnick said he would talk to the undertaker about it? Yes. He had. They had taken his Linda Sue away. Three years. He had only known her less than three years. Such a short time. There was so much to do, so many arrangements — but not today. He would think about them tomorrow.

For two days Martha tended him. She made him eat twice a day. She fed him gallons of coffee. She talked to him as if he were responding. Johnnie had packed her bags at the hotel and brought them to the small frame house. She didn't care what the neighbors said. Someone had to look after Allen.

The neighbor who kept the two children, Mrs. Jenkins, came by from time to time and saw how stunned Allen still was. She approved of the arrangement and said she would keep the children until Allen was himself again.

Martha had made a bed on the couch for Allen, and he spent most of the two days there. She made him come to the kitchen to eat, then he would go back and hold his face in his hands. Twice he sobbed uncontrollably. She let him cry it out.

Martha had slept in the bed in the back room, which she guessed was where the children usually slept. She hadn't been in the sickroom since that first time.

The third morning, she woke Allen and gave him a cup of coffee. He sipped it, then stared at her with the blank eyes she had seen for three days.

Martha slapped his face.

Allen jumped, his eyes flashing fire, his hand coming up to defend himself. Then he blinked and sighed.

"Yes, Martha, it's time I begin living again. Today we'll pack up Linda Sue's things. Mrs. Jenkins next door can help us. We'll give most of her things to Mrs. Jenkins. Will you mind doing that?"

"No, Allen. Now get dressed, then I'll have some hot cakes and syrup for you. After that, you need a good hot bath and a shave."

The three of them worked all morning packing up the dead woman's clothes and personal things. In the covers of the bed Martha found a hair necklace with a small leather pouch fastened to the bottom. She frowned. She had seen something like that before, but where? She put it in the pocket of her apron and tried to remember.

Later that afternoon she remembered where she had seen a hair necklace. She showed it to Allen, but he said he'd never seen it before. Martha told Allen she had to go to the store, and outside she found Johnnie waiting near the carriage. She told him to drive her to Dr. Warnick's office. There was a worried look in her eye.

At the office she waited a moment and then got to see the doctor. He looked at the strange necklace a moment and nodded.

"I see you found the thing. Linda Sue had it gripped so tight in her hand I couldn't get it away from her. She kept looking at it and mumbling some French words I didn't understand."

"She had it the first time you saw her?"

"Yes, and the rest of the times. She finally must have got so weak that she dropped it and couldn't find it in the bedding."

Martha thanked him and went out to the carriage. She didn't know how or why, but now she was sure that Johnnie Laveau had done something to Linda Sue. The necklace she held was almost an exact duplicate of the one Johnnie had given her over three years ago.

Johnnie Laveau had a lot of explaining to do, and he had better do it right now!

CHAPTER TWENTY

Martha sat in the carriage unmindful of the sparkling blue sky and the warmer temperatures. She could only stare at Johnnie with a soul gripping anger such as she had never known before.

"Johnnie, how could you do it? How could you use that hair necklace to hurt Mrs. Cornelius?" She pulled out the *gris-gris* and held it up so Johnnie could see it.

"Johnnie no hurt. Silly white trash hurt self."

"I know something about this voodoo, this Caribbean ritual. I've read about its being practiced down in Louisiana, in New Orleans. I never connected it with that necklace you gave me three years ago. I'm sure now that you tried to put a hex on Linda Sue. You voodooed her and she died."

Johnnie shook his head. "No, *mon*. She plenty silly woman. She *think* she voodooed. All Johnnie do spill cat blood on back porch, put *gris-gris* on front porch. Silly white woman, she *believe* she voodooed."

"But you did it so she would be frightened, so she might make herself sick. Or maybe you wanted her to run away. Right?"

Johnnie shifted in the seat of the buggy. She had never seen him so nervous or uncomfortable.

"Johnnie no can tell what silly woman do."

"But you deliberately tried at the very least to frighten her, and you did. You made her so scared that she couldn't eat or sleep or drink. You made her sick. Now even if all that sickness was in her head, it was still your doing, because you gave her the idea in the first place. Johnnie, I'm shocked and ashamed of you, playing on a person's fears and superstitions. That's bad. And because you've done this bad thing, I'm discharging you. I'm sending you back to my father with a complete report. I'll do all I can to keep you permanently out of the company."

Johnnie looked at her, his face emotionless again.

"Right now, you drive us back to the hotel. There you will get your baggage and I'll see that you get on the next boast headed for San Francisco. *Right now,* Johnnie!"

The carriage drove away toward the hotel.

Martha could say no more. Johnnie and

his voodoo certainly didn't kill Linda Sue. Yet, in a way it had. It made her so ill and so weak that the pneumonia found an easy target and struck her down within twenty-four hours.

Martha was so shocked and upset that she didn't know if she could ever face Allen again. She would have to tell him. There was no other way. He had to be told. She wanted Johnnie out of town first. Allen might try to kill Johnnie. That could only mean more trouble for all of them.

The funeral was set for that afternoon. Doc Warnick had postponed it until he thought Allen was sufficiently recovered. It was at two o'clock. Martha had planned on being there, but now she wondered if she should go. This was no time to tell Allen what had really happened. Could she face him without telling him the truth?

Johnnie came out of the hotel with his suitcase and they drove to the docks. A ship was set to sail at noon, and Johnnie barely had time to get abroad. Johnnie stared at her before he left the buggy.

"Johnnie only try help, Mrs. Dyke. No want hurt anyone. Johnnie's job to take care Mrs. Dyke." Then he turned and walked up the gangplank and into the passenger section of the ship.

Martha stayed at the dock and watched as the last lines were loosened and the vessel pulled away in a light breeze.

She drove back toward the hotel. There should be plenty of time before the funeral. The first thing she had to do was move out of Allen's house. She drove back there, dashed inside, and without seeing Allen, repacked her suitcases and carried them out to the carriage. Allen came out and helped her put them in the rig.

"Going somewhere?"

"I thought I'd better move back to the hotel now that you're feeling better. You'll want to get a housekeeper for the boys. I'll talk to you about it at the funeral. I'll meet you at the church."

As she drove away she could see a dozen questions on his face, but she left quickly before he could voice them. At the hotel she got another room and stretched out on the bed. She was exausted, emotionally drained. It was too early to go to church, and she had no intention of going now so she could talk to Allen. It would be hard enough after the casket was in the ground. How in the world could she tell Allen what had really happened, about the *gris-gris* and the cat's blood and the voodoo?

For a moment she drifted off to sleep, but

woke quickly when she heard her door open. Or did it open? It was closed now, and she saw nothing. She started to sit up, but a rough hand clamped over her mouth and forced her back on the bed.

Martha screamed but no sound came out. Her eyes widened in terror as she tried to see who held her. Another hand wound around her waist, pinning her to the bed. She twisted her head to one side and saw him. It took her a few seconds to recognize the man with his moustache and small beard. But the eyes were the same, and the firm set of the thin lips: she was staring at Josiah West! He was the man she had been engaged to, whom her father had fired because he had deserted his wife in Seattle. She hadn't even thought about him.

Josiah laughed. "Well, little princess, you know who I am. The shoe is on the other foot now, don't you think? You don't have a big company president pushing people around for you now, do you?"

He moved his hand from her waist and quickly wrapped a heavy cloth around her mouth and tied it in back of her head. It was impossible for her to talk, let alone scream.

His hand brushed her breasts and she pulled away at once.

"Still touchy, ain't ya? Well, hell, you got a good body to protect. I should know. A damn good body, and I've seen it naked." He laughed, and it made her cringe.

"Your old man really smashed me down, now, didn't he? Fired me, ran me out of town, even tried to turn Seattle against me. But I got good friends up here. I never abandoned my wife and family, you know that? We'd kind of separated a while, and then she was getting ready to move down when I discovered the little queen bee who had gone to work at my store all secret-like. My wife June and me, we decided to wait and see what happened. Something might work out we both could take advantage of." Josiah laughed.

"Goddamn, I never expected to get as far as I did. You went up in the company in a rush, and I knew why. I never hoped to bed you, let alone be engaged to you. So all the rest of it was pure profit. Then your father and his damn detectives got busy."

Martha mumbled something through the gag. He sat her up on the bed and tied her hands in front of her with another piece of cloth that had been torn from something — the bedsheets, maybe.

"Oh, no, I'm not going to let you talk. Scream is what you'd do. I ain't even gonna

451

take your clothes off, because I'd just have to make you get back into them before we left the hotel. You and me are going for a little drive." He laughed and Martha could not remember ever hearing a more angry sound.

"June and me, we got a little party all set up for you in our house. Oh, thanks for the money — that five thousand certainly came in handy. We got most of it in the bank, and we spent some. It's better than working. Now June and me figure we got a great chance to get a whole lot more."

He took a whiskey bottle from his pocket, tipped it up for two swallows, then capped it and put it away. "Oh, no, no chance I'm going to get myself drunk. Not any. I got plans that are just too big for that."

He reached over and rubbed her breasts. "Christ, do I remember these! *Beauties!* But time enough for that later, right? I figure about three o'clock or so, when things quiet down, you and me will take a walk down the back stairs, I'll have my six-gun under my jacket with the muzzle two inches from your back. One word from you and your whole backbone will blast right through your stomach. Understand that good, pretty little princess."

Martha bobbed her head.

She tried to stay calm. How in the world had he known she was in Seattle? Then she figured out the answer. In a small town like this, everyone knew what everyone else was doing. There wasn't anything else to do or talk about. He had probably found out the first day she was there.

Martha tried to evaluate her situation. It wasn't good. She was gagged and her hands were tied. He expected to take her down the back stairs and out of the hotel. She had to run, get away now. But he still had the gun. She wasn't going to dive out a second-story window. Neither was she going to try to scream when he had that gun in her back as they went down the steps.

She looked around. There was nothing, no weapon, even if her hands were free. She scowled and realized he had planned this well. She was trapped and she couldn't get away.

"Oh, yes, little princess, Martha. We do have a surprise for you. Nothing fancy, but interesting. I was down at the docks the day you hit town and I couldn't believe my eyes. That big nigra with you was more than I wanted to tangle with right off. But I kept waiting, and you finally sent him off on the ship today. Gave him a good tongue-lashing, too. He's probably going to smart all the way back to your father's office. So suddenly your protection was gone and I had a free hand. Now wasn't that nice of you? I just moved my schedule up a few days and here we are, snug as two lovers in their honeymoon bed." His fingers crept down her side and she shoved them away with her bound hands.

"You weren't near so touchy when you thought you had trapped me into marrying you." He grinned. "Now that was something, in the office on the carpet. Bet you never did tell your mother about that time, did you?"

Martha turned away.

"Well, time we got moving. You won't need to bring your bags. Yes, we're moving a little early. I figure most of the good folks of the town will be in the church by now for the funeral. We won't be missed at all, going out the back door and down the outside steps."

He pulled her to her feet, took a pistol from his belt, and showed her how he could push it against her side while holding her arm and have the gun hidden by his jacket. "I can shoot you here, or in the hall, or on the steps, if you say a single word. You sure you understand? Now just be a good girl and you won't end up dead." He untied the gag, threw it on the bed, then held her arm and placed the muzzle of the weapon against her side. He tested it, was satisfied, then untied her hands and they marched out into the hall.

It went just the way he said it would. Below the back stairs sat his buggy. They stepped inside, and a few seconds later they were driving away. Josiah laughed.

"Easy as pulling down the bloomers on a brand-new widow," he said.

It was the first time she was able to talk. She scowled at him. "You can't get away with this. Allen has already missed me at the funeral. He'll think the outlaws came to town and caught me, and he'll turn this place upside down and crossways until he finds me."

"Not likely, little witch. We got near a thousand houses here now. He going to search every one of them? He'll figure you just found a better man and you're bouncing on your mattress in your hotel and would rather not be disturbed. Men understand things like that."

She evaluated what he was saying. Now was no time to get emotional or to cry. He was an intelligent man who used his mind and could do good planning. She had no doubt now that he had planned this whole thing quickly but well. She hadn't even thought about him being in Seattle. She should have taken some kind of precautions. It was easy to understand how he must hate her after what had happened — not that it was her fault. Her father had done the damage, but Josiah would be quick to take out his hatred on her to spite her father.

Yes, it made sense. But what could she do now? Before she could come up with a plan, the carriage stopped beside the back door of a two-story frame house, and he hurried her into a half basement and closed the door. It was unearthly dark for a few moments until he struck a match and lit a lantern.

The thin light showed an earthen floor covered with boards and with water seeping up between all of them. In the far corner was a partially constructed room made of raw lumber. She looked at him.

"If I had that pistol I think I'd be able to shoot you, Josiah."

"After all we meant to each other?" he asked, feigning surprise. "After all those intimate moments, that physical thrill. All that petting and rolling around in your bed?" Josiah scowled at her. "And I'm just as able to shoot you, so don't try anything smart."

He pushed her toward the wall and the half finished room. Then she saw what it really was. It was a cell, eight feet square, built into the corner made of raw two-by-four timbers. It went from floor to ceiling. The boards were spaced so closely together it would be impossible for her to escape. An opening at the corner swung out, and he pushed her inside.

He followed her into the cell, took out a straight razor and began cutting off her clothes. At first Martha fought, then she realized that was futile. He was stronger, he had a vicious weapon, and she was sure he wouldn't mind cutting her with the razor if he had to in order to rip every shred of clothing from her body.

She cringed, watching the razor cut through straps, cloth and laces until she was naked. She resented his stares, the way his eyes glittered as he watched her body. Then he pushed her toward the far wall. She stumbled, slipped, and sat down suddenly in four inches of cold, muddy water. Josiah roared with laughter.

She sat there for only a moment in the cold water, got to her knees, and then stood up, shivering. She was beginning to understand the depth of the hatred Josiah felt toward her and her father. She knew there would be no limits to the steps he would take to vent his rage. However, she did not fear for her life. He had indicated that he wanted much more money, and he could get that only through a ransom — and for that she must be kept alive. She might be ill, tortured, beaten, violated — but Josiah was a careful man and would be sure to keep her alive.

"Jesus, this is good. Miss Princess herself, the richest bitch I've ever bedded, caught and naked, and she can't do a thing about it. All her damn money is no good to her now, and she's just hoping that I let her spend some of it to get free before I take a knife and rip out her guts."

Josiah closed the door and nailed it shut, and with each sound of the hammer, Martha felt that her fate was being sealed. She had felt trapped before, but never anything like this. Nailed into a cell! It threatened to make her lose control, but she steadied herself, hung on and refused to break down; there was to be no crying.

"Jesus, what a body! I don't even know why I came out of there. But we'll save that for later. About time you meet my favorite wife." He went out the door and a few minutes later came back with a huge woman behind him. She towered over him like a douglas fir over a vine maple. Her shoulders were as wide as any man's, and her hair was cropped short, close to her head. She stared at Martha from small, dark, narrowly spaced eyes. The hint of a moustache darkened her upper lip.

"God-amighty, but she's a skinny little thing, ain't she?"

"Skinny only in the right places, Dora."

Dora scowled. "Josiah, ain't you got no respect? Don't talk that way around a lady. This is the flower of young womanhood. We got to be nice to this rich gal." Dora snickered. "Suppose the bitch is in heat?"

Josiah guffawed. "Damn, I wonder? Now wouldn't that be a good one, send her back home pregnant as a jersey cow?" They both laughed and Martha turned away. Dora was the most mannish woman she had ever seen. She'd heard that some women were like that, and that they enjoyed sex with other women, but she'd never seen one before. It was so disgusting that Martha could hardly imagine it.

"Hey, rich girl. You with your bare bottom hanging out. Turn around here," Dora said.

Martha ignored her and moved to the far corner where the two earth sides of the wall met. She was as far from the woman as she could get.

Dora laughed and walked to the closest edge of the two by four bars to Martha and set down a bucket of water. She took a dipper full of water, reached through the wooden bars and splashed the cold water on Martha's back.

Martha gasped, but caught herself before she screamed. She wanted to turn and strike at the woman, but she didn't. Instead she faced the wall and waited, knowing there would be more. She took another dipper of water and gasped again, then saw the puddle of water behind her and near the cell boards. She turned, and just as the woman reached through the bars with the dipper of water, Martha kicked at the puddle again and again, splashing the muddy water from the floor through the bars and on Dora.

Josiah jumped back out of range, but Dora dropped the dipper in surprise. Martha darted forward and skidded, but got to the dipper inside the cell. She used it to hurl water at her tormentors from the puddles in the cell.

Dora fumed and screeched. "You god-damn bitch. Just wait until I get my hands on you. You'll wish to hell you'd never done that. You prissy bitch, wait, just you wait! Thought you could bribe us into being quiet, did you? Thought your stinking money would undo the harm you done us?" She was panting from her fury. She turned to her husband. "All right, Josiah. Go in there and show me how you work. Take her right now and do it so rough she'll scream. Let's hear that goddamn rich whore bellow for mercy!"

Josiah picked a small mattress off the wall where it hung on pegs and carried it to the cell door. He used it as a shield against Martha's splashing as he pulled the nails out of the door. The next step was to push the mattress through the opening and throw it on the dryest part of the floor. Then he charged Martha, caught her and they both slipped and fell in the mud.

Josiah laughed and threw her on the mattress, then leaped on top of her squirming nude body.

Martha didn't know much about fighting, but now she kicked and scratched and clawed with an innate understanding, trying to punish him as much as she could. He slapped her face hard, and she screamed at him. He slapped her again and again until the whole room went fuzzy and her arms fell at her sides. She was almost unconscious. Martha was vaguely aware that Josiah had opened his pants and pulled them down. She tried to fight with him again, but he slapped her, and a huge white cloud boiled up in her brain and she wasn't sure what was happening.

He used her body roughly, once, then quickly again, with Dora shouting encouragement.

Martha knew exactly what was happening at last. She glared at Josiah as he panted and gasped for breath. She leaned up and bit his cheek, bringing blood. He hardly noticed, and collapsed at once on top of her. She found his ear near her mouth.

"Josiah, you let that woman in here and I'll kill her, you hear? I learned a dozen ways to kill with my bare hands in Tahiti, and I'll sure do it to her. I'll knock her out and strangle her before you can help. Keep her out of here!"

Josiah lifted his head, stared into her eyes, then nodded and got up off the muddy mattress.

Before she knew what was happening, Josiah picked up one side of the wet mattress and rolled Martha off it back into the muddy water. He dragged the mattress out of the cell, and as he did, Dora threw the full bucket of water on Martha where she sat in the mud.

Martha sat there in the chill wetness, and for the first time the hint of a tear came to her eyes, but she fought it back, stood and went to the corner as far away from them as she could get.

"Martha, I'm going upstairs to write a letter. When I get it just right, you're going to copy it and sign it and I'll send it to your father. If you want to stay alive and see your family again, you better do exactly what we tell you. Do you understand what I'm saying?"

"Yes, Mr. West. I understand perfectly. And before this is all over, I promise you that I'll be standing here looking down at your corpse, and I'll be wondering just why you tried it. You really think you can get away with it, knowing my father, knowing the power behind the company?"

"I know I can. Your old man will do *anything* to get his baby daughter back home safe and sound."

"Josiah, you know, you're betting your life on this. What if you lose?"

"I've already lost once, bitch. That's plenty. I don't intend to lose again." He went out the half-basement door, shooing his wife ahead of him and leaving Martha in the darkness.

She shivered. Martha had never been so cold, so angry, so miserable, so humiliated in her life. Everything was back to the basics of survival, the way it had been on Rapango. First she had to live, to stay alive. What came later didn't matter so much right now. If there were to be any "later" at all, she must survive now!

It was over two hours before Josiah came back. He had a tablet of cheap paper, a wooden pencil, a small table and a wooden chair. He unnailed the door and took the things inside the cell. Josiah drew out his razor, its six-inch-long honed sharp blade glinting in the lamp light.

"Martha, you are going to do exactly what I tell you. If you don't, I'll make an inch-long cut somewhere on your body. It will hurt like hell and it will bleed. I can probably make five hundred such cuts before you bleed to death. I'd suggest you do exactly what I say."

He waited for a reaction, but she gave none.

"First, sit down at the table on the chair and put your hands on top. There's a towel there, which I want you to use to wipe off your hands and arms so you don't get the paper dirty. A princess doesn't have dirty hands."

Martha did as she was told.

He put the pad of paper and the pencil

down, and a hand-written letter beside them.

"Copy the letter exactly the way it is there, and don't try to disguise your handwriting. I know it very well."

Martha looked up at him and glared, then read the letter he had written. She crumpled it up and threw it into the mud.

The searing, sudden pain on her back brought a scream of agony from Martha. She leaned forward crying on the table and felt a trickle of blood work its way down her back.

Josiah turned her face toward him by catching her chin. "I told you not to do that. Now sit perfectly still while I get the paper. It will be harder to copy now, but that's your problem."

Josiah put the crumpled sheet of paper on the desk.

"Martha, I suggest you work carefully, with no mistakes." His hand fondled her left breast. "Because if there are any more problems, the next cut will be on your pretty bosom."

Martha shivered, straightened out the sheet of paper and began copying it. There was nothing else she could do. The message was what she had expected. Only the amount of her ransom surprised her. He was asking for five hundred thousand dollars in gold.

Delivery would be made at sea in Canadian waters far up along the inland passage in the Straits of Georgia above the small town of Vancouver. It was a clever, perhaps a foolproof method of collecting the ransom.

Martha copied the letter, marking it exactly the way Josiah had indicated she should. Twice more his hands came down and played with her breasts. She tried to ignore his touch, but at last pushed him away. Josiah laughed.

"Father will never believe this is my handwriting."

"He won't have to. Your company lawyers will convince him. And I'll send your small purse and your handkerchief with the family initials on it. Altogether they should do a very good job of identifying you. First he'll send detectives to check to see if you are still in your hotel room. That will take several days. Then another week for him to be sure, and the third week when he sends the small ship with the money. Until then we have to keep you fed at 'east. All the water you want to drink, but little food." Josiah laughed. "Then, too, I'll be sure that I take care of your other needs. I plan on using you at least once a day, and whenever

I feel like it — unless of course you start showing me that you enjoy it too much!"

His razor came out again and he laid it against her breast.

"Now, Princess Martha, stand up and move over to the far side of the cell. I wouldn't want to have to slice you open right there, would I?"

Martha moved, getting used to the slippery floor now, and wondering if he would bring the mattress back in so she could sleep on it. As soon as he had the table and chair out of the cell she asked him about the mattress.

Josiah lifted his brows. "It would be a shame for you to catch pneumonia and die on me, wouldn't it? Yes, I think it might simply be good business to give you the mattress and a blanket at night. The rest of the time I want you naked. I never get tired of looking at that marvelous body of yours."

Martha turned her back to him as she stood in the corner. She had won one small battle, and she didn't want him to see her cry with joy and relief. She would take the rest of the problems as they came.

CHAPTER TWENTY-ONE

When Johnnie Laveau walked up the gang-plank and boarded the *Pacific Spirit* bound for San Francisco, with Martha Pemberton Dyke watching him, he had no thoughts of staying on board. He quickly hired one of the seamen to take his suitcase off the ship by the forward crew's boarding plank. Johnnie watched his chance, and when Martha turned away from the ship for a moment, he walked across the crew's gangplank with half a dozen visitors and made it quickly to shore before the first lines on the ship were freed. He found his bag and ran with it two blocks up the street to be out of the path of Mrs. Dyke's carriage.

Johnnie rented a room at the Seven Seas Hotel, a low-class place catering to out-of-work seamen. He changed into an old woolen shirt, black pants and ankle-high boots, then bought a bill cap such as he had seen many of the loggers wearing. It would be easier to go unnoticed by Mrs. Dyke dressed this way.

Johnnie trotted along the street a block away from where Allen Cornelius lived. He stayed just far enough away so no one could recognize him, but so he could be sure Mrs. Dyke was there. Johnnie leaned against a big hemlock tree a block away and watched the buggy he had so recently driven. It was at the Cornelius house, and he had just seen Mrs. Dyke coming back to it with a small suitcase. She returned a moment later and Allen was with her, helping her put her luggage into the rig.

The two talked for a moment. Then she got into the buggy and drove away, heading back toward the center of town.

Johnnie ran easily, parallelling the buggy a block away. He guessed she was returning to the hotel, which seemed reasonable. He refused to think about any of the things she had accused him of. She simply did not understand.

When Johnnie had made certain that Mrs. Dyke had checked back into the hotel, he went to have some food. It had been a long time since he had eaten.

Less than half an hour after Josiah West captured Martha and led her down the back stairway, Johnnie decided he should go to

Martha and tell her he had not returned to San Francisco as she had wished. He ran up the steps to room number twelve, which the clerk had indicated was Mrs. Dyke's. He knocked on the door but got no response. After three more knocks he tried the handle and found it unlocked. Cautiously, Johnnie eased the door open and looked inside. No one was there. He stepped into the room and closed the door. Something was wrong. He wasn't sure what.

He saw the cloth lying on the bed and looked at it carefully. It might have been anything — a strip of material that had been tied at the ends and was wet in the middle.

Lying on the small dresser was Martha's daytime purse. She never went anywhere without it. He opened it and found over fifty dollars there.

Johnnie checked the rest of the room, but saw nothing else that seemed out of place or unusual. There was no evidence that she had left quickly other than the purse and the rag. He looked at the cloth again. It could have been tied around her mouth, which would account for the center of it being wet. But who would do that — and why?

Johnnie went out the door and to the far stairs, where he positioned himself. He stayed there for an hour, then checked the dining room. Martha was not there. The funeral was set for two. Could she be there? Not without her purse. He had never seen her go anywhere without a purse.

Johnnie went back to the second-floor hall and waited. She would be back soon. He was getting worried for nothing. Still, this was not like Mrs. Dyke at all.

At four o'clock he talked to the hotel clerk who said he had not seen Mrs. Dyke since she went up to her room sometime just after lunch, when she checked in.

Johnnie ran up the stairs this time, opened the door without knocking and knew now that something was wrong. He had searched for Mrs. Dyke when she had been missing before, but he had had a little more to go on then. Now it was all a blank. She was last in this room. He looked around again and picked up the cloth which might have been used as a gag.

A scent came to him, a perfume Mrs. Dyke often wore behind her ears. He sniffed the cloth again and noticed that the scent was in two places, at about where it would cover her ears if it had been a gag.

He put the cloth down. Suppose she had been abducted? Why? And to where? He went into the hall and walked away from the main steps. At the far end of the second-floor hall he found a door to an outside wooden stairway that led down to the alley. Johnnie ran down the steps and found fresh carriage tracks in the soft mud of the alley, as well as several small shoeprints and some larger, heavier ones in the same place. A woman and a man had got into a buggy here.

Could she have been shanghaied as a ship's woman? Johnnie felt a growing anger as he ran toward the docks. He had known of some captains who picked up women in one port, kidnapped them and used them during long sea voyages. They were sometimes passed around to the officers and even the crew. In the end they were dumped in a foreign port or simply dropped overboard so there could be no charges brought against the captain or crew. It was a crime almost impossible to prevent or to prove.

But if he could catch them before they left port . . . Johnnie ran faster, and surveyed the ships at the dock. Four were tied up there. He asked an old fisherman if any ships had sailed that day, and the old man said only one, the *Pacific Spirit.* That had been the ship Johnnie had almost sailed on. He thanked the man and ran to the first ship where he talked to the mate. She was owned by Mormons and was heading for

Hawaii. There would be no ship's woman there. At the next boat he found the captain, a cantankerous man in his seventies. When Johnnie explained he was searching for a missing woman, and asked if the first mate might have smuggled her on board, the old captain laughed.

"Sonny, I wish I was young enough to enjoy the likes of a beauty, but 'fraid I'm not. What I don't get, my officers don't get, neither!"

Johnnie had no better luck turning up Mrs. Dyke on the other two ships. He decided she was on none of them, and not set to be brought aboard just before sailing time.

He then hurried to the sheriff's office. Deputy Abner Irvin listened to his story.

"That lady sure has been getting herself in trouble, ain't she?" He pushed the black, low-crowned hat back on his head. "We'll sure keep a watch out for her. I ain't heard nothing about finding a body or anything. You think she's been kidnapped?"

"Shore, *mon,* look like. Gag mouth, back stairs, carriage tracks."

"I'll keep a watch out. You say she's pretty, about twenty-one years old, and five feet three or so with long black hair. Right, we'll watch."

Johnnie went back to the street. Five thousand people, and any one might have kidnapped Martha. But why? He could think of no reason. She was the daughter of a rich man. Kidnap her for treasure, ransom? Yes, possibly.

By now it was starting to grow dark. The funeral had been over long ago. Mr. Cornelius would be back home living with his grief. He should not tell him, not yet.

Johnnie went back to the hotel, where he told the clerk he thought Mrs. Dyke had been kidnapped. The clerk could remember no one asking about her room number, but the register was right there on the desk and could be read by anyone.

"Who stood after Mrs. Dyke check in?"

Together they looked at the register. Only two persons had signed in after Martha — one a hardware drummer, the other a ship's captain.

The clerk was about thirty, with close-cut hair and spectacles. Now he was getting frightened.

"Anybody could have walked up and looked at the register. We can't keep it hidden all the time. It ain't my fault if somebody found out what her room number was."

Johnnie left him and went upstairs to

check on the two rooms that had been rented since Martha moved in. He knocked on the door of room eight and was invited inside. The sea captain lay in bed with a naked woman who had red hair and a large body. She hid her face. Johnnie saw that Martha couldn't be there, laughed and backed out. The other room was unoccupied. Johnnie used a stiff piece of wire, unlocked the simple mechanism and looked into the room. Martha was not there.

He went back to Martha's room and sat on the bed. The buggy track had to be a clue. He ran back down to the outside stairs and followed the buggy tracks down the alley and saw them turn north. That was away from the direction of Mr. Cornelius' house. But there were over three hundred homes in the northern section of town. Once in the muddy street, he soon lost the narrow tracks in a jumble of broad-wheeled wagon tracks and horseshoe marks.

He went back to the rear stairs of the hotel and sat down. The end of the trail. It would be dark in half an hour. He looked up and down the alley, and noticed the usual back doors of businesses, including the rear entrance to the Lumberjack Saloon. For a moment he saw nothing in the thickening dusk. Then a loud belch sounded from behind a trash barrel and Johnnie ran to the spot.

The man hiding there was in his fifties, and clutched a wine bottle to his chest, looking up suspiciously.

"Get yer own bottle, this damn one is all mine."

Johnnie squatted beside the man, who wore layers of clothing, all dirty and ragged with numerous gaping holes in them from his sweaters and shirts to his old coat. His inch-long beard was matted and turning gray, his eyes watered over a nose that dripped yellow mucus.

"*Mon,* you here long?"

"What the hell's it to you?"

Johnnie took out a coin purse and extracted a small one-dollar gold piece. He held it in front of the drunken man.

"How long?"

"Since noon. Found this bottle, and I'm taking good . . . taking good old care of her."

Johnnie gave the gold coin to the man who sat up, wiped the yellow slime off his face and blinked. "I seen things."

"What you see, *mon?*"

"Carriage, stopped over yonder."

"Who got in carriage?"

"You got more money?"

"No. Who got in carriage?"

"No more gold?"

"No."

"Lady, small lady, black hair, pretty."

Johnnie took out a two-dollar gold piece and showed it to the drunk. "Who was with her?"

"With her? Hell . . . oh, yeah." He reached for the gold. Johnnie pulled it back. "Who . . . man, not too tall, medium. About thirty, maybe thirty-five. Big ears. Biggest damn ears I ever seen on one mortal man."

"He make woman get in carriage?"

"Yeah, sure. Had a gun at her side." The drunk reached for the gold piece, and Johnnie gave it to him.

"Who was the man? You know him?"

"Yeah, he's a local guy. Don't know his name."

Johnnie stood and frowned down at the wreck of a man. There was nothing more he could get from him. Where did he start looking? Just because the man was "local" didn't mean he would be easy to find.

Josiah had taken the lamp out when he gave Martha dinner. She had a stale slice of bread, a glass of water and half an apple. She remained in the corner with her back to them until Josiah pushed the mattress in the cell and dropped a thin blanket on top

477

of it. Then when they left she sat on the mattress, huddled in the blanket and ate. She tried to keep warm, but it seemed impossible. Martha had no idea how cold it would get at night, but she knew it would be too cold for her.

She dried her feet and hands on one corner of the blanket and kept the rest of it dry. Martha sat cross-legged on the mattress to conserve her body heat and tucked the blanket around herself tightly. In a few minutes some of the chill was shut out, and she was feeling a little warmth. But she could shiver at the slightest thought of cold. She had to think of happier times, warmer times. Rapango! That delightful island, with its beautiful sun and the lazy days of eating and swimming and just sitting in the sun letting it warm you through and through. Glorious!

She relived the gentle, beautiful parts of her days on the island, and soon nodded off. Martha almost fell into the mud. She worked the mattress back against the wooden bars and leaned against them so she could sleep.

They had taken the lantern out hours ago, and now it was starkly, mine-tunnel black. She kept thinking about Tero and Mirani and the lovely island as she dropped off to sleep again.

Martha sensed that someone had come into the half-basement. She didn't wake up completely, but blinked when she saw the swinging lantern, than heard a high laugh. A bucket of cold water sloshed through the bars, soaking her, the blanket and the mattress. The sudden shock set her teeth chattering and she screamed in surprise and alarm. Martha saw only the shape of Mrs. West as she continued to laugh and went out with the lantern, slamming the door behind her.

Martha cried.

She didn't know what else to do. Now surely she would catch a bad cold, maybe consumption. She prayed it wouldn't be pneumonia. Slowly she realized she couldn't sit in the wetness all night. She stood and wrapped the dripping blanket around the two-by-fours, then tipped the mattress to pour off as much of the water as she could.

She wiped the water off her body with her hands, then examined the dripping blanket. She felt of it, searching for dry spots. At last she found one side that was comparatively dry. Again she sat down, crossed her legs and brought the dry part of the blanket around her. Part of the wet section came on her back, but she decided her body heat would dry that out eventually. It was better than catching pneumonia.

Each time Martha awoke during that long, cold night, she stared at the spot where she thought the door should be, hoping she might see a crack of dawn. A dozen times she woke, then slept fitfully, and woke again. She was cramped, sore and sneezing by the time she at last discerned the first signs of daylight through the loose-fitting door.

Martha got up and walked around the cell to get her legs working. She tested the door and found that Josiah had done a good job of nailing it shut. Without some kind of tool, she would never get it open.

There was nothing to do but wait.

She smelled coffee upstairs, and then the aroma of frying eggs and bacon drifted down. It was too much. She felt tears at her eyes, then running down her cheeks. She hadn't cried from all of the hate, anger and abuse that Josiah and his wife heaped on her, but now in a weak moment the smell of bacon made her weep. Life was one continual series of surprises.

She had always been a great one at planning. What could she work out now, some way to bargain with her captors? But the more she thought of it, the more strongly the realization came that she had absolutely nothing to bargain with. Josiah held all of the cards. He owned everything of value. All she could do was wait — wait and hope.

For a moment she wished she hadn't sent Johnnie Laveau home. If only he had stayed, at least someone would be looking for her. Poor Allen was in no shape even to think of her, let alone wonder where she was. Now there was simply no hope until the negotiations were completed for the payment of the ransom. *Three weeks!* Could she maintain her sanity for that long?

An hour later Josiah brought down her breakfast, a glass of water and two slices of bread.

"That's your ration for today, Martha, sweetheart," he said. "Dora didn't want me to put any butter on the bread, but I did. I'm just soft-hearted I guess. I've got to go down to the docks and get your letter to your father sent off on the first boat to San Francisco." He smiled, wrinkling his forehead. "Now, I'm sure you want me to hurry, don't you? No sense in making you stay in my hotel here any longer than you need to."

He went to the door. "Don't go away, anywhere. I'll be back as soon as I can." He laughed as he left, and Martha was sure she had never heard a more evil sound.

She ate the bread slowly, chewing it

completely, savoring each bite, sure that he would not give her any more food. She heard the door open and spun around, but when she saw Dora come in Martha retreated to the far corner and hid her bread.

"Well, showing me your backside again, sweetie? I don't see why you hate me so." Dora smiled — at least it was a smile on her. She walked to the edge of the bars.

"Honey, you and me could have a real good time. You know what I mean? I bet you've never tried it with another woman, have you? What can it hurt?" Dora hooted and laughed, but it didn't bring a rise from Martha.

"You want some more training, girl? You're gonna be here for three weeks. I got me lots of time. And remember I can come in there any time I want to. I'm bigger and stronger than you are. Just remember that."

Martha wouldn't even look at Dora. She went on talking. For fifteen minutes Dora tried to convince Martha that she should turn around and come out of the corner. Martha tried not to listen.

The cold splashing water came so suddenly that Martha gasped and screamed in shock. Again and again the dippers of water splashed on her. Martha kicked water as before, but this time she was blinded and couldn't see where Dora was.

Dora laughed and emptied her bucket, then retreated to the doorway.

"That's just a sample of what I have for you, sweetie. I've got some friends who will want to play with you. You won't be able to say no to them!" Dora went out and closed the door.

Martha was relieved when the semi-darkness of the windowless half-basement closed around her again. She picked her way toward the blanket but found that it had been thoroughly soaked again. She hung it on the two by fours, tying the top corners so the blanket could dry.

Martha sneezed. She realized that her nose was stuffed up and her breathing came hard. She had a cold, a bad one, and it had come on so quickly. It frightened her. She kept seeing the image of Mrs. Cornelius lying on her bed, wheezing, sweating, and making those awful sounds. No, it just couldn't happen to her!

Again Martha wiped as much of the water off her body as she could with her hands. Daylight had brought slightly warmer temperatures, but the room was far from warm. She shivered, her teeth chattered, and once more she tried to think about more pleasant things.

■ ■ ■ ■

Johnnie Laveau rapped on the plain wooden door at Allen Cornelius' home. It was time to tell the man. He should know. He'd had all night to get over his grief. Now it was daylight and almost a full day since Mrs. Dyke had vanished. The door opened.

"Johnnie Laveau," he said removing his cap. "Mrs. Dyke not here?"

"Why, no, Johnnie, she moved back to the hotel."

"Yes. She no there. Mrs. Dyke vanish, kidnapped yesterday afternoon. I no find."

Allen frowned and shook his head. "Did I hear you right? You're telling me that Mrs. Dyke is missing? That she isn't in her hotel room and that no one has seen her since yesterday afternoon?"

"Yes. Somebody hate Mrs. Dyke?"

Allen leaned against the door. He wasn't ready for anything like this yet. He thought he'd had enough shocks and tragedies for a while. What was happening now? He asked Johnnie into the house and they sat down. Then slowly, step by step they went over the entire story, from the time Mrs. Dyke put Johnnie on the boat, right through the story of the drunk in back of the Lumberjack Saloon. When he was through with the story, it was almost noon.

Allen sat back and rubbed his chin. There had to be an answer, at least a clue somewhere.

"Who would want to capture Martha?" he asked. "Who could gain from that? Somebody might hold her for ransom, but who? I can't think of anybody in Seattle who might want to harm Martha." He scowled. "But you can bet your life, Johnnie, that we're going to figure it out, and damn soon!"

CHAPTER TWENTY-TWO

Martha thought she was going out of her mind. All afternoon Dora West had sat outside the cell and thrown cold water through the bars. Half of it hit Martha. The rest made the floor of the cell so slippery that she could hardly stand. The blanket and mattress were soaked and couldn't provide comfort or protection now.

Her nose dripped. Martha could never remember a time in her entire life when she had let her nose drip. It felt terrible, but she had no strength to try to stop it. Her head felt light and the cough she had developed that morning came more and more often now. Each time it sounded she thought of Linda Sue Cornelius.

Where was everyone? Were they going to let her sit there and die?

Dora chuckled, watching Martha. She enjoyed seeing this naked bitch suffer. Served her right. Dora had told Martha a dozen times how she could be dry and warm and loved. In another day or two Martha would be begging for a dry blanket, and there was only one way she would get it. Dora grinned and threw another dipper of water. It hit Martha squarely on the head, sending more water down the long ropes of black hair that hung down her back.

Josiah had been down about an hour ago and made Dora stop throwing the water.

"Think I want to let you kill my half-million-dollar princess?" he shouted at her. Josiah hit Dora on the arm, then slapped her face, and she groaned in delight. She turned her backside and Josiah kicked her hard.

"Now look, you, I don't want you to throw any more water on Martha! Is that clear? No more damn water! We can't let her die too quick. After we get the goddamned money we don't care, but right now use your head for a change!" He stormed out and Dora had only grinned.

Her bucket was empty. Josiah wouldn't be back for another hour, maybe two. He had gone downtown to buy something. It must be getting close to four o'clock now. This was the time.

Dora went out of the basement door and into the house. In the back corner of her bedroom she picked up a small wooden crate she had bought from one of the neighbor boys only that morning. She carried it gingerly to the kitchen where she found a pair of heavy leather work gloves and then took the crate to the basement.

Martha looked up as the woman came in, not bothering to turn her back now from where she sat on the sodden mattress. She didn't care any more. Everything was so wet, so damp, so cold.

Dora put down the box and looked at Martha. "Hey, naked woman, I sure hope you like little friends, cause I got a few for you."

Dora went to the edge of the cell, took a dozen crusts of bread from her apron pocket and threw them into the cell. Back at the wooden box she pulled out a board and let a pointed nose with black eyes poke through the hole. When the head came out she grabbed it with the heavy gloves and pulled the animal out then dropped it into the cell.

Martha screamed. It was a rat, an eight-inch rat with a long tail and sharp teeth. It looked at Martha, then its nose picked out a better scent and it scurried through the wet and mud to the crusts of bread. Martha kept screaming, and stood on the mattress. Dora laughed, delighted to see Martha upset so much by the rat.

Dora tossed five more rats into the cell, then she threw a handful of bread slices at Martha's feet and watched as two of the big rats scurried over Martha's bare feet after the bread.

Martha screamed again, holding on to the two-by-fours of the cell, knowing the rats weren't after her, but unable to calm her fears. She tried to step up on the rough wooden studs, but slipped and jolted down on the mattress, stepping on a rat. It turned and bit her toe.

Martha shrieked and ran off the mattress. She cringed in the far corner away from the rodents. She knew it was stupid, the little animals weren't interested in her, but she was frightened of them. She always had been. Even a mouse could do it.

"Oh, come on now, fancy lady. Play with your little friends. Why be so uppity? They hardly ever bite, unless you step on them like you did. Only trouble is when the bread runs out they still might be hungry. Then they could show some interest in all that soft pink flesh of yours." Dora laughed again.

"One way you can get out of there. And you know what I mean. I can pull the nails out of that door in a rush, and then get you all dried off with a nice fluffy warm towel and take you upstairs to a nice soft bed. Hell, you'll like it. Now ain't that a decent trade? You'll get warm for a while, have a nice nap and a wild time too."

Martha heard only one phrase: "Pull the nails out of that door."

She knew what Dora wanted, but once the door was open, maybe she could kick Dora or gouge her eyes, get a knife, maybe get that hammer, anything to use as a weapon so she could escape. But she couldn't let it look like she was giving up too easily.

"Please get me out of here. Please."

"Go upstairs with me?"

"Go . . . well, I've never done anything . . . I mean . . ."

"Believe me, you'll love it. Almost no difference, I know, I like it both ways. Come on."

"Well. I —" Martha screamed again as a rat ran toward her. She jumped in the mud, splashing it and scaring it away.

"That ain't gonna work for long, sweetheart. Why don't you just come over to the door easy-like and let me feel of you for a minute, kind of warm you up some."

"Oh, no, I couldn't do that." Another rat sniffed toward her. Martha screamed and shied six feet toward the wooden door. It had to look accidental. Another rat moved toward Martha and she backed up. When she stopped she was against the cell wall next to the door, and Dora's big arm circled her chest, her hand clamped over one breast.

"Well, so you got here, anyway. Now, just relax, Martha. Those overgrown mice won't hurt you a bit."

Martha wanted to scream. She hated the woman's touch, and her hand over Martha's breast seemed to burn. But this might work. At least she had some kind of chance. She seemed to sag a little, and Dora laughed.

"Oh, yes, I think you do like it. Will you come upstairs?"

Martha looked at the rats, then back at Dora, and nodded.

"Goddamn!" Dora shouted. She let go of Martha, found the hammer and quickly pulled the nails out of the door and swung it open. Martha took unsteady steps now, wanting to appear stiff and feeble from confinement. It was twelve feet to the outside door. Martha stepped through the cell door, deciding a throat punch would be best. She doubled her fist behind her back and stumbled along. Why didn't Dora put down the hammer?

Dora watched Martha carefully. She had to be sure Martha wasn't bluffing. Damn sure. She looked weak, probably from the cold. Dora put the hammer down on the chair and pushed Martha head of her.

"Just walk right out the door, sweetheart, and we'll go up the stairs and have ourselves a wild time. You don't even need to tell Josiah . . . if you don't want to."

Martha jumped to one side, darted backwards around the huge woman and grabbed the hammer off the chair. Now Dora was between her and the door, but Martha had the hammer.

"Son of a bitch, so it was a trick. Hell, you ain't no match for me. You hit me once, sure, but then I smash you down and pound the hell out of you."

Martha held the hammer in front of her. She knew it wouldn't do any good to hit Dora's massive arms or shoulders. She had to hit Dora's head to do any real damage.

Martha swung the hammer once or twice, advancing on Dora. There was no other weapon. The chair, a wooden straight backed type, was too heavy. Dora jumped forward, remarkably quick. Martha hit her forearm with the head of the hammer, and Dora yowled in pain. The claw hammer had the claws extending almost straight back from the head, not curved as most were. Martha turned the tool so the claws would hit first.

This time Martha darted forward, swinging the hammer, and forced Dora to take a step backward. The big woman shrieked and dove forward. Martha swung the heavy hammer with all her strength and drove the claws into Dora's forearm. Dora stopped suddenly, shocked by the pain, and Martha jerked the hammer free as Dora stared in terror and disbelief at the blood spurting from her wounded forearm. Martha surged forward, taking advantage of Dora's surprise. Martha swung the hammer again, putting all her weight behind the blow. Dora threw up her injured arm, but the handle caught her wrist, knocked it down and the heavy prongs of the hammer drove past and hit Dora just over her ear and penetrated her skull. The claws stuck there.

Martha let go of the hammer and watched Dora sink to her knees, then sprawl on the floor, her eyes closing, one hand reaching toward her head. Martha stood frozen over her, unable to move. She should be running, but she could only stare down at the wounded woman who had been so powerful. Martha wanted to vomit, but she knew she couldn't. There was no time.

She looked for her clothes — any clothes. There were none. She jerked the apron from Dora and tied it around her own waist. Then she saw a man's old coat hanging on a nail near the door. She grabbed it and struggled into it.

Now Martha realized she was crying. Tears dripped down her cheeks. She buttoned the coat, and saw that it came almost to her knees. That would be good enough until she could run to a neighbor's house.

Martha went to the door and pushed it open cautiously. Before she could step out a form appeared in front of her and pushed her back. She slipped on the wetness and fell in the mud. When she looked up she saw Josiah glaring at her. His gaze took in Dora's bloody head and the hammer.

He roared at Martha, picked her up and shoved her into the cell. Josiah hardly noticed the rats. Gingerly he removed the hammer from Dora's temple and hammered the nails back into the door of the cell.

Josiah knelt in the mud beside Dora. He felt for her pulse, grunted when he found a faint one, then listened to her shallow breathing. When he looked up, his expression was neither of anger nor surprise, rather one of resignation. "Damnit, Dora, I told you not to try for Martha. I told you she wasn't easy to handle. Now you've got yourself hurt, bad."

Martha ignored him. She took the wet blanket, folded it in half to make a weapon, and began swatting at the rats until she drove them away from the bread. Then she threw the bread outside the cell and the rats followed.

With the coat on, she felt much warmer. Martha hadn't yet realized the full consequences of her attack on Dora. It had been necessary, her only hope, and if Josiah had been gone another five minutes she would now be free.

Josiah stood and stared at Martha for a long time. "I really didn't want to do this, Martha. You're good in bed. I figured on having you many more times. But now, I can see that's too damn dangerous. I hoped I could wait until I had the money, then I'd send you back to your loving father with a .44 slug right through your forehead. Now, my plans are changed."

He took a revolver from his belt and cocked the hammer. Enough light came in through the half-basement door so that Martha could see him plainly — see the fury in his eyes. She knew that he meant what he said. Martha stared at the black hole of the pistol wondering if each second would be her last.

The crashing roar of the pistol shot inside the basement sounded like a dozen cannons going off. Martha felt something hit her hard and spin her around, slamming her to the floor. It hurt, so at least she wasn't dead. She lay still, wondering if he planned on shooting her many times to see her suffer. Then the pain in her arm forced a groan from her lips.

Martha heard feet pound down the steps into the basement, heard voices, and then looked up to see Johnnie Laveau's beautiful face staring at her through the wooden bars. He kicked at the middle of one of the two-by-fours. Then he jumped in the air and kicked again, and the wood splintered in half. A moment later he was beside her, holding her head in his lap.

A few seconds later Allen pushed through the hole in the cell and kissed her cheek. She looked and saw another man, one she didn't know, who held a gun that was still smoking. He was looking at the floor. Martha struggled to sit up so she could see what had happened. She looked through the bars and saw the stranger reach down and touch a body on the floor. It was Josiah West. The stranger looked at Allen and shook his head.

Then they all began talking at once.

EPILOGUE

Martha lay in her bed in the hotel holding Allen's hand. It was the morning after Deputy Abner Irvin charged into the basement and shot Josiah West dead. Martha remembered standing there over Josiah and looking down at him. "I told you so, Josiah," she had said softly, then let them help her out of the basement to a carriage. She had still worn the old coat.

Her arm hurt. The bullet from Josiah's weapon had been pulled off target by Deputy Irvin's shot and had dug a deep hole in her left arm just below the elbow. Doc Warnick had treated it and doused it with some salve, then wrapped it up tightly. The lead had missed the bone and had not cut any large arteries or veins. It should heal without any problems, but there would be a pair of scars there for the rest of her life.

For a moment Martha wasn't sure what else had happened last night. They had taken her to the hotel and helped her into bed. Doc Warnick had given her some sulphur packs and put a mustard plaster on her chest. Just inhaling from them was enough to make her more ill. Still, they must have helped. She had used up a dozen handkerchiefs blowing her nose and promptly gone to sleep while both Allen and Johnnie sat with her. Her bed was so warm and she felt so snug and protected that she hoped she would never have to get up.

This morning she had ordered up a bath, found Johnnie sitting outside her door, and used another dozen handkerchiefs for her running nose. But there was no more cough, her lightness of head had vanished and she felt she was recovering nicely. There would be no more mustard plasters. By noon she was feeling well enough for company. Now she sat up in bed and ate something from each of the dishes in front of her without appetite.

Allen moved to a chair and watched her eat.

"So, now, tell me what else happened," said Martha. "How in the world did you ever find me? Josiah had planned it all so well, and was so secretive about the whole thing."

"Johnnie did most of it. He figured how

you must have been taken away, and found a drunk in the alley who did see you leave. The old sot got a good look at the man with you, claimed that the abductor had the biggest ears he'd ever seen on a man."

"But Josiah didn't have big ears."

"That's what threw us off for so long. As soon as Johnnie told me about it, I thought about Josiah because he'd had that trouble with you in San Francisco. We had an official notice about him saying we should under no circumstances hire him in any capacity. So I knew he must hate you and your father. But the big ears thing slowed us up by a good two hours. At last we went to the sheriff and asked him to come check out Josiah just in case he might know something about it. There was no one home upstairs, and Deputy Irvin was walking around to check on the back door when he heard Josiah threatening you."

"How is Mrs. West?" asked Martha.

Allen looked at Johnnie.

"Maybe yes, maybe no live. Bad hurt."

"I'm sorry. She really wasn't an evil person. But she certainly did have a mind of her own. It was my only chance to get away. I knew Johnnie was gone, and Allen — you were in no way responsible for taking care of me. I knew I had to do it all by myself. Sometimes we all need a little help."

"You're safe now, and that's all that matters," said Allen. "We can forget everything that's happened and start out fresh."

Martha wished desperately that she could. With all her heart, she wanted to do exactly as Allen suggested, but she still had a large stumbling block in the way. She had to tell Allen about the voodoo. Now was the best time, before he made any commitments, so he could just walk away if he wanted to. She'd die if he went, but he had to know. Allen must have the chance to understand what had really happened to Linda Sue.

"Allen, there's one more thing we need to talk about. It's Linda Sue. I know what the sickness was she had that left her so weak."

Allen looked at Johnnie who stood and walked to the window.

"Martha, what is past, is past. I know what you're going to say, and it's not very important any more. Yesterday Johnnie told me all about it. He said he was sure you would want me to know. That was before we knew if we would ever find you."

"But, Allen! If Johnnie hadn't interfered that way, then Linda Sue would be alive and happy right now!"

"That might be true. But she might have caught pneumonia anyway. Doc says sometimes people catch it for no good reason at all."

"Allen, Johnnie caused this directly. If he hadn't done —"

Allen cut her off. "No, Martha! Stop it. We can make up 'ifs' all night. If I'd never met you, you wouldn't have been up here and you wouldn't have been captured. If I hadn't taken you to the mill that day you would never have been captured and molested by that man. Ifs can go on and on and on. They don't make any difference. They are a dead end. I won't hear any more."

"But, Allen, I think that Johnnie should . . ."

"No, Martha. Johnnie and I talked it out. He was not harming her. What he was trying to do was scare her, to make *you* happy. He was doing something *for you,* not *against* Linda Sue. My wife really believed in voodoo. We talked about it now and then. She didn't know much about it, so the *gris-gris* frightened her. But it was her own doing."

He touched Martha's arm, then took her hand. "Martha, I loved Linda Sue with all my heart — but that was because I couldn't love you. Now she's gone, and that part of my life is over. Now all I'm concerned with

501

is making up to you these last three years that we've missed."

He bent and kissed her lips.

When Martha opened her eyes after the kiss she saw that Johnnie was gone.

"And you're really not angry at Johnnie?"

"No more than I would be at anyone who made a mistake that led to a tragedy. It wasn't his fault. We've made our peace, the two of us. Now I want the same kind of understanding from you."

Martha looked up at him, her eyes shining, her chest filling with an all-powerful love she had only felt once before.

"Darling, hurry over and lock the door." She moved the lunch tray and slid to the far side of the bed. When Allen came back she patted the place beside her and he lay there, his lips searching for hers. They covered her mouth, then touched her eyes and nose, her throat, and all the time he was whispering the words she had wanted to hear from him for so long.

"My darling, you're the sweetest woman in the world. You're the only love for me. I've waited for years and now at last you're here and we're both free. You must have known from the very first how I loved you, how I always have loved you and always will, no matter what happens."

Martha snuggled down in the comforters, reaching for him, sure now that her life was only beginning. After this, she would always say that her true love — her whole life — began on this very day.